# THE WHITE MARRIAGE

Charlotte Bingham

BANTAM PRESS

LONDON · TORONTO · SYDNEY · AUCKLAND · JOHANNESBURG

TRANSWORLD PUBLISHERS
61–63 Uxbridge Road, London W5 5SA
a division of The Random House Group Ltd
www.booksattransworld.co.uk

First published in Great Britain
in 2007 by Bantam Press
a division of Transworld Publishers

A CIP catalogue record for this book
is available from the British Library.

ISBN 9780593055953

Addresses for Random House Group Ltd companies outside the UK
can be found at: www.randomhouse.co.uk
The Random House Group Ltd Reg. No. 954009

The Random House Group Ltd makes every effort to ensure that the papers used in
its books are made from trees that have been legally sourced from well-managed and
credibly certified forests. Our paper procurement policy can be found at:
www.randomhouse.co.uk/paper.htm

Typeset in 11/15pt New Baskerville by
Falcon Oast Graphic Art Ltd.

Printed and bound in Great Britain by
Clays Ltd, Bungay, Suffolk

2 4 6 8 10 9 7 5 3 1

THIS NOVEL IS SET IN ENGLAND
AFTER THE SECOND WORLD WAR

I wonder by my troth, what thou, and I
Did, till we lov'd?

John Donne

# Prologue

There was a time, believe it or not, when it was perfectly possible to know very little about the birds and the bees, unless, or until, it was necessary. There was a time when Christmas meant a tangerine, some nuts and a second-hand book; when to own a whole length of tinsel was almost unimaginable; when to pin together a paper bell to hang from a light fitting was exciting; and to see a man carving a turkey was to be filled with an inestimable feeling of good fortune.

It was at about this time that Sunny finally finished growing up in Sussex. Her parents, Mr and Mrs John Chantry, lived in a thatched cottage overlooking the green in the ancient village of Rushington. Not many people had motor cars in those days, in fact hardly anyone had a motor car, and if they did it was more or less guaranteed to be on blocks in the garage waiting until such a time when petrol rationing was over, or the owner could afford to buy some new tyres, or someone could be found to come out and get it started.

Sometimes Sunny would go into her parents' garage, with its upper storey that housed what always seemed like acres of home-grown apples and onions, and stare at her father's

Vauxhall 12. It was covered with a large tarpaulin tightly pulled together. It might have been a sad sight to someone else, but to Sunny that strangely shaped fawn object was full of promise. She knew that one day soon that tarpaulin would be coming off, and the bricks upon which the axles were resting would be removed, and they would all push the pre-war motor car outside into the sunshine. She would help her mother wash and polish it, and her father would dart about from one side of the car to the other pointing out bits that they had missed, as he always did when they were helping him.

Sunny was less like her school friends than she would have liked. She had no pony of her own, nor did her father do 'something in the city'. Her father worked for a company that helped restore old buildings, which was why, because of the post-war building restrictions, he was not at all rich, which was also why her mother had a service altering and refashioning ball gowns and cocktail frocks, because dress materials too were rationed, and a bolt of cloth found in the attic was treasure trove, and if there was just a hint of a party coming up, clothing coupons were saved for months and months beforehand.

So you see, it was very different from now, and yet – and yet to Sunny, little though there was, and little that she perhaps had, it seemed almost too much. She was that happy.

## Chapter One

It was a miracle that Mary Chantry had never choked on a pin. It was one of the many things about her mother that Sunny found fascinating, because not only would Mary inevitably be found at most times of the day with a couple of pins in her mouth, but she was quite able to carry on a conversation with the pins still in residence as she busied herself with some alteration.

'Gracious, a motor car has just come to a stop outside the cottage, Sunny.' As usual Mary was speaking through several large dressmakers' pins, but nodding towards the window. 'I think you had better see if the driver needs help.'

Sunny, sporting a stunning pre-war bias-cut satin ball gown, which her mother had been busy pinning on her, stepped down from the dining table where she had been standing in for the owner of the gown, and stared out of the latticed window at the motor car.

'It's not a motor car, Ma, it's a Bentley.'

No one in Rushington owned a Bentley. Sunny pulled on the latch of the thick, black, iron-studded oak front door, only to find herself confronted not with a chauffeur, as she had half expected, but a tall, expensively dressed gentleman wearing a stylish belted pale wool cashmere coat into the pockets of which had been driven two brown leather driving gloves.

He stared at her before removing his hat in greeting.

'Good morning. My name is Gray Wyndham, and I am so sorry to trouble you.' He smiled, exposing an almost shocking set of princely white teeth, which set off his light tan, his thick dark hair, and the beautiful light blue of his shirt and tie. 'It is really rather a bore, I dare say, but my motor car has broken down, and right in front of your cottage. I expect it must be bothering you, blocking the view and so on?'

'Good morning,' Sunny replied. 'And really, I do not mind at all if you bother us, or block the view. As a matter of fact I know Pa will be only too delighted if you will stay bothering us and blocking the view, because he so loves motor cars, and if he comes home and finds that he has missed seeing such a splendid one as yours, he will probably kick the cat.'

'Does he kick cats often?' the stranger asked, looking startled.

'No, no, it's just something he always says, you know? Besides, we don't even have a cat, although I would like a cat. But we don't even have a dog yet, although I would like a dog too. But if we get a dog, he has to come first, Pa says, and the cat second. But all that is in the future, as it must be until the building restrictions are lifted, Pa says. Because we have so few pennies.'

Despite feeling frustrated that his car had broken down on the way to a Friday-to-Monday with Dilke and Leandra Fortescue at Maydown Manor, Gray Wyndham started to look amused, as why wouldn't he? This was honesty indeed.

'So your father says a good deal, does he?'

'Oh, yes, he is a chatterbox. I get it from him, Pa says. Ma is not a chatterbox.' She leaned forward, lowering her voice as she did so. 'Too busy dressmaking, too many pins in her mouth, I say.'

'And you are?'

'I am Sunny Chantry.'

'How do you do, Sunny Chantry?' As she stared at him staring at her, the stranger added, 'As I say – my name is Gray Wyndham.'

'How do you do, Gray Wyndham?'

Sunny frowned. It was a strange name, but she had to admit it did have a ring to it.

'Such a nuisance when a new motor car gives out on you.'

'Yes, what rotten luck, but do come in. We have a telephone, so as it happens you have actually broken down in front of just the right cottage. You can telephone to Mr Arkwright of Arkwright's Garage. He dearly loves a breakdown, but when he sees it is a Bentley, he will love it even more. In fact you will make his day, if not his week.'

Sunny indicated for Gray to step into the hall, after which she pointed at a telephone on the hall table. It was polished, it was dusted, and it stood on a mat.

'There's the telephone,' she told him, indicating it with just a hint of pride in her voice, because it was one of only half a dozen in the village. 'Shall I dial the number for you, since your hands are a bit grubby?'

'I should like that very much,' Gray admitted, and he stood by patiently as Sunny looked under A in her mother's thin, dark blue leather-covered telephone book.

'Ah, there we are. I always think it's Rushington two four oh, but it's Rushington two four two.' She dialled the number, and as she did so Gray noticed that she had long fingers, and no nail polish.

'Mr Arkwright?' A far away '*Yes?*' was bellowed down from

Rushington two four two over whatever was happening so noisily in Arkwright's Garage. 'This is Miss *Chantry*.' Sunny raised her voice and spoke slower. 'A gentleman by the name of Mr *Wyndham* has broken down outside our cottage – at least he hasn't broken down, his *car* has. It is a *Bentley*, Mr Arkwright.'

There was a long silence.

'Are you there, Mr Arkwright?'

'A Bentley you say, Miss Chantry? Are you sure?'

'Oh, yes, Mr Arkwright, I am very sure. It's right outside our door even now.'

'Well, I never. A Bentley. Stay you there, Miss Chantry, don't move, and I will be out to you all in a jiffy.'

Sunny carefully replaced the telephone and stared at it for a few seconds in reverential silence, before turning to Gray and giving a satisfied sigh.

'Mr Arkwright is leaving now; he is coming straight out. He can't wait.' She smiled at him. 'I am not sure if he has even seen the new Bentley yet, except perhaps in pictures, but he is a very good mechanic. He was in the war as a mechanic. He mended motor cars all over Europe. He went right from the toe of Italy up to the French coast, on a motor bike or in an army van, mending cars all the way. He was invaluable to the army, Pa says, because he is so quick. But he will be a few minutes now, I expect. Would you like a cup of chicory coffee, or a cup of tea? Or a sherry perhaps? It is nearly lunch-time, and I know Pa and Ma like a sherry before lunch – sometimes.'

'I would love to wash my hands.'

Shortly after Gray Wyndham was shown to the downstairs cloakroom, Mary Chantry opened the dining-room door where she had been busying herself with trimming a satin bolero that went with the gown that Sunny had been modelling for her.

'How do you do, how do you do?' She began removing the customary mouthful of pins and sticking them into the pin cushion on her wrist when Sunny introduced Mr Wyndham. 'How dreadful for you to break down in such a beautiful motor car. Almost too much to bear, I would say. Take the gentleman into the sitting room, Sunny; don't leave him standing about in the hall. Oh, and ask him if he would like a sherry, dear. So upsetting, a motor conking out on you.'

Mary firmly but quietly closed the dining-room door again.

Sunny pulled up the latch on an old oak door, and Gray followed her into a sitting room that seemed to be filled with flowers, probably because so many of the linen covers on the furniture were floral. Easy chairs round the fireplace gave an air of expected comfort, and there were horse brasses and an old brass warming pan hung about the old oak surround. Further down the parquet-floored room, a baby grand piano stood by the latticed French windows, which themselves opened out on to a garden filled with spring bulbs, which on a May day was really quite a cheering sight.

Gray walked down the room, looking round appreciatively at the Victorian watercolours on the wall, at the tweed-covered books on shelves either side of the fireplace, at the highly polished fire irons, at the neat pile of kindling, strips of newspaper, and raggedly cut items of wood from every and any source.

'Do you play?' Gray looked at the piano, lifting the lid momentarily to inspect the immaculately maintained keys, before closing the lid and gazing across at Sunny.

'Oh, yes, I play, but I am no Dame Myra Hess, I do assure you.'

Sunny raised a glass decanter, and poured Gray sherry into a tall waisted glass. She walked as gracefully as she could back down the length of the small sitting room, suddenly aware that, dressed as she was in an evening gown, she must look more than a trifle strange to Gray.

'I'm sorry I'm dressed like this—'

'I do assure you, I'm not.'

Gray looked at her with open appreciation, but Sunny pulled a little face.

'I act as a mannequin for my mother: she remodels old dresses like this for the ladies of the county, for balls and cocktail parties, and such like.'

Gray stared at the yellow dress, head on one side.

'As a matter of fact I think I can date the one you are wearing – nineteen thirty-three, or 'thirty-four, perhaps.'

Sunny looked down at the dress.

'It might as well be *eighteen* thirty-three or 'four, as far as I am concerned.'

They both laughed lightly.

'You're not having a sherry?'

'Oh, no, visitors only. F.H.B.'

'F.H.B?'

'Family hold back.'

Sunny's perfect pink and white complexion grew rosier. She was not ashamed of her parents' lack of wealth, but just at that moment she could think of no other way of hinting to this Mr Wyndham person that a schooner of sherry at Pear Tree Cottage was considered something of a luxury. Sherry was only to be offered to visitors, or enjoyed by her parents and their friends on a Sunday after church, but to state this too overtly might be what her mother and father and their friends called *infra dig* – in other words, laid you open to being sadly embarrassed by your financial straits.

'As an uninvited visitor, I am honoured.'

Gray smiled and gave a little bow, and as he did so Sunny frowned. Mr Wyndham was a stranger, and yet somehow he seemed almost familiar, as if she had known him in another life.

'Ah, that was the bell. It must be Mr Arkwright.'

Sunny did not know why but all of a sudden she found she was only too thankful to leave the room and answer the door. As she passed the dining room, her mother popped her head out, several pins once more in her mouth.

'Any more excitements around the place?' she asked in her usual bright way.

'No, no, I'm afraid not. Everything just as it was a few minutes ago. The handsome stranger is still in the sitting room, Ma, and I did give him a sherry.'

'Jolly good, Sunny. Anyone as handsome as that must be given every kind of encouragement,' Mary laughed. 'Oh, look, there is Mr Arkwright at the door, come to mend the handsome stranger's Bentley motor car.' She turned back to her daughter. 'I told you when I saw that tea leaf floating in your cup this morning that a handsome stranger would call,' Mary murmured, with a distinctly satisfied look in her eye, before closing the dining-room door again.

Sunny opened the front door. Mr Arkwright stood on their doorstep looking immaculate in a startlingly clean pair of overalls, a black bowler hat on his head, which he now removed in greeting to Sunny, and held to his chest.

'I will not ask myself in, Miss Chantry, seeing as what I am in my overalls, but if you yourself would care to ask the owner of the motor car to step outside . . . ? He may be able to explain to me the nature of the problem with the, ah, Bentley.' The last word was uttered with such reverence it was clear that Mr Arkwright thought of the Bentley as being the undisputed monarch of the road.

'The owner's in the sitting room, Mr Arkwright. He is drinking sherry – you know how it is?' Sunny added inconsequentially. 'One should always offer refreshment to people travelling by road, especially if they have broken down. Awful for him, really, because his motor car is quite new. If it was a Rolls-Royce I dare say they would have sent someone out to him by now.'

'I'm sorry if I kept you waiting, Miss Chantry.' Mr Arkwright dropped his voice as Sunny moved away from him. 'But I had to change my overalls – for a Bentley, you understand?'

Sunny nodded. Of course she understood. If a Bentley did not warrant clean overalls, what did?

'Of course,' she agreed, dropping her own voice. 'And for my part you must excuse me for being in a long frock, but I was modelling this gown for my mother when the breakdown happened.'

Mr Arkwright looked understanding. The whole village knew that Mrs Chantry did alterations to help bring home the bacon, until such time that the building restrictions were fully lifted and Mr Chantry could get going again, but it wasn't something that was talked about, except of course by the ladies who took her their dresses for remodelling and alterations.

Sunny pushed open the sitting-room door and put her head around it.

'I wonder if you would care to come to the door, Mr Wyndham? Mr Arkwright is here.'

Gray put down his half-finished schooner of sherry. 'Why, certainly.'

At the door he shook Mr Arkwright's hand. 'It was very kind of you to come out so quickly to me, Mr Arkwright.'

Now it was Mr Arkwright's face that grew rosier. He was too shy to say to someone he didn't know that it was a privilege to be called out to a Bentley Mark VI.

'I only hope I can be of assistance.'

He stepped aside to allow Gray to walk up to the car, which stood by the kerb, looking like some great patrician lady who had suddenly, and most unexpectedly, been taken ill and was at pains to look dignified despite this.

Meanwhile, Sunny went back into the dining room and quickly changed out of the ball gown, handing it back to her mother who they both knew had to get it finished for Lady Finsborough as soon as maybe.

Once more in her navy-blue skirt and neatly darned twin set, Sunny hurried out to the front where the two men now stood gazing into the Bentley's engine.

Sunny listened to them talking for a while, but as soon as Mr Wyndham stood back to let Mr Arkwright peer happily at the relevant parts in the immaculate engine bay, she could not help showing off.

'This is one of the first Mark VI's to be factory built, isn't it?'

'No, this is coach built.'

'Oh, I didn't think they were coach building them—'

'A few have been—'

Sunny nodded, pretending not to be impressed as Gray too tried not to look impressed.

'You know a great deal about motor cars, perhaps, Miss Chantry?'

Sunny shook her head. 'No, no, not a great deal, but I know a little about these particular "queens of the road", as my father calls them. He will be so sorry he missed seeing this one. But I will tell him all about it.'

'What will you tell him?' Gray prompted.

'I will tell him it was a Mark VI, which means that it has, I think, a six-cylinder in-line F-head engine with inlet over exhaust and a four point two five seven capacity. I think that's right,' she finished.

'Has your father got a Bentley, Miss Chantry?'

Instead of laughing at the very idea, Sunny carefully shook her head, pushing back her long dark hair as she did so, as the expression in her grey-green eyes became serious. Cars, after all, were *frightfully* serious.

'No, Pa has a Vauxhall, but ever since he arrived back from Burma – you know, after – after . . .'

'Of course, once peace was declared,' Gray finished easily for her.

'Well, ever since then he has always insisted on teaching me about motor cars. And one of these is his dream – when his boat comes in, that is.' She smiled, her eyes still on the Bentley as she went on artlessly, 'You see, Pa always says that he wants me to be the first woman in his life to know how the combustion engine works, to know how to change a wheel, and to know everything about every new car that is produced, because he thinks motor cars are works of art, just as much as paintings, or – or sculptures. He thinks motor cars have souls, and that they respond to different people in different ways, that they can be heard to sigh sadly when driven badly, and to purr with delight when they're driven well. That is what Pa thinks.'

At that moment a singularly happy sound filled the quiet Sussex air, a glad sound, a good sound; it was the sound of the Mark VI leaping into grateful life once more.

'A split hose,' Mr Arkwright called out from the driver's seat. 'Thought it might be. So often is with these thoroughbreds.' He climbed out of the motor car and, wiping his hands carefully on a clean piece of rag, he stood back. 'She's all yours now, sir. All yours once more.'

Gray sighed with some relief.

'You always feel such a fool breaking down in a brand-new motor car,' he confided to his two roadside companions as they all stared at the beautiful motor car, sunshine bouncing off her bonnet, the blue sheen of her immaculate paintwork a tribute to her makers.

'She's a grand lady, she is, and she'll be all the grander for you carrying on with your journey, sir. She will do you proud from now on, I guarantee it. She feels ashamed of herself, letting you down like that, she does.'

Mr Arkwright removed the cloth he had placed on the driver's seat to protect the leather, and stood by the open door, holding it for Gray.

'It's been a privilege, sir,' he went on, smiling and holding his bowler hat against his chest the way he always did when marching for the British Legion in the village parade on Remembrance Sunday.

Gray stepped back from the open car, and instead of climbing into the driver's seat he carefully removed a slim leather wallet from the inside pocket of his overcoat, but before he could do more, Mr Arkwright shook his head, holding up his hand as if he were a policeman stopping traffic.

'No, sir – please.'

Mr Arkwright's expression was a mixture of distress and embarrassment.

'Come, come, Mr Arkwright. I must owe you something, surely?'

'No, sir, really. It's been a privilege, truly it has.'

Gray stared at the mechanic, but since he could see that to insist on paying Mr Arkwright would be truly to wound his feelings, he shook the mechanic's now cleaned hand.

'Thank you very much, Mr Arkwright. I am most grateful to you, really I am.' He turned to Sunny. 'And thank you, Miss Chantry. To say that you have both made my car breaking down a positive pleasure is to say the least.'

He smiled and climbed into the driver's seat. Mr Arkwright closed the door, and the car left them, gliding smoothly out into the main highway, leaving Sunny and Mr Arkwright waving until it quite disappeared from sight, although certainly not from memory.

'I hope that she stays sound until she reaches the end of his journey, Miss Chantry, I do really.'

Sunny liked the fact that Mr Arkwright still used horsey expressions like 'staying sound' about motor cars, maybe noting that a car was 'lame on its off side'. It was understandable really, since his father, and his grandfather before him, had run the livery stables in the village, until motor cars took over from horses and the stables were turned into a garage. Yet somehow the language of the stables had stayed around Arkwright's Garage, even though the horses themselves had gone.

'I would say that she *will* stay sound, Mr Arkwright,' Sunny reassured him. 'My father always says –' Sunny assumed a deep voice, her eyes sparkling – 'he always says,' she repeated doing a passable imitation of her father, "When George Arkwright mends a motor car it stays mended, and always did, and always will." '

Mr Arkwright looked shy. 'Now petrol's come off rationing, Mr Chantry will be bringing the Vauxhall down to see me, Miss Chantry, no doubt?'

Sunny nodded. 'The old girl's coming out from under her cover soon, Mr Arkwright, or so my father told me.'

'I shall look forward to that, Miss Chantry. It's been a long time since we had the privilege of seeing the Vauxhall.'

They both nodded, and turned away. Mr Wyndham's Bentley might have been a Court occasion as far as Arkwright's Garage was concerned, but Mr Chantry's Vauxhall was a well-loved member of the village, remembered from the old days before the war with affectionate respect. Its first outing would therefore be remarked upon, even discussed in the Fox and Hounds pub. People would observe to the landlord, 'I see John Chantry's Vauxhall is off its blocks.' It would be something of an occasion in the village, something that would make them feel excited, hopeful even, something that they would remember in the ensuing years. The day John Chantry's Vauxhall made its first post-war outing.

Sunny went quietly back into the house, and, having changed, let herself into the sitting room. She sat down at the baby grand piano, the light of her mother's life. The sitting room was filled with sunshine, the garden was filled with flowers, and her mother was nearly finished with Lady Finsborough's dress, and yet Sunny felt vaguely unsettled. She started to play a Chopin prelude, but found it too beautiful for her mood. She began again, this time playing a waltz. She imagined herself dancing in the dress she had just been modelling for her mother. She imagined herself moving about a large ballroom in the arms of a tall, dark handsome stranger, and then she stopped.

Daydreams were dangerous; her mother had often told her that. Daydreams led to people having false ambitions, being discontented; putting themselves on the rung of a ladder they could never hope to climb. Ma believed only in keeping your feet firmly on the ground, whereas Sunny was always longing for them to be swept from under her. She wanted to reach for the blue sky that she could see beyond the latticed French windows of her parents' cottage; she wanted to know more than just Rushington, but the darns in her pullover, her low-heeled shoes, and her navy-blue skirt, once a part of her old school uniform – everything told her that her mother was right. To long for what could never be was to become permanently unhappy. It would be as silly as leaving a pebble in your shoe after you walked up from the beach.

She stood up abruptly. She must make her mother some lunch before going back to studying her shorthand note-book. It was college again on Monday, and that was no daydream.

Leandra Fortescue stared at herself in the mirror. She was looking particularly beautiful, which was just as well since she had planned a large house party of people, all of whom were also really rather beautiful. She glanced down at the guest list in the dark blue leather book laid out for her by her housekeeper.

To the house would be coming the Earl and Countess of Bridlington, the Hon. James and Mrs Metcalfe, Mr and Mrs Herbert Chambers. Also Celia Hopwith, Ginny Braithwaite, and Randy Beauchamp (bless him!).

Last and not least, there would be her husband, Dilke Fortescue, and herself, and of course Gray Wyndham, every-one's favourite house party guest, most particularly Leandra's.

It was a satisfactory list, and although the restrictions from the war still hung over even the most prosperous British house-holds, happily at Maydown they seemed to manage really quite well. There would be lobster, smuggled in from France (not difficult in Sussex-by-the-sea), pâtés, brought in from the same location, and pies and soufflés made from their own produce on the Home Farm. No one would go without butter at breakfast where the pats would be the size of golf balls, and no lady would have to come down to breakfast, but rather each would have a beautifully laid tray taken up to her. An embroidered white cloth would be spread across her sheets before the tray was stationed above her lap, and an ironed copy of the *Daily Telegraph* placed carefully on the night table beside her.

All this organisation, all this luxury, was due entirely to her husband, Dilke's, wealth. Dilke was American by birth, but he had been brought up in England, spoke like an Englishman, hunted and shot like an Englishman, while living like a Southern gentleman, albeit married to Leandra, a real Englishwoman.

'Mr Gray Wyndham has arrived, Mrs Fortescue.'

Leandra, having moved to the drawing room, looked up from reading a fresh copy of the *Tatler* and nodded at her butler.

'Please show him in, Rule.'

Her butler gave a short bow, and closed the door once again. Leandra stared at the door for a second. Rule was a treasure, a great treasure. More than that, he was her friend in a thousand ways that she could not name; he was her rod and her staff, far more than her husband, dear Dilke. Dilke did not concern himself with the running of Maydown, his interest lying solely in the stables. For this reason just a tiny part of Leandra always slightly dreaded a large house party. After all, it was not unknown for a guest, or guests, to steal not just a good, but a brilliant butler from under the noses of their best friends. Not Randy Beauchamp, or Gray Wyndham, of course. Being bachelors, they had no large country houses to run, only

London apartments in Belgravia or Grosvenor Square, flats that were convenient for the clubs, the theatres and restaurants, and all the usual amenities required by unmarried men of undoubted good looks and charm. But for the rest of the guest list – Leandra could not be quite certain. They all had houses to run. They might take Rule aside and whisper blandishments in his ear. She shook the thought off. The very idea of Maydown without Rule was beastly beyond words.

'Ah, Rule. And how are we? Am I the first? I hope so. I love to arrive unfashionably early, as you know.'

Gray stared at Rule. The butler was wearing his professional servant-as-mandarin expression.

'Yes, Mr Wyndham, you are indeed the first.'

Gray handed Rule his coat, shooting his cuffs as he did so.

'It has been a beautiful day, Rule, a beautiful day even for breaking down in a brand-new Bentley.'

'Have trouble with the great lady, did we, sir?'

'A hose, Rule, a hose gave out; the good man who mended the new beauty informed me that hoses are to a motor car what laddered nylons are to the ladies, oft occurring, but none the less distressing for that.'

As Rule opened the drawing-room door for Gray Wyndham they both knew that the lady inside, Mrs Leandra Fortescue, would never be found sporting a laddered nylon. Indeed, in the event of such an unlikely thing happening, there would be a short ring on the house telephone before a quick exit was made up the wide, shallow-stepped staircase to the floor above, where Mrs Fortescue's maid would be already waiting with a fresh pair of precious nylons.

'Mr Gray Wyndham, madam,' Rule announced again.

There was a fire burning in the grate, despite the warmth of the spring afternoon. There were great bowls of flowers brilliantly arranged on tables by the long windows, and books arranged on other tables, and a small easel that held a delicate drawing of a child's face.

At the windows hung yellow taffeta curtains, swagged and draped with gold cords, the tassels themselves fastened by three matching rosettes – or as Leandra would call them 'taffeta choux'. The large room, its fine windows leading on to a stone terrace and vistas of distant rounded hills, was painted a brilliant yellow, so to walk into the room at any time of day gave the visitor a distinct feeling of walking into sunshine, and that was before they noted the paintings of children playing on beaches, of vast bowls of flowers, of jewel-collared dogs, all the paintings hanging from the cornices on grey silk taffeta ribbons. The furniture was eighteenth century, a mixture of French and English. There was a mahogany writing table set about with small china dogs, and elegant little boxes, which probably held only paperclips. There were lyre-backed chairs placed casually near the windows, themselves filled with marble-topped tables bearing yet more flower-filled vases.

Gray was less interested in the details of the ornaments, in the drapes, or the taffeta choux, than he was in the effect the elegant room had on the people who entered it. The result of the supreme elegance of the surroundings was that the room frowned or smiled on the people who came into it. Anyone badly dressed, or too dull and ordinary would look out of place in Leandra's drawing room; on the other hand, bravely shabby would not be out of place; nor indeed elegantly eccentric.

Leandra herself always looked exquisite and, to give her every due, she made quite sure to give the impression of being totally unaware of it. Today her rich chestnut-coloured hair was coiffed gracefully to touch the collar of her *Directoire*-style jacket, which, in its turn, covered a slim dress of silk faille.

'Gray?' She extended her hand to him, and he kissed it continental-style, which he knew she always enjoyed. 'Some tea, or?'

'Some tea, thank you.'

'Some tea, Rule.'

'Thank you, madam.'

'Thank you, Rule.'

Leandra turned back to Gray.

'You are slightly, if fashionably, early.'

'I truly cannot tell you how, since a few hours ago I was slightly, if unfashionably, broken down.'

'The new motor?'

'The new motor.' Gray sighed.

'Something special?'

'No, nothing very special, just a hose.'

'You made sure to break down somewhere convenient, I hope?'

'As a matter of fact I did. A dear little gentleman in a bowler hat and immaculate overalls arrived within minutes, and mended the hose in a trice.'

They both laughed. For some reason 'dear little men' in bowler hats were always quite funny in Society, perhaps because they lived in such a different world. Or maybe they were just funny anyway. Or again, perhaps the image was funny, in a Charlie Chaplin kind of way. Who knew? Possibly none of these. What they both did know was where to laugh lightly and appreciatively.

'Shall I read you the guest list?'

Leandra asked this as Rule opened the drawing-room door once more and, with a maid following with a tea tray set for one, pulled up a small black pug made of papier-mâché and supporting a table of just the right size to hold the wooden inlaid tray with its Meissen tea service carefully laid.

'Lemon and one lump of sugar, sir?'

Gray smiled his assent as Rule poured the cup of tea and withdrew, the maid following solicitously.

Leandra opened a large leather folder embossed with a gold coiled serpent, its head supporting the initials 'LF' on the front.

'Very well. We have coming for our Friday-to-Monday the Arthur Bridlingtons—'

'Don't know them.'

'You'll like them, Gray. Truly, you will. James and Lavinia Metcalfe, whom you know. Herbert and Betty Chambers, Celia Hopwith, Ginny Braithwaite, darling Randy Beauchamp, and last but not least – Gray Wyndham.'

'Now let me see – Gray Wyndham? Do I know him? Oh, yes, I fear I do. Rather a dull fellow, isn't he? But good for making up numbers,' Gray added lightly.

Leandra closed her folder with its immaculately laid-out menus and notes, and smiled. 'That is for you to say.'

'Yes, I think I do. I think I know him just a little. He's quite a good fellow. A member of Brooks's Club, rides well, plays tennis well, dresses quite well—'

'Dresses beautifully,' Leandra put in.

'Can be quite amusing.'

'Is always *very* amusing.'

'And one way and another, very occasionally, gets *asked*.'

Leandra laughed. 'Everyone wants you at their house parties, Gray, you know that. For that reason it is always so hard to get you. Last week you were with everyone, including the Suffolks, in – where was it?'

'Norfolk, actually.'

They both laughed again.

'Next Friday-to-Monday I expect you will be somewhere much more exciting than poor old Maydown.'

'No, no, there can be no more exciting place than here. Where else is the company amusing, the food exquisite and the atmosphere so relaxed that we all give of our best?'

'Saying which, I think I can hear the Bridlingtons arriving. They are always a little early. Their house is still so cold, you know? I think they can't wait to come here because we are at least warm, if nothing else.'

Rule stood by the door and announced, 'The Earl and Countess of Bridlington,' from the door.

Gray noted that Rule did so in rather louder tones than those he had employed when 'Mr Gray Wyndham' was announced; so inevitably the thought came to him that Rule might well raise his voice, or drop it, according to the exact importance of a guest's title, which would surely mean that when announcing royalty he would *bellow*.

Perhaps the Bridlingtons were not the only guests who wanted to warm up at Maydown, for they were closely followed by the Metcalfes, and the Chamberses, by Miss Hopwith, and Miss Braithwaite, and finally – off the train and looking madly dishevelled – Randy Beauchamp, gaiters spattered with mud, monocle dangling, three or four bright white hairs standing up at the back of his head in an alarming manner.

Now the tea table at the far end of the room was laid out for everyone, with small drop scones, home-made strawberry jam, and butter that looked to Gray as if it must have come from France, since it was light coloured and not farm yellow. Besides the scones, there were tiny biscuits shaped as farm animals, with which everyone amused themselves, biting off their heads and tails and then pretending to be shocked at what they had just done. Small coconut and chocolatey cakes were also laid out invitingly, their coloured paper cases giving the tea table fleetingly a look of a child's party.

When Gray and Ginny had finished laughing at their headless biscuits, Ginny's eyes strayed to the maids, who were busy hovering with plates of teatime delicacies.

'I remember my *mother*,' she dropped her voice. 'I remember my *mamma* telling me that during the First World War, she was forced to write to Lord Kitchener to ask him to cease conscription at once for young men, because it was having a bad effect on her household. Never before, she said, *never* before had they had to have *maids* rather than *footmen* to wait on them at Chaseley.' She paused. 'Can you imagine that now?'

Both she and Gray shook their heads, because of course neither of them could.

'You hardly see footmen now, outside of royal or ducal circles.'

'Hardly.'

Gray turned his eyes on the small cake he had just taken from a proffered plate.

'I don't know when I last saw footmen in a private house in London, but then I don't get asked much in London,' Ginny went on.

'Such a pity not to have footmen any more, I suppose; but all those uniforms and bulging calf muscles – would we really want them now?' Gray asked of no one in particular, because he knew that Ginny could hardly afford a maid, let alone a footman, let alone a butler. Nowadays few people were as rich as their weekend hosts.

'It all depends on what you happen to be wanting them *for*.'

Ginny was straight-faced, but only for a second, because they both laughed again.

Gray popped his cake into his mouth and his gaze wandered

off to take in the rest of the party, some of whom were now putting down their teacups preparatory to climbing the wide staircase up to their suites of elegantly appointed and brilliantly comfortable rooms.

Somewhat thankfully Gray followed suit. He liked Ginny Braithwaite, she was good-hearted, even if she was a bit of a hunt bicycle. He just wished that her moustache was not quite so heavy, and her voice a little more musical, her chest less flat, and her eyes less hard.

Later, as he came down, changed into dinner jacket and black tie, and stood around murmuring pleasantries, his eyes strayed to Leandra's immaculately designed yellow taffeta drawing-room curtains, and inevitably, because they were yellow, he found his thoughts straying back to earlier in the day, to the young girl in the pre-war yellow satin dress with all the pins down the side. And as he stroked one of Leandra's four toy poodles, he could not help remembering the look of longing in the girl's eyes as she spoke of one day being able to afford even one dog, let alone one dog and one cat.

Dinner came and went, with all the usual vaguely scandalous conversations kept for later when the ladies retired to powder their noses, and the men were left with the port. Who was doing who, but much more importantly *why* – dominated the ladies' conversations; while who was making *how much* money and why – dominated those of the gentlemen.

Eventually the sexes came together once more, and this reunion was followed by cards for some, and more gossip and tittle-tattle for others. It was all very decorous and delightfully elegant. The food was delicious, the women decorative, and Gray was, as always, the perfect guest, but as he finally climbed the stairs once more for bed, he found himself feeling vaguely claustrophobic, and the prospect of Saturday and Sunday seemed to stretch ahead almost endlessly, certainly longer than they should, the whole weekend not so much a Friday-to-Monday, as a Friday-to-Friday.

He must be tired, he told himself as he surveyed his pyjamas laid out carefully on the bed, turned down so that the linen top sheet seemed to have been ironed. He knew that beneath the sheet and woollen blankets would be found an old-fashioned stone hot-water bottle dating back perhaps a hundred years. He usually adored staying at Maydown, never wanted to go back to London, certainly never normally longed for Monday to come. After all, as everyone he knew would agree, if you tired of Maydown and Leandra Fortescue, it could well be said that you had tired of life.

'Of *course* you're tired,' Leandra told Gray the following day. 'You have so much to think about, so much in that handsome head of yours that you are turning over and over. You are also tired because you are, as they say, on the horns of a *dilemma*. You know you are happy, but you also know you have to have, *must* have, a future but you don't quite know where it lies, and that is always and ever worrying.'

Leandra was wearing a sapphire-blue silk dress with a wide belt that showed off her tiny waist. The dress had long fluid sleeves, which in their turn showed off the beauty of her sapphire ring, just as the shirt collar of the dress, worn standing up, showed off her matching sapphire earrings.

'You look beautiful, Leandra,' Gray told her, all of a sudden.

Leandra smiled. 'I feel beautiful this morning,' she told him with quiet satisfaction. 'Oh, look, there's Dilke.'

Her smile widened as her tall, if ample, husband strolled across the lawn towards the terrace where they were seated.

'Darling, what can I do for you?'

'You can tell me how much you're going to miss me now that I'm off to have luncheon with that rascal Percy Yatcombe.'

'Of course I shall miss you, sweetheart. We will all miss seeing you at luncheon, won't we, Gray?'

Gray nodded obediently, only to be dismissed from his host's view by a peremptory nod. Gray was quite used to this, just as he was quite used to the way Dilke Fortescue said his name, on a sigh – which was a signal to all and sundry that Gray Wyndham was a friend of *Leandra* Fortescue, but certainly not of *Dilke* Fortescue.

'Of course we will miss you. Leandra would never forgive us if we didn't,' Gray told his host, but by that time Dilke had turned to leave, walking across the lawn with the speed normally associated with a far slimmer man.

'Dilke is amazingly light on his feet,' Leandra murmured, watching him. 'As always with a man with small feet and a tall frame, he dances beautifully too.'

Gray tried to look interested in the size of his host's feet and failed.

'Now,' Leandra turned her large violet-blue eyes back on Gray, 'now is the moment we must return to the subject upon which we touched last night at dinner, namely your father and his indifference towards you. What would it take to change his attitude, do you think?'

Gray's eyes wandered from Leandra's beautiful face and out to her flower-filled garden. 'I don't know,' he stated lazily, without the slightest attempt at truth.

'I think you do, Gray. And I think I do too. I think we both know what would change your father's attitude to you, what would change your future.'

Gray's expression, normally good-natured if reserved, turned to one of all-too-evident concern. 'Yes, you are right,

I do, Leandra. I know what will change his attitude towards me.'

'In one word?'

'Marriage.'

'Exactly.'

Gray stood up, pushing out his chair behind him impatiently, then starting to walk up and down the terrace.

'I cannot marry, Leandra. You know my feelings on marriage. It is impossible for me to marry, being as I am – you know my secret.' He stopped, looking at her with intensity. 'Feeling as I do, I cannot marry.'

Leandra watched him, her head on one side, allowing him to stroll up and down for a while, before patting the seat beside her.

'Come and sit near me.'

Gray sat down. Leandra was so beautiful, it was difficult to sit down beside her and not give way to his feelings.

'Gray, look at me?'

Gray looked at her. At that moment it seemed to him that Leandra matched the sky. She was certainly as beautiful as her surroundings.

'There are ways around this.'

Gray found this vaguely amusing. How could there be ways around a marriage? It would be like saying there were ways around dying, or the law. He was, however, careful to keep his expression serious. It was so terribly 'Leandra' to be so careless of marriage, one of the most sacred foundations of civilised society.

'Leandra, I know that you can work miracles. But of one thing I am quite sure and that is that even you cannot find a way to work round the marital status in our society. It is simply not possible. Marriage is marriage, and just as the sun comes up in the morning and goes to bed at night, marriage is the sensible, safe and sacred centre of our society, and try as we can to overcome this, it is impossible.'

'And that being so, I have thought of a plan.'

'If you are going to suggest I marry someone and then divorce them – then no, I cannot. Divorce may be recognised by the law, the people, the police, whomsoever you care to name, but in the Wyndham family it is *un*acceptable. I come from a very, very stuffy family. We have never borrowed money, and we have never, and will never, have anything to do with divorce. That is all there is to it – alas. To do so means a severance of any connection with the family trustees, which is a fairly polite way of saying – ruin.'

Leandra waited for him to finish his short speech, a tolerant expression on her face, and then began again.

'My plan for you is that you should make a white marriage, Gray. If you think about it, a white marriage is the one marriage that never, ever enters the lists at the divorce courts. A white marriage would you keep you both safe, and in the black!'

They both laughed.

'You mean marry in church? The bride in white, the brides-maids in white, white flowers and white faces, not to mention the father's whitened face when he sees the bill?' Gray went on, determined to be facetious.

'Silly old bear,' Leandra murmured. 'You know very well what a white marriage is! It is a marriage of convenience, such as the French, and indeed the Americans, have always made. You know that very well.'

'Indeed I do, but really, I cannot see myself being able to live with a woman who does not like men. I am far too – how can I say? – I am far too loving a personality to live with someone who will be permanently upset by my presence in her house, who will want me to spend not just my days but my nights at my club, who will be pained by my albeit not particularly overt masculinity.'

'As always you go too far,' Leandra laughed. 'No, no, bless you, my plan is that we should find some nice person who will marry you on the understanding that you can never have conjugation, that you will lead fashionably separate lives. It can all be arranged in a very civilised fashion. They do it all the time in France.'

Gray rolled his eyes expressively. 'They do a great many things in France, Leandra, that we would surely not attempt here. We are not a sophisticated society like the French.'

'No, but we are civilised, and it is most important that we should remain just that.'

'So you propose we find some young woman who will consent to marry me, lead her own life, and generally remain civilised, in return for what?'

'In return for everything you can give her, of course,' Leandra stated smoothly. 'It happens all the time. Why, in Paris I know of two or three such unions, and they are not just successful, they are very happy.'

'Are they indeed?'

'Of course, yes. After all, they have gone into the union with their eyes open. They do not have their heads filled with romantic nonsense.'

Gray went to say something, and then stopped.

'You were going to say . . .'

'Nothing of interest,' he returned quickly. 'Really nothing of interest.'

Leandra smiled at him, her expression protective.

'You had a brilliant war, that you have suffered from it is

undoubted, and that is something I can never understand about your father—'

Gray stopped her. 'Before you go on, Leandra, there is nothing *to* understand about my father. He is everything to himself, but not much to anyone else, believe me.'

Gray sighed inwardly, and his eyes drifted towards the outer limits of the garden, and eventually towards the distant hills, rounded, green, and perfect. He had fought his way through six years of war, somehow surviving unscathed, although only God, and God alone, knew how. Eventually arriving home at midnight in late 1945 he had been greeted by his father the next morning at breakfast with the immortal never-to-be-forgotten words, 'Don't hog all the marmalade, will you, Gray? There are other people on this earth, you know.'

Gray had wanted to reply, 'Yes, and I have just finished killing a great number of them,' but instead he had remained silent, knowing that to say anything at all was worse than a waste of time; it would be to court yet more pain.

'No, Leandra, there is nothing to understand about my father at all, except that he is, as far as his son is concerned, unloving and unlovable. He does not even love himself. As a matter of fact I think he does not even like himself.'

Leandra pulled a little face. 'Gracious. That is sad. Most of us are able to love ourselves, sometimes inordinately.'

'Very well, let us go back to our conversation. Supposing, just supposing, we find this young woman who will consent to this marriage. What happens if – if she falls in love with some-one else once she has married me, knowing that we can never love, poor thing?'

'Precisely nothing, Gray darling, precisely nothing. She will abide by the rules.'

'Which are?'

'The old rules – as the Edwardians used to say as they nipped in and out of each other's marital beds – *à chacun sa chacune*! To each his own. People like Dilke and myself stay married, and observe civilised behaviour. It is our duty. If we wish to pursue other interests, that is our affair.'

'And you think this poor innocent will consent to all this?'

'I am sure of it.'

'Because?'

'Because by doing so, you, and she, will become very rich indeed, and let us be practical, poverty is the root of all evil, not money.'

'Supposing *she* is already very rich?'

'She won't be, believe me. Anyone suitable to fill the position will not be considered—'

'You make it sound like hiring a maid—'

'Anyone suitable not only will not be rich, she will be innocent and well-behaved. We shall make sure of it.'

'I see.' There was a pause before Gray finally finished, 'I don't know why, but I feel as if I am planning a murder.'

'Anyone suitable will agree to our plan because it will seem very, very easy, which of course it is.'

'Again – because?'

'Because you will be offering her a very nice, and a very happy life.'

'Supposing she is not nice and has no intention of having a happy life, and we discover this far too late?'

'She will be nice, if I have anything to do with it.' Leandra touched Gray lightly on the cheek. 'Leave it to me. This is what my father always called "women's palaver". Now, tonight there is a dance at the Norells' – Harcourt House? Remember, we went there for drinks when you stayed at Christmas?'

'Yes, yes, of course.'

'We will dine here – there will be another eight of us coming over from Stapleton Court – and then we will all motor on to Harcourt House. It is only fifteen miles from here. You will take the Bridlingtons, and Ginny, and Randy. I will see to the others. We will be about six cars.'

'Let us pray my hose does not split again,' Gray said in a suddenly pious tone.

'Yes, Gray darling, let us pray.' Leandra paused, the expression in her eyes softening. 'Let us pray for many things, most of all to find someone suitable for you to marry so that the Trust will be released, and all will be well for you. Time is, after all, running out. Your father is no spring chicken.'

Gray nodded. If his father died, and he remained un-married, his very married cousin Barrington Wyndham would inherit everything. He frowned suddenly.

'Just one thing, Leandra. If this is to be a wholly white marriage, *à la française,* what happens about – you know – an heir to satisfy my father's all-abiding desire to pass on his estate in the male line?'

'You adopt abroad, darling. Everyone does it. There are so many babies being born where or when they shouldn't be, because of the war. It is simple, truly it is. Quite, quite simple. Everything can be arranged.'

Gray sighed. Really, Leandra should have been given the country to run. If she had there would have been no rationing, everyone would be employed, and all England would be as beautifully run as Maydown.

Mary Chantry replaced the telephone on its cradle, and turned to Sunny, who had just come in from a walk.

'Lady Finsborough is unable to go to the ball tonight on account of her mother being taken ill, Sunny. It seems that the poor lady, who, as you know, lives in the Dower House on the estate, is far from well.'

Mary turned away.

'After all that work on the dress, what a shame for her, and for you, Ma.'

Sunny followed her mother back into the dining room, and they both looked up at the beautiful, old-fashioned, yellow satin, bias-cut dress and bolero at which Mary had worked so hard over the last thirty-six hours, and which was now hanging from the dining-room picture rail.

Mary turned to Sunny. 'Lady Finsborough did suggest to me that you might like to go in her stead, because you are known to the Norells of Harcourt House – remember you used to visit the twins, and they used to come over here and play Monopoly sometimes?'

'Yes, of course I remember the twins coming over.'

The contrast between Pear Tree Cottage and the grandeur of Harcourt House had been all too evident to all of them, and yet the Norells seemed to love coming to Pear Tree Cottage because, as Jennifer Norell used to murmur to Sunny, her eyes rolling with delight at the prospect, 'You have such lovely food at your cottage. We get nothing to eat at home except gristle and fat. Nanny starves us!'

Mary Chantry was continuing, 'At any rate, knowing that you don't really like grand people, I thanked Lady Finsborough, but said I thought you were busy. I must say I thought she sounded a little disappointed, but there we are. No point in going somewhere if you're going to feel awkward.'

'Lady Finsborough wanted me to go in her stead? Are you sure?'

'Oh, yes, ducks, she did indeed, but as I said, I didn't think you would want to go.'

'Why ever *not*, Ma?' Sunny stared at her mother.

Mary stared right back at her, slowly removing the pins from her mouth.

'Of course I want to go, of course I do!' Sunny caught her mother by the arm as she was turning away. 'Of *course* I would like that sort of thing. In fact, I am quite sure I will. I just say things like that about grand people – well, because I've just never been asked, I suppose.'

Her mother followed her out into the hall. 'Well, if you're sure, dear. I must say, Lady Finsborough was very charming about it all. She even suggested you could wear her dress since you are both so much the same size.'

'So I could. I modelled it for you, didn't I? Oh, yes, how wonderful, I could wear the dress.'

Before Mary could say any more, Sunny had opened the leather telephone book and started to dial Lady Finsborough's number, drumming her fingers on the telephone table as they both stood listening to what now seemed like the endless ring-ing of the telephone. Sunny's fingers drummed faster and faster, as if she could encourage someone the other end to answer, which they finally did. 'Hallo, yes. I wonder if I could speak to Lady Finsborough? . . . Sorry? . . . Yes, of course. It's Sunny Chantry.' Sunny covered the telephone and mouthed, 'Her butler . . .' at Mary, who by now was feeling dreadfully awkward for several reasons she could not quite understand, but these feelings were soon followed by relief as she listened to the telephone conversation that followed.

Finally Sunny put down the telephone.

'You heard, Ma? I'm to go to the Manor this evening, and join the Brownes' dinner party, and then on to the dance.'

Sunny started to jiggle up and down on the spot out of excitement, which was really rather a childish habit that Mary

knew she ought to have grown out of, but like so much to do
with Sunny, she never had the heart to stop her because, when
all was said and done, one day she would get older, and the
jiggling would stop anyway.

'Will Pa be able to take me? Will the Vauxhall be off its
blocks by then? Will there be someone else who could take me
if Pa can't?'

'Best not to let Pa take you,' Mary said quickly. 'You know
how it is, such a terrible thing if you break down, like that poor
man yesterday morning, and in a Bentley too. No, best if Mr
Arkwright takes you, and then your hostess will make sure
there is someone to bring you back to Pear Tree Cottage, as
they do.'

But Sunny wasn't listening. She was already pushing her way
back into the dining room to gaze at the beautiful dress.

'I say, Ma, can you imagine? I shall be going to the
ball in Lady Finsborough's dress! Who would have thought
it?'

Her mother nodded, taking the dress down and holding it
against her daughter once more. She knew she had done a
good job on it, knew that Sunny, with her pretty looks, would
look beautiful.

'Just be careful not to let anyone spill anything on it, Sunny,
that's all.'

'Of course, of course, I shall treat it like spun gold.'

Sunny took the dress from her mother and held it against
herself.

'The only thing is – I mean, what I don't understand, Ma, is
why Lady Finsborough thought of me; why she thought I might
like to go in her stead.'

'She's a very kind woman, Sunny, she probably knew.'

'What? What did she know?'

Her mother frowned. 'Something, I imagine. People like that, they always know *something*.'

The dance began at ten o'clock. 'Breakfast', as it was still always called at balls and dances, although in reality a late night supper, would be served from twelve thirty onwards – and motor cars would be sent for at one thirty, although like 'breakfast', they were still referred to in the old way on formal invitations, as 'carriages'.

The ballroom at Harcourt House was already a lively scene when Leandra and Dilke arrived with their house party, the dancers waltzing gracefully to the sound of a small orchestra, the clusters of candles at either end of the room burning brightly among great banks of flowers, while the overhead, electrically lit chandeliers provided just the right amount of light. It was an undeniably pretty sight, a sight that reminded both the dancers and their onlookers that no matter what Hitler had thrown at them, style had at last returned to England. He might have brought the country to its knees for six years, but now they were up on their feet once again, and what was more and what was better, old and young alike, they were dancing, just like in the old days before the war.

'This is the time when I feel the need for a quizzing glass, as in Regency times,' Gray murmured as he stood on the top step of the stairs.

He turned to Randy Beauchamp, who was looking even more startled than usual as yet more of his prematurely white hair was standing up on end, matching his old-fashioned stand-up collar.

'No one's wearing white tie any more,' he complained a little too loudly. 'The whole place is awash with dine-at-home black ties,' he groaned.

46

'That's how it has been since the war, Randy,' Gray told him, adding a moment later to himself, 'As a matter of fact, since *both* of the wars.'

'I still think it looks frightful; black tie at a ball looks frightful,' Randy went on inexorably. 'Quite frightful. And I dare say from the look of the young men half of them are wearing made-up bow ties at that. I dare say none of them even knows how to tie a bow tie.'

'Oh, I don't think they would dare wear already made-up bow ties, Randy – not if they knew you were coming.'

They were passed by couple after couple, all heading for the dance floor, but neither of them was tempted to turn round and search out a dancing partner for himself, preferring instead to lean against the banisters of the staircase and watch the pageant below.

'I must say, the women and the girls look quite sweet, and Barbara Goalen looks more than sweet – she looks ravishing as usual,' Randy finally conceded. 'But for the rest, yes, I must say, they look really quite sweet.'

He turned to look up at Gray, who was now staring past him at someone below them.

'I say, you're looking a little strange, old chap. Seen someone from your past, come back to haunt you?'

'No, no, just a rather sweet face.'

Gray moved slowly down the staircase towards the dance floor just as the music came to an end, and just as Sunny was bobbing a little mock curtsy to her partner and turning to leave the floor.

She stopped as she saw Gray coming towards her, and laughed.

'Good heavens, Mr Wyndham! First yesterday morning, and now this evening. I dare say you are more surprised to see me than I am to see you; but I am the one out of my ground, I dare say. How is the motor car? Did Mr Arkwright do it all right? He is a splendid mechanic, but he has never done a Bentley before. As you probably gathered, we do not see many Bentleys in Rushington, truly we don't, so I do hope you made it all right. Well, stupid of me, really – of course you made it all right, or you wouldn't be here,' she finally finished.

Gray stared at her. Sunny was wearing the same yellow evening dress that she had been wearing the day before when she had opened the door of her parents' cottage to him, but she was also wearing her long dark hair up, and tied with a brocade ribbon at the back, which, for some reason he couldn't quite work out, had the effect of making all the other women in the room, in their jewellery and splendid ball gowns, look overdressed and a little tired.

'Who are you, might I ask?' Gray finally asked, poker-faced. 'Have we met before? Now let me see, I seem to remember . . . where was it? Ascot? Henley? No. No . . . Oh yes, of course, I remember now. You are – you are, yes, you are Miss *Chantry*. I am sorry, for a second I really didn't know you in that dress without the pins down the side. You look really quite different without the pins.'

Sunny gave her kitten-like smile. 'I dare say I might never have known you without your motor car, if I hadn't met you first without it. You know, like people without their shops, or when you meet someone on the Downs, and you recognise their dogs, but not them,' she retorted.

'Touché,' Gray laughed. 'I suppose it is really rather a miracle you know me without my Bentley,' he added a little ruefully.

'You have obviously only just arrived,' Sunny went on airily.

'Yes, I have only just arrived. I am staying at Maydown, a

Friday-to-Monday with the Fortescues. And you? Are you staying nearby, perhaps?'

'Oh no, I don't like staying with people when I can be at home,' Sunny replied, turning away to look at the other dancers because she felt she might be losing their exchange. 'As a matter of fact I have been here for hours and hours because, being in a much older party, I arrived unfashionably early.' She leaned forward and whispered, 'Actually, I am only here because Lady Finsborough's mother fell ill and there was no one to wear the *dress*! So she rang up my mother and suggested that I come here in her stead, because I have known the Norells for years and years – they used to come over to Pear Tree Cottage for Sunday lunch and play Monopoly. They loved the lunch because their nanny only gave them mutton with lots of fat and overcooked carrots and tapioca, all of which they hated, whereas Ma always managed roast beef, because of knowing the farmer up the way, and having done his wife's wedding dress, not to mention altering all his clothes when he came back from the prisoner-of-war camp.'

'Is that so?' Gray stepped back a little from Sunny as if to allow for her torrent of dialogue. 'Well, I must say, joking apart, that is a very pretty dress, and I am very glad you wore it, even if it really belongs to Lady Finsborough.'

'Since it is quite an old dress I don't suppose there is anyone else here who would have wanted to wear it, which is probably why she thought of me. I like it so much.' She looked down at the dress, and then up at Gray. 'Mind you, I do rather miss the pins.'

Gray laughed. 'Would you like the next dance, without pins?'

'Well, yes. But shouldn't you dance with your hostess first?'

'Of course, but on this occasion I am sure she will

understand. I will explain to her later that I would not be here if it were not for you.'

Gray led Sunny on to the dance floor. It was a waltz. He didn't know why but it seemed suddenly really rather appropriate to be dancing with such a sweet, old-fashioned girl in an old-fashioned frock.

As he waltzed Sunny past a group standing chatting to the side of the ballroom, he saw Leandra staring at them both, taking in the youthful figure in his arms. He smiled across at her and it seemed to Gray that Leandra's look to him was saying, '*Could this be the one perhaps?*'

## Chapter Two

Mary Chantry looked up from her sewing machine and stared out at her front garden, as she always did between bouts of turning the machine's wheel. Someone was coming up to the cottage door, and she knew straight away from the vaguely bohemian look of her – amber beads, long black skirt – that it was Sunny's friend Arietta Staunton.

'Come in, come in, Arietta dear, come in – do,' Mary begged her, holding open the front door while speaking as always through pins. 'What a beautiful morning. And God created Rushington, wouldn't you say?'

Arietta followed Mrs Chantry into the hall, but not into the dining room.

'Is Sunny here?' she asked, pronouncing her words rather over-clearly.

Mary turned at the dining-room door. 'Yes, dear, she is here, but she is still fast asleep upstairs.'

'Oh.' Arietta smiled broadly at Mrs Chantry. 'Lucky thing,' she went on, nodding and smiling even more broadly.

'Go and wake her up, if you can, Arietta, but stand well

back, because she can be lethal when woken too suddenly!'

Mary laughed, but Arietta did not, though she smiled ever more broadly.

Mary carried on into the dining room, and then stopped and returned to the hall.

'*Arietta!*' She paused, taking the pins from her mouth one by one, quite carefully, as if they were fish bones, and sticking them, also one by one, into the pin cushion strapped to her wrist. 'Arietta, you have had your braces off! My dear, this is too exciting for words.'

Arietta's smile was so wide now it was practically splitting her face.

'What do you think?'

Mary leaned forward, the better to appreciate the smile.

'Perfect, just perfect. Your teeth are so perfect I dare say you could do advertising for an American toothpaste company, really you could.'

Arietta finally stopped smiling and let out a sigh of such deep feeling that Mary felt compelled to pat her reassuringly on her arm.

'I had them off on Friday afternoon, and I haven't stopped smiling since.'

'Well, of course, you wouldn't have done, you poor child. Braces are such a burden, I often wonder how anyone puts up with them, really I do wonder. Not that Sunny has ever had to have a brace, but if she did I know that she would feel just as you do. Now, go up and wake her with your new bright smile. I dare say she will have to shade her eyes to look at you.' Mary nodded up the stairs. 'She is sleeping off last night's party – well, not a party so much, a ball really. Lady Finsborough, you know? She couldn't go, so Sunny went instead, because Sunny stands in for all Lady Finsborough's dress fittings, especially for the Season and Ascot and the rest, their measurements and height being precisely the same, so as she couldn't go to the ball she very kindly insisted that Sunny went in her stead. She also insisted that she wore her dress, would you believe? Mind, it is pre-war, but even so – such generosity is almost unimaginable, you must agree.'

Arietta was halfway up the short flight of polished dark oak stairs long before Mary had finished speaking.

Mary smiled, went back into the dining room and shut the door. There would be so much for the two of them to talk about. Although now she came to think of it, she had heard nothing from Sunny since she had returned at two o'clock in the morning. Mary had heard the door of the car that must have brought her back slammed in such a way, and their own front door opened and shut so quickly that she knew, as mothers do, that Sunny had been only too glad to get out of the car and into the house, which had made her feel a little anxious about who could have brought her home.

Still, much as she longed to know whether or not Sunny and the remodelled ball gown had been successes, she could not spare the time to go up and ask Sunny all about it. She had to finish altering Mrs FitzWarren's cocktail dress and matching coat.

Mrs FitzWarren was giving a reception in honour of the committee organising the funding for the village war memorial. The cocktail party was to be held at the Manor House, Rushington the following weekend. Everyone who was anyone from Rushington and nearby Bexham had been invited. It was a worthy cause, Mrs FitzWarren kept saying, most especially since so many of the fallen had no other memorial, nothing to remind their families, or anyone else, that they had died for their country, just a telegram and a collection of black-and-white photographs in a family album.

Mary bent once more over her sewing machine, turning away from looking back, looking only to the future, for really there was very little that you *could* do. She knew that John had taken the covers off the Vauxhall, and that after Sunday lunch the family would probably go for a spin around the lanes, and then up to the Downs. That was something to which she could really look forward, just as she could look forward to cooking the first piece of pork they had been able to obtain since heaven only knew when. And a very fine piece of roast pork it was going to be, with the crispiest crackling, accompanied by a flavoursome apple sauce, and golden roast potatoes, and vegetables from the garden, which would be followed by a floating island pudding. All in all it would be quite a day.

Upstairs, Sunny was sitting up in bed, her hair tangled, her large eyes staring at Arietta as if she had only just seen her, which in a way she had.

'Oh goodness, Arietta, I can't *believe* it, really I can't. It makes you look so different! What does it feel like? It must feel wonderful, gracious heavens. I mean to say, really, you are a different girl now. How marvellous, how particularly marvellous! I can't get over how different you look, truly I can't.'

They both laughed and Sunny leaned forward and hugged Arietta as if she had just passed a really difficult exam, which in a way perhaps she had.

'I should jolly well hope you can't get over how different I look,' Arietta stated. 'It would make anyone look different, not having all those wires in their mouth. Of course, the good thing is that it has finally worked. My teeth are finally straight now, I think they truly are.'

She bared her teeth at Sunny, who lay back against her pillows, smiling.

There was a short silence. Sunny carried on smiling, and Arietta smiled back, although she could not yet understand what there was so very much to smile about. It was just so fine being able to try a large smile, knowing that your teeth were showing and not the brace.

'So.' She stared at Sunny once she had stopped smiling. 'So? Are you going to tell me about the Norells' ball, or are you going to go back to sleep again and leave me dangling on the end of a very long piece of string? Did you dance every dance? Were you the belle of the ball? Did you fall in love with a handsome stranger? Please answer all the questions, leaving a wide margin at the bottom of the paper so I can make footnotes.'

'I don't know,' Sunny said, shaking her head, and she stared past Arietta, seeing something that she couldn't explain to her. 'I don't know – it was just magical, but I don't know how to explain why it was so magical because it all happened in such a hurry. I mean, I didn't realise I was going to go to the Norells' ball, let alone in Lady Finsborough's dress. I don't know how to explain how I felt.'

'Well, of course you do,' Arietta put in impatiently. 'Oh, tell, please, do, or I shall go home and cry and cry.'

'No, don't cry, please. It will spoil the look of your new teeth if you have a red nose. Very well.' Sunny looked serious as she recalled the best evening of her life so far. 'To begin at the beginning, of course, I was not the belle of the ball. I couldn't possibly have been because there were hundreds and hundreds of beautiful women, wearing gowns by Hardy Amies and heaven only knows who, and you have never seen such jewels. But I did dance every dance, and I never had to sit out, not once.'

'Well, then!' Arietta clasped her hands over her knees and swayed backwards exultantly. 'How perfectly marvellous, how perfectly perfect. Imagine, your first ball and you never had to sit out once, *and* you were wearing Lady Finsborough's dress.'

'You should have seen the jewels that were there. They were so perfect, all matching their gowns. Barbara Goalen was there too, looking stunning, just like in the magazines. She is such a beautiful mannequin.' Sunny shook her head. 'Actually, all the women were beyond the beyonds, my deah,' she said, mimicking the county ladies who called on her mother for dress alterations.

'And what then? Did a handsome stranger fall in love with you? Were you swept off your feet?'

Sunny looked away, her eyes straying to the view beyond the window. Somewhere out there she imagined that *he* would be getting up and having breakfast. Perhaps he might already have had breakfast? Perhaps he would have a valet to lay out his clothes? Older men so often did have valets, even now.

'No,' Sunny stated firmly, sitting up and twisting her hair into a knot on top of her head and fastening it with two Kirbigrips from her bedside table. 'A handsome stranger did not fall in love with me, but the handsome stranger whose Bentley broke down outside here the other morning, well, he *did* dance with me quite a bit, and he did say he wants me to have lunch with him quite soon, although I expect he will forget completely.'

Arietta let go her knees and fell backwards on to the eiderdown on the bed, her arms dramatically outstretched.

'Oh, heavens! You'll probably be married before the end of the month!' Arietta announced, staring up at the ceiling.

'Oh, no, no, no, nothing like that. No, it was just that we had met before; that was the only reason he asked me to dance the first dance after he arrived. As I just told you, it was because his car broke down outside here, and Mr Arkwright came and mended it, and he is so grateful to me for calling out Mr Arkwright, and all that kind of thing.'

Sunny lay back against her pillows once more, thinking, for perhaps the fiftieth time, that really, all in all, it was a strange sequence of events that had led to her going to the ball, and dancing with Mr Wyndham.

'I don't believe a word of it. He has not asked you to lunch about mending his Bentley,' Arietta asserted, sighing happily, her eyes half closed. 'He has asked you to lunch because he has fallen in love with you, I know he has. I just know that is why he has asked you to lunch.'

'Don't be silly.'

'No, I know he has,' she insisted. 'I know from the look on your face he has fallen in love with you. You have that look. My cousin had it last year, when she'd had a whirlwind romance, and been swept off her feet, and now she has gone to live in a castle in Spain.' Arietta paused. 'Mind you, her mother is furious because she says she will never, ever be let out of Spain again, because apparently Spanish noblemen don't let their wives even go to the shops; they have to send their maids in their stead. At any rate, looking at you now, I would say that you definitely have the same look as my cousin.'

Sunny turned away and stared out of the window once more.

'Don't be silly, I don't have any look. I would know if I had a look,' she replied, but Arietta continued to smile up at the ceiling.

'I always knew something wonderful would happen to you soon, Sunny. There's something about you that makes you so different from the rest of us, there really is. And I tell you what – it makes everyone who knows you want something wonderful to happen to you, including me, and I'm horrible, so that is how wonderful you are, Miss Chantry.'

Sunny lay back against her pillows once more.

'You are dear, Arietta,' she murmured, but then she quickly changed the subject because she didn't really believe her. 'I say, Pa's taken the Vauxhall off its blocks. Stay to lunch, and help with the car, won't you?'

Gray stood up as Sunny reached the restaurant table. It was a long time since he had lunched with someone as young as Miss Chantry, and now she was here it seemed to him that she was even younger – and this despite the fact that she was wearing a white-trimmed straw hat and a pretty floral dress and jacket, and three-quarter-length gloves, and high-heeled shoes and carrying a formal handbag.

'You look very pretty,' he told her appreciatively as the waiter pulled out her chair for her, and she sat down.

Sunny smiled. She knew she did look quite pretty, but that knowledge did not stop her feeling nervous.

'It was very kind of you to ask me to lunch.'

Gray looked around the light and spacious dining room, with its heavy white linen tablecloths and matching napkins.

'I doubt that it was kind; I doubt that very much,' he stated, his eyes observing the other couples lunching, noting that they were all much older than himself. 'This is really rather too grown up a place for me,' he observed, 'so it must be far too grown up a place for you.'

'I think it's lovely,' Sunny put in quickly. 'And it's only older in here because places like this, places around about, like Napley Hill and Rushington, are full of older people, and they like to have lunch here when they change their library books, and that kind of thing.' Sunny gave an affectionate look round the restaurant, and lowered her voice as if she was emotionally in charge of the rest of the dining room and therefore protective of them. 'They're actually all trying to keep their spirits up, after all that has happened, and I think they're doing rather well,' she ended proudly.

Gray stared at her, and then shook his head as if for some reason he could not quite believe what he had just heard.

'What would you like to drink? Are you allowed a drink at lunch-time?'

'Of course. I would like a—' Sunny hesitated. 'I would like a—'

'Dry sherry?'

'A medium dry sherry.'

'As I remember it from when my motor gave up the ghost outside your house, your family are rather fond of sherry, aren't they?'

'Only for visitors. If there are visitors, of course we offer sherry, but at lunch, at the weekends, they drink beer. Everyone round here does.'

Gray ordered the drinks and then turned back to Sunny, knowing that it was his duty to find out more about her. They had been together barely more than a few minutes and already a large part of him wished that he had not taken Leandra's advice and asked Miss Chantry to lunch. He had never had any real intention of carrying through Leandra's plan, which had seemed to him to be far too outrageous for his taste; but then part of him was glad that he had done as Leandra had suggested, because if Miss Chantry was one thing and one thing alone, she was certainly refreshing.

'What would you be doing normally, if you weren't having lunch with me?'

Sunny pulled a little face. 'Normally? Normally I would be doing something very normal, normally.'

'And what is, er – normal, normally around here?'

Sunny bit her lip, hesitating. She hated to admit that she was studying to be a secretary, of all things, and yet she hated to lie even more – in fact she couldn't lie, wouldn't lie. She finally decided that she would give it to Mr Wyndham between the eyes. He wanted to know how normal or ordinary she was? So be it, she would let him know just how normal and ordinary.

'I would normally be at secretarial college, and you can't really get more normal than that,' she told him, after which, to cover her embarrassing admission, she quickly picked up her schooner of sherry and sipped at it.

Gray stared at her.

'Of course you would. That is – well – that is really quite normal,' he agreed in a kind voice, while at the same time he couldn't help hearing Leandra's voice saying, '*Anyone suitable not only will not be rich . . .*' Girls who went to secretarial colleges had to get jobs, and girls who had to get jobs were not rich. They were expected to work in offices and look elegant, or at least neat, and then leave to be married. 'Will you enjoy being a secretary?' he finally asked.

'Oh, no.' Sunny shook her head. 'Not at all, but Ma says I have to do something. She doesn't know I am here. I told her I had toothache and was going to the dentist, which was naughty, but she would never have let me come otherwise, and I told the college secretary the same. So here I am, and going a beastly puce from the effects of this sherry.'

She picked up her water glass and held it first to one cheek and then the other.

Gray watched her. She was so artless, so honest, so poor – certainly compared to everyone else he knew – and, naturally, so young also compared to everyone else he knew. She couldn't be more than eighteen, might be only seventeen. Again Leandra's words came back to him: '*Anyone suitable . . . will have to be innocent and well-behaved.*'

'Shall we order?'

He picked up his menu and gave it a cursory glance. Sunny put down her water glass, picked up her own menu, and started to read it in silent, reverential concentration. She felt so hungry.

'We had roast pork for the first time on Sunday,' she murmured.

'And it was delicious?'

Sunny nodded, still not taking her eyes from the dishes on offer. 'Oh, yes. It was just as perfect as Ma and Pa always said it was, before, you know – before the war.'

It seemed to Gray that the menu was not so extensive that it would take a sophisticated person more than a few seconds to choose from it, but such was not the case with his luncheon companion. Sunny was reading the choices of dishes very, very carefully, hoping, he sensed, not to make a mistake, because what she was about to eat, and presumably be thankful for, mattered that much to her. He thought of the food he had enjoyed at Maydown at the weekend. He thought of the enormous breakfast table laden with kedgeree and meats and fruits of every kind; of the choices of drinks of every kind; of the sophistications on offer to all the guests; and in the presence of this slip of a girl who was so obviously excited by the really very limited menu on offer, he felt oddly guilty, as if he had come on from some kind of bacchanalian orgy.

'And you would like . . . ?' he prompted.

'Would it be all right to have roast chicken?'

Chicken was very, very expensive, and always spoken of in hushed tones in Rushington.

61

Gray smiled. 'You may have anything you like, Miss Chantry,' he said, and he found himself staring at her in such an odd way that he didn't even look at the waiter as he was ordering, only kept on looking at Sunny, who was once more pressing the water glass against her cheeks.

'I'm afraid it *is* the sherry,' she explained apologetically. 'I do like sherry, but it does make me horridly red. I think it's because I don't have it very often – well, only really at Christmas, and then only after church.'

'It doesn't matter, really—'

'Oh, but it *does*. It's such a woeful thing to happen. No one wants to go red over lunch, do they? I mean, when you're sitting at home thinking about going to lunch with someone you don't know very well, you don't *exactly* say to yourself, "*I do hope I go reddish purple as soon as I sip my sherry,*" do you?' she finished with sudden indignation.

'No, no, of course not.'

'There that's better.' She put down the water glass and pushed the sherry away from her. 'I don't think I will have any more. Just water. You're lucky, obviously you can drink what you like and it doesn't make you look like some sort of old publican with a bottle nose and a wife and six children.'

Gray kept what he hoped was an admirably straight face.

'Do you know many bottle-nosed publicans with six children?'

Sunny, who was still feeling hopelessly out of her depth and yet at the same time looking increasingly indignant, because a great part of her was blaming Mr Wyndham for suggesting that she drank the sherry, frowned.

'Well, no, I can't say that I do. But I don't see what that has to do with anything.'

'No, I don't suppose it has got anything to do with anything.

I must confess to you, I am actually beginning to feel rather out of my depth,' he confessed.

'Well, you would do,' Sunny said, looking suddenly sympathetic. 'I mean, it's not often someone like you takes out someone like me, who just doesn't know how to go on, and what is more,' she added, starting to look mildly indignant all over again, 'who can't even take a sip of a medium dry sherry without going purple.'

'Pink, not purple.'

'Well, say whatever colour you like, but it is most discomforting, and not at all what someone like you is used to,' Sunny sighed. 'I did hope I would do better than this,' she added, lowering her voice, as if Gray was not her host, but someone in whom she was confiding – in other words talking *to* him *about* him.

'You are doing beautifully and you are once more a normal colour, I promise you,' Gray reassured her, as the chicken arrived.

'Masses of bread sauce, and a lovely thick gravy, how heavenly,' Sunny announced dreamily, her mood changing as her eyes dwelled approvingly on the sauce boats being offered.

In the pause, as they were being served by the ageing waiters, Gray heard his own voice saying to Leandra, '*Supposing she is not nice and we discover this far too late?*'

He couldn't quite remember Leandra's reply, but he thought it might have been something vaguely dismissive to indicate that if she, Leandra, had anything to do with it, his future wife-in-name-only would be as nice as pie. Certainly, if this young girl whom he had met by chance *was* going to be Leandra's choice for him, she was not just nice, she was almost impossibly nice.

He sighed inwardly. He should always trust Leandra to make

everything perfect for him. She, after all, had perfect taste in everything, which was one of the many reasons why he loved her.

Gray put aside the thought of Leandra, and her multitude of attractions, and turned his attention back to Sunny. She was sitting in a pool of sunshine, and her colour, with the aid, obviously, of the glass of water, had gradually returned to normal. He noticed that she sat quite still, did not fiddle with the knives and forks or keep turning and looking around, and that her eyes were large and thoughtful, staring at him as if he was someone from another planet.

'Are you enjoying yourself?' he asked, after a pause.

Sunny stared down at her plate of delicious-looking chicken, and then all too briefly at him, before her eyes returned to her plate.

'I haven't really been enjoying myself up to now, but I think I might be just about to.'

Gray laughed. Miss Chantry was nothing if not honest.

Arietta let herself back into her mother's cottage, hoping against hope, as always, that Audrey Staunton would not be in, or that if she was she would not hear Arietta coming back but would continue ironing and listening to one of those radio programmes that, for some reason that Arietta could never quite work out, always made her mother excessively depressed. For if Sunny's mother always seemed to be in a good humour, sewing and busying herself in house and garden, if she was always at pains to be looking towards a brighter future, confident that somehow or other good would ultimately triumph over bad, Arietta's widowed mother was quite the opposite, which was probably why Arietta always found herself sidling into their cottage, hoping that she could reach her bedroom without her mother hearing her.

'Ari-*etta*? Is that you, Arietta?'

Arietta paused on the stairs, one foot poised to mount the next step. Her mother must have just switched the radio off as Arietta's foot hit the squeakiest board on the narrow rickety old oak staircase.

'Yes, Mummy, it is me.'

Audrey came into the hall, removed her spectacles and stared up at Arietta, frowning.

'What are you doing, Arietta, may I ask?'

'I'm just going upstairs to study my shorthand.'

'Study your shorthand? You're always studying your shorthand; never have time to sit down and talk to me, never a moment.'

'It's not that, it's just that I thought if I could do the course in half the time, I will be able to get a job sooner, which means you can stop worrying about bills because I will be bringing you home my wages.'

Her mother turned away from her. 'I don't worry about bills. There's no point,' she said flatly. 'And I certainly can't imagine you making any kind of secretary! You're really not the type! You're far too dreamy! Far too much of an unmade bed! I mean, look at you!'

Arietta nodded in agreement. 'I know what you mean, Mummy, but now I have my brace off I do look a bit better, more the thing, don't you think?'

Her mother turned back to face her. 'The money that brace cost, it doesn't bear thinking of,' Audrey sighed, and then made to go to the kitchen. 'I suppose you want something to eat? There's a rissole in the fridge.'

'No, really,' Arietta called as the kitchen door swung shut behind her mother. 'Really, I don't want anything. I'm trying to lose weight.' After which she positively leaped up the last steps of the staircase, and quickly closed her bedroom door. 'I hate rissoles even more than I hated my brace,' she murmured to her small bedroom.

She lay down on her bed. She wished – oh, how she wished with all her heart – that she had a mother like Sunny's. Mrs Chantry was always laughing and smiling, sewing things for people, being kind, not always grumbling about money. It was not as if her mother had even had to pay for Arietta's upbringing. She did not understand why her mother grumbled so much about money since they both knew very well that Arietta's Uncle Bob, her dead father's brother, had paid for everything for his niece, poor soul. Not that Uncle Bob could have got out of it should he have wanted to. Audrey being so particularly adept at extortion, she would ask him to lunch once a month, and grumble at him so long and so hard that Uncle Bob would inevitably find himself writing out an even larger cheque than on his previous visit.

The theme, the constant theme that had dominated Arietta's childhood was that she was a ball and chain anchoring poor Audrey to their cottage, forcing her into a life of washing and ironing, of drudgery and care, a life that without Uncle Bob might have reduced her poor mother to 'living in a slum'. It seemed that had not her mother had the misfortune to give birth to Arietta, Audrey could have been an elegant woman attending fashionable parties where hostesses entertained glamorous guests, where life was easy and sophisticated, where attractive women met rich men who whisked them away to lives of luxury. All this would have been possible had Audrey Staunton not been left a widow with a *child*. No man wanted to take on a woman with a child, let alone a daughter.

'If it wasn't for you . . .' Audrey would begin, and then she would sigh, and Arietta would try to think of something that would please her mother, try to make up to her for the deprivations her existence had caused.

Strangely, Arietta perfectly understood her mother's point of view – perhaps because there was no other point of view on offer, or perhaps because, being a practical girl, she could perfectly see that Audrey *would* have been far better off if she had been left a childless widow, which was why Arietta was in such a hurry to leave secretarial college and strike out on her own, earn a living, send money home to Audrey who would, at long, long last be able to be what she had always wanted to be: a glamorous single woman.

Leandra picked up her white telephone receiver and was unsurprised to hear Gray's mellifluous voice at the other end.

'You are back from luncheon, and at your apartment?' she asked, careful not to say his name in front of the maid, who was clearing her coffee tray from her desk.

'I am.'

'And how was it all?'

'It all was – interesting, and amusing too.'

'As suitable as we thought it might be?'

The maid had now closed the door behind her. Leandra lay back against her chair. She loved the time between lunch and dinner, time which could be spent in any way she chose, when there would be no guests expected and no one to whom she had to be charming.

'It is quite as suitable, but terribly young. Hardly eighteen, you know. Almost half my age, Leandra. Really it doesn't seem right to take a young sweetie like that and throw her into the maelstrom of Society. It does not seem at all right.'

'Has the person other plans?'

'Certainly she has. She has plans for the future which do not include marrying a man of well over thirty and leading a separate life.'

'What are her plans?' Leandra always kept her voice low when speaking on the telephone, for many reasons, one of them being that she knew only too well how many maids listened at doors, knew how they could be in the pay of other households whose mistresses would be glad to know anything about Leandra, from her clothes to her menus to her lovers.

'Her plans are to become a secretary, and then save up the money she makes from that and open a flower shop.'

'*Tiens! Mon Dieu!* What innocent ambitions.' Leandra smiled. She had a very pretty French accent, which was why she often used French expressions. Besides, it was very fashionable. Nancy Mitford was living in Paris, everyone that was anyone was going there for Friday-to-Mondays, and coming back with glorious tales of heavenly meals, and shopping trips to Dior.

Leandra would not go to live in Paris; she was too aware of her reputation. She did not want to encourage the sort of adverse publicity that others of her kind had attracted by going to live lives of ease elsewhere. She was always careful to stay in England, to look and seem patriotic, to divide her time between London and her country house, not to do anything that was not thoroughly English. Dilke had too many business affairs for her to want to be seen to be anything but exemplary. Besides, she knew that Dilke was beginning to harbour political ambitions, which, since he had recently become a British citizen, were not beyond the realms of possibility.

There was a pause. Leandra allowed the pause to lengthen. It was one of her strengths, one of her many social skills, that she knew never to fill a pause hastily in case it made her seem ill at ease or, at the very least, neurotic.

'Supposing I take the person in question to lunch, and learn a little more about flower shops and other notions?'

'What can I say? I am putty in your hands.'

'I am very glad to hear it. *Quatre ou cinq?*'

This was their code for meeting up at tea-time. Despite the fact that she employed only Spanish maids in London and country girls at Maydown, who would not know a word of French, Leandra would not risk saying anything remotely suspicious on the telephone.

She replaced the telephone on its cradle, and then she stood up, and strolled towards the window of her beloved sitting room. The room that Dilke had allocated to her, to do in it as she wished when she wished was one of her favourites. It was where she kept her long lists of amusing guests, important guests, dull but rich guests, newly arrived celebrities, and every other kind of personality. Her sitting room – or sulking room, as Dilke always affectionately referred to it – was in reality the engine room of their social and political life, which was why she never left it without locking the door.

She pulled aside the net curtain and gazed down at the street below. London still looked so awfully post war, people hurrying along in old-fashioned clothes bravely altered, clothes with which they nevertheless sported fashionable hats, for which no clothing coupons had been required. Opposite Leandra's apartment block, a window cleaner was propping up a ladder. Even from her distant point of view she could see that he was painfully thin, no black market produce coming to *him* then. A car passed. A large car with a gleaming body and with a silver lady on the front – the famous Rolls-Royce Spirit of Ecstasy.

Leandra dropped the curtain. It was time to change. How glad she was that Dilke and she had never wanted to have children, because it meant that despite being in her late thirties, her body was still that of an eighteen-year-old – everyone said so, Dilke and Gray particularly. She was very lucky. She had two men who loved and adored her, but in such very different ways. One way and another she really had the perfect life.

'I don't really like the sound of her, Sunny.' John Chantry looked round at his daughter, a worried expression on her face. 'She sounds rough again to me.'

'At least she's going, Pa, and that really is something after all this time, don't you think? I mean last weekend you couldn't get her to even start, could you now?'

Sunny was standing in wide-bottomed slacks, a favourite old cardigan done up around her, a pair of old white gym shoes on her feet. Her father stared at her, not really seeing her, listening instead to his old girl, his beloved Vauxhall.

'She may be going, Sunny, but she's running rough.' As the engine suddenly stalled, a look of triumph came into John's eyes. 'See? See? I told you. Better telephone Clem Arkwright and get him out to us. I didn't want to call him out, because he never will send me a bill, as you know, ever since my father did his father a turn with saving his favourite horse, which makes me feel worse than dreadful. I mean to say, that was in the Ice Age, but they say the Arkwrights never forget a favour, and so it would seem.' He patted the Vauxhall as if it was a horse. 'Poor old girl got a touch of the colic – I expect that is what Clem will say. But what a dratted nuisance, what a bother. Still, we must not expect too much of the old servant. She is, after all, of a certain vintage and, what is more, a really rather special one. Best if you pop indoors and telephone Clem Arkwright to come out to her, would you, Sunny?'

Since Sunny did not move to do his bidding. John turned from comforting his car and stared at her.

'Well, go on, go on, girl, or we won't be able to go to this *do* tomorrow that your mother has talked us into, and I will never hear the end of it. I will be in hot water for the rest of time.'

'Mr Arkwright's already on his way, Pa.' Sunny smiled. 'Ma told him to be sure to be here for you at ten thirty. After what happened last Sunday, she thought the old girl might need a bit of help.'

John shook his head and then smiled suddenly with satisfied understanding.

'Your mother is a wonderful woman, Sunny, a really wonderful woman.' He turned as he heard the front gate clicking. 'And here is Clem, large as life and twice as horrible. Gracious, Clem,' John went to hold out a large blackened paw before hastily withdrawing it to wipe it on one of the many rags that were now littering the drive, 'I have only to rub the magic wand on my spanner, and here you are! Been working on her since last weekend, but I am dearly afraid I have not your magic touch, Clem.'

Clem Arkwright smiled, standing back a little way from the old Vauxhall.

'Good to see the old girl with her rugs off, though, isn't it, Mr Chantry?'

'It certainly is, Clem, it certainly is.'

They both stood for a few seconds in reverential silence, gazing at the motor car, remembering her in her glory days before the war.

'My father bought this from your father for my birthday, didn't he, Clem?'

'He did, Mr Chantry, he certainly did. And I daren't think what he paid for her.'

'Worth every penny. I learned to drive in her, and you know how I learned to drive in her, Clem?'

Clem Arkwright, despite knowing only too well, shook his head. 'No, I don't remember, at least I don't think I do.'

'When I stopped driving into the ditches round Rushington, falling into the hedges, and reversing into farm gates, that's when your father and my father considered I had learned to drive! Golly, but those were the days, Clem. Couldn't do that now, not with this lot turning the country upside down and inside out, making laws for this and laws for that, turning England into some kind of police state.'

They both nodded in agreement. They were as one on everything were John Chantry and Clem Arkwright.

'Nothing like a new car when you're young, eh, Clem?' John asked, after a short pause.

'No, Mr Chantry, nothing like it.'

Clem Arkwright started to peer into the engine, which was a sign for Sunny to slope off back into the house, engines being what her mother always called 'chaps' talk'.

'For you. A Mrs Fortescue?'

Sunny stared at her mother. She was holding their telephone out to her and waggling it uncertainly as if it had something in the earpiece, an earwig or a wasp, that she wanted to get out.

Sunny took the telephone from her and, covering it with her hand she whispered to her mother, 'It must be for you. I don't know a Mrs Fortescue, do you?'

Her mother mouthed back to her, 'No,' and then quickly disappeared back into the dining room, where she had two bridesmaids' frocks and a wedding dress to finish altering before the following morning.

'Hello, Sunny Chantry speaking.'

'Hello, Miss Chantry. My name is Leandra Fortescue. I do
hope you don't mind me calling you, but I am a friend of Gray
Wyndham. You may remember you had lunch with him
yesterday?'

'Yes, of course.' It was embarrassing but just the mention of
Gray Wyndham's name made Sunny blush, and feel really glad
that her mother was not in the hall, or even Arietta or someone. She stared at the white of her gym shoe. Staring at
something white often helped to make the red go out of her
face.

There was a short pause.

'I was wondering,' Leandra went on eventually, 'if you would
like to come to lunch with me, at Maydown? Nothing formal,
just the two of us. It would give me such pleasure. Mr
Wyndham has told me so much about you, I feel I know you
already. But of course it might be dull for you, in which case I
quite understand.'

It was the mention of Maydown that did it. All of a sudden
Sunny realised to whom she was speaking. This was Leandra
Fortescue, the legendary socialite and hostess, a woman of
such style that even personalities such as Beatrice Miller were
known to go to her for advice. Mrs Dilke Fortescue was the
acme of everything that was stylish and beautiful in post-war
Britain, and she wanted to ask Sunny Chantry to lunch with
her.

'I would love to come to lunch—'

'Well, that is excellent. Shall we say one o'clock on Tuesday?
The Friday-to-Monday guests would have gone by then, and we
can have the place to ourselves.'

Sunny replaced the telephone and stared around the hall.
Leandra Fortescue had asked her to lunch with her. Why? She
felt dizzy. The hall seemed suddenly smaller and more

enclosed. She stared down at the parquet flooring, shiny with polish and vigour. Everything was just the same. Her gym shoes were just as white, her wide-bottomed slacks just the same navy blue they had been before, but everything was quite, quite different, because Mrs Dilke Fortescue had telephoned to ask her to lunch.

'Ma!'

Sunny burst into the dining room, but her mother, well used to her daughter's impetuosity, did not look up from her sewing machine, only kept her feet pedalling, and her eyes down.

'Ma, I've been asked to lunch by Mrs Dilke Fortescue.'

'Have you, dear? When?'

'Next Tuesday.'

'But what about secretarial college, Sunny? What will the principal say to you?'

Sunny shook her head. 'I'll have to have a cold. You'll have to tell Mrs Chandler I'm poorly.'

'Can't tell a lie, Sunny, you know that. I am George Washington's direct descendant, always have been, always will be.'

'Very well, you can say that I am going to have to be excused because I have to go to a very important appointment, which is true.'

'But how could it be very important, Sunny?'

'Mrs Dilke Fortescue, you know. *Mrs Dilke Fortescue, Ma!* You were pointing her out in *Vogue* only last month, remember? The article about style in post-war Britain – she was picked out as the one with the most, remember? It was in Chez Gaston; you were having your hair permed. You *must* remember.'

'I still don't think Mrs Chandler will be very pleased if I ask for you to take the day off, Sunny, really I don't.'

At that moment there was a shout from the drive.

'Come on, Sunny, we're ready for the off. Come on!'

Sunny dashed out into the drive and jumped into the Vauxhall beside her father.

'Hold on, Sunny, wave to Clem – shout thank you!'

Sunny did as bidden as the old Vauxhall once more sailed triumphantly into the empty road outside their gate, and Sunny sat back in her seat and stared ahead of her.

'Got her up to twenty-five already!' her father shouted excitedly. 'How about that, Sunny? What a wonderful old girl she is.' He beamed proudly at the road ahead. 'What a morning for a spin,' he said, lowering his voice as the excitement of the moment transformed momentarily into something calmer. 'What a morning. I dreamed of this when I was in prison camp, you know – dreamed and dreamed of the first morning in late spring when I could take out the old girl for a spin. Nothing will detract from this moment, Sunny, nothing.'

Sunny stared ahead of her, not replying. She hated her father mentioning being a prisoner of war, knew that he still had nightmares, knew that his experiences would haunt him for ever, but at that moment all she wanted to think about was that Mrs Dilke Fortescue had asked her out to lunch at her famous house, Maydown. She was going to have lunch with a woman who advised editors of magazines on what was good taste and what was not, who was worshipped by the fashionable world for her style. If her father could not believe that he had the old Vauxhall going, his daughter could not believe what had just happened to her. She had just been telephoned by *Mrs Dilke Fortescue.*

'Oh God, she's stalled – she's broken down.'

As the car came to a reluctant and shuddering halt, which made Sunny cling to the side of her leather seat, John pulled on the handbrake and leaped out of the driver's seat.

Then, Sunny heard him say in surprise, 'Oh look, there's Clem.'

Sunny smiled with relieved satisfaction. She knew, even if Pa didn't, that Mr Arkwright would never let Pa out in the Vauxhall for the first time without making sure that he really had been able to get the old girl going. He had obviously followed them down the road, just to make sure.

'Oh blow, seems that she must have a bit of indijaggers, Clem. Bit of a tow needed, would you say?'

'Might be a good idea, Mr Chantry.'

They both smiled ruefully.

'At least we got her as far as the crossroads, Clem!'

The short return journey stopped momentarily outside the Chantrys' cottage to let Sunny out, before continuing on to Arkwright's Garage.

Sunny let herself back into the house, making sure that she made as little noise as possible, before creeping up the stairs to her bedroom where she sat for the next hour gazing out of the window in a trance. What was happening to her life, and why? Something – but what exactly it was, she could not have said.

The question of Sunny missing a day at college came up again over the weekend, but Mary Chantry remained intransigent. She would not ring and make an excuse to the secretarial college, and what was more and what was worse, she thought that Sunny should really reconsider whether she should go to lunch with Mrs Dilke Fortescue.

'She is out of your league, Sunny, really she is,' Mary insisted, while John remained silently disinterested, wondering only if the reason that his old girl had misbehaved herself was plugs, dirt in the petrol, or too long on blocks in the garage.

Sunny was silent.

'I cannot insist that you ring and cancel, Sunny, but I do advise you that you should,' her mother went on.

Sunny still said nothing, so Mary left her at the kitchen table and went back to her sewing in the dining room. Sunny stared at the beetroot salad, at the piece of jellied tongue and the undressed salad leaves from their garden.

She did not want to think of Mrs Dilke Fortescue as being out of her league, at least not for ever. After all, if you always thought of everyone as being out of your league, then you would never go anywhere or get anywhere, or do anything. She was sure of it, and yet at the same time she was reluctant to upset her mother, who rarely if ever took a stand about anything. For some reason that she could not understand, Mary did not want her daughter going to Maydown to lunch. Of course, this made the whole idea even more exciting. Sunny started to clear away. She would go to Maydown. She just would not tell her mother she was going to go. She would probably become all too occupied in her next bout of sewing and would forget all about it, as she so often did, and Sunny would be able to go and come back without her remembering.

She laid her plans carefully. All through Monday, during her classes she took care to act as if she was not feeling very well, swallowing aspirins in front of teachers at given moments, and powdering her face with talcum powder so she looked becomingly wan.

The following morning she put on what she wanted to wear to lunch at Maydown beneath what she would normally wear for college. It was exhausting and hot, and meant that she had to pass her mother very, very quickly when she popped her head out of the dining-room door to say goodbye.

' 'Bye, Ma, 'bye.'

Once in the drive, all was well, and she managed to stagger

towards the Greenline bus, and climb aboard without too much trouble, stepping off at exactly the same stop as she always did, and watching for the bus to disappear from sight before doubling back to the station where she went to the ladies' cloakroom, and stripped off her college clothes.

It was a nuisance, but when she saw how nice she looked in her sprigged muslin dress and matching jacket, she smiled at herself. Now all she had to do was to leave the bag of clothes and college books in the left-luggage place and wait around the tea-room until the appropriate time, and then catch a train and a taxi to Maydown.

Rule opened the front door before Sunny had time to ring the bell, which was strangely disconcerting, as if he had been waiting for her all morning.

'I hope you had a safe journey, Miss Chantry?'

As Sunny followed the butler through the hall she tried to put the memory of the two hours of boredom she had endured in the station tea-room, the dirty train, and the bumpy taxi ride out of her mind. She knew from the butler's smile that, since she had arrived in a taxi, he must know just what a series of hoops she would have gone through to get to Maydown, which was not easily accessible, to say the least. He would know that she was poor, because not only was he the butler, but because he would be used to seeing their more normal guests stepping out of motor cars – the doors of which would have been held open by chauffeurs.

Sunny frowned as the butler waited for a reply to his question. 'It was very interesting,' she said finally, looking round the hall as Rule took her jacket from her. 'Although there were quite a lot of people eating rather black bananas on the train. I hate bananas when they go black, don't you?'

Normally Rule's coat taking and door opening were done in one smooth movement without pause. Now, however, he was forced to pause, albeit only fractionally, as he stared at Miss Chantry, at the same time struggling not to laugh.

'Quite so,' he agreed, having cleared his throat.

'When someone starts eating an overripe banana you do so often find yourself praying that it will all be over in a minute, don't you?'

'Naturally, one does,' Rule agreed. 'Would you like to follow me, Miss Chantry? Mrs Fortescue is expecting you in the Blue Room.'

If Sunny was feeling nervous she certainly did not show it, but followed the butler across the hall, which was actually more like a very grand drawing room. She could not help turning and gazing back at the vastly opulent decoration. The walls carefully painted in what even she knew the Pre-Raphaelites called yallery-green, the gold and white marbled insets, the red-velvet-coated gentleman over the fireplace, the equally carefully matching red-velvet-covered sofas and chairs placed artlessly around the fireplace on a vaguely faded rug, itself made up of colours that toned in quite exactly with the rest of the décor. Sunny took in all this in a few seconds, just before she turned right, following Rule down past a bust on a plinth, and so on to the Blue Room, where she found herself stepping into a sea of such blues that she was only too glad that her sprigged muslin dress and jacket were white with small pink flowers picked out, and not *blue*.

Leandra too was not dressed in blue, but in palest apple green, which set off her justly famous chestnut hair to perfection, as it was meant to do. One glance at her told Sunny that here was a great beauty who knew just what to expect of life, and what was more, the best way to achieve it. Sunny thought her grandmother, when she was alive, might have described Mrs Fortescue as 'a bit of a go-getter'.

'How nice to meet you. I have heard so much about you from Gray Wyndham.'

Sunny held out a gloved hand and shook the ungloved hand of her hostess, before sitting down and removing both gloves and placing them carefully in her handbag. Leandra watched her with some interest. Miss Chantry was a much prettier girl than Gray had led her to believe, but then she had always found that the male of the species was never really very good at describing the female of the species, unless they were particularly voluptuous, at which point they tended to go to town and *over*-describe them. Just as they were hopeless at remembering what someone had been wearing at a particular event, unless they were sporting a colour they loathed, or a truly ridiculous hat.

If Leandra herself had been asked to depict Sunny Chantry, she would have described her as a young girl of medium height, with rich dark brown hair, large grey-green eyes, and an elegant slender figure. She noted with interest that as the young girl sat down, the expression on her face was of an almost mischievous interest, and she exuded the kind of enviable confidence of someone who has never known unkindness. To say that she looked innocent would be to give the wrong impression of Miss Chantry, Leandra decided, as they exchanged the usual introductory banalities. Miss Chantry did not *look* innocent, she *was* innocent, which meant that she was just what was wanted for Leandra's purposes.

'So-ooo.' Leandra paused, her head tipped slightly back, her own famous violet-blue eyes looking at Sunny with an increasingly amused expression. 'So-ooo, you had luncheon with Mr Wyndham?'

Sunny nodded, at the same time adjusting the skirt of her muslin dress minutely. 'Yes,' she agreed, 'I did have lunch-eon.' Just in time she remembered to add the last bit. There was a long pause, which neither jumped in to fill. 'Yes, I had lunch-*eon* with Mr Wyndham, and the food was *delicious*.'

Leandra, like Rule before her, found herself struggling not to laugh at Miss Chantry's insouciant manner.

'Oh, good, I am so glad it was delicious.'

For a second Leandra allowed her mind to trot through all the young ladies and women who would give their eyeteeth to lunch with Gray, but she could not think of one whom she could imagine saying afterwards that the *food* was delicious. That *Gray* was handsome and charming, yes, but not – well, never mind. Miss Chantry herself was quite obviously, if nothing else, an original.

'Yes, and we had a jolly good chat.'

'Well, that was good.'

'Yes, he told me all about how he is going to help bring Britain back into the forefront of everything. He and lots of other people are going to start some sort of design pro-gramme. They want everything that we handle every day to be original and beautiful as well as functional, so they are dying to get going. My father too is dying to get started on rebuilding, but the restrictions are so tiresome, he thinks he will be an old man before they are fully lifted, and that life is doomed to go on being post-war dreary.' Sunny looked round the room in which they were sitting, noting the vast arrange-ments of hothouse flowers, the large blue vases, the marble columns, the carved gold picture frames, the vast eighteenth-century rug. 'Not that it is dreary here,' she finally added a little hastily, after which she smiled and cleared her throat.

Rule entered. 'Luncheon is served,' he said, speaking quietly from the door.

'*Ah, madame est servie?*' Leandra asked, as she always did.

'Yes, madam.'

Rule bowed slightly. He did not like French except on menus, but if Mrs Fortescue insisted on speaking it now and then, there really was very little that he could do about it.

Leandra stood up and Sunny followed her. They walked across the beautiful room into a small conservatory, where a table was laid for two, silver, cut glass, eighteenth-century polished knives and forks with the initials 'DLF' discreetly engraved into the handles, and stiffly starched napkins placed in front of each setting and tied into the shape of a water lily.

'It is so pretty it seems a pity to unwrap it,' Sunny stated, admiring her napkin before unravelling it, and spreading it over her knees.

'So,' Leandra said again, as a maid walked in and placed a plate of beautifully arranged melon in front of each of them, before holding out small silver dishes, one Sunny found to be holding ginger and the other caster sugar. 'So, you enjoyed a delicious luncheon with Mr Wyndham.' She waited until the maid had left. 'Did you also enjoy his company, may I ask?'

Sunny stared at the melon, wondering if she had put too much ginger on it, before speaking.

'Mr Wyndham is very nice. We had already met, you know, at the ball, and then he rang to ask me to lunch-*eon*, because he wanted to thank me for helping him, or rather for getting Mr Arkwright to help mend the hose in his motor car. At any rate, it all went very well, and we parted the best of friends, I think. Not that you can ever be sure with an older man, if you see what I mean? I mean, older men always make one feel so much younger, so one has to work awfully hard to impress on them that one is not as wet behind the ears as they perhaps think. I expect I failed dismally, but then how would I know, because although I wrote and thanked him, I cannot know what he thought. It is awfully difficult with a man like Mr Wyndham, because he is so easy to talk to, and yet he doesn't really let one know how it's going his end. He was probably bored stiff, poor chap. But at any rate, we did laugh a lot, mostly –' she leaned forward confidentially – 'mostly, I am ashamed to tell you, about the people at the other tables, who were even older than Mr Wyndham, and very, very proper, so we had to keep our voices down in case we said something to upset them. I will say he caught on very quickly, because actually it is a good game.'

Sunny stopped suddenly, possibly because she had come to the end of her melon, or possibly because she had suddenly become aware that she might have said rather too much.

'Mr Wyndham can be most amusing,' Leandra agreed, but she did not continue because the maid had returned to remove the plates, and replace them with fresh ones.

The second course was the lightest fish pie that Sunny had ever eaten, but because the sun was now shining on the conservatory it had grown hot, and she found herself having to lift the glass of water in front of her to her cheeks once more to cool them. This time, however, she felt that an explanation was needed.

'I had to do this when I had lunch – when I had lunch-*eon* – with Mr Wyndham, but then it was because of the sherry! A sip of sherry and I turn the colour of that geranium!'

Leandra imagined Gray faced with this young girl applying her water glass to her cheeks to cool them, and wondered for a second at the scene. Gray was so sophisticated she feared he might have found such behaviour embarrassing.

'It is quite hot in here. Really conservatories were only

meant to be used in the winter, as winter gardens, as you know.'

'No, I didn't . . .'

Sunny stared around her. The scents on the air were delicious. The whole scene with the dark blue china and the dark blue flowers, the maids serving them, and Leandra wearing apple green was so beautiful, and so different from life at Rushington, where sophistication meant napkins with rings, and mats with men shooting pheasants on them, and a daily cleaning lady who called you 'madam' and went home at twelve.

For a second it seemed to Leandra that her young guest's face had clouded over, and that she had, in a spiritual sense, left Maydown and gone back to Rushington.

'My dear,' Leandra put her head on one side and smiled, 'can I be very honest with you?'

'Yes, yes, of course. I like people who say that, because you know it is never very easy to be honest with people, that you have to like them so much that they won't mind the truth, wouldn't you say?'

Now it was Leandra's face that seemed to Sunny to have clouded over.

'Oh, I say, I am sorry. Have I said the wrong thing? I talk too much. I get it from my father. I told Mr Wyndham that when we first met, when he came to the house the day his Bentley had a broken hose. Pa is a chatterbox, except when he is cross, which luckily for Ma and me is not very often.'

Leandra beckoned to the maid, who was now hovering once more, preparatory to removing their plates, which she did, replacing them with fruit plates.

'Do have a peach. They're from our own hot-houses, and really, they are so delicious.'

'Shall I need to wear a mackintosh to peel them?'

84

They both laughed, and in fact Leandra noted that Sunny peeled and ate her peach using her fruit knife and fork in a commendably elegant fashion.

'I was about to be honest, wasn't I?' Leandra asked her guest. 'So what I wanted to say to you was this. You impressed Mr Wyndham a great deal, so much so that he wants to – he asked me to ask you – to . . .' She stopped. 'Well, it seems he has it in his mind to marry you, if you should so wish.'

Sunny put down her fruit knife, and carefully wiped her fingers on her napkin. 'Why would he want me to marry him?' she asked eventually, frowning. 'We have only met twice.'

As she tried not to look too astonished at what Mrs Fortescue had just said, Sunny could not help realising that her feelings were, to say the least of it, mixed. On the one hand she believed that stranger things happened to people than someone asking for your hand in marriage after only two meetings – she had, after all, been told of a wartime romance when two people met at one railway station and left the train at the next in order to marry by special licence – on the other hand that had been during the war, and now was now.

Not that she did not find Mr Wyndham attractive. After dancing with him at the ball, she had even dreamed about him, but the idea of marrying him was vaguely ridiculous, like marrying a film star, or royalty.

'Mr Wyndham was very impressed with you. He feels he could make you happy, but since he is rather older than you, he wanted me to act as his go-between in the old way, which is why I asked you to luncheon today.'

There was a long silence, during which Sunny tried not to stare at Leandra, and failed. After a few seconds her face mirrored the amazement of her feelings.

'It's quite old-fashioned to ask someone to ask someone else to lunch to tell them that they want you to marry them, isn't it?' Sunny ventured, finally. 'I mean it is a bit like something in an opera, wouldn't you say?'

Leandra raised an eyebrow, considering this. 'Yes, yes, I suppose it is,' she agreed finally. 'Although that is how the royal family go on. I believe they still send an emissary to ask for someone's hand in marriage.'

The maid had reappeared with the coffee, which she now, at Leandra's direction, placed in the drawing room next door, after which they both stood up, and went to sit either side of the chimneypiece.

'It is old-fashioned,' Leandra went on, once the door had closed behind the maid. 'But what I should perhaps explain is that Mr Wyndham enjoys what I would call rather unusual circumstances, and it is these that he especially wished me to tell you about. He wants to be honest, but, quite naturally, he does not want to embarrass you.' Leandra handed Sunny a gold-decorated coffee cup, and offered her some brown coffee sugar. 'Mr Wyndham had a good war – MC and all that – but it left him . . . how shall I say?' She lowered her voice to hardly more than a murmur. 'It left him unable to be a man – in the proper sense of the word.'

As she finished speaking and saw the expression on Sunny's face Leandra could have kicked herself. The poor girl looked more than embarrassed, she looked mortified. But perhaps that was good? Perhaps it meant that she was modest and well brought up?

In fact Sunny was blushing not because she was either particularly modest or especially well brought up, but because she and Arietta had always remained determinedly vague about the details of how a man *was* a man, neither of them liking to think that when it came to procreation the human animal was no different from any other.

'You mean Mr Wyndham can't have children?' Sunny finally offered, after a determined sip of her coffee, which in the absence of a glass of water did nothing to lessen the colour in her still burning cheeks.

'No, my dear, more than that.' Leandra lowered her voice still further, so that she was barely audible. 'He is not able to be a man in any sense of the word, if you understand me.'

Sunny put down her cup of coffee, and her heart flooded with sympathy for the handsome, debonair man with whom she had enjoyed lunch only a few days before.

'I see,' she said, despite the fact that she didn't at all, but she couldn't think of what else to say. She clung to the idea that she could surely iron out the fine details of the implications much later. 'In that case, if he is unable to be a man, why would he want to be married to someone, if you don't mind me asking?'

'You may well ask, Miss Chantry. I suppose in one sense, despite having a very full social life, he feels lonely, and then in another way, as his long-time friend, I know that he has always yearned for a settled relationship with someone whom he *could* love as a *friend*, and after your luncheon together he told me that despite the more than ten years' age gap, he felt that you could well be that person but, quite naturally, he felt shy of discussing the more intimate details of his life with you personally.'

Sunny stared at Leandra. Now everything really did seem to be happening as in a dream. Perhaps it *was* a dream, just like the one that she had that had starred Mr Wyndham. Quite soon she was sure she would wake up in her own little bed at the cottage, and the sun would be trying to burst through the old pale blue curtains, and there would be downstairs-sounds coming up from below the window: her father mowing the lawn, her mother's radio playing *Music While You Work*. She was silent for a moment, trying to decide how to be, and finally settling, as she nearly always did, for complete honesty.

'I feel as if I might not be going to understand you,' Sunny confided to Leandra. 'I mean, I feel as if I have wandered into another world, like Alice in Wonderland, a world full of kings and queens and perhaps even a mouse in a teapot.'

She nodded round the sumptuously furnished room as she finished speaking, and Leandra too nodded.

'That is not surprising, but perhaps if I explain a little more you will understand what is being asked of you. You see, Gray not only felt that you were young enough not to mind his particular situation, but he felt you were also young enough and charming enough to help him regain the affection of his father, who is something of a surly old curmudgeon with little affection for anyone but himself – and I can say that with my hand on my heart, as I have known him since I was quite young.'

'His father? He wants me to be nice to his father?' Sunny asked, surprised.

'It is necessary to appease his father, who is really rather difficult, and nothing has changed him – not the war, not his son going missing, nothing. He is a sad, bitter old man, who does not show the least affection for Gray, but whom Gray hopes might change towards him if he gets married, if he has a wife, albeit in name only.'

Leandra stopped, wondering if she had gone too far by calling Jocelyn Wyndham a sad, bitter old man, a description that was actually not hers at all but one that Randy Beauchamp had made to her about Mr Wyndham Senior some months before, when she had been in Randy's bookshop, choosing Christmas presents.

'Gracious.' Sunny looked impressed. 'He sounds a bit like some kind of crusty old earl in a book.'

'I am sure that is a very good comparison,' Leandra said easily. 'But now you know the truth of the story, and why Mr Wyndham wants to make a white marriage with you, you will need to go away and think it over, will you not? It is not a step to be undertaken lightly, as you can appreciate, but there will be many gains, of course – not least that you will have a husband who is kind, elegant, handsome and amusing, and that after all, is not nothing.'

Sunny nodded. 'Yes, of course, but, as you say, it isn't something you could just rush into.'

She turned away and for a second her eyes left Leandra sitting opposite her on her velvet sofa, and wandered to the view outside the window, to the blue sky, to the green of the countryside, and it seemed to her that she was suddenly older, because the truth was that she didn't like to think of Mr Wyndham as some sort of war victim. He had seemed so handsome and urbane and charming, and very much a man.

'Is something troubling you, Miss Chantry?'

'Yes,' Sunny admitted. 'You see, I really liked Mr Wyndham, but now you have said what you have said it seems to me that I am being asked to feel sorry for him, and that really rather changes quite a lot.'

Leandra stood up and went to sit beside Sunny on the opposite sofa.

'Oh, my dear, dear girl,' she said, her beautiful Fabergé-blue eyes seeming to spill with sympathy. 'There is no known reason to feel sorry for Gray Wyndham, really there is not. He is handsome, rich, and lives his life in a pat of *butter.*' As Sunny frowned, not understanding, she went on, by way of explanation. 'His circumstances do not, believe me, stop him enjoying himself. He is asked everywhere, not just Maydown, but everywhere. So, please believe me, while you are thinking over his offer of marriage, do not trouble to feel *sorry* for him. Promise me?'

Sunny nodded. Mrs Fortescue's words were sincere. Sunny believed her, but even so, that feeling of being let down, of confusing attraction with pity would not go away. Besides, what would she explain to her parents? She was meant to be going to secretarial college, not getting married to some older person who could never be a proper man. She glanced quickly at her tenth birthday present, her wristwatch.

'I must be going,' she said, realising with a sinking heart that she would have to be very lucky to catch the right train and return home at just the same time as she always did. Not that it mattered really. She had hoped that with the invitation to lunch with the famous Leandra Fortescue would perhaps come a future offer to help her find a post as a social secretary, or working in an auction house, or for an old duke, something like that. She had not expected to have to consider an offer of *marriage*. It was, of course, quite out of the question. 'Thank you so much for lunch-*eon*.'

They shook hands.

Leandra walked her to the drawing-room door.

'You will think it over, won't you? And let me know? There is no hurry, of course there is not; although I do know that Mr Wyndham is anxious to know how you feel. He did so love your company at luncheon, and I know the last thing you will want is to hurt his feelings.'

Sunny smiled, and the drawing-room door closed behind her, as did the whole idea. Or so she thought.

## Chapter Three

Arietta stared at Sunny. They were sitting in Mrs Caerphilly's teashop, a favourite meeting place for both of them. Whenever they felt flush, they could indulge in what Arietta always thought of as a perfect orgy of tea drinking and cake eating, although at that moment she was less interested in cakes (and that took a great deal) than absorbing Sunny's news.

'What did you say?'

'I said, this chap, this Mr Wyndham, the one I told you about, he wants to marry me.'

Arietta pushed her thick brown fringe of hair to the side and continued to stare, this time wordlessly, at her best friend.

'He wants to MARRY you?' She put down her cake fork. 'Oh, but that is so lovely! I told you, I *told* you, he had fallen in love with you.'

Sunny shook her head.

'No, no, he hasn't fallen in love with me. He wants to marry me because I am suitable. It's not love Arietta, it couldn't be. We have only met three times. No, it's not love at all.'

'Of *course* it is!'

Sunny shook her head yet again.

'No, no, no! No, you see . . .' She paused, clearing her throat. 'Something terrible happened to him in the war, and he can never be a man, but he needs to marry to help his father like him better, and that sort of thing. He is handsome, urbane and asked everywhere, so he doesn't mind too much about not being a man, but he still needs a wife who won't mind his terrible problem.'

Arietta struggled not to look crestfallen. They both knew about dreadful things that had happened during the war; most of all they knew *never to talk about them.*

'So, so, so.' Arietta stopped. 'So, he wants to *marry* you but he can't be a husband to you?' She dropped her voice. 'You don't suppose he's "different", do you?'

'Oh, no, he's not different. No, I think it was a war accident, a bomb blowing up near him or something; or perhaps he was tortured? But really what would it matter? I mean, if you agree to marry each other, you don't always . . . well you don't *have* to be a husband with your wife, I don't suppose, do you? You can just be good friends, I should have thought, wouldn't you? Like brother and sister and all that kind of thing.'

Arietta frowned. She was as vague as Sunny about the exact details, the hard facts surrounding the marital bed, probably because she, like Sunny, was an incurable romantic.

'Yes,' she finally conceded, 'I think you *could* just be really good friends, and perhaps it might even be better because you wouldn't have to have babies and die in childbirth, and all that sort of thing. My mother's sister died in childbirth and my mother has never got over it.'

Arietta had grown up with the endlessly repeated story of her mother's sister dying while giving birth, in the most *agonising* way, which meant that, unsurprisingly, Arietta herself had become convinced that marital relations and giving birth were possibly two of the worst things that could happen to anyone.

'So what is going to happen next?'

'I don't know.' Sunny looked away. 'There's been the most awful row about everything, you see.' She nodded at a passing waitress. 'Some more cakes, please.'

'Certainly, miss.'

'Why has there been an awful row? Surely your parents don't know about . . . about . . . ?'

'No, no, they don't know about *that* bit, but Ma caught me coming back from lunch – lunch*eon* – with Mrs Fortescue, and she was livid, quite rightly, I dare say, because I deceived her and went against her wishes, and all that.'

'Oh, but she shouldn't mind, really not. No one notices if you don't turn up at Princess Secretarial College, really they don't. Not unless you have been gone about a fortnight, and then not at all during Ascot week.'

'No, but Ma minds terribly if I miss even a day, because of the huge amounts of money they are spending on me being there, which they can't really afford, and which Pa would prefer to spend on the Vauxhall. At any rate, she met me at the door, and sent me to my room, and then Pa came back and *he* was furious, and so it went on, and it all ended up with me saying I was going to marry Mr Wyndham no matter what, which I really didn't *mean*.'

'Why did you say it, then?'

Sunny stared past Arietta out into the village street. People were hurrying by, holding precious baskets of shopping, the sun was trying to make a rather late entrance, shining patchily on the old Tudor façades, the red brick Georgian frontage of the White Swan Hotel, the one car parked in the street outside the grocer's. The whole scene was so dear and familiar that she found herself wishing to heavens that Mr Gray Wyndham and his Bentley had never broken down outside Pear Tree Cottage.

'I suppose . . . I suppose I said I *did* mean to marry him because they were in such a fluff about my going to have lunch with Leandra Fortescue when they had told me they didn't think I should. I suppose I said it because, well, because I was in such a bate about being found out! I just found myself saying that Mr Wyndham was everything I had always wanted! And Ma was furious and rang Mrs Fortescue and told her to tell Mr Wyndham that I would not marry him, because she would not let me, which sounded as if I really wanted to, even though I didn't really, at least not at that moment. I just said the first thing that came into my head. And Pa is furious and practically ready to call Mr Wyndham outside, or whatever men do when they are frightfully angry. At any rate, he has asked him round to the cottage to sort everything out.'

'What a pickle.'

'A whole jar of pickles, actually, Ari. Because the next thing I knew I was rung by Mrs Fortescue, saying that both she and Mr Wyndham were thrilled that I wanted to marry him, and that I was not to worry about my father being so furious because he would soon come round. So what happened was that Ma's telephone call to Mrs Fortescue meant that she and Mr Wyndham took what I had said to my parents to be the gospel truth, instead of which I was just being a bit of a Bolshevik, really. At any rate, Pa is blue-steel angry now, and that is not very, well, not very nice actually.'

Arietta swallowed hard. Sunny's father, as they both knew, was what was always called in Rushington 'a darling' – humorous, and generous to a fault, all things to all men, unless challenged on a point of honour, whereupon he became St

George on a charger, his hand on his sword hilt ready to slay just about anyone, let alone dragons.

'I say, they don't know your pa, do they, Sunny? I mean, I would hate to be Mr Wyndham if your pa is furious. Talk about entering into the swallowing-hard department. Not funny at all.'

Arietta took a small chocolate cake from the new plate of cakes that had arrived. It was very small, not very much more than about an inch square. Even so, she took her cake knife and started to cut the tiny offering as if it was a full-size cake, and then taking each little slice she savoured it as if it was her last, which, since the war began and rationing, she always did think it might be going to be.

'Golly, Sunny, I say, if your pa is cross,' she repeated, her large eyes widening as she stared at Sunny, 'I should really, *really* hate to be Mr Wyndham.'

'Me too.' Sunny tried to look brave. Since the awful row with her parents she had spent the days hiding in her room, so much so that it seemed to her that even the pattern of the wall-paper was now imprinted on her mind, and to such an extent that she could not look at anything, not even Arietta, without seeing its outline reflected over everything. 'Well, at least Mr Wyndham will probably talk nicely to Pa. He is very charming,' she finally offered. 'I mean, I dare say another man, especially an older one, can deal with Pa in that mood.'

'I dare say,' Arietta agreed, but she did not manage to sound very convinced.

Instead she took a pink iced cake from the plate and pro-ceeded to cut that one too into tiny little slices. The cake-cutting ritual was a comfort, and it took her mind off the idea of Mr Chantry calling Mr Wyndham outside – although what men did once they *were* outside she had no more idea than Sunny. She too now stared out of the window. It suddenly seemed that Sunny and she did not know anything very much at all, which was a pity because she had really rather hoped that they did.

Sunny and Arietta might put John Chantry's intransigence down to the war, but Mary, his diligent, hard-working wife, knew that it was just a part of his character, as much as his blue eyes and his fair hair. The slightest opposition to his declared will, and his mouth would set so firmly that his lips might have been two parallel lines drawn in concrete.

Gray did realise the exact gravity of his situation because it had been communicated to him by Leandra. He had hardly rung on the front doorbell before Sunny had opened the door to him, so he guessed that she must have been waiting all too anxiously, and probably for some time, in the hall. They stared at each other, the age gap shrinking instantly as they became bonded by the fury of her parents.

'My father is in the sitting room, Mr—' Sunny stopped, realising that if she was going to continue to insist on marrying this tall, handsome, elegantly suited man, it would sound really very odd to address him so formally as 'Mr Wyndham', so she quickly changed it to 'Gray' for the first time and they both smiled fleetingly, because they recognised that it was a sort of breakthrough.

Gray stared down at Sunny. She looked enchanting, despite the fact that she was obviously very tense.

'Stop looking white to the lips,' he whispered. 'They're not going to kill me.'

'If I was you I would not be too certain,' Sunny whispered back, bossing her eyes to make Gray laugh, which he did.

After her luncheon with Leandra, Sunny and Gray had spoken several times on the telephone, but now that she was standing beside him, Gray, who since the war was not in the habit of thinking very much beyond enjoying himself as much as possible, now found himself wondering what on earth he was doing.

It had all seemed so simple at Maydown – but then taking Leandra's advice always did seem simple – whereas now, seeing the tension in Sunny's face and how her hand shook as she leaned forward to open the sitting-room door, it seemed to him that Leandra's plan was about to backfire.

Before Sunny could turn the handle of the sitting-room door, Gray leaned forward and kissed her swiftly and delicately on the cheek. Sunny stared up at him.

'Good luck,' she whispered, as Gray passed her.

For the second time Gray found himself going into the Chantrys' sitting room, wondering at its cosy, welcoming ambience, its lack of pretence, its Englishness.

'Mr Chantry, I don't think we've met. How do you do?' He smiled and held out his hand.

John Chantry put his hands behind his back. 'How do you do, Mr Wyndham?' he said, and nodded his head instead of extending his hand.

Gray smiled. 'Quite well, thank you.' He stared humorously for a second or two at his hand. 'I can't blame you for not wanting to shake my hand, Mr Chantry,' he went on easily. 'But if it is of any comfort to you, today my hands are at least clean. The last time I was here they were far from being so, covered in oil, from my motor car. Sunny was so kind to me that day, you know. Sweetest girl in the world, isn't she? No wonder I fell in love with her the moment she opened your front door.'

John Chantry's eyes narrowed. He was not in the mood to be cajoled, charmed, or talked *down* to. In fact he was in no mood for anything except stating his case, which was that he absolutely refused to have Sunny marry this Gray Wyndham, whatever kind of case he made out.

'Mr Wyndham, my daughter is only eighteen,' he began. 'If it wasn't such an abhorrent idea I would be quite prepared to take you to court for trying to seduce an underage girl.'

Gray's large eyes widened. 'Far from trying to seduce her, Mr Chantry, I have hardly held her hand, except, unlike you and me, to shake it. No, I have no desire to seduce your daughter, only to marry her. She seems just the girl for me.'

'How very satisfying for you. Well, in that case you will have to be quite prepared for her to reach twenty-one, Mr Wyndham, because as of this moment I propose to make her a ward of court, and to make sure that when she is twenty-one she will be as far away from you as possible.'

'May we sit down?'

'No, we may not. At least you may not.'

Gray frowned. He had expected opposition, but not such ill manners.

'Very well, in that case let us consider what we have to discuss, er, standing up.' He crossed to an armchair and stood behind it, leaning on it. 'First of all there is Sunny. Now Sunny is an enchanting, innocent girl, with no ill intention towards anyone – at least not as far as I can discern – and this enchanting innocent girl has, as you know, consented to marry me. I, on the other hand, am an older man and I have only honourable intentions towards this lovely creature. I can provide for her.' He looked carefully round the small sitting room with its homely touches. 'Frankly, I can give her a lovely life, full of luxury. Two houses, a flat in London, her own maid, a car, and a chauffeur, whenever she should need one.'

'I am not interested in your wealth, Mr Wyndham, only your suitability. You are not suitable to be my daughter's husband.'

'I had a good war, though not as distinguished as yours, I am sure. Nevertheless MC and bar – that sort of thing.'

John Chantry looked openly appalled. In his book, anyone who mentioned their war gongs was an absolute bounder.

'I hardly think that a gentleman would mention such a thing about himself to another gentleman, Mr Wyndham, any more than he would keep on his wartime ranking rather than returning to plain "mister".'

'I agree with you. And you are quite right about mentioning wartime gongs, but you forced my hand. I was merely trying, albeit in a rather crude manner, to tell you that much as you are determined to think the worst of me, I did at least fight for my country. I do assure you that it is not something that I would normally mention.'

Gray cleared his throat, realising that he had been forced into a corner.

'Whatever you say, the answer is the same. I do not, categorically, give you my permission to marry my daughter at this time, and there is an end to it.'

'In that case, there is nothing I can do or say, sir, other than to wish you good day.'

Gray turned on his foot and let himself out of the sitting room.

Sunny was still in the hall. She had gone from looking tense to horrified, because of course she had overheard everything.

Inside the sitting room, Mary had appeared at the other end of the room from the conservatory. John knew at once that she had heard it all. For once Mary had no pins in her mouth, which was perhaps why she was able to open it and sigh loudly and theatrically.

'Well done, John. Now you have given Gray Wyndham every reason to run off with Sunny!'

*

Following Gray Wyndham's visit, the atmosphere at Pear Tree Cottage changed almost overnight, as it might be expected to do. Sunny, too frightened of her father to do anything else, went back to attending Princess Secretarial College with Arietta.

Unlike Sunny, Arietta was surging ahead in her shorthand and typing tests, and seemed primed to be able to leave long before anyone else had reached halfway through the course. Not that this impressed Audrey.

'I fail to see how anyone will employ you now that you *have* finished,' was Audrey's only comment when Arietta burst through their front door to inform her mother that she was now fully qualified. 'I mean, look at you.'

Audrey's eyes moved slowly up and down Arietta's tense young body.

'It's all right, Mummy. I am going to find a job as soon as possible.'

'Looking like that, I very much doubt it. You will not be able to find anyone who wants to take on someone so young and, frankly, unversed. Typing and shorthand are not enough, you know. You will not be an asset in an office, or other secretarial situations. The whole idea is ludicrous.'

Audrey turned on her heel and stalked off to the kitchen, where she began to prepare a cup of tea, for one, in a tiny pot.

Arietta had never liked or enjoyed tea, preferring orangeade, if she could get it, or coffee, so she was only too relieved not to have a cup of tea made for her. Instead she rushed upstairs and lay down on her bed. It somehow didn't matter if her mother was still full of doubt as to her possible future. All that mattered was that she had passed her exams in one term instead of three. She was now fully qualified and she had a certificate to prove it, which meant that she could get a job – any kind of job – and once she had a job she would have money, and once she had money she would be able to leave Rushington, because even if she did not *quite* believe in fairies, she did believe in happiness.

With all this in mind she called at the Chantrys' cottage the following day.

'Oh, hallo, Arietta.' The pins were back in Mary Chantry's mouth, and she was holding a large, very stiffened black taffeta skirt in one hand. 'How are you?' She turned to go back into the dining room, and Arietta followed her.

'I am very well, Mrs Chantry.'

Mary sat back down behind her sewing machine, which in some strange way suddenly appealed to Arietta as being a kind of altar to fashion, and Mrs Chantry its attendant priestess.

'Sunny is not very well, as you know, Arietta.'

Arietta nodded. She did know. Sunny had not been to college for some days now, so she would not know about Arietta, or her results.

'I heard she had some sort of fever.'

'Yes, she is running a bit of a high temperature in the mornings, but no other symptoms.'

The wheel of the sewing machine was now turning faster and faster as Mary bent to her work. It seemed to her that her sewing machine was the only thing of which she could be truly sure in a mad, post-war universe. At least if she finished a dress, it stayed finished. It did not, unlike so much in the house, have to be done over and over again, endlessly, it seemed to her, and all too often pointlessly. Nothing else was quite as good as it should be, neither her cooking, nor the flowers, nor their few savings. Only her sewing stayed as she had designed it, either on or off her grateful customers' elegant bodies.

'Mrs Chantry?'

'Yes?' Mary called over the sound of the sewing machine.

'I was wondering if you could make me a suit.'

The machine continued, the wheel going as fast as ever, but Arietta knew that Mrs Chantry must have heard her question, because she was frowning.

'You want a coat and skirt?'

'Yes, that's right, a coat and skirt. It is very necessary, if I am to get a proper job, which I must do to help out at home, and that sort of thing. It is also very necessary that I don't look like an unmade bed, which Mummy says I do most of the time.'

Mary stopped the machine. She liked Arietta so much. Just lately she had actually found herself wishing that she had a daughter more like Arietta, and less like Sunny. Not that she did not love Sunny with all her heart, but she did not understand her. Could not understand how she could have set out to deceive her and John by agreeing to marry a man she hardly knew, just to irritate her parents, or more likely to get out of going to secretarial college, or because she did not want to have to earn her living. Whatever the reason, it was quite definitely a shallow one, and one of which her mother could never approve.

'My dear Arietta, you never, ever look like an unmade bed. You always look nice, and . . . and smart, but if you are to be a career woman – however temporarily – you must *look* the part, we both know that. Moreover, my dear,' Mary eyed her daughter's best friend with a kind, firm look, 'you must not look as if you need the work. That is the most important aspect of going for an interview. You must look enthusiastic, but not – never, ever – as if you need the work.'

They looked at each other, silent for a second. Part of what Mary had said was true, and another part of it was not true.

Arietta always did look nice, but she certainly never looked smart, and because she had no smart clothes she had to go for the bohemian look. And she not only needed the work, she was desperate for it.

'You are perfectly right, Mrs Chantry. That is why I need a coat and skirt, Mrs Chantry. Because I need to work so very much.' She smiled with sudden nervous enthusiasm, and her colour heightened. 'I can't go for interviews in my old school skirt and cardigan, and that kind of thing. I really cannot. As you say, I must try to look the part, or I will never have a chance.'

Mary remained looking at Arietta rather than her clothes, afraid that if she glanced down it might look critical.

'Yes, as I have said, at the risk of sounding repetitious, the key to this sort of thing, if you don't mind my saying so, Arietta, is to look as if you will find the situation that is being offered amusing and interesting, but not completely necessary – which, of course, we both know it is if you are to help your mother. One just must *not* let on.'

Arietta knew at once that Mary Chantry was trying hard to mark her card, and as always she was terribly grateful. She made a mental note to rehearse looking casual, but enthusiastic.

Mary stood up. 'I always think that grey flannel is so useful, and so awfully safe, don't you, Arietta?'

Arietta nodded, her heart sinking. Grey flannel was not cheap. Grey flannel would be way beyond her Post Office savings. Besides, decent materials were still difficult to find.

'Oh, yes,' she agreed. 'I do so think so, I do so agree, grey flannel is always so elegant, and perfect for all but the most wintry of days.'

Mary went to the cupboard where she kept her precious French patterns.

'There is something by Jacques Fath that I have here, sent to me from Paris last year. I know it is here somewhere . . .'

Arietta watched as Mary's slim well-dressed figure moved slowly past shelf after shelf of patterns. Somewhere in the background the wireless was playing organ music. Somewhere above them Sunny was lying in bed with a temperature, perhaps dreaming of marriage to Gray Wyndham. At their cottage across the green, her mother would be reading the *Daily Telegraph* and drinking a cup of chicory coffee, whereas here in the room with Mrs Chantry was Arietta, holding on to a dream of how her life could be about to be changed by a beautiful French pattern made up in a material that she would never, in all her wildest dreams, ever be able to afford.

'Ah, here we are.' Mary had grown vaguely flushed with the concentration of the search, but was now brandishing the pattern. 'I can't guarantee you *will* like this, but I think you *might*.' She placed it with a look of concentrated respect on the dining-room table. 'I did not, as it transpired, make it for the lady in question, because following her order, she went to live in America.'

Arietta did not know it, but she suddenly looked out of her depth, and because she was nothing if not sensitive, Mary realised it and, knowing of the poor girl's circumstances, she concluded she had to quickly find some way to help her. It came to her within a few gratifying seconds.

'Gracious, Arietta, a thought has come to me. The lady from Wisteria House who went to live in America, so unexpectedly did she depart, she also left behind with me the material she had bought for the pattern.' Mary looked excited. 'It is not, alas, grey flannel, but it *is* black and white worsted, and I think that will prove just as smart and useful to you, really I do.'

Arietta swallowed hard. Black and white worsted sounded even more terribly costly than grey flannel.

'I am sure I can pay her for it, eventually. I have some savings in the Post Office that my godmother sent me,' she murmured.

'Of course you can, dear,' Mary agreed, leaving the room. 'But not unless and until she comes back, which is certainly not on the cards at present, since the lady in question ran off with an oil millionaire and is now living in high luxury near – near, oh you know, near one of those places where oil millionaires live. Houston, I think. At any rate, have a good look at it while I go up to the attic and find the parcel. Oh dear, how exciting. Goodness, to think that had you not arrived I might have left it there until kingdom come.'

As Mary left the room and hurried upstairs, Arietta stared at the figure of the lady on the front of the pattern. She was tall and slim, and perfectly made up, and her figure was everything that it should be – as it would be in a fashion drawing. Oddly, this did not daunt Arietta, who knew that she too was quite well made; rather it excited her. It was something to aim for. The suit itself was the epitome of everything for which Paris stood. It was tightly sculpted to show off the silhouette of the wearer, and to this same end, fastened with large buttons. The collar was neat, but not small, and there were two double seams that might have been pockets, but were not. The waist was cinched tightly, and the bottom of the jacket flared, just covering the hips, while the long slim near-ankle-length skirt emphasised the cut of the jacket. Altogether it was heaven in the shape of a pattern.

'And here it is. Here is the material!'

Arietta looked up as if from a dream. Mrs Chantry was

standing in front of her with a parcel of cloth, which she was now placing on the dining-room table and quickly unwrapping.

'This pattern is so heavenly, Mrs Chantry. Really, so heavenly.'

'Feel that!' Mary held out a section of the cloth for Arietta, who felt its perfect surface. 'Petit point worsted,' she said, dropping her voice reverentially.

Arietta felt the cloth. She had seen her mother's tailor do the same when her mother had gone for post-war alterations to a pre-war coat and skirt.

'Such nice quality,' Mr Shoreham had murmured. 'You will never find such quality now, Mrs Staunton. This cloth is of a quality that only royalty wears, and even they cannot find such cloth nowadays. Why, my mother had cause to take the coats of the Queen and Princess Margaret when they visited the theatre where my mother is privileged to work in cloaks – and the linings of their coats were such, there was so little sateen left, so much had they been mended, she gave it as her opinion that if one thread was caught, the whole mesh of mending would have sunk to the floor with a glad sigh. No black marketeering for our royalty – no, God bless them. They have gone without along with their people, so they have; not like some what we know of, who have lived it up through the war like rajahs and princes of the blood. No, our royalty know how to go on.'

The tailor's speech had made Audrey smile. She liked to think that in Mr Shoreham's mind there was a corollary between herself, Queen Elizabeth and her daughter Princess Margaret; that in all probability the tailor was in the habit of thinking of Mrs Staunton and the Queen in the same way – that he could see no difference between her suiting and that which was being worn by those supreme beings.

'I am sorry it is not grey flannel, which would have suited your purpose a great deal better,' Mary was now saying. 'But nevertheless I believe that this will make up into just the right kind of coat and skirt that will be most useful to you, Arietta, really I do.'

'I may have some savings—'

'Never mind your savings, dear, really. Never mind any of that for now. You will need them for gloves and shoes, and train fares, for going up to London to see people, for cups of tea on the train, and so on. One's money goes nowhere when one is in search of work. I will guarantee that once we have you looking as you should do, you will land a very good position as someone's social secretary. We don't want you letting down the side, now, do we? You must put your best foot forward for Rushington, eh?'

Mary patted Arietta on the arm. It was only a very light pat, but as far as Arietta was concerned it might as well have been a bear hug, so much did it mean to her. She now knew that Mrs Chantry wanted her to do well, that she thought she *could* do well, and what was more and what was better, she was prepared to help her.

For the next few days Arietta came in and out of the Chantrys' cottage for fittings, and both Mary and Arietta became more and more excited as the suit – or coat and skirt, as Mrs Chantry called it in the old way – took shape. In the excitement, Arietta quite forgot to ask after Sunny, and Mary was only too relieved not to have to talk about her.

As Arietta stood having first the pattern, and then the toile, followed by the material with linings, and all the other para- phernalia, tried and fitted, refitted, and retried, and she stood in front of Mrs Chantry's dressing mirror, Mary talked to her instead about the kind of more sophisticated fittings that would take place in Paris.

'Now if this was a gown being constructed at Dior, dear, first would come Brivet's tulle, then Abraham's organza – to prevent the scratching of the silk stockings – and finally silk pongee to line the skirt.'

Arietta did not like to admit that she did not know exactly what silk *pongee* was, so she did her best to imagine it, and quickly came to the conclusion it must be a very special French silk.

'Of course, that is only the beginning,' Mary went on, speaking as always through her dressmaking pins. 'The dresses fit so beautifully because they make corsets individually for each of their ladies; these fit inside each individual piece. To look at a woman in a Dior dress one would almost imagine her to be perfectly made, which of course she is not. The average wealthy woman who goes to the House of Dior is just as short-legged, flat-chested, or over-plump on the hips as the average poorer woman – the only difference being that at Dior they can so mould the corsets fitted *inside* the gowns that they can deceive even the men paying the bills that they are married to perfectly proportioned ladies!'

'How nice that must be,' Arietta sighed.

'I cannot rival Dior, alas, but I shall try to make this suit your elegant little figure,' Mary added, holding up the skirt to view the tacking. 'Besides, the long flowing lines are so pretty on the young, and no need for a young girl with your silhouette to have to do much more than wear really well-cut clothes with a good silk lining. Now, if you don't mind going up to see Sunny, dear . . .? Nowadays she seems to spend the whole time in her room.'

Arietta went upstairs, and found Sunny, who was seated in a

chair staring out of the window at the distant view of the Downs. The room was small, and there was no other chair, so Arietta sat down on the bed.

'You look a bit peaky, you know, Sunny,' Arietta told her after they had greeted each other in their usual way.

'I do, don't I?' Sunny agreed in a vaguely triumphant voice. 'I've hardly been downstairs since Pa lost his rag with me. I keep out of his way. Talk about icicles coming from the ceiling. He is not at all amused at the moment. Doesn't even ask me to go out for a spin with him in the Vauxhall. And my so-called fiancé has gone off the radar map as a result, I should think.'

They both contemplated John Chantry's parental fury and its aftermath, which appeared to have contributed to Mr Wyndham going off the radar map.

Sunny looked out of the window again. 'Growing up can be a bit beastly, can't it?'

Arietta couldn't agree. She thought growing up was wonderful. It offered a chance to escape from Rushington, to make her own way.

'Remember when we used to go for bicycle rides across the Downs, stopping off to buy lemonade and crisps? How wonderful it all was, not complicated like now.'

'It's not complicated, Sunny. It's just become a bit complicated because of – you know – because of you getting yourself into a bit of a stew about this Mr Wyndham person. Do you think you really want to marry Mr Wyndham?'

'I don't know.'

'Well, you must.'

'I don't see why,' Sunny stated obstinately. 'He is very handsome, and he wears really lovely clothes. You should see his cashmere driving coat. It is so stylish.'

Arietta frowned. She loved clothes, but she wasn't *quite* sure that admiring a person's coat was a good reason for marriage.

Leandra seldom frowned. She was too aware that extremes of expression caused wrinkles, and for this reason even smiling was kept to a minimum whenever possible.

'Would you not consider *me* going to see Mr and Mrs Chantry, on your behalf, darling?' she asked Gray.

Gray smiled. 'Leandra, you may be beautiful, you may have eyes the colour of Fabergé blue, and you may be the most talented hostess in London and Sussex, but not even you could change John Chantry's mind. He is adamant.' He took Leandra in his arms and whispered in her hair, 'Let us forget the Chantrys and concentrate on matters nearer to both our hearts and bodies.'

Leandra smiled over Gray's shoulder. He was a brilliant lover, and he was looking particularly handsome that afternoon. He was wearing perfect grey suiting, a white shirt with a stiffened collar and just the right amount of cuff showing gold links of an impeccable design. As befitted a gentleman, Gray's aftershave lotion was subtle, not overpowering, and from Trumper's, but for once she was less than interested in Gray's style, or his physical attributes. Without his perhaps realising it, he had challenged her, and if there was one thing Leandra could never resist, it was a challenge.

Who was this John Chantry, she asked herself after she had checked her appearance in her drawing-room mirror.

Leandra and Gray were about to go to an art exhibition of some rather outré sculptor, and she wanted to make sure that her dress was everything that it should be because there would be everyone who was anyone there. The dress she had chosen to wear was very pretty, the top made of white organdie with a wide turn-back cuff, and the skirt billowing out from a slim silk belt into a mass of silk pleats, the whole hand-embroidered with flower garlands.

Who was this John Chantry, she repeated to herself, as Gray undid the belt on her dress.

'Gray . . .'

He eased her out of the whole delightful creation, which she had just finished admiring, before starting to make love to her.

'We will be late for the . . .'

But she had already forgotten what it was that they were going to be late for as she followed him through to her dressing room, with its Madame Récamier chaise longue, and its eighteenth-century paintings of French courtesans.

Nevertheless, as they lay together a little later, and despite his having pleased her inordinately, the question of 'Who is this John Chantry that he should stand in my way?' returned to her mind.

And again it came back as they attended the opening of the art exhibition, looking very much the perfect couple. Mrs Dilke Fortescue, and one of her regular escorts – Mr Gray Wyndham. Everyone in polite London circles accepted that Leandra had many different escorts, that she attended art exhibitions, first nights, and race meetings with a variety of elegant men. It was just how it was.

Even so, the notion of John Chantry continued to dominate her thoughts. Who *was* John Chantry after all, she asked herself as she stepped into the back of the Rolls, followed by Gray.

John Chantry was no one, no one at all. And since he was no one she would deal with John Chantry herself. She would render him powerless. By the time she had finished with him he would not be able to see the wood from the trees; so much so that in a few weeks, at most a few months, Gray would find himself married to his daughter, and his future quite secure.

*

Mary looked vaguely frightened.

'It's, er, you know, *that* woman,' she whispered to John.

John knew at once from his beloved wife's expression who '*that* woman' was.

'I'll take it.'

He cleared his throat, and walked up to their hall telephone, shoulders straight, his expression solemn as if being summoned by the colonel of his wartime regiment.

'John Chantry speaking,' he said in what Mary recognised as his best army tone, rather than his normal civilian voice.

'Oh, Mr Chantry, how sweet of you to come to the telephone . . . so kind, so dear. I *doo* so appreciate it.'

John Chantry removed the telephone receiver from the side of his face, frowned at it, and then replaced it to his ear. What on earth . . . ? What the devil . . . ? What was the woman *on* about?

'I know you are such a busy man, because your darling Sunny, your darling, darling daughter, told me herself, so I am thrilled that you could find the time to speak to me, but could you possibly find the time to also come to luncheon with me? I am so terribly at a loss as to how to cope with a little matter with which I think, in some way, we are both involved. I truly need your help. Will you come to luncheon with me, Mr Chantry?'

'Of course, yes, if that is what you want,' John Chantry heard himself saying, while all the time knowing that was definitely not what he had wanted to say.

'Oh, but that is so kind, so sweet, so dear. Would tomorrow at half-past midday be too soon?'

'No, no, of course not.'

As he finished speaking John Chantry frowned almost violently at his own image in the vaguely pink hall mirror. What was he saying? And why was he saying it? It was because the woman was speaking in such flowery language he was finding himself saying 'yes' when he probably meant 'no'.

As she could not hear what was being said the other end, Mary found herself standing by the dining-room door, staring at John instead of getting on with what she was meant to be doing. What had happened *now* with this wretched woman? Oh *dear*, she had the feeling that everything was getting on top of her – everything, that was, except Arietta's coat and skirt, which were now finished, and which she really could not wait for her to try on. She was almost sure it was going to be one of the best things she had ever done.

'What did she have to say?' she finally asked.

John replaced the telephone and looked up. There was a short pause.

'To tell you the truth, dear, I have no idea at all. She wants me to go to lunch with her tomorrow. God knows why. It's not going to change anything, you know, nothing at all.'

Mary turned away. She was not so sure, but the truth was, just at that moment, probably because she was expecting Arietta, she was more interested in the fit of the coat and skirt than the fact that this silly woman that Sunny had taken up with had asked John to lunch. As far as Sunny and this Gray Wyndham were concerned, what would be would be. But the fit of the coat across the shoulders – well, that was something else altogether; that was really quite exciting.

'Goodness.'

Arietta stared at herself in the long dressing mirror that Mary always kept for her customers in what was ostensibly the Chantrys' dining room, but nowadays served as Mary's fitting room. To this purpose the dining chairs and table were set down one end of the room, and rarely used, the family making do instead with eating on their knees in the sitting room, or at a table in the conservatory.

'Goodness,' Arietta murmured, for the second time.

Mary smoothed the fit of the jacket across Arietta's shoulders yet again. If only she could capture Arietta's expression for posterity. It was simply wonderful to see. A look of surprised, almost pained, fascination had run across the young girl's face the moment Mary had turned her towards the dressing mirror so that she could see herself. To say that the clothes had changed her was to say the least: the clothes had *transformed* her. Mary stood back from Arietta, her head on one side.

'Well, Arietta dear, if you don't get taken up by someone immediately, I shall want to know the reason why. You really look every inch the social secretary in that coat and skirt. I know I would take you on if I was that kind of person.'

They both smiled at each other in the mirror.

'I can't wait for Mummy to see me. She will be so surprised. I will be a made bed at last!'

Mary's heart sank. She knew that really that would *not* be the thing, for Audrey Staunton could always be relied upon to make a remark of the kind that would put poor little Arietta off the coat and skirt for ever. It would probably end up in the back of the wardrobe unworn and unloved after Audrey had finished making one of her sarcastic remarks. But what could she do? Audrey was Arietta's mother. What could she *do*?

'I am not at all sure that your sainted mother will like this coat and skirt, Arietta,' Mary finally stated, plucking up her courage, after a short inner struggle, to say what she thought should be said. 'I am sorry to say this, Arietta, but your mother has never been an admirer of my work, and while that is entirely her prerogative, and I quite understand that one cannot please everyone, nevertheless I think once she knows that I have made this for you, she might become difficult about it.'

Arietta coloured. She knew how hard it must be for the really rather diffident Mrs Chantry to pluck up the courage to say what she had just said. She also knew that she was completely right, but what to say in return? If she agreed with Mrs Chantry, it would mean that she had betrayed her mother. If she did not agree with her, it would mean that she had lied.

'I will not wear it in front of her,' she said simply.

'Won't that be difficult, dear?'

Arietta shook her head. 'Not really. She has started going out a great deal to see friends and so on, and as a consequence she sleeps in late, so I can leave for interviews before she sees me. If I get any interviews, that is. There is very little work at the moment, my uncle told me.'

'It might be best, dear, for Audrey not to see the coat and skirt, just until you are offered a position.'

'You have been so kind, so kind. I – er – I—'

Arietta stopped. She knew she *must* mention remuneration, but she didn't know how to bring the matter up without sounding impertinent.

Mary guessed poor Arietta's thoughts and, reaching forward, she patted her gently on the arm.

'Oh, and by the way, Arietta, the making, and the material for the coat and skirt, *both* are my present to you for your future, and I only hope they bring you the greatest of good luck, dear. You certainly deserve it, whizzing through your exams like that. Really, I think you have been quite plucky in your attitude.'

Arietta would have liked to have hugged Mrs Chantry. She knew that in her place Sunny would certainly have done so, in her usual spontaneous way, but Arietta was more inhibited than Sunny, and anyway, Mrs Chantry was not her mother.

'The coat and skirt are so beautiful, Mrs Chantry. I will always treasure them, and I will never forget this present of them you have made me.' She smiled suddenly and brilliantly at Mary. 'I know they will, they *must*, bring me luck. I feel so different now. I feel – I feel as if I could do anything.'

That particular morning had passed so pleasantly for Mary that she took the rest of the day off to potter in the conservatory and to tidy up her workroom. She even made a pie, something that she normally never had time for, but the following morning reality struck as she waved John off in the perfectly polished Vauxhall, while all the while crossing mental fingers that his car would not conk out before he arrived at Maydown.

She knew that whatever John and Mrs Fortescue said or decided about Mr Wyndham and Sunny, the truth was that the end result was always going to be dreary. If John gave in and allowed Sunny to go ahead and marry this Gray Wyndham, that would be less than satisfactory, and if he fought his corner and did not allow anything of the sort, Mary would have a listless daughter on her hands for the foreseeable future, which was really quite a miserable prospect.

'You are far too young to marry,' she had said many times to Sunny, but Sunny took no notice, staying in her room where she played her gramophone, usually the same songs over and over again. So much so that Mary thought if she heard one more song about the sun being high in the sky and the wretched corn no doubt too, she would go dotty, but she could think of nothing to end the whole horrible cycle.

She had a shrewd suspicion that Sunny, being Sunny, was clinging stubbornly to a situation out of which she was refusing to extricate herself, while Mary herself could think of nothing that she could do to help, short of giving Sunny a hard shake, while John, poor chap, was facing down this Society woman, and that *was* something. Mary was comforted by the thought of John standing up to Mrs Fortescue. She knew that he would. He was, after all, made of stern stuff, and had come through the war, if not unscathed, at least more or less sound of wind and limb.

Rule was courtesy itself when he took John Chantry's coat.

'Mrs Fortescue is expecting you, sir, in the Blue Room.'

John followed the tall, good-looking butler down a long corridor lined with beautiful gold-framed paintings. It was difficult not to feel shabby when you were faced with such splendour. Walking from the hall, with its great elaborately framed paintings and its marble chimneypiece and exquisite furniture, down the specially woven carpet they were now treading, he was hard put not to feel inferior, and really rather certain that he was going to look so. Never mind being poor and proud, everyone felt smaller when they were faced with a display of such wealth wisely spent on beautiful effects.

Leandra waited for John to walk halfway down the room, and then she stood up and went towards him with hands outstretched.

'It is so good of you to come, so good. In what must be such a busy life, to spare the time to come and see me, and to have luncheon with me, I cannot tell you how flattered I am.'

Even as she finished speaking, Leandra saw at once, not just from the expression on his face, but from the sort of man that he was, that she was going to have her work cut out with Mr Chantry.

To begin with, the room, which was always so critical of everyone – being eighteenth-century, and perfect in both its proportions and its decoration, it tended to find out the least pretensions – was now telling Leandra that here was not a shabby genteel man standing in its midst, but a man of strength. He was wearing an impeccably cut, if old-fashioned suit, which showed off an athletic figure. He was tall, and good-looking. His signet ring was small, and gold, and made no pretensions to grandeur; his shirt collar perfectly ironed. His shoes, although old, must have been handmade since they were still elegant to a degree, and highly polished, and his handshake firm, without being a knuckle breaker. In short, to Leandra's astonishment she was finding that Mr Chantry was an extremely attractive man, and not even she, or the Blue Room, could fault him.

'How do you do?'

John Chantry's formal delivery of the customary greeting acted as a reproof to this Society woman, as it was indeed meant to do. He then cleared his throat a little too loudly.

Leandra smiled.

'Do sit down, Mr Chantry. I am sure you will feel like a nice glass of something after your journey.'

Rule was hovering, a look of expectancy on his face.

'Thank you.' He turned to the butler. 'I will have a gin and Schweppes.'

'My usual, please, Rule.'

Rule disappeared behind a Chinese screen where he kept various alcoholic beverages at the ready, and promptly re-appeared with perfectly prepared drinks on a silver tray.

John did not say 'cheers' as he would have done in the village pub, he merely raised his glass, a few seconds after Leandra had raised hers, and they both drank.

'It is such a beautiful day, I trust your drive was enjoyable?'

'Of course.'

John had resolved that he was not going to give an inch to this famously beautiful woman. He might be a man, and as vulnerable as any man to the wonders of woman's wiles, but now primarily he was the father of a daughter. He was Sunny's father, and he was not going to stand by and have her life ruined by the rich set, who believed that whatever they wanted they could get; and much as he could not help admiring the fit of Leandra Fortescue's tightly waisted jacket, and the marvellous spread of her skirt when she sat down, not to mention the drift of sophisticated French scent that was reminding him of weekends in Paris before the war, nevertheless he knew he was there on a mission, and that was all there was to it.

Leandra turned and gave her brilliant smile to the butler. 'You may leave us for the moment, Rule.'

Rule bowed and absented himself from the room, although not from the corridor outside.

In the silence that followed, John Chantry gazed round the room, and once again cleared his throat.

'And shall Trelawny die?' he murmured. It was a phrase that he always used to fill in gaps, to cover moments of hesitation, before some idiot could chip in with, 'It must be either twenty past or twenty to.'

'Quite so.'

Leandra tried not to look as she felt, which was momentarily wrong-footed, if not startled. She began again, determined to get down to business before it was too late.

'Now, Mr Chantry, I think we must come straight to the point, don't you?'

'Of course,' John said again.

'We have a strange situation here. My husband and I have an old friend, as you doubtless know, a Mr Gray Wyndham, and he has fallen in love with your daughter, and wants to marry her – very much. The problem, from your point of view, is that your daughter is far too young to know her own mind and might well live to regret it. However, the fact is that at the present time she does seem to think that she wants to marry Gray Wyndham, and he does want to marry her, so we have an impasse here, which cannot, it seems, be resolved easily.'

Leandra had long ago learned that by sympathetically laying back before your adversary their own case, you could very quickly make them come to realise that there *could* be another way. If, on the other hand, you were foolish enough to contest their point of view, you would only be met with intransigency and obstinacy, not to say aggression, most particularly if your opposition happened to be of the opposite sex.

'Frankly, Mrs Fortescue, I think the whole situation is faintly ludicrous. Mr Wyndham has not met my daughter more than three or four times – a meeting when his Bentley broke down, a dance or two at the Norells' ball, a luncheon, and that about makes up the length of their relationship. How can he possibly know he wants to marry her? Equally, how can she, a mere eighteen-year-old, know her own mind? She hardly has one yet; she is certainly no bluestocking, that I can tell you. Education has passed over her like the French over the gin in a gin martini.'

Leandra smiled again, stifling any sense of shock that Mr Chantry's words might have caused, and waited for a second or two to pass.

'Well, I am sure, Miss Chantry *does* have a mind, Mr Chantry, but we are not really here to discuss her scholastic abilities or otherwise. We are here to talk about emotion, and while you say you find this situation ludicrous, I myself find it enchanting. Two people who could, when all is said and done, be perfect for each other – what could be sweeter?'

John took a large gulp of his gin and tonic, thinking that he rather hated anyone describing something as silly as this particular situation in which they were finding themselves as 'sweet', but he said nothing.

'I myself,' Leandra continued, realising that she had not provoked him into a reply, 'am a firm believer in love at first sight, probably because it happened to me when I was just your daughter's age. I went to a ball, aged seventeen, my future husband saw me, I saw him, and frankly that was it.'

'I am sure I am very happy for you and your husband, and your marriage has obviously lasted a long time, and made you both very happy, but one ice cream doesn't make a sundae, does it?'

'It was not my present husband, Mr Chantry. No, this was my first husband, who alas was gathered only a year after our wedding, almost to the day, but it was a year during which I knew happiness of a very rare kind.'

Leandra's gaze drifted from the man sitting on the sofa opposite her and fixed itself on the view beyond the windows. They had lived in heaven, Tom and she – in heaven! And after he had been taken from her, so suddenly, so horribly, she had not hoped to be so happy again, in fact she had given up any hope of so being long before she met Dilke. Happily, Dilke and she had been sensible enough to know not even to attempt a romantic marriage, and had quickly settled for a loving friendship, getting along amicably, living their separate lives, until

Gray Wyndham came into hers. Then things had changed overnight, as she realised happiness once again, for despite Dilke's interest lying very much elsewhere, Leandra had to take care to be as discreet as any wife pursuing an affair behind her husband's back. Dilke might not want Leandra, but neither did he want her finding happiness with someone else. It was an awkward situation, but manageable.

All had been well, with Leandra taking care not to upset Dilke, until the last year, when things had begun to look a little shaky. It was not that Dilke was running out of money, it was just that however fast the money came into their account, it was having a very hard time catching up with Dilke. Deauville, Trouville, Paris, gold trinkets, junkets to Venice – he could deny his present love nothing, which meant that Leandra, ever practical, soon realised that something had to be done before it was too late and they all went under.

It was not long before she decided that the solution could lie in Gray's father's fortune, which, according to the family trustees, should pass to his only son while the father still lived, to avoid death duties, but only providing that Gray was married. It was a simple situation that could be easily resolved to the satisfaction of everyone concerned, if only the immovable old goat sitting opposite her could be persuaded to give his consent to young Miss Chantry marrying Gray.

She turned her attention back to John Chantry. It seemed he was apologising for being tactless about Tom. Well, that at least was a start. She resolved to play on his embarrassment ruthlessly.

'I suppose it is because I have known great love, Mr Chantry, I believe in it so ardently,' she said softly.

John looked away from Leandra. He did not come from a background that mentioned emotion, most particularly not one's own emotions. Everything in his upbringing and education, his wartime experiences, everything was repelled by such feminine frankness on such a delicate subject.

'I am perfectly sure that Sunny is not experiencing the kind of emotion to which you refer, Mrs Fortescue. To be frank, I think Sunny is going along with the whole situation to annoy her mother and myself, and to get out of secretarial college, just as young women in the war married and became—' He stopped and, reluctant to mention pregnancy or babies, altered what he had been about to say. 'Just as young women,' he began again, 'just as they married and had children to get out of being in the WRNS or the ATS, or something similar that they were not enjoying. Young women do this all the time. It is not reprehensible, but it can be foolish and impulsive.'

He had used the right words, and he knew it. For a second he saw Leandra's eyes drop. It would be useless for her to deny that Sunny and Mr Wyndham were being, at best, impulsive, and at worst, foolish.

'Let us go into luncheon.'

They moved, as Sunny and Leandra had done, into the conservatory, where they were waited on by two maids and Rule, and where the food and the wine proved to be so good that, much against his better judgement, John started to mellow, as he was meant to do. He had not eaten food, or drunk wine as good as this since before the war. It took him back to his honeymoon with Mary, to all the jaunts they had enjoyed in France before the great catastrophe of surely the worst world war mankind had ever fought.

Now John found he was fighting his emotions. He tried not to be impressed with the flowers and the food, with the maids and the butler, but after all the deprivations that he had suffered both as a prisoner of war, and now during the post-war austerity years, it all proved too much for him. He started to become animated, he started to enjoy Leandra's company, to laugh quietly at her charming jokes, to enjoy her stylish clothes, her beauty. It was impossible not to. He felt as if he had been terribly cold, really frozen to the marrow, and was now being immersed in a warm bath. At first every part of his being tried to fight these feelings. The lightness of the food, the perfection of the wines, their choice, even the glitter of the Waterford glasses, and the solid-silver knives and forks, all combined to seduce him, until, as they moved back into the Blue Room, he found he had not stopped enjoying himself for almost two hours. Worse than that, he had laughed and talked as he had not done for years and years. All the grind of the war, all the disappointment of returning to a country that could not organise itself into any kind of workforce, the sheer weight of it all had dropped away from him.

'So, Mr Chantry, what decision do you think you should come to about this little matter of Mr Wyndham and your daughter?'

John tried valiantly to sober up and look as stern as he had when he first arrived at Maydown, but once again his emotions failed him.

'I have to tell you, I have not changed my mind,' he said eventually, after two or three sips of strong coffee. 'And the reason I have not changed my mind is that Sunny is so very silly.' As Leandra stared at him intently, he continued, 'She is just such a typical eighteen-year-old, doesn't really know her own mind, doesn't really care to know it either. She is just like the foal in the field opposite our back gate, loves life, wants to keep kicking up her heels just for the sheer joy of living, but doesn't really know anything.'

Leandra picked up her elegant silver coffee pot and

carefully poured herself another cup of coffee, quite purposefully ignoring John Chantry's now empty cup.

'Oh, I think you will find that Sunny has a mind, all right, Mr
Chantry. But really, once again, I find I have to remind you, it
is not Sunny's mind of which we are speaking, but her heart.'
She then took John's cup and placed it on the tray, before saying, looking him straight in the eye, 'I believe she is rather
unhappy at the moment.'

John moved uncomfortably on the sumptuously upholstered
sofa, and looked away. Mary had murmured that she thought
that Sunny was determined to be ill, that she might starve herself to death rather than give in over her determination to
become associated with this Gray Wyndham character.
It was absurd – the whole notion was absurd – but nevertheless
he knew enough about female hysteria to know that
damsels in the nineteenth century when thwarted in their
infatuations were always throwing themselves off cliffs or into
lakes.

'As I just said, Sunny is being awkward, sitting about like a
wet Wednesday in Worthing. Really, that is all.'

'Mr Chantry?' Leandra leaned forward and smiled her justly
famous brilliant smile, and her blue eyes seemed to grow even
larger in her beautiful heart-shaped face. 'Mr Chantry,' she
repeated softly as the subtle aroma of her scent wafted towards
John, 'why do we not arrive at a truly British compromise? Why
don't we give Mr Wyndham and your daughter six months in
which to prove to you that they are sincere and suitable for
each other?'

'Not six months, no – twelve months, and then they can
marry. That is my last offer, and if they contravene the agreement I shall go after Mr Wyndham in a way he would not like.
I am not a man to cross, Mrs Fortescue.'

The look in John's eyes returned to its original expression, so that Leandra was able to observe with some interest that the set of his mouth once more resembled a line drawn not in flesh, but in stone.

'No, I am sure you are not, Mr Chantry. I am quite sure you are, as you say, a man of your word.'

'I will give them a year, and then I will reconsider.'

'Very well, just as you wish, Mr Chantry. We will give them an agreed twelve months. Twelve months in which, with your blessing, they can go about as an unofficially engaged couple, and prove to you and your wife that they are truly devoted to each other, and deserving of your blessing.'

John nodded briefly. He did finally believe in good old British compromise rather than conflict. It would be best for all if he gave a little. To do otherwise might seem ungracious. He stood up.

'Thank you for a most entertaining lunch, Mrs Fortescue, and for your wise counsel. Mary and I would hate to cause unnecessary suffering, but on the other hand, given that Sunny is so young, it is only understandable that we are feeling cautious, in the extreme, over this matter.'

'Of course, of course.'

Leandra walked John to the door of the Blue Room behind which, as always, Rule was lurking.

'Ah, Rule,' she said smoothly, giving him the secretly significant look that she always exchanged with him when they had succeeded with a particularly awkward guest, 'Mr Chantry is leaving.'

Rule produced John's hat and perfectly rolled silk umbrella as from nowhere, and walked him to the front doors, where he waited until he had driven away.

Leandra, meanwhile, closed the Blue Room door and went

straight to her perfectly white telephone, picked it up, and dialled Gray's number.

'Darling, it's me,' she said, even though they both knew that it was. She waited a few seconds as Gray was obviously waking from a post-lunch-at-the-club sleep, and then she said, 'Congratulations, Gray, you are, as of now, unofficially engaged to Sunny. You can take her to meet your sainted father, and tell him the good news that you will be marrying a nice girl, in twelve months' time.'

There was a long pause.

'So what happens now?' Gray asked.

'Well, it might be a good idea to telephone to your fiancée and tell *her*!'

They both laughed.

'Do you know, I think I shall do just that.'

Leandra replaced the telephone, and stared at it for a few seconds. It was all working out so well, it was almost too good to be true. Pretty soon she would have everything just as she wanted it, which only went to show that if you approached matters pleasantly, things went your way.

In the pantry off the kitchen Rule went about his routine tasks in his usual manner, doggedly and efficiently, while Cook and the maids chatted and laughed in the kitchen. He breathed on the cocktail shaker, which he was polishing up for the evening. He now knew, if only from Mrs Fortescue's expression, that she was moving towards a situation that would suit all and sundry very well indeed. He knew this, because not only did he know his mistress, but he knew his social history, as he should do since his father too had been a butler.

'Study your history, my son,' he would say, when they took a turn around his garden of an evening, Rule Senior puffing on a large Havana (taken from his master's thermidor, naturally).

'Study your social history and you will see mistress and maid, lord and lover, things have changed very little over the centuries, but always beware the domestic situation that appeals as being perfect. Unlike Icarus, who flew too near the sun and burned himself, people who think they have everything burn not just themselves, but everyone around them.'

Rule blew once more on the cocktail shaker and gave it yet another brisk rub with his duster. He would have to keep an eye on the situation upstairs. It might start to get too complicated and affect his position.

## Chapter Four

The house in which Gray's father, Mr Jocelyn Wyndham, lived was Edwardian, built by a pupil of Edwin Lutyens and surrounded by a garden designed by Gertrude Jekyll. It should have been most appealing. In fact it *was* most appealing, from the outside, so that Sunny, dressed to the nines in clothes chosen and paid for by Leandra, had every reason to feel in high good humour as she stepped out of Gray's pristine Bentley into the summer sunshine of a midday morning.

Gray too, as he glanced sideways at Sunny, had every reason to be in high good humour. Leandra's melting of John Chantry had been masterly, or – in her case, and rather more accurately – mistressly. Not only that but she had taken Sunny shopping, and transformed her into something so chic and adorable that she was a feast for the eye. Indeed, if Gray's heart had not already been taken long ago, he felt sure that he might have been quite vulnerable to Sunny in her sprigged muslin dress, her straw hat decorated with matching muslin, and short white gloves and flower-decorated handbag. The truth was that she looked not just young and beautiful, she looked innocent as the flowers that were chasing each other all over the faded brickwork of Chelston Manor.

Gray paused for a moment before beckoning Sunny to accompany him up the shallow stone steps to the oak front door. It was all very well bringing Sunny to Derbyshire to see his notoriously bad-tempered, cold-hearted father, but what in the name of all that was unholy would the old man make of her?

They were shown through the hall, with its charming tiled floor, to the drawing room, with its wide French windows that opened on to trim lawns, brick paths, old trees, and wide herbaceous borders whose scent immediately seemed to be beckoning them to step outside and enjoy their colourful beauty.

The aged manservant whom Gray addressed as 'Jones', whose bent frame precluded them from seeing his expression, nodded towards the Knole sofas and muttered, 'He'll be down in a minute,' and shuffled out.

'Jones is not exactly Rule,' Gray murmured to Sunny, who smiled, but instead of seating herself she moved about the room examining the paintings.

'Your father has very good taste in paintings,' she told Gray, appreciatively.

'No, not my father, my late mother,' Gray corrected her, at which point the drawing-room door opened.

Sunny turned and her eyes widened, as they would do, because framed in the doorway, tall, white-haired, and immaculately dressed, was a much older replica of Gray.

'You've arrived,' the newcomer stated in a cold voice, seeming for a moment content to stay framed in the doorway.

Gray glanced at Sunny, prepared to be protective of her, but to his astonishment she was staring at his father as if she was looking at someone she already knew.

'Yes,' she piped up cheerfully, after a short silence. 'We *have* arrived, and we had a wonderful journey. How do you do?' she went on, going straight up to the still unmoving Jocelyn Wyndham as if he too was smiling, not scowling. She waited for him to extend a reluctant hand, and then shook it gently. 'It was so kind of you to ask me to come and meet you, Mr Wyndham,' she continued. 'I have heard so much about you from Gray.'

'I doubt that very much,' came the reply.

'How are you, Father?' Gray asked quickly, before his father could continue in his usual unpleasant way.

Gray went up to the still unmoving figure, and he also shook the reluctant hand, but his father did not look at him. He was determinedly looking everywhere except at his guests.

'How long are you staying?'

He walked past them towards the terrace, as if he could not wait for them to leave, and was hoping that they would not follow him out to the garden, but turn and go back to the Bentley and drive off.

'We are here for the night, Father. Jones and Mrs Jones do know this.'

'Not staying until Sunday? Well, that's something, at any rate.'

'No, not staying until Sunday, Father. No, we are going on to stay with Aunt Bessie, as a matter of fact, near Bakewell.'

'Aunt Bessie? She still alive, is she?'

'At this minute, yes, I believe so.'

They were out on the terrace now, followed by Jones carrying a butler's tray held at a more than dangerous angle. Sunny, who had sat down on one of the large wooden benches with high backs and sloping designs, immediately stood up and went to him.

'Let me help you,' she offered in a lowered voice, removing two of the more perilous items.

Jones turned his head and smiled, and with good reason, Gray imagined, since it was probably a hundred years since anyone in the house had made the slightest attempt to help him.

'Thank you, miss.'

Jocelyn watched as Sunny busied herself on Jones's behalf.

'Isn't she used to servants?' he asked Gray in a rather too loud voice.

'Servants she is used to,' Gray lied. 'Bad manners she is not.'

He threw his father a look that Jocelyn Wyndham would probably have liked to have thrown straight back at him, but it seemed he was too astonished at being answered back by Gray to do anything except redden and look away.

'How beautiful everything is looking. You must love your garden very much,' Sunny stated, when, having finished helping Jones, she sat down beside Jocelyn, who was staring furiously into the far distance.

'I keep three gardeners. If you want to compliment them, please go ahead.'

Sunny smiled. 'I should love to,' she said, and turning to Jones, she added, 'Where may I find a gardener to compliment him, Mr Jones?'

Jones, who had not been addressed as 'Mr' in public life before, almost straightened up from the shock.

'I believe Mr Cradock is working in the Italian Garden this morning,' he said in a properly sepulchral tone.

'I shall go there at once, and since the morning is so hot, I will take him a glass of this perfectly delicious lemonade.' Sunny poured a glass of lemonade from the tray. 'I dare say you will prefer to stay with your darling father,' she said to Gray, nodding happily at Jocelyn, who was currently exhibiting an expression more akin to a gargoyle on the side of a cathedral than a doting parent. 'I can see the Italian Garden from here, down those steps, so no one need disturb themselves. So formal always, aren't they? My grandmother had one, but it was only small, in Surbiton, but she used to charge visitors sixpence each and give the money to the local hospital to buy toys for children. It was in thanksgiving for her son having been saved by them – the hospital not the children. So you see,' she added, nodding around to three already amazed males, 'such good comes out of Italian gardens as we never even think about, or of which we have never dreamed.'

She tripped off down the steps to the formal garden beyond that in which the Wyndhams were seated, and found Mr Cradock, who was only too grateful both for the lemonade and a repetition of the story of Mrs Chantry Senior.

'She resembles nothing more than a parakeet. You are engaged to a parakeet,' Jocelyn muttered.

'Sunny by name, sunny by nature, Father.'

'Your mother never stopped chattering. Got on my nerves so. Morning, noon and night, didn't matter where you went there was always the sound of chatter, natter, chatter.'

'And laughter, Father, and laughter.'

Gray fell silent, staring around him. If his mother had been alive they would all be sitting on the terrace laughing and talking. Alas, his mother had been killed in the war as she was driving to help the victims of one of the now notorious flying bombs, or 'fly bombs' as they were then known. The effect on his father was that he locked himself away and became bitter. And God, was he bitter!

'Glad to see you're still driving the same car, not throwing your money about, so that at least is something,' Jocelyn remarked.

Gray was just about to say that far from being his old car, he was actually driving a brand-new Bentley, when he remembered that his father suffered from what could only be described as 'car blindness' and, Gray's last car being dark blue, his father was obviously under the impression that he was still driving the same one. The necessity to form some sort of reply to Jocelyn's remark was removed from him by the happy return of Sunny.

'I have just been talking to Mr Cradock,' she said, sitting down opposite Jocelyn with the artless grace of a young filly settling comfortably into lush summer grass. 'He thinks the world of you, Mr Wyndham, as you know. He says there's not a single flower or tree in the place that you don't know and love.'

Jocelyn Wyndham's thick eyebrows, already low over his steel-grey eyes, now lowered themselves further, not frowning, but hiding the expression in them, an expression at which Gray could only guess.

'Cradock,' he stated eventually, 'is an old fool, and I am an even older one.'

'I wish you would teach me the names of all your flowers. It would be so interesting to try to learn them,' Sunny said, staring around her. 'As a matter of fact, you could begin on the terrace with this rose. It is so extraordinarily pretty, more like a blossom on a tree than a rose, and yet it is a rose, isn't it?'

Jocelyn nodded, standing up and going to the rose in question.

'This,' he said, the timbre of his voice changing suddenly. 'is a banksia.'

Sunny jumped up, and went to his side, and the timbre of her voice changed too, and took on the tone of someone in a church.

'It must make you very proud to see such a rose blooming

against your house, Mr Wyndham. I know if it was me I should feel ever so, *ever so* proud, because it means that you are a nice person. Banksia roses, my grandmother always said, hid from you if they didn't like you, but then they came back again, if you were kind.'

'My wife planted this – *Rosa banksia* "Lutea",' Jocelyn conceded. 'Although why it should keep on going for my sake, I wouldn't know, because she was a genius with flowers. I could only look on when she was around, but after – after – well, I had to learn, for the sake of the flowers, you know. For their sake perhaps more than anything I had to learn their little ways. I expect your grandmother knew that too?'

'Oh, yes, she certainly did. She had a theory that so many flowers died of heartbreak if their loved ones didn't return.'

Jocelyn was walking along the side of the terrace now, and it was just the two of them, himself and Sunny, and he was talking to her as he probably talked to the flowers, or to Cradock and the other gardeners, more in a murmur than in his usual cross voice, but he didn't realise it, because Sunny having fallen in love with his favourite rose, he was being swept along with his own love for it.

'Your grandmother was obviously a very wise woman, Miss Chantry. I have known healthy, hardy shrubs go to the wall once the gardener they loved went.'

Gray, who had been left alone on the terrace, turned as he saw Jones coming towards him with yet another perilously balanced tray.

'Ah, Jones—'

'Yes, Mr Jocelyn?'

'I am the younger one, Jones. I am Mr Gray.'

'Yes, of course, sir. Sorry, sir. May I fetch you another drink?'

'You can fetch me at least another two, Jones,' Gray told him in a low voice. 'It seems that my father is determined to take Miss Chantry on a tour of the whole garden.'

Jones straightened up slightly, and a slow smile formed on his thin lips.

'Do you know, Mr Gray, it is years since I saw Mr Jocelyn going round the garden with a visitor. They normally have no interest you see, sir. No interest at all.'

He turned and shuffled off back to the drinks tray, leaving Gray to stare after him.

Audrey stared at Arietta.

'You want *what?*' she asked, having heard the first time and knowing very well what it was that Arietta wanted.

'I did warn you, Mummy, I might need some money towards my journey to London.'

'You will need the money for where?'

Arietta felt her throat tightening. 'I just need the money for a third-class ticket to London,' she said, after a pause during which she cleared her throat. 'I told you yesterday, I need the money for a ticket. This friend of Sunny, Mrs Fortescue, has obtained an interview for me with this Mrs Ashcombe-Stogumber. The interview is at four o'clock today.'

'Well, this Mrs Hoojit will just have to wait, won't she? I hardly think she can't wait. She is only a human being, after all, even if she is rich.'

Such was her panic Arietta found herself pulling off one of her precious new gloves, and then pulling it on again.

'And where you found the money for your suit, and the gloves and the handbag, and the shoes, I wouldn't like to know and hate to ask.' Audrey sniffed.

Arietta knew that she must not tell her mother that Mrs Chantry had made her the suit and given her the material for it. To do so might risk being made to take it back. A feint, a verbal distraction, anything, was suddenly necessary, most particularly something that would irritate Audrey, take her mind off the coat and skirt. Arietta alighted on the very thing – a mention of poor old Uncle Bob always did the trick.

'Uncle Bob sent me a postal order.'

She did not say that she had telephoned Uncle Bob and he, guessing what her situation might be, had come up trumps.

Audrey stared at her daughter, a look of growing fury in her eyes.

'Bob should have sent the money to me, not you. I need it more than you. My need is far greater than yours; he should have known that.'

'And then you gave me my Post Office book – because of being eighteen.'

'I wouldn't do such a thing.'

'It was when you came back from the Gorsleys' cocktail party.'

It had been Arietta's eighteenth birthday. There was no celebration, but she had been asked to the Chantrys for supper, which was jolly, while her mother went out. However, earlier in the day her mother had taken considerable pleasure in clearing everything to do with her daughter into a suitcase and presenting it to Arietta with an old-fashioned birthday card. That had been her birthday present, not much to boast about, but happily it had included the Post Office book.

'Your Post Office account, of course. I should have taken eighteen years' rent from you. After all you have cost me, all these years, what you have cost me, a poor widow, I don't like to think. I should have taken a cut from you.'

Arietta nodded, and then, saddened beyond measure, she turned towards the front door.

'Where are you going now?' Audrey called.

'I am going to catch the train.'

'How can you catch a train without money?'

'I think I have just enough money for the ticket.'

Arietta closed the front door behind her and began the long walk to the station. She would have liked to have stopped off and asked Sunny if she could lend her a few shillings, but Sunny was away with Mr Wyndham, visiting Mr Wyndham's terribly cross father, so that would be a waste of time. And Mrs Chantry had been so kind to her already, she really could not ask her for even one more favour.

As Arietta turned into the main road that led to the village station, thankful that her new shoes fitted properly, she thought about how her mother had been with her all the time she was growing up, and how much she resented her daughter, and it seemed to her that it might have been quite different if she had been a boy, until she remembered that her mother was the same to everyone, and so she quickly rejected the idea that her life might have been different, and concentrated instead on trying to keep her hat straight.

Arietta had not lied when she told her mother that she had enough money for a third-class ticket. She did have enough money, but what she had not told her mother was that it was only enough for one way.

As the train pulled out of the station she stared around her at the other passengers. They were all dressed for travel, their well-worn, belted coats or mackintoshes done up to the neck, some of their outer wear probably covering no more than their vests, such was the poverty that she could read in their faces.

The war had made everyone very thin. As far as train travel was concerned, this was a most happy side effect of a most unhappy six years, for it meant that there was plenty of room for everyone, and as each new passenger climbed on board at each new station no one thought too much of squeezing up to each other and making room for some new angular arrival. This was done with abundant good nature as precious oranges and bananas and knitting were taken in and out of much-worn brown paper bags and faded holdalls, and their owners silently peeled fruit, or pursued their knitting with a fervour that made Arietta imagine that they must be knitting for dozens of shivering children or siblings at home, for the day had become overcast and cold, despite its being June.

From her window seat Arietta could see the gardens of the houses that backed on to the railway lines. They sported washing that she imagined could not stay clean for very long, and vegetables and flowers arranged in straight lines. Bean canes and rounded potato beds gave a feeling that the future might be brightening up, as did marigolds planted among the vegetables. As she stared out of the window, Arietta appreciated that she had never known the kind of poverty that the occupants of those houses backing on to the railway must still be enduring, but she had known what it was to be without. She had known what it was to be hungry, all right, and still did. Audrey was very figure-conscious, caring little for food or cooking, so Arietta knew what it was to be sent to school in clothes that were too short, and shoes that were too small, while her mother saved whatever money they had to buy herself a new cocktail frock for some dim and distant social event to which she always seemed to be looking forward.

'Like a piece of orange, dear?' The lady opposite her held out a segment.

Arietta shook her head, looking with longing at the proffered piece. She would have loved a piece of orange, but it would never do to turn up for her interview smelling of fruit.

'I would love it, but orange doesn't like me,' she said diplomatically.

'Go on, duck, you must. Slake your thirst no end.'

Everyone in the train carriage stared as they realised the extent of the woman's generosity, and Arietta knew she would have to accept.

'You got a good appetite, I expect, but you haven't eaten in days I warrant, too busy banting to get into that smart suit of yours.'

Everyone in the carriage nodded and laughed at this, because Arietta's fashionable look stood out like a sore thumb among the utility clothing around her.

'My friend's mother is a dressmaker,' Arietta explained, staring round the train carriage at all the interested faces. 'She made this for me for a present, because I am going up for a job, and I must look the part, or I will not have a chance.'

The occupants of the carriage all looked across or around at each other, obviously finding Arietta's explanation acceptable. The young lady was obviously very young, and equally obviously not a snob, or else why would she be in a third-class carriage? And then too the fact that she had needed a suit in order to go up for a job made her appearance, oversmart as it was, understandable.

'Well, I 'opes you gets it, duckie, really I do.'

'So do I.' Arietta looked ruefully round at her audience, who were evidently all quite interested in her chances. 'Because if I don't, I will surely have to walk home, and that is the truth.'

'You make sure they gives you your journey money, dear,' one of the knitters said, waving a knitting needle at her. 'That's your rights, that is, your journey money.'

'Oh, I think they will,' Arietta said, but she dropped her

eyes. No one had mentioned journey money, not Sunny, nor Mrs Fortescue when she had telephoned her about the interview.

As the train drew into Victoria Station, and while it was still moving, a man in the party threw open the carriage door and jumped out.

'Ooh, I do wish Bert wouldn't do that,' one of the women remarked. 'Talk about a foot stinger!'

But Bert merely sprinted on beside the train and as it stopped he promptly stopped, and carefully handed out each of the occupants of his carriage.

'My party piece, that is!' he said, winking at Arietta. As he stepped back he hastily refastened the top of his mackintosh, covering the lack of a jacket and tie underneath. 'Good luck with the interview, miss. Hope you get the job.'

Arietta turned and smiled and waved a newly gloved hand at him. 'So do I,' she agreed, before turning back to glance at the station clock.

She had an hour to find Mrs Ashcombe-Stogumber's house. It should be plenty, even in new shoes.

The house was a tall one, with a black painted front door. It was the only house in the street whose balcony was festooned. It was while Arietta was standing on the other side of the road, waiting for the hand of her old second-hand childhood watch to reach two o'clock, that she came to appreciate the significance of the floral decorations. They told the world that Mrs Ashcombe-Stogumber was a woman of wealth who must have a country estate, because the flowers were obviously rare and beautiful and they bloomed and tumbled in such a glorious manner it was a wonder that a crowd had not gathered beneath them.

A few seconds after two o'clock Arietta crossed the road and stood in front of the immaculate front door. It sported a large heavy brass knocker, so large and so heavy that Arietta immediately felt defeated by it, and instead of raising it and dropping it, she leaned forward and pressed the brass doorbell with its china centre that announced 'BELL'.

A butler opened the door to her. He was tall. He stared at Arietta, who was not tall. Arietta stared right back at him from under her new hat set firmly straight on her head. ('Never, ever wear a hat on the back of your head, dear, always straight on, or tilted forward,' Mrs Chantry had instructed her when she had given her the retrimmed hat.)

'You have come for the interview?' he asked in a kindly tone.

Arietta stared up at him from under her hat, which meant that she had to hold on to it with one hand.

'Yes, I have come for the interview,' she agreed in firm tones. She was sure that she must be one of many girls and young women coming up for the job, so she had already determined that she would not allow herself to become nervous, for it would only prove to be a waste of time, most especially since she probably had no chance of being taken on by this Mrs Ashcombe-Stogumber.

'If you would like to follow me, miss . . .?'

The staircase was narrow, as in so many Mayfair houses, but it led to a wide landing, and although the boards creaked and groaned under their feet, the carpet and the rugs were delightfully tasteful, of a delicate pattern, but not pronounced. The butler threw open the door in front of them.

'A young lady come for the interview,' he announced from the door, and then held it open for Arietta.

Arietta stepped into a surprisingly large and light room, at the end of which was a large ormolu-mounted writing table at which sat a small woman in a grey light tweed fitted jacket with a flat collar, beneath which lay a discreet strand of pearls. For a few seconds Arietta stood and watched as the butler closed the door, and the woman finished writing something. She finally looked up.

'Sit down,' she said, nodding towards a nearby sofa.

Arietta sat down carefully and with due consideration to the usual niceties: no crossing of ankles, skirt to be arranged decorously, gloved hands held loosely in the lap.

The woman went on writing with renewed vigour. Arietta felt grateful for the time to compose herself, and allowed her eyes to wander round the room. It was large and decorated in a purposefully unselfconscious manner. The furniture, like the stairs and landing outside, like the paintings on the walls, was not shabby but delicately worn, nothing looked too new but sat about the room in a confident manner, as if it had been there for some time and was aware of its appropriate beauty, its perfect setting. In contrast to such good taste, Arietta felt all too new, as if her very smartness, her new suit, her new hat, her new shoes and gloves were an affront to the sumptuous ease of the room and its owner.

'Very well.'

At last the older woman looked up and, having placed her pen in a china holder in front of her blotter, she cleared her throat and put on a pair of spectacles.

'Come here, gel.'

Arietta stood up and went towards the desk, although from the way the woman had addressed her, it might as well have been an ormolu-mounted throne.

Arietta stood quite still, looking at Mrs Ashcombe-Stogumber firmly in the eyes.

'Turn round, gel.'

She did as she was told.

'Now go and sit down again, gel.'

Mrs Ashcombe-Stogumber took another piece of writing paper out of the china folder and picked up her pen once again.

'You have come a long way on a train, or in a motor car?' she asked, as she wrote.

'In a train, Mrs Ashcombe-Stogumber.'

'So, you did not have a motor car to bring you?'

'No, I do not have a motor car.'

A slight pause followed this, although the pen kept travelling across the paper.

'Would you like a motor car?' Mrs Ashcombe-Stogumber asked, not looking up.

'Yes, I would.'

'Good. That is good. It is always good to want things. It means one stirs one's stumps and does not sit about waiting for an apple to fall on one's head like Isaac Newton.'

Arietta frowned slightly. She had never before realised that the defining of the theory of gravitation had been the result of some kind of reprehensible inertia on the part of Isaac Newton.

'So, here we are.' Mrs Ashcombe-Stogumber looked up at last. 'You and I. You without a motor car, and I without a social secretary, the previous incumbents time and time again having proved so very unsatisfactory. Shall we be suited, you and I, do you think? Will you, unlike they, be able to last more than a few weeks?'

Arietta stared at Mrs Ashcombe-Stogumber, but she knew enough not to fill the silence that followed. She also knew enough to know that even a few weeks would be good experience, being in Mayfair and working for such a grand lady, even if Mrs Ashcombe-Stogumber sacked her after only a short time.

Mrs Ashcombe-Stogumber removed her spectacles and stood up, coming out from behind her desk to reveal the bottom half of her suit, which was a full skirt of a becomingly cartwheel shape that showed off her undoubtedly elegant figure.

'I think we will be suited, really I do. When would you like to start? As soon as possible, as far as I am concerned, since I am utterly without anyone.'

Arietta cleared her throat. 'Tomorrow, if you would like?'

'Certainly. I certainly would like. Do you know why I would like you to start so soon?'

'No, Mrs Ashcombe-Stogumber.'

'I will therefore tell you. I would like you to start because you are quiet, you do not fidget, and you do not cross your ankles when you sit down.' She turned back to her desk and, having pressed a button underneath it, quietly examined the contents of a small drawer. 'How much would you like for your journey money?'

Arietta stared. She had not even had to mention the cost of the ticket, and now she was being offered a reimbursement.

'It's very kind of you but—'

'Don't be silly, gel. There's no kindness in me, ask anyone.' She placed a five-pound note in Arietta's gloved hand. 'That is for your luncheon and tea on the train, and make sure that you never ever travel third class again.'

Arietta missed any inference that might or might not have been intended. She was far too fascinated by the, to her, quite extraordinary sight of the five-pound note. It was unimaginable money.

'Thank you very much indeed,' she said slowly. 'Thank you, but I don't think you need to—'

'No, my dear Miss Staunton, it is for me to thank you, and of course I need to reimburse you, and of course I know it is far too much, but if you knew how many fast-and-loose types have sat where you have been sitting, you would know what I mean. It's the war, of course. I keep saying that to Joseph and Mrs Joseph. The war has played fast and loose with the morals of young women, but we must not dwell on that now we have found you. You will have a room at the top of the house, and the run of the place when we are in London, and when we are in the country, the same applies. You will have Saturday afternoon and the whole of Sunday off in town, and Sundays only if we are in the country. You will have a certain amount of your wardrobe paid for, and a certain amount you will pay for yourself. Your starting salary is to be arranged between you and my Mr Balcombe, who adds up little things in columns for me. We will not dwell on vulgarities, but I do assure you it will be fully enough to compensate you for leaving hearth and home and taking up residence here with me. You will, I can also promise you, earn your salary. What you will not be, however, is bored. That I can absolutely guarantee. I have a very active social life, and am known as a great hostess, so you will, of course, meet all sorts of exciting people, but discretion will be your guide. Remember, in Society it is always better to be known as a person of few words rather than too many. And – and this you must never forget – loyalty is everything. If you remain loyal to me, I will remain loyal to you, and I think we will have a happy time of it. So now, nothing better to be done than wish you a safe journey, and we will expect you tomorrow afternoon after lunch, and before tea.'

She nodded her dismissal.

Arietta hurried off down the windy London street, clutching her handbag with the large white five-pound note now hidden in its depths. She hurried along, trying to come to terms with the realisation that she would actually be able to take a taxi back to the station. After which two questions arose in her mind. First of all, what on earth would her mother say when she told her she was going to start a new job, in London, on the following day?

And next, and most puzzling of all, why would such a person as Mrs Ashcombe-Stogumber choose Arietta, of all people, to be her social secretary?

'Taxi!'

Seated once more at her ormolu-mounted writing desk, Mrs Ashcombe-Stogumber raised her white telephone to her carefully coiffed head, with its swept-back dark hair beautifully arranged in a chignon, and started to dial Leandra Fortescue's number. She must thank her for the recommendation. The young gel could not be more suitable. She was quietly spoken. She was pretty without being a beauty. She wanted to please. She was afraid to upset. The fact that she smelled vaguely of citrus fruit showed that she was not extravagant, that she had preferred to travel up third class with poor people who ate oranges rather than charge a potential employer too much money for her journey. All in all, she could not be a better choice. And by the time Alice Ashcombe-Stogumber had finished with her, she would not know herself, and that was the truth.

For the journey home Arietta did as Mrs Ashcombe-Stogumber had advised and treated herself not just to a first-class ticket, but to tea on the train, served by waiters who seemed quite able to stand swaying wildly over the crockery while pouring tea without spilling a drop.

As she revelled in the tea, the sandwiches, and the cake and biscuits, Arietta could not help staring at her own reflection in the window of the carriage. There she was, Arietta Staunton, seated in a first-class carriage, eating toast and drinking tea, just like someone she might read about in one of her mother's library books and, what was more and what was better, on the following day she would be coming back along the same track. The wheels of the train going along the track might sound like clickerty clack, clickerty clack to the other passengers, but to Arietta they seemed to be saying, 'You're going back, you're going back.'

'I know before you say anything, I know just what you are going to say.'

Arietta stared at Audrey. She was standing in the hall as if she had been waiting for her return all afternoon, which couldn't be true, surely?

'You have spent all your money on the ticket, and want a loan to go after another job. Well, before you say a thing, the answer is *no*.'

'Actually, Mummy, *my* answer is no.'

Audrey continued as if Arietta had not said anything, 'You may have finished your course, but as I said to Mary Chantry just now, I know how this is going to turn out. It's going to turn out that you cost me more than when you were at school. You'll have to get a job doing housework or some such, until such time that you can land a job as some secretary to some poor benighted person of low intellect.'

Arietta stared at her mother, but before she could say anything in reply, Audrey had turned her back on her and was heading for the kitchen.

'I am going out to dinner. The Tredegars have invited me at

the last minute – someone must have dropped out – so you will have to make yourself something. There's some soup some-where, I think; some soup in a jug under the meat safe, and there's a roll in the bread bin. That will do you, won't it?'

Arietta's look had now turned into an expression that would have shocked even Audrey, but instead of following her mother into the kitchen, she turned and went upstairs. She would start packing straight away. The sooner she left Rushington for Mrs Ashcombe-Stogumber's house, the better.

Eventually her mother called up to her, 'Don't expect me back until late.'

Arietta waited until she heard the front door shut, after which she mouthed silently to her reflection in her small dressing-table mirror, '*Oh, good.*'

And then she continued to pack the suitcase that had long ago been assigned to her, but which she had only had cause to use when going to spend the night with Sunny at the Chantrys' cottage.

The following morning she woke up early, too excited to stay in bed. She crept downstairs to iron one of her two blouses. She was busily making them look as good as she could when she heard a car arriving back. She went to the window and stared out. It was Audrey, and she was waving someone good-bye. Arietta looked round the kitchen. She had to get out. She switched off the iron, snatched up her ironing, and fled back upstairs.

Once again in her room she stared around it as if it was somewhere she had never been before. What was her mother doing coming back, still in her cocktail dress, all black lace and matching cape, and high-heeled shoes, at six o'clock in the morning? Why had she not come home before?

She started to dress in a panic-stricken manner. She knew

that Audrey would have walked to the Tredegars' house, which was just across the village green and then down a quiet road, hardly a walk at all; so why, in heaven's name, however late the dinner party had been, would her mother come back in a car, and not just *a* car, someone *else's* car?

Arietta heard Audrey's bedroom door close quietly, and then for no reason at all, since she had already been up and had intended to stay up, and was almost fully dressed, she slid under the eiderdown of her own bed and stared up at the ceiling as the increasing sound of the dawn chorus floated through the half-open window.

Later Audrey opened Arietta's bedroom door and stared in. 'What are you doing?' she asked in a flat, bored, tired voice. 'I am packing, Mummy.'

'*You're packing, Mummy*, are you?' Audrey imitated Arietta's voice, a habit of hers for some years. 'Been invited to go to the Chantrys yet again, have you?'

Audrey stood pale-faced in the doorway, the vivid colour of her Chinese dressing gown with its mandarin collar making her look even paler as she snatched at a glass of water from Arietta's bedside table and, taking the two aspirins that she had been carrying, she swallowed them down with the water.

Arietta waited until her mother had drained the glass and replaced it on the pale blue table, with its faded design of teddies and trains, making such a sharp smacking sound that Arietta blinked in surprise, before going on,'No, no, I haven't been asked to the Chantrys yet again. Sunny is away with Mr Wyndham, her fiancé-to-be.'

'Fiancé-to-be! Really, you young girls – your ideas . . . really, you are so extraordinary. Do you honestly think that John Chantry will even countenance Sunny getting married to that man? Of *course* he won't. The whole idea is ridiculous. Mind you, I will say one thing for Sunny Chantry, she is busy keeping the whole village on tenterhooks with all this talk of her engagement. No one could talk about anything else at the Tredegars' dinner party last night. Gerry is even running a book on it. I had a little flutter.' She laughed suddenly, remembering. 'Just a little flutter – seemed such a pity not to.'

She turned and started to walk back to her own bedroom across the landing.

'So what is it now that you are going to the Chantrys for? If Sunny isn't there, what is it now? Mary making you model a cocktail frock for one of her swanky ladies? Honestly, the way that woman works, sews her fingers to the bone, God help her. Rather her than me. So what is it?'

Arietta stood at her own bedroom door. 'No, Mummy.'

For perhaps the thousandth time Arietta found herself wishing to goodness she could call her mother something other than 'Mummy'. It suddenly sounded so babyish.

'So what is it?' Audrey demanded yet again.

'I told you, *I am not going to the Chantrys!*' Arietta stated, speaking with uncustomary force.

'Don't shout, Arietta. My head hurts.'

'I am not going to the *Chantrys*, I am going to London. I have a job. I am leaving home. I have a job.' Without realising it Arietta's voice had taken on a tone that was exultant.

Her mother stared at her. 'Don't be ridiculous. Going to London, got a job? Don't be pathetic, Arietta. Only a mad person would want you!'

Arietta turned and very slowly snapped the locks on her cheap suitcase.

'Well, actually,' she paused, avoiding the word 'Mummy', 'a very nice lady wants me to work for her, in Mayfair.'

'In Mayfair?'

Audrey stared at Arietta and it seemed to the daughter that the mother's jaw was dropping. Mayfair, with its quiet streets and elegant houses, was not somewhere that Audrey knew at all, although of course, because it was the London home of the patrician classes, she had read about it in books and gossip columns.

'Yes, in Mayfair. It is a tall house with very elegant rooms, and the lady has a very nice butler, Mr Joseph, and Mrs Joseph, his wife, and they look after her in London. She also has a beautiful house in Surrey, where royalty have stayed.'

Arietta buttoned up the jacket of the suit that Mrs Chantry had made her, and taking a small hat and placing it on her brown hair, and pulling on some cotton gloves she finally straightened and faced her mother.

'Just think, Mummy, you're going to be free of me,' she stated gravely. 'What you have always wanted.'

'Don't be idiotic, Arietta. That is such a hurtful thing to say. Of course I shan't be free of you. You're my daughter. It is a fact. I am your mother. That also is a fact.'

Audrey sniffed and started to turn away as Arietta picked up her suitcase.

'I didn't mean to be hurtful, Mummy, but I know that I have been such a burden to you all these years, costing you so much money, as you always said, so now I have a job, you will be free of the worry of me. It will be so good, won't it, not to feel worried by how much I eat, or the cost of my clothes, or fees for college? All that is now behind you. I am no longer your burden, which is good, isn't it?'

Audrey did not choose to dispute the fact that Arietta had always been a burden. Instead she changed tack.

'I don't believe you will hold down this so-called job for more than a second. You'll be back to plague me, mark my words, and probably within the week.'

Audrey crossed the landing, went into her bedroom and slammed the door.

Arietta stood for a moment staring at the door, remembering how often as a small child she had been dragged into it to be punished, until the day she bit Audrey on the hand. It was an event that had somehow brought about an uneasy truce. She remembered the look in her mother's eyes as the pain registered, and Arietta flung herself down the stairs and through the front door and out on to the village green, from where she fled across to the Chantrys' cottage.

Mrs Chantry had stood in the doorway, looking down at the six-year-old, her hair awry, her small chest heaving with emotion.

'Mrs Chantry, I wonder if I could come in for a while?'

'Of course, dear, come in, do.'

She sat Arietta down in the kitchen where, her small body still shuddering with suppressed emotion, the little girl had found herself the object of Sunny's amazed interest.

The silence in the kitchen had been broken by Mary Chantry's voice calling to her husband, 'I'm just going to pop across to Audrey Staunton, John. Keep an eye on the girls until I get back, would you?'

She had not been gone long.

'You will be staying the night with me, Arietta. Your mummy has agreed,' Mary Chantry said in a commendably kind voice. 'Now who would like some toast and golden syrup?'

Never had toast tasted so good, nor would it ever again. Nor would Arietta ever forget the kindness of Mrs Chantry as she walked her up to the bathroom and ran a bath for her.

'You can manage, can't you, dear?' she asked tactfully, before half closing the door.

Arietta had undressed herself, stepped into the warm water, and then suddenly overwhelmed and shuddering with suppressed tears, she had put a flannel on her face. She knew now, somehow she just knew, that from now on her young life would get better.

As she remembered this, not slowly, but in a few seconds – the smell of the soap, the borrowed nightdress, the bliss of going to bed with another little girl in the room, not all alone – Arietta gave a great sigh, knowing, as she had all those years before, and with the same strange certainty, that her life was about to get better. She went slowly down the stairs and out into the fresh air.

She closed the front door behind her, realising that she would never have to open it again except by choice, for even if Mrs Ashcombe-Stogumber did not like her work, even if she failed at her new job, Arietta knew that she would rather scrub floors, work in a factory, anything – *anything* rather than go back and live with her mother.

Sunny was enjoying Sunday lunch with Jocelyn and Gray, and not just because the food was delicious, and she had spent a heavenly morning walking round the grounds with the old man, but because she knew now that she was a success with him. The truth was that he could not take his eyes off her.

'You remind me of my mother, Miss Chantry,' he had said earlier as they walked past the lake with its fountains and grottoes, and on to the fields above it, from where they paused to stare down at the ten-acre garden in all its summer radiance. 'She was dark-haired and small-framed like you. And she loved to laugh. I can see you love to laugh, that you have a happy nature.'

Sunny smiled at old Jocelyn and pulled down her hat a little lower to avoid becoming sunburned.

'We are not put on this earth to be sad, are we, Mr Wyndham?'

Jocelyn had stared at her and then, avoiding her question, but only because he didn't know what to say in reply, he said after a short pause, 'I see you're sensible too. Don't want to ruin your complexion with this fashionable tanning business.'

Sunny continued to smile at him from under her hat, but he, finding her smile unexpectedly affecting, dropped his gaze and stared down towards the gardens. It was odd, but he had woken up that morning feeling as if he had recovered from a long illness. He had not sprung out of bed – he was too old for that – but he had run his own bath, and chosen his own clothes, which he normally left to his valet. Then he had been the first into the dining room, and what was more and what was better, he had eaten a good breakfast – a hearty breakfast for him – after which he had walked out into the garden and picked some roses for Miss Chantry which he put into a jug and placed by her table setting, something that he had always been in the habit of doing for his wife when she was alive.

Sunny had changed into a white linen many-folded skirt and a green linen jacket with large white buttons up to the neck.

'You cannot go to stay at Chelston Manor without several changes,' Mary had murmured, and although her voice registered disapproval of Sunny's proposed visit to Jocelyn Wyndham's house, she had set about altering three or four outfits – yet more discarded pre-war clothing given to her by her customers – to suit Sunny.

Sunny did not know it but, seated between the older and the younger Wyndham men, she looked as fresh as the roses that Jocelyn had picked for her, and just as a film director, to enhance the beauty of his female star, will first slip in a close-up of an older, uglier woman, so seated between her host and his son, Sunny looked younger than springtime itself.

'What on earth are you doing with my son, Miss Chantry?' Jocelyn demanded as, lunch being over, they once more walked off down the gardens.

Sunny coloured slightly and found herself hesitating before she could find a suitable reply. She did not mind the old man being so direct; what she minded was the possibility that she might have to tell a lie and so run the risk of the old man knowing that she was not telling the truth, and thinking less of her because of it. She wanted to keep his respect.

Finally, after the pause that had become almost too long, and during which it seemed to her she could hear every sound in the garden, from the humming of the bees to the birds in the trees, becoming louder and louder until it became a symphony as insistent as anything that had ever been written, she turned to him.

The look in the old man's eyes was too shrewd, too anxious, too direct.

'I am learning to love him in the only way that I can, Mr Wyndham.'

Jocelyn gazed at her briefly, before starting to walk on.

'Ah,' he said softly, appreciatively, giving a brief smile. 'I thought as much. I thought you could not be in love with him. I must be honest, Miss Chantry. In a way I hope that you never will be in love with my son. It would be hopeless. Gray cannot love you in return, you know – the war changed all that. He shut up shop as a man. I saw it the moment he came into the dining room that first morning back. He was no longer the same person, but someone quite different. I would not have known him. I would not have known my boy.'

Sunny looked away. It did not seem right for a father to be talking about his son in that way. On the other hand, it was only what Leandra Fortescue had told her, so it was obviously not something that grown-ups, as she still thought of them, found in the least embarrassing.

Perhaps that too was a result of the war? Perhaps, after all the bombs and the killing, older people did not mind referring to such things? Perhaps it was something to which she too, one day, would be able to refer quite openly and casually? She could not imagine it, but she knew, nevertheless, that she had to at least embrace the possibility, if not the prob-ability, like having grey hair, or walking with the aid of a stick, which she sometimes tried to imagine, and failed.

'Gray is very sensitive,' she suggested.

Sunny knew that being sensitive was a good thing. She knew this because it was always spoken of in Rushington with quiet appreciation. Someone who was sensitive was a good person, a person who was aware of others, of their happiness and unhappiness.

'He is pleasure loving,' Jocelyn announced of Gray, after a pause during which he stopped and frowned for no particular reason at some wild flowers that they happened to be passing.

'Perhaps that is a result of the war, Mr Wyndham?'

That was something that everyone in Rushington had been in the habit of saying. If there was an unexpected divorce, or someone took to the bottle, or a husband ran off with another woman, the inevitable conclusion was that their behaviour was a direct 'result of the war'. It was Rushington's way of brushing anything uncomfortable under the carpet.

'Everything is a result of something, Miss Chantry, but it does not make it excusable.'

'No, not excusable,' Sunny agreed, 'but understandable, don't you think?'

That was something that her mother was always saying.

Sunny frowned, realising with an odd feeling of guilt that she seemed incapable of saying anything original.

'You are very mature for your years, Miss Chantry.'

This remark served only to increase Sunny's guilt as she realised that far from being mature she was really just a parrot.

'I am afraid I am not at all mature, Mr Wyndham,' she confessed, staring ahead at the summer sky, at the swallows swooping above a distant pond, at the variegated greens of all the trees, all seeming quite determined to subtly capture the eye, while flattering their surroundings that they were staying hidden. 'I realise that everything I say is really rather second-hand, which is actually quite a lowering thought.'

The old man stopped and turned towards Sunny, his resident frown deepening into two granite-like furrows.

'Nothing that you say, whether second- or first-hand, matters beside the fact that you are a very truthful young woman, Miss Chantry, and as such, if I were you, I should reconsider your relationship with my son.' He leaned forward. 'Indeed, if I was your father there is only one word I would say to you, and that is – run!'

## Chapter Five

For Arietta, arriving in London for the second time was a revelation. This time she was not nervous; this time she had a destination.

'Number forty-two Upper—'

She stared up into the taxi driver's lined face. He was wearing a smart if old-fashioned hat, probably the kind of hat that his grandfather had worn when driving a hackney carriage.

'I've had a sudden blank.' She fumbled in her handbag and produced the address written on a piece of paper. 'There, here.'

She went to show him a piece of paper, but the driver had already climbed out of his cab and, taking her suitcase from her, he carefully strapped it into the luggage space before looking at the piece of paper with the scribbled address.

'Oh yes, I know.' He nodded at the piece of paper without taking it. 'Matter of fact, I just came from near there, Curzon Street. A nice old gent, saying goodbye to his town house, he was. Can't afford it any more. Has to sell. Imagine, he said, the bombs missed it, Hitler missed it, the doodlebugs passed it by, only for the government to get him with their supertax. It's a shame, really, for people like him, a crying shame.' He held open the door for Arietta. 'In you get, dear, and don't you worry about a thing. Old Arthur will get you to your address in no time.'

He shut the door, and as he did so Arietta sat back in the seat, half closing her eyes. She was here at last. She was in London. She was going to be happy. She knew it.

It was as if she had become a part of everything, and everything a part of her: the train, the passengers, the station, the bombed-out buildings they were passing, and then as they grew nearer and nearer to Mayfair, the elegance of the people walking along the street, the doormen opening and shutting car and taxi doors, the London pigeons strutting in the roads, hardly bothering to move before the oncoming traffic, until at the last minute they neatly sidestepped into the gutter, only to reappear in the middle of the road once more.

'I'll take you past the park, then you can see the 'orses in Rotten Row,' the driver called back to her. 'Lovely sight, that is, specially for a country girl.'

Arietta would have liked to have asked him how he knew she was up from the country but, the roads being empty at that time of day and the streets uncrowded, the taxi drew up in front of number forty-two before she had time.

Mr Joseph took her suitcase from the driver, and Arietta made sure to tip the driver, who very promptly gave her back the coin.

'You'll be needing your pennies in London, dear, more than what I do, I assure you.' He winked at her. 'Good luck with your new job.'

Arietta blushed, and smiled, and then waved to the receding taxi, before turning to walk after Mr Joseph. Was it that obvious that she was a hayseed? It must be.

'I, er, I brought Mrs Ashcombe-Stogumber some flowers.'

She had dampened the newspaper that directly surrounded the flowers to keep them fresh, and then wrapped them about with Christmas paper, carefully ironed.

Mr Joseph stared at her offering, took them and laid them on a silver salver beneath a vast arrangement of hot-house blooms.

'Mrs Ashcombe will be most pleased with your offering, Miss Staunton. I will have them brought to the kitchen and arranged and placed upon her breakfast tray tomorrow morning. She dearly loves the flowers of field and garden.'

Arietta knew the butler was being kind, he knew he was being kind, and at the same time they both knew that it was most likely very true that, amid all the hot-house blooms, the carefully picked garden flowers, a mix of roses and sweet peas, of lavender and cornflowers, would indeed be very welcome.

'Perhaps they will be a change?'

'If you will follow me I will take you to your room.'

Arietta was fit and young. Mr Joseph was neither, so that by the time they both reached the top of the house and the attic room that was to be Arietta's small kingdom, he was breathing so heavily it was frightening.

'This is your room, Miss Staunton, and opposite, the usual offices. You will be quite alone up here, you will find. My wife and myself are in the basement – when we are not in the country with Mrs Ashcombe, that is. Mrs Ashcombe, by the way, Miss Staunton, does not use her full name except in Society. At home, here and in the country, she uses only the first surname, never the second. That is the rule.'

Arietta could hear his heavy tread going down the steep, creaking old London staircase, and as she did she felt a sudden desire to run after him, and ask him not to leave her alone at the top of the house, to stay with her as she unpacked.

Once she had hung all her clothes in the curtained cupboard and put her few things tidily in the chest of drawers, Arietta went to her bedroom window and found herself staring at yet more London pigeons. She opened the window and secured the latch. They cooed, they moved, but they did not fly away, seeming, like their relatives in the roads below, to be filled with an admirable confidence.

'If I am to stay in this town, I am going to have to become like you, aren't I?' she asked them, but they, being pigeons, paid no attention, for pigeon-business is all too preoccupying.

Arietta turned to her mirror. Her coat and skirt, worn for the interview, were her only good clothes. She hoped that Mrs Ashcombe, as she must now think of her, would get used to seeing her secretary in the same clothes, day in and day out, until such time that she could save up to buy another outfit. She certainly could not wear her Rushington clothes for work. No lady of influence would want her secretary to be taking dictation, answering the telephone or going on commissions for her in skirts and jumpers.

She walked slowly down the stairs in search of her new employer.

'You never knock on a drawing-room door, Miss Staunton.'

Mr Joseph's low tones came towards Arietta before she could even reach out and commit the *faux pas*.

Mr Joseph did not wink at her as the taxi driver had done, he merely sidestepped and, going in front of her, he pushed open the door.

'Miss Staunton, Mrs Ashcombe.'

The drawing room seemed both bigger and smaller than when she had last been in it, and Mrs Ashcombe's desk further away, and nearer than it had been before, so that as Arietta stepped up to it, it seemed to take an age, and yet at the same time be upon her before she could say 'good morning'.

'It is after midday, dear, so officially it is afternoon.'

Arietta blushed, and held out her hand. Mrs Ashcombe ignored it.

'Sit down.' She nodded towards a high-backed chair, and Arietta, since the older woman was holding out a notebook and pencil, realised at once what was being asked of her, pulled the chair up and, taking the pad and pencil, prepared to take dictation.

'To the Lady Percival, Shalcombe Castle, Shalcombe, near Swiveliscombe, Dorset. No, put Dorset*shire*, she likes that . . .'

The art of taking shorthand notes, Arietta had swiftly discovered, was to shut out everything except the sounds coming towards you, and allow them to be translated into quick pencilled squiggles. What was being dictated to you should be of no interest, until you typed it up.

'Very well, that will be all. I am going to the Berkeley for luncheon now. I will be ready to sign the letters when I return.'

Arietta nodded, silently glad that she had passed out of Princess Secretarial College with such good speeds.

'The typewriter is through there.'

Mrs Ashcombe plucked up her crocodile handbag and sashayed quickly out of the room, an elegant figure in figure-hugging jacket and Dior-length skirt.

Arietta followed her directions and found herself in an almost claustrophobically small office dominated by an ancient typewriter such as the secretarial college had used, and of the type that she had ardently hoped never to have to use again.

Beside the typewriter was a pile of monogrammed writing paper, a pen and a bottle of ink. Just as she was about to roll the first piece of paper into the typewriter there was the sound of a throat being cleared in the doorway of the little office.

'Mrs Ashcombe doubtless explained that all her personal letters must be written by hand. Only the business letters are expected to be typed.'

Arietta stared at the space that Mr Joseph had momentarily occupied before closing the door behind him as quickly as he had entered it. They both knew that Mrs Ashcombe had explained no such thing. She stared at the pot of ink, and taking another piece of writing paper she started to address the envelope by hand, and then write the first of the required letters.

> Dear Lady Percival, Mrs Ashcombe wishes me to thank you on her behalf for your kind invitation to support her charity, a donation for which she would be grateful if you will find enclosed. She has the highest regard for the sentiments expressed in Lady Percival's letter, and wishes her every success in her charitable venture.

Arietta stared at her shorthand book, realising now that almost every letter dictated to her was in reply to a charitable request, and while the replies did vary in tone and length, nevertheless in every case a donation was to be enclosed, and the letter signed on her employer's behalf by her secretary.

'Very well. You have passed with flying colours, Miss Staunton. Flying colours,' Mrs Ashcombe repeated as she studied each letter in the folder that Arietta was presenting to her. 'You have no idea how dreadfully ignorant some of my secretaries have been, *typing* personal letters. Imagine!' She nodded and, taking a small key out of her desk, she undid a drawer. 'Now for the donations.'

Arietta fell silent as she realised just how many cheques were being placed at the back of the letters and inside the fold of the envelopes, ready for her to fold and send off.

'You will find stamps in the box in the hall, and Mr Joseph will send a boy to post them in the box for you.' Mrs Ashcombe nodded. 'Good.'

Arietta turned with some relief to go back to her small office, but it seemed that her employer was not finished with her.

'There is a matter of some delicacy to which I find we must address ourselves, Miss Staunton.'

Arietta stopped and turned.

Mrs Ashcombe sighed. 'I hear you have no clothes.'

Arietta blushed possibly more heartily than she had ever blushed. They both knew from whom Mrs Ashcombe must have heard that Arietta had no clothes.

'Mr Joseph makes it his business keep me informed of everything to do with the house and its running,' the older woman continued. 'It is not a matter for embarrassment, I do assure you. Most of London has no clothes, but since you represent me, and I have clothes, it is incumbent on me to provide you with whatever it is you might need.' She pushed a card towards Arietta. 'Go to Shotcombe Street, and ask for Mrs Pomeroy. She will help you with everything you need. Oh, and tell her to send me the account.'

'Do you wish me to go now?'

'Of course, of course. We can't have you in rags for a minute longer.'

Rags! A lump came into Arietta's throat as she wandered down the steep London staircase to the street outside. It did not seem possible that her beautiful coat and skirt could be described as rags. The hours that Mrs Chantry had spent in the fashioning of the coat and skirt now seemed utterly futile. As she walked dutifully into the heart of Mayfair, it seemed to her that everyone was staring at her 'rags'. She ached with homesickness, so much so that if her mother had not come back that morning looking like something the cat had brought in, and in some stranger's motor car, she *would* have gone home. As it was she found the house number that she needed, and dutifully rang the bell.

'Yes, dear?'

A small, plump woman dressed in a black silk frock stood in the entrance of the doorway. Beyond her, wafting gently out to the now warm afternoon, came delicious, foreign smells of unimaginable delights.

'Yes?' she demanded again.

Arietta extended one gloved hand. 'You don't know me. I am Arietta Staunton. Mrs Ashcombe sent me to you, for – for—' Arietta stopped, and frowned. 'She sent me to you,' she ended finally, colouring, 'for – for – clothes, because she doesn't like mine.'

'Yes, yes, of course, Mrs Ashcombe just telephoned to me. I know all about you. Come in, my dear.'

Arietta stood in the hall as Mrs Pomeroy closed the door behind her, and for a second as they stood in the darkened space with only the fanlight over the door creating a pool of light, Arietta felt anxious and the smell of the older woman's perfume threatened to overpower her, until she walked ahead a short way and flung open a door through which, feeling just a little like Alice passing through the looking-glass, Arietta followed her.

Now they were embraced by a room of startling elegance.

Pale greys and blues dominated the furniture, all of which was elegant, French, eighteenth century and curiously uninviting. It was a room in which no one would ever be found to be seated comfortably chatting, at ease in its perfectly upholstered chairs. They might sit bolt upright, or walk over to admire the oil paintings of flowers in vases, or boats in an overcast harbour, and they might, on occasion, be found to be murmuring, often and in low tones, at the loveliness of it all, the exquisite taste, but once enjoyed they would not hurry to return to the room's preserved atmosphere. They would have 'done' it, as a tourist might 'do' a museum. It would not entice them back to its elegance; it could not embrace them with its warmth – because it had none.

Mrs Pomeroy crossed the highly polished wooden floor with quick, light steps followed, at a polite distance, by Arietta. Another door was opened, and Arietta, with a strange feeling of relief, stepped into a cornucopia of colour. Here every kind of fabric was displayed on boards in neat clusters; or pinned on dummies of female forms of enviable outlines, around many of which were also pinned toiles and paper patterns of every kind of shape and design.

'*Eh, voilà*, here we have the engine room of the house.' Mrs Pomeroy, who spoke perfect English with the lightest of Gallic accents, smiled. 'Mrs Ashcombe, she is anxious that I should dress you with a new wardrobe, *n'est-ce pas*?' Mrs Pomeroy nodded towards one of the models. 'That is Mrs Ashcombe there.'

They both stared in silent reverence at the dummy standing in for Arietta's employer. It was small and elegant, but unlike Mrs Ashcombe, it was headless. Mrs Pomeroy twitched the almost complete dress that had been pinned to the dummy.

'This is for Ascot. Mrs Ashcombe suits bright colours. She has the courage to be herself.'

Arietta admired the very tight waist, the bodice gathered into a thick waistband of stiffened velvet, the sleeves three-quarter length and the skirt full and pleated.

Mrs Pomeroy turned to her. 'Now we must dress you,' she said, and her eyes quickly took in Arietta's figure as she spoke as a cook's eyes might take in the freshness of some newly arrived fruit. 'The workroom have all gone home because today was a feast day in Genoa, and they must prepare special gâteaux and many delicacies for the evening, but we can start to prepare some dresses for you from last year's collections, and I will pin them on you, and my ladies will not take long to do the alterations tomorrow. If you will undress a little, please – to your petticoat. There will be day dresses, suits, and cocktail dresses required. Also I think a housecoat in case your toilette is interrupted by some *crise* in the house, *n'est-ce pas?* You would not want to be embarrassed called down to Mrs Pomeroy in a dressing gown found only in a boarding house,' she ended, giving a light laugh. 'Of course, there will be more, but for the moment it will be enough, I think.'

As Arietta stood waiting for Mrs Pomeroy to slip the first of many dresses over her head, she started to appreciate how many times a day a Society lady must change her clothes.

First, after her early morning tea, she must change into her housecoat for breakfast in her boudoir, then she must bath and change into a suit in which to give or take lunch at home or in someone else's house; and then a cocktail dress in which to go to drinks, after which a ball gown, or opera coat and dress might be required. At all times a lady in Society must be made up perfectly, not a hair out of place, and not a chipped piece of nail varnish on either hand or foot. Her hats must match her outfits, and her gloves be clean and of varying lengths: short for day, longer or three-quarter length for evening. Her stockings, of silk or nylon, must have seams that are always straight, and her shoes be of just the right height or design to go with her myriad choices of clothes. In short, a Society lady has to be a picture of perfection to reflect her husband's and her own wealth and standing.

'You appreciate Mrs Ashcombe would like you to always be smart.'

Arietta realised at once from the look in Mrs Pomeroy's eyes that she, like the rich ladies about whom she had read in magazines and newspapers, must reflect Mrs Ashcombe's wealth and standing.

'This is very smart.'

How many times Arietta said that in the next hour, she could not have said, but eventually, very eventually, after much pinning and tucking, and pulling and twitching, a great pile of clothes had been laid aside waiting on the arrival of the seamstresses in the morning.

'Tomorrow we will take you out for your shoes and et ceteras, and then we will take you to André for your hair, and after that, when we come back we will find everything will be ready for us, for my ladies will attack the alterations first thing.'

As a result of her visit to Mrs Pomeroy's house, Arietta returned to Mrs Ashcombe's feeling younger and shabbier than ever. After climbing the stairs to her attic room she took off the treasured jacket and skirt made for her by Mrs Chantry, and having smoothed it, hung it reverentially in the curtained cupboard. She was in London now. She had turned her back on Rushington and all its happy ways, its lack of sophistication, its appreciation of even the smallest luxuries. She lay down on her narrow bed, and after a while she fell asleep, only to dream of going home and finding no one there.

The following day Mrs Pomeroy called for her. After a visit to

Mr Rayne for shoes and handbags, and to Fortnum and Mason for handbags and gloves, not to mention Mr André the hairdresser, she made her way back to Shotcombe Street in Mrs Pomeroy's triumphant company.

Once again she was fitted with clothes now newly altered especially for her, before finally being advised to stay in a navy-blue suit with a stiff white collar and cuffs. The rest of the clothes were swamped in tissue paper, packed into large boxes and sent round to her new home. She followed them there a little later, once more in the company of Mrs Pomeroy.

'My dear Mrs Pomeroy,' Mrs Ashcombe murmured as soon as they were ushered into her drawing room. 'You have done marvels.' She walked towards Arietta. 'I should never have known Miss Staunton. She is a revelation, truly she is.'

Mrs Pomeroy beamed proudly. She felt very happy – more than that, she had managed to make the transformation of her little protégée in less than twenty-four hours.

'Nothing could please me more,' Mrs Ashcombe continued. 'I now have a social secretary who not only is the part, but looks it. You are to be congratulated. Go, Miss Staunton, walk to the top of the room and back.'

Arietta, having spent a homesick-filled night in her attic room, was only too pleased to do as bidden, and to see that the two older women were smiling happily at their protégée.

'This evening we are having a cocktail party,' Mrs Ashcombe told Mrs Pomeroy. 'Thanks to you, Miss Staunton will now be able to attend *and* look the part.'

'We have set aside four cocktail frocks, two day suits, four day frocks, two top coats for spring, and two for autumn, and one ball gown and an opera coat and dress can be on their way when necessary.'

Mrs Ashcombe nodded. Mrs Pomeroy took her leave, and

Arietta followed her employer down to the dining room where they lunched, after which she took dictation, and Mrs Ashcombe retired for an afternoon rest.

The excitement of the thought of her first cocktail party kept Arietta's spirits up as she ploughed her way through first the letters to be handwritten, and next those to the trades-people, which had to be typed. Of one thing she was rapidly becoming aware, and after only two days as Mrs Ashcombe's secretary, and that was that her employer seemed to be known to everyone in England, up to and including the royal family.

'It is certainly a very difficult thing to have the interest of so many people,' Mrs Ashcombe had murmured earlier, between bouts of dictation. 'A very difficult thing. Everyone seems to want a bit of you,' she added, just a trace of a martyred look coming into her eyes.

Arietta dressed herself in a ravishing cocktail dress – net skirt slightly raised at the front, tight bodice, rounded shape above the bust, and very pretty butterfly sleeves – in a state of great excitement. Her long hair having been pulled back into a chignon by Mr André she had been careful to step *into* the dress rather than attempting to pull it over her head.

There being no full-length mirror in her attic room, she was only able to check her hair and makeup before making her way downstairs. She would always be required to be down in the drawing room waiting for guests before her employer, so she found herself hurrying a little, only too anxious to do exactly as she had been told, only to come to a sudden full stop in front of a full-length mirror hanging on the wall of the land-ing below.

As soon as she saw her reflection in the rust-marked old looking-glass, Arietta gave a small intake of breath. It was hardly surprising, for instead of being surprised, or thrilled by her new sophisticated appearance, she felt only a dull sense of *déjà vu*, for the mirror reflected someone she was getting to know all too well. From her Rayne shoes to her silk stockings, to her nipped-in waist, full skirt, and classic highly styled chignon, she was a junior replica of Mrs Ashcombe. She stared at herself in vague horror, before turning and starting to walk sedately downstairs to the lower floors. It was here that she started to discover that even her walk had changed. The sound of her tread on the stair, the swish of her new taffeta under-skirts, all told her that the person that had been her, Arietta Staunton, was gone. Clothes might maketh the man; they certainly drowned a girl.

Sunny's life had become more fractured than she could have thought possible. On the one hand she was required, daily, to attend secretarial college, study, and help around the house, just as if nothing had happened in her life, just as if she was not engaged to Gray Wyndham, just as if she had not scandalised the neighbourhood by acquiring a fiancé at what was generally considered far too young an age; just as if she had not won over Jocelyn Wyndham's heart, and so much so that he now sent his chauffeur to Pear Tree Cottage with flowers and fruit for her every Monday morning.

The truth was, during the week, she was appallingly lonely. She had made no friends at college, and with Arietta in London there was no one in whom she could confide. She would have loved to have talked to her mother, but engagement or no engagement, Mary Chantry seemed quite determined to carry on treating her daughter as if she was some kind of delinquent on whom she was obliged to keep a reluctant eye. And so in the grey atmosphere that now pervaded her home, Sunny's days had become tediously unhappy, one day seeming to take a fortnight, as she divided her time between disapproval at home and boredom at college.

Unsurprisingly the idea of running away or falling ill came to her regularly every Monday morning, as she faced yet another tedious week, but then as Friday approached and she realised that an invitation to Maydown might be imminent, she always found she was grateful that she had rejected the temptation.

'Going to lunch with Mrs Fortescue?'

Mary looked her daughter up and down. It was really rather obvious from the way that Sunny was got up that she certainly wasn't preparing to help her father in the garage.

'Yes, Ma, you know I am.'

'Yes, of course I do. Shall we expect you back for dinner?'

'I will telephone you if I am invited to stay for dinner at Maydown, Ma,' Sunny stated, purposefully using the same kind of formal language that she had heard Leandra and Gray use.

Mary nodded and sighed, and then made her way with slow and deliberate tread to the dining-room door wherein lay her beloved Singer sewing machine. Once in the room, the door closed, she nodded at nothing in particular, and sighed again.

It was no good pointing out to her daughter that going to lunch at Maydown with Leandra Fortescue was turning Sunny's head, that she was becoming oversophisticated, overconfident and, in her mother's opinion, a proper little pill as a result. Telling Sunny anything at that moment was about as much use as begging John to stop ignoring his daughter and start treating her as a normal young girl, not someone who had been caught out on the tiles, or become pregnant out of marriage.

*The day that Bentley broke down outside this cottage was a bad, bad day.*

It seemed to Mary that her emotions were so sudden and so strong, as if she had sworn that she might actually be hearing her thought played out aloud. But then, as always, as she saw the work waiting for her, pins to be placed or removed, patterns to be cut out, her mood instantly lightened.

As long as there was something to be done, something busy to keep her mind off everything out there, beyond the door of her little kingdom where the two people she loved might be going about in silent resentment of each other, then here, with Mary Chantry, would be found only smiles of appreciation and often happy laughter, as her customers came and went with what was now increasing regularity. Here she knew she was needed and, what was more, could do good. Out there she was powerless to do anything except stand by and watch the two people she loved hurt each other.

At Maydown Leandra was inspecting the newly arrived Sunny with open appreciation.

'My dear, that dress is most becoming. Your mother is something of a genius with her needle, is she not? I should never have thought that such a long point on an organdie blouse could look so elegant, and the fullness of that skirt with the bands of ribbon echoed in the hat, that is most becoming.'

It would be ridiculous not to compliment Sunny on her appearance. She was looking as beautiful as she surely had ever done, but so youthful that Leandra felt a dart of pain as she remembered that, as she stood in front of her mirror that morning, the early morning light had seemed just a little harsh.

'Thank you very much, Mrs Fortescue,' Sunny smiled.

It never occurred to her to compliment Leandra on her appearance, because she always looked beautiful, but now, for some reason, she realised that something might be needed, otherwise it was really rather one-way traffic.

'I only want to live up to you, Mrs Fortescue,' she admitted, her eyes shining with admiration. 'You are my heroine, Mrs Fortescue, truly, you are. Every time I leave you I go away wondering how best I can look to live up to how *you* are, because you are everything I would like to be.'

Leandra smiled and indicated a sofa.

'How very dear of you, Miss Chantry,' she murmured, but even as she repeated the last part of the sentence and sat down, she could not get rid of the feeling that she was ageing. Perhaps it was Sunny's manner of addressing her really rather too frequently as 'Mrs Fortescue', or perhaps it was just that, the day being hot, she felt a little tired, but she was vaguely irritated by it. Goodness knows, no one appreciated conventions more than herself, but somehow being addressed so formally, together with Sunny's constant use of her name, was distancing, and, it had to be admitted, ageing.

'I know I can learn from you, and I know that everything that I do learn from you will please Gray all the more, and I want to please him very much.'

As far as Leandra was concerned, Sunny had been pleasing Gray all too much. She had not only pleased Gray on their weekend visit to Chelston, it seemed she had even managed to please old Jocelyn Wyndham too. Gray had returned full of the success of the visit.

'Not only did she twist the old man round her little finger, she managed to twist my old Aunt Bessie round it too. The child is something of a genius when it comes to charm, Leandra, really she is. You are to be roundly congratulated. No one but no one could have chosen better.'

Leandra had suppressed her feelings of jealousy at Sunny's

success at Chelston Manor. She had even forced herself to feel pleased at the way Sunny had won over Jocelyn, but what she could not feel pleased about was the way that Sunny, artlessly and without realising it, made her feel suddenly older.

Leandra stood up before Rule had even come into the room to announce that lunch was ready. She felt hot and impatient, restless and discontented, but at the same time only too happy that Sunny Chantry was having lunch with her. If she were not, Leandra might have worried that she was having lunch with Gray, who would normally have arrived by now.

Not that he had said anything that she could not believe. His late arrival was, it seemed, because he had to have lunch with an old army friend, someone who'd been in Italy with him.

'But I shall be down with you as soon as I can after that,' he had told her gaily. 'Looking forward to seeing the two beautiful girls in my life.'

Leandra had laughed at that. As why wouldn't she? She liked to think that she was still a girl, but when she replaced the telephone she had stared ahead of her, silently furious.

*Two* beautiful girls?

Something was going wrong. Gray was not meant to find Sunny Chantry beautiful. He was meant to find her sweet and endearing. Whatever happened, he was not meant to find her anything more than that. He certainly was not meant to bracket Leandra and the Little Puppy, as Leandra had nick-named Sunny, as equally lovely. Leandra was the beauty; she was the person whom Gray worshipped, not the Little Puppy.

That perhaps was why Leandra was feeling so restless, so uneasy, so unable to appreciate either the sunshine, or the lunch, or the company.

'I am looking forward to seeing Gray,' Sunny confided halfway through lunch. 'I miss him now I'm back home.'

'Of course you do,' Leandra smiled. 'That is just how it should be,' she lied.

'He is so handsome, isn't he?' Sunny continued. 'And so *brave*. No one could have been braver in the war than Gray, and particularly seeing what happened to him, I don't suppose there is anyone braver.'

She smiled innocently at Leandra, who went to say something quite quickly as a response, and then stopped, allowing herself to frown. Seconds later Sunny too frowned, remembering the old man telling her to run from Gray rather than stay engaged to him. She still could not understand why, but she imagined that it too was because of the war, everything coming between people's understanding of each other.

'I don't think Mr Wyndham realises that Gray is much happier now than when he came back from the war, I truly don't, but by the end of the weekend he seemed more content. Do you know that ever since that weekend, Mr Wyndham sends me flowers and fruit from his garden every week? Isn't that so awfully kind of him?'

Leandra had started to feel vaguely sick. She pushed her plate away from her. When she had laid her plans – and they were good plans, not complicated, but perfectly good and manageable – she had not taken into account that Sunny Chantry might become a success in her own right, perhaps because, like so many socialites, she had a very limited imagination. She had only seen that Miss Chantry was a peach, round and pink and ripe for the plucking; that she was an innocent; that she came from a background that was less than monied; that she was exactly right for their purposes.

What she had not *ever* thought was that little Miss Chantry would become a glorious success, that Gray would start to find the Little Puppy beautiful, that he would speak of her in the same breath as Leandra, and use the same tone of voice about her. It was not a thought that had ever occurred to her, and now that it had more than occurred to her, now that she realised that the bud was starting to become a flower, she also knew with complete certainty that something would have to be done. The bud would have to be snipped, and well before it flowered.

Arietta had stood her ground and greeted the guests arriving at Mrs Ashcombe's first-floor drawing room as if she had been doing it all her life. She had no idea from where her courage came, but as guest after guest arrived and was announced by Mr Joseph, and no Mrs Ashcombe appeared, she received them, introduced herself, introduced them to each other when necessary – and thankfully she found it was hardly necessary at all as they all seemed to know each other – and kept on hoping and silently praying that their hostess would make a delayed entrance.

'In case you couldn't catch what Joseph was saying above the din, I'm Randy Beauchamp – how do you do?'

'How do you do?' Arietta held out her hand to the tall white-haired man.

'Quite well, thank you. And you are?'

'I'm Arietta Staunton. Mrs Ashcombe's new secretary. I'm sure she will be down in a minute.'

'Well, you are more optimistic than I, my dear. I am quite sure she won't,' Randy told her blithely, but in a low tone.

Arietta stared at him. 'I'm sorry?'

'Oh, don't be. I always hear the bad news first. I don't know why – it is just one of those things. I really ought to go about wrapped in black drapes like something in a Greek tragedy. No, my dear, you will not see Alice Ashcombe this evening. None of us will. Mrs Ashcombe is quite, quite ruined.'

Arietta stared at him, for a moment unable to say anything. 'I am so sorry?'

'As well you may be, but not as sorry as she will be feeling at this moment. I am afraid the net is not closing in on her, I am very much afraid it *has* closed in on her.' His eyes searched the room in nonchalant style. 'Sad to say but I doubt that she will any longer be able to throw parties such as this. Even as we speak, I understand the bailiffs are calling.' He cocked his head towards the drawing-room door. 'Maybe we can even hear them at the front door now? No, perhaps not here, but certainly they will be calling at the Surrey place in the next few days.'

'But how terrible. Are you sure?'

'Quite sure, my dear. I never speak out of turn. It is one of my greatest virtues, and my worst faults. As the French so rightly remark, often and sometimes endlessly, we all have the faults of our virtues, and the virtues of our faults. Let us face it, without the one we would be as nothing, and without both, completely characterless, which has to be some sort of comfort when one wakes in the night, one must suppose.' He beckoned Arietta away from the rest of the crowd in the room. 'Follow me, my dear, and I will tell you all.'

Feeling very much like a conspirator, or even a lamb to the slaughter, Arietta followed him down the room to a window seat, where he sat down, encouraging her to join him by patting the cushion beside him.

'I have known Alice Ashcombe for years. She is a wonderful woman, generous to a fault, but I am afraid that is the trouble. Her generosity *is* a fault. She has done nothing but entertain for years and years, come hell or high water, and right through the war. This place alone was home from home to young officers all day and all night, but an end to everything has to come, and tonight I happen to know, on the grapevine – where else? – that a certain person has called on her, mercifully briefly, we hope, and told her that the cupboard is bare. There is to be no more credit, alas, and no more parties, also alas. Alice has never owned her houses, not this house nor in Surrey, but she has always insisted on keeping up this magnificent display of wealth, which was really founded on nothing more than a fantasy of generosity and social climbing. From an early age she wanted only to be part of Society, and Society a part of her and, bless her, she has succeeded in that anyway.' He paused to light a cigarette before continuing, 'I expect you are wondering how I know all this?'

He smiled briefly at Arietta as the smoke from his cigarette curled up between them before disappearing over Arietta's shoulder into the half-open window behind them, as if the noise from the party was too much for it.

'I will tell you how I know what I know. I am Mrs Ashcombe's bookseller, and traditionally the bookseller is, and always will be, the last person to be paid – most especially in Norway, where it seems it is the custom to disappear up into the mountains with shoals of books, and then laugh at the poor bookseller who cannot, of course, reach one with his bill until such time that the snows melt.'

He paused again.

'I have not been paid by Alice for nearly four years. You can imagine how much that is now. What with Christmas and birthdays to her friends – she is very generous on my behalf – and furnishing all the rooms in her houses with ancient vols of the classics. I know now, of course, that I shall never be paid by Alice, although she did pay me once in nineteen forty-five, which *was* nice; but, bless her, she has always recommended me to her friends, some of whom have obliged by sending in funds. On reflection, knowing what I know now, I may well ask Alice for a few of my books to be returned to me.' He sipped at his champagne. 'Vintage. Delicious. I have no idea where she gets it from, but that too I must ask before she is hauled off to the debtors' prison.'

'Surely she will not have to go to prison?'

'No, no, of course not, but she might have to go to somewhere almost as bad.' As Arietta stared at him, Randy leaned forward and whispered, 'She might be banished to Surbiton, where she will be put into the care of an ex-governess on a lowly wage. How long have you worked here, you poor soul? *You* will never be paid – of course you know that. I am quite sure that Joseph and his wife haven't been paid for months, if not years.'

'I have only been here two days.'

Randy laughed. 'Well, not too bad then. You will have to get a new position, of course.'

Arietta nodded, dumbstruck. She had imagined that she might be sacked, that she might make a mess of things, but never that poor Mrs Ashcombe would go bankrupt.

'If it is any comfort, none of the previous incumbents ever got paid either. That is why they were in and out of here like cats through a kitchen door.'

Almost at once Arietta remembered Mrs Ashcombe's speech when she had been interviewed: how the older woman had deplored all her previous social secretaries. The brevity of their employment now made perfect sense.

'But never mind, my dear. You look just what I need.' Randy leaned back a little from Arietta. 'My assistant has run off with a sailor, silly trollop. You are here, as by design, beautifully dressed, and coiffed to a T too. Would you like to come and work in my bookshop? It is very fashionable, and you will have to learn a great deal about folios and such like, but I can see you have an intelligent eye, and the fact that Alice took you on is reference enough for me, quite apart from the fact that, having been left high and dry, I am, to be honest, actually desperate.'

Arietta knew that she had to be honest too, if only because Mr Beauchamp was being so.

'I am afraid I am like Cinderella, Mr Beauchamp. These are not my clothes, and although this *is* my own hair, it was styled courtesy of Mrs Ashcombe. Everything will have to go back. Well, not my hair, but everything else.'

Randy looked at Arietta with sudden intimate affection as if he had known her for years.

'Never mind the clothes, my dear. I will buy them off old Mrs Pomeroy for you. That will be where they were purchased, I would guess? Old Jeanne Pomeroy has done a brisk trade in second-hand for years now. And as for all the rest, never mind that either. It can all be sorted out, I am sure.'

They continued to talk, Randy making suggestions as to how they should go about their new, what he termed, 'unholy alliance', while observing that no one seemed to mind or notice that their hostess was not present. After a while the fashionable crowd hurried off in small chattering groups, all of them intent on going on to yet another cocktail party, finally leaving Randy and Arietta and Mr Joseph as sole occupants of the drawing room.

'Well, Joseph?' asked Randy. 'And how is Mrs Ashcombe?'

'After the earlier visit of a certain gentleman, Mrs Ashcombe has taken a sleeping draught and is lying down.'

'Ah, yes, just as well, perhaps.'

From the expression on his face Arietta quickly understood that Mr Beauchamp must know the old butler really very well.

'Yes, Mr Beauchamp.'

The butler indicated the bookshelves. 'I should take what is yours, sir, while the going is good.'

'Very sound advice, Joseph.'

Randy took a pair of spectacles from the top pocket of his suit and nodded at Arietta, before threading the delicate gold-rimmed affair past his ears, and pushing them gently up his nose.

'Stay with me, my dear, and I will start to attempt to teach you how to sort books, handle them, and stack them. It is an art, believe you me.' He frowned at the spines of the leather-covered books in front of him. 'Alas, we will have our work cut out this evening, for I do believe the books are catalogued in subject rather than alphabetical order . . . Ah me. Never mind. Into the fray we go!'

Arietta followed Mr Beauchamp up to the shelves. It seemed that her life had taken on yet another sudden and very strange turning but, as with everything, she knew that she must, whatever happened, follow the immediate path until it either ended in a cul-de-sac or led on to another path. It took only a few seconds for her to realise that there was, after all, very little else that she could do. What she could not do, would not do, was to return to Rushington and Audrey's mockery. She would prefer to walk naked down Piccadilly rather than do that.

## Chapter Six

Gray arrived promptly for dinner at Maydown to be greeted as always by Rule.

'Mrs Fortescue is in the Yellow Drawing Room, sir.'

'Thank you, Rule.'

Gray smiled. He had been delayed in London by a business deal he was putting through on behalf of the family trust. Aware of the time, he fairly sprang through the drawing-room doors towards Leandra, smiling with his usual urbanity, hands outstretched.

'I am so sorry that I am late, but not so late as to upset Cook, I hope?'

'No, no, of course not.'

They smiled and kissed each other on the cheek briefly.

'Dry martini, sir?'

'Splendid.'

Gray looked round, but it was not for his drink, which he knew Rule would bring to him, perfectly made, exactly how he liked it, but for something else.

'Are we alone tonight, Leandra?' he asked in a surprised voice.

'Dilke is in France,' Leandra said, her head on one side. 'And I am afraid Sunny could not stay.'

Gray's face fell. 'Oh, is she not well?'

Once again Leandra felt a sharp but, she hoped, fleeting pain as she registered Gray's expression.

'She is perfectly well, but not able to stay. I think it was something to do with a complication at home.'

'Oh, well then, in that case, I will telephone her.'

'She won't be home, Gray.' Leandra looked at him, making sure to wear her sweetest and most tender expression. 'She will be out tonight, with, well, I can only call it – a complication.'

Gray turned as Rule held out a silver tray for him. He took the martini glass and raised it to Leandra, keeping the look in his blue eyes as unemotional as it had ever been.

'A complication? Really?' He sipped at the martini a little too quickly. 'Well. Here's to everyone, Leandra. Including the complication,' he stated in a purposefully even voice, and then he walked off down the drawing room to the garden where he sat down, without Leandra, who, surprised by his sudden exit, finally followed him out into the balmy summer evening air, knowing that her inference about Sunny had been picked up all too quickly, as it was meant to be, but not knowing quite how it had affected Gray.

'Darling,' she said in a low voice after a minute or so, when she had settled herself beside Gray, 'you have to understand, there are bound to be complications with such a young person. It is only understandable. She is, after all, much younger than you.'

'Of course,' Gray agreed. 'Of course. I just wonder how it will affect our arrangement. She is such an enchanting creature.' He smiled. 'Even the old man fell in love with her, you know? He became putty in her hands. I don't think she meant to wrap him round her little finger, but she did, and now nothing must be but he must send her fruit and flowers from the garden every week. He has never done that for anyone else. And when he was with her, wonder of wonders, he actually laughed and smiled. The first time I heard him laugh I thought it must be someone else. In fact I looked round for someone else, but no, it was my *father*, laughing. But when I asked Sunny what it was that had made him laugh, she only gave that funny little shrug of her shoulders, you know the way she does? And that mischievous look came into her eyes, you will know the one, and she said, "Just a joke I told him." '

'And did she tell you the joke?'

Gray stared ahead. 'Yes,' he said. He turned to look at Leandra for a second, before saying, solemnly, 'And it was very funny.'

'May I hear it?'

'No. I wouldn't dare risk telling it again.' He sipped his martini, and then, the flat tone returning to his voice, he said, 'It wouldn't seem funny now. It was the way she told it, the look on her face, really more than anything, I think, that was what made it seem funny, why even my father laughed.'

Leandra was unhappier than ever, but at pains not to show it because she knew it would upset Gray even to glimpse her jealousy. Of course it had been a risk to tell him a lie about the reason for Sunny's absence, but if all went well and Leandra soothed him in the ways that she, and she devoutly hoped she alone, knew best, everything would all turn out satisfactorily.

'Would you like to know what is for dinner?'

Gray shrugged, and drained his martini.

'It's almost too hot for food, don't you think? I doubt that either of us have much appetite, have we?'

It was Leandra's turn to shrug. Just as Gray had described

Sunny as making the lightest of shrugs, so was Leandra's the lightest of shrugs, a mere indication of feigned indifference to Gray's resistance to the idea of eating.

After a few seconds, however, Leandra murmured, 'What a pity. Cook had some crevettes, freshly delivered from her private source, and then she has been slaving over that velouté sauce that she knows you love . . .'

The expression in Gray's eyes changed, and a minute or two later they were moving into dinner at really quite a fast pace, Leandra smiling, Gray looking more cheerful.

Rule walked ahead to pull out their chairs, his expression as always professionally inscrutable, despite the fact that one word, and one word alone was dominating his thoughts – *trouble.*

Mrs Ashcombe, as Mr Joseph had stated, had indeed taken a sleeping draught, but it seemed that she had taken too much. It was a mistake, of course. The doctor wrote 'heart failure' on the death certificate.

As soon as she knew that her employer of two days was dead, Arietta wanted to run back to Rushington, but instead she telephoned Mr Beauchamp.

'Start packing up everything, my dear, before the bailiffs arrive and take over, because, believe me, they will commandeer everything, up to and including your chic little chignon. I will call a taxi immediately, and come round and help you move from your smart Mayfair attic room to "down-town Bohemia", otherwise known as Chelsea.'

Arietta started to do as she had been told, and within the hour she heard Mr Beauchamp climbing the stairs to her room. He arrived in a dark coat, clutching his hat, and a little out of breath, but commendably calm.

'I don't wish to sound like a magistrate, Miss Staunton, but I am very much afraid that we will have to return those items of apparel that you have not worn,' he said, looking round at the many boxes that had made their all-too-brief appearance in Arietta's attic room.

'Of course. I already thought of that.' Arietta nodded towards a virtual pyramid of precious boxes all filled with new shoes and new handbags, and other delights that she had been looking forward to enjoying.

'If we leave them in the downstairs hall with a note that they should be returned to their shops, it might be the best solution, do you not think?'

Arietta nodded again, and quickly started to collect up all the boxes preparatory to taking them downstairs, returning several times until she had stacked everything neatly in what now seemed like an oddly empty hall.

'I have already worn one of the suits and one of the dresses from Mrs Pomeroy,' she finally confessed.

'No matter. We will take those and I will make sure Jeanne Pomeroy is suitably reimbursed for her remakes, my dear. Now we had better skedaddle while the going is good, as they say in the movies.'

Arietta stared for a second into Randy Beauchamp's round, smooth, unlined yet middle-aged face.

'Why are you doing all this for me?'

Randy smiled. 'Because I know my types, Miss Staunton. The moment I clapped eyes on you I saw that you were intelligent, attractive, although not a beauty, and very, very good-natured. You have good nature written all over your face. Believe me, I can spot a good 'un from a mile the way my father would spot a winner. Trouble was, he always forgot to back them.'

Arietta was left speechless.

'It's all right, you needn't say anything,' Mr Beauchamp went on cheerfully. 'We all need each other in this world, and I happen to need you, as of now.'

'Well, well, I had better say goodbye hadn't I, I mean—' She stopped. 'Well, I mean, to Mr Joseph, at any rate. I had better say goodbye to him, at least?'

'No time for those sorts of niceties, my dear,' said Randy. 'Besides, the house is completely empty. To my certain knowledge Joseph and Mrs Joseph have fled, as is the way with servants when disaster hits. I dare say they have taken with them those items that will compensate them more than adequately for not having received any wages for the past heaven only knows how long. And who can blame them? I think it is called rough justice, or maybe just barter? Who knows? But skedaddle time it is, that I do know.'

He opened the front door, but as he prepared to hurry out to the waiting cab, closely followed by Arietta, they were met by two heavyweights in fawn mackintoshes.

'May I know who you are, sir?'

Randy paused, and shot the bullet-headed man a sombre look.

'Yes, of course, I am—' and coughing and indicating his black tie he murmured – 'I am sure you appreciate, sir, that we had to call for certain small items.'

He lowered his eyes pointing an elegant hand to Arietta's one shabby suitcase.

The bailiffs, responding to the gravity of Mr Beauchamp's expression, promptly removed their hats as if poor Mrs Ashcombe had been placed in Arietta's suitcase, and without further comment allowed them both to step into the waiting taxicab.

As the taxi turned the corner into Park Lane, Randy smiled.

'One tip my dear old father gave me: if you want to do well in business, always wear a dark tie, winter and summer. It gives one an air of authority.'

It was most likely very true. Certainly Mr Beauchamp's expression being so solemn, and his manner so smoothly sombre, it was really not very surprising that the bailiffs had deferred to him.

'I shall remember that,' Arietta replied, wondering what the female version of a dark tie might be, before turning her thoughts to what lay ahead of her. There was no point in worrying, of that she was quite sure. She was not in any kind of position to worry. She just had to cast herself on the waters of life, and hope for the best. After all, Mr Beauchamp did not look or sound like some sort of white slaver. In fact, there was only one option open to her and that was to start to try to enjoy the reckless quality of everything that was happening to her. She had no idea where she was going, and all of a sudden she cared less. After all, when all was said and done, there was very little that she *could* do, except cling to the lifeline that she hoped she had just been thrown.

'Here we are,' Randy murmured in a vaguely triumphant voice as the taxicab drew up outside a house in a side street on which stood many other identical houses. 'Life has to get better for you here, my dear. Mayfair was far too old for you, too many crumbling biddies with ageing servants. Here you will find people of your own age, all trying to make their way in this great metropolis of ours, as is only proper, for we do not want them spending their time in idleness and luxury, or worse, enjoying themselves.'

He paid off the cab, and started up the flight of stone steps that led to the black-painted front door, which he promptly opened with a small gold key. Arietta followed him, and seconds later she was climbing a flight of stairs to a large room, the door of which was opened with a similar type of key.

'You will be utterly private here,' Randy told her, looking round with commendable pride at the clean, neat sitting room, with its dark blue checked curtains, and pale yellow carpet. 'Through here is the bedroom, bright white and pristine. And through there the bathroom, ditto. I am your landlord, which could be bad, but is actually very good, because if you have a burst pipe you can come to work and moan at me. Below and above you are yet more similar little flats, and one again in the basement, which is occupied by one Sam Finnegan, painter and jazz drummer, the latter occupation being the reason why he has been confined to the basement, as you will soon appreciate if you ever walk by the basement on a summer evening when the windows are open. I will wait downstairs while you tidy up, and then off we must fly to my beloved bookshop.'

'What is it called?'

Randy smiled and sighed, a look of affectionate pride coming into his eyes.

'It is called Beetle after my favourite character in *Stalky and Co* – Beetle's Bookshop. You see, I always felt that Beetle would become a bookseller once he had knocked about the world a bit, possibly a bookseller of some note. He was so much the type, don't you think?'

'He was "stalky" all right, wasn't he, Mr Beauchamp?' Arietta agreed, glad to be able to show off her literary knowledge.

'He was. Really we all should be, and then the world would be a better place. What does "stalky" mean, Miss Staunton?'

'It means,' she said, after a few considered seconds, 'it means being clever and wily.'

'Do you speak stalky?'

'I can, I think,' Arietta admitted. '"Biznai" is one of my favourite stalky words.'

'And mine.' Randy gave her an approving look. 'I knew when I saw you trying to cope with Alice Ashcombe's soirée that you would be stalky.' He gave a small sigh of contentment. 'That is another thing about bookselling – shrewdness must be practised at all times; boxing and coxing is not enough. One has to trust one's judgement instantly, knowing a rare first edition before looking inside for corroboration – or, as in your case, the kind of person who knows her *Stalky and Co.*'

As soon as Arietta arrived downstairs a few minutes later, Randy swept her ahead of him into a taxi, even though they were barely half a mile from their destination, and it was definitely not raining, something which Arietta found stylish and impressive.

The bookshop was in a back street. It was not smartly painted, perhaps because paint was still in short supply. Indeed, it was unremarkable in every way, until you stepped inside, and then, as Randy remarked every now and then to customers who commented on his shop, 'It's not until you step inside that you get the picture.'

And what a picture it was! Ever since she was a small child, Arietta had been a bookworm, which was just as well since her mother's idea of having fun in the holidays was to get her daughter to look after the house while she lay in bed and read novels of a certain kind. Arietta knew that they were of a certain kind because she read them so quickly.

As a change from such things as dusting and polishing, twice a week Arietta was graciously allowed to go into town to the library, where she found a new world waiting for her, a world where no one else could go, a world of untrammelled vistas, and endless opportunities, the world of the imagination.

'However many books are there here?' she asked Mr Beauchamp, glancing round, while immediately regretting the question because it sounded stupid.

'Far too many,' Randy told her, and his eyes followed hers as he glanced affectionately round at the hundreds of volumes stacked on shelves that reached right up to the high ceiling. They were stacked so high that only the tallest of stepladders would reach, a single set of which she noticed were propped, ready and waiting.

'What can I do?' Arietta asked quickly, feeling that she had already made a bad start by asking a silly question.

'You, my dear, can begin by making us each a cup of coffee, and then I will show you the ropes.'

Mr Beauchamp's expression was solemn. 'Selling books is both absurdly easy, and terribly difficult. You will find that you can sell a dear old body a copy of some classic for their grandson, and yet be unable to shift a so-called best seller that has been boomed and logrolled by every literary bod in the country.' He paused, adjusting his thin gold spectacles with a small punctuating movement. 'What no one in this country will ever admit, except perhaps the bookseller, and then only to himself or his mother, is that a book sells because there is something in it that suddenly sparks, and once that little spark is lit, however small, other little sparks start to fly about, until finally an incendiary follows, and that is what we call a *best seller*. But really and truthfully, no one, but no one, understands why or how it happens. It is a mystifying business, and that is precisely why being a bookseller is really so wizard, and I use that word advisedly. You have no idea when the magic fire will catch, but you have *every* idea that, when it does, you will have ordered far too few of whatever it is that everyone suddenly wants.' He laughed good-naturedly. 'Now, Miss Staunton, stop looking so worried and I will show you how I like my coffee – and then we can begin.'

Gray had not telephoned Pear Tree Cottage for a few days, as a consequence of which Sunny went about trying to pretend that she hadn't noticed, and failing dismally.

Every time the telephone did ring, she would stop whatever she was doing and pray, 'Please, please, let it be him,' but it never was, and now it seemed it never would be.

Even Mary Chantry noticed the lack of a telephone call, but she said nothing, just as Sunny said nothing.

Sunny imagined that her mother was choosing to pretend not to notice, while all the time hoping to goodness that Gray's lack of communication would continue – for ever.

Nowadays they walked around each other, catlike and carefully, not wanting to upset each other, but at the same time keeping to the squares within which both of them had decided to imprison themselves.

Sunny was well aware that her mother considered a year a very long time, which of course it was, and now that only a few weeks of it had gone by and Gray was not telephoning his young fiancée, it seemed that she would probably be proved right. She herself was too proud to telephone him, but finally, hurt by his neglect, she telephoned Leandra.

'My dear, how nice to hear from you.' Leandra's voice could not have sounded warmer. 'How are you?'

'I am very well, thank you.'

'Are you sure?'

'Oh, yes, of course.'

'My dear, you sound a little low. Why not come round to

luncheon tomorrow? I am sure you can get off that silly old college for a while, can't you?'

Sunny nodded silently into the telephone, finally managing to say, 'I would love to.'

'Come about one o'clock and, if it is fine, we will sit in the garden and enjoy a light luncheon under the trees on the lawn, eh?'

'I would love to,' Sunny managed again.

'Good. I will look forward to it,' Leandra finished, but before she could say any more the telephone had clicked the other end. She stared at it. The Little Puppy was unhappy. Was that good or bad? It was something that she would decide tomorrow.

The following day, lunch being over, and Sunny having started to look more like her name and less like a wet week, she finally came round to the subject that was most troubling her.

'I think I may have done something to upset Gray.'

Leandra put her head on one side. 'Oh, no, my dear, surely not?' she asked in a tender voice.

'Yes, I think so. You see, he hasn't telephoned since – well, for quite a few days, and I don't want to telephone him. It seems so ... so presumptuous, and anyway, my mother has always said you must never telephone a man, that it gives them the wrong ideas.'

Leandra suppressed a smile. It was too sweet and silly of the Little Puppy to think that it was possible to give someone to whom you were engaged the 'wrong ideas'. Still, let her think away, it could do no harm.

'I know Gray has been very busy – very, very busy – with business affairs to do with the family estate.'

Sunny nodded, trying to understand how busy a family

estate might be, so enthralling obviously that it stopped someone telephoning you.

'I thought it must be something like that. Of course, that must be the reason. Just so long as I have not upset him. You see I am so much younger than he, I felt I must be rather dull, and then the arrangement between us is – is so fluid, as it were, that I wondered if he would rather let the matter drop now? And I wouldn't blame him, I wouldn't really, because after all, quite a few people might not want to marry someone who felt sorry for them, and that kind of thing. I mean, since he is not quite what he would wish, he might not want to go on being with someone who knows this, and that would be quite understandable. Besides which, my mother and father are still very against everything, and he might feel that too, mightn't he?'

Leandra put a cool hand on Sunny's arm. 'Why don't I, in a very roundabout and discreet way, find out from him? If there is anything to find out, which I am sure there is not.'

'Could you? Would you? I mean poor Mr— I mean poor Gray, he might want to drop the whole idea, as I have just said. He might be having second thoughts, particularly since he is older. He might not want to enter into an arrangement with someone who could not keep up with him in conversations, and is really ignorant compared to him. It's not that I feel any different, because of course I want to do the right thing by him, but at the same time I look up to him so much I would not want to drag him down, if you see what I mean?'

As Sunny finally finished, her expression being one of such unvarnished idealism, even Leandra felt a small dart of guilt, but more than that, she sensed that Sunny rather than Gray might be having second thoughts, which would not do at all. She wanted to keep the Little Puppy on her leash, to keep her idealistic, grateful, but above all determined to go against her parents' wishes.

'My dear, I will do everything I can to help you in this matter. Now I must go back to organising this wretched ball in aid of war orphans which I have let myself in for, and you, in your turn, must go home and stop worrying. Above all, remember that the golden rule in life is to follow your heart, and let no one and nothing dissuade you from that.'

Sunny leaned forward impulsively and kissed Leandra on the cheek, something that she had never done before. Leandra coloured slightly, not quite knowing how to take it.

'My dear—'

'Thank you, thank you so much for *everything*, Mrs Fortescue, really. You are so *kind*. I've never known anyone so kind, really I haven't. I have learned *so* much from you today, and in a way I knew I would.'

She fled back to the house, where Rule called her a taxi. After a hot and crowded train journey, she arrived back at Pear Tree Cottage to find her mother waiting for her with a tired expression.

'The college has telephoned, Sunny, yet again—'

'I know, I know, Ma.' Sunny stopped suddenly and, facing her mother in the small dark hall, she heard herself saying, 'I have to tell you I am going to take Mrs Fortescue's advice and follow my heart, and – and so – I thought about it so much on the train, and I know I can't go back to college. That's it, I'm not going back to college any more, Ma. I hate it. It is a complete waste of time doing something I hate, and a waste of your precious money, besides bringing me down.' Leandra Fortescue's kindness to her had given Sunny sudden courage. 'I am going to do something else with my life. I don't know what, but something – something that maybe I can be proud of – sewing, perhaps? Like you.'

'You're not talented enough to sew, Sunny. You've never paid enough attention to sewing to be good at it.'

Sunny nodded in agreement, unsurprised by her mother's reaction. It was true. But she must think of something, anything, rather than go back to that wretched college. She had thought about her life all the way back from Maydown, in the taxi, and in the train, and the conclusion that she had come to was that it was because she was doing something so dull that Gray was not telephoning her. She had nothing new to tell him. It must be that. It could be nothing else. She was dull and boring, and talking to her on the telephone had proved only too dull and boring; and even if that was not the reason, it was nevertheless a fact. No, she had made up her mind. She was never going back to Princess Secretarial College, and no one could make her.

'So what *are* you going to do, Sunny?' her father asked her in a bored voice the following weekend.

Sunny knew that her mother must have talked everything over with her father, and the fact that nothing had been said meant that they were still hoping that she would come to her senses, whatever that meant.

'I am going to London, and I am going to model clothes.'

'Going to be a mannequin?'

His voice told Sunny that in her father's eye that was tantamount to being a tart.

'Yes, Pa, I am going to be a mannequin.'

'Is there someone who might want you?' John turned briefly at the door, his eyes on Sunny, his mind already on starting up the Vauxhall and going for a spin, because somehow driving about took his mind off everything better than staying around the house.

'Well, yes, as a matter of fact Arietta has a lady who she thinks would like me to model clothes for her. She does the same sort of work as Ma, except on a bigger scale. Arietta thinks that because I am quite tall I might get some work with her.'

'Arietta does, does she?' John shook his head. 'Well, let's hope Arietta is not stringing you along, Sunny, because I'm not prepared to keep you twiddling your thumbs in London, really I'm not, and the sooner you understand that the better.'

It was a hot summer evening and London had a quiet, almost empty feeling to it, as Arietta, her first hard-working week at Beetle's Bookshop at a close, made her way back to her new one-bedroomed flat in the downtown house with the black-painted front door.

In Rushington she knew that the flowers in the cottage gardens would be swaying in a slight breeze, but in the row of terraced houses to which she was making her way, the geraniums in the window boxes would be under-watered and unmoving, their leaves yellowing a little, their flowers drying. In Rushington husbands and fathers, boyfriends and sons would be making their way steadily towards the pub, and what they would consider to be well-earned gins and tonics, whereas along the King's Road, respectably dressed men were walking slowly back to bus stops, or catching taxis to some other part of town where they would change into evening dress before 'going on'.

'This is London's bohemia, my dear,' Mr Beauchamp had explained earlier in the week as they walked down the King's Road. 'Here the painters and the writers, the artists and the poets all go to their locals and talk a lot of claptrap. Happily they only come out at night, since they are all late risers, and by that time the rest of us have vamoosed back to our cosy gardens, or taken off to the West End to see our proper friends, for if there is anything more boring than hearing one artist arguing with another about something that neither can prove, I do not know it.'

'What about writers?'

'Oh, writers are so conceited they don't acknowledge anyone else even exists!'

From these brief observations Arietta had assumed that Randy Beauchamp had little or no time for the artistic community who frequented his bookshop.

'Don't you like the people whose books you sell?' she had ventured at lunch-time that day, when Randy had opted to put 'CLOSED FOR LUNCH' on the door and retired to the backroom for Arietta's sandwiches.

'One loves one's writers, my dear, of course one does, one really loves them, of course,' Randy had answered beaming. 'But one doesn't really want to get *involved* with them. It has to be a doctor-and-patient relationship. The bookseller as doctor can be a most helpful and creative figure in a writer's life, guiding him towards healthy sales and away from self-indulgent literary habits. I tell my customers just what I think they will enjoy and what they will hate – I have to, even if it should get back to the author. It is my bounden duty. You will learn the same after a while. You must get to know your customers, keep their shelves stocked, and shoot from the hip when an author has gone off. It is just how it is.'

Probably because it was the end of the first week, and she had been paid three pounds – which seemed like unimaginable wealth – Arietta thought about all this as she walked along the King's Road, savouring the summer air, the people, the sounds of taxis stopping and starting, until she finally approached Randy's lodging house.

As Randy had predicted, and because it was a hot summer evening, the basement windows of the lodging house were open, and the sound of a lively jazz trio was floating up to the street.

Arietta looked into the open window in the basement below. Underneath an overbright light made of cheap plastic could be seen a closely grouped trio of piano, bass and drums.

Arietta stood by the iron railings that enclosed the basement area, staring down at the scene below. Since the window was open, and the curtains were not drawn, it occurred to her that this entertainment must be in the public domain.

As she watched the musicians she started to tap her foot, while noting that the contents of the room were all too reminiscent of a café rather than a sitting room. Everywhere were positioned wine bottles with candle grease collected thickly around their tops, from which old, bent, used candles peered as if, old and bent and used as they were, they were still intent on climbing out of their surroundings towards the central light fixture. Unframed posters decorated the walls, some of them advertising plays, some concerts, and others such things as seaside towns on the South Coast.

One, advertising 'A Day by the Sea', seemed to be something the occupants found amusing because they had cut out black-and-white photographs of themselves, or perhaps their friends, so that the advertisements now contained their cheerfully grinning faces, smiling incongruously above the bodies of quite alien people holding buckets and spades.

'Good set, fellas.'

The drummer stood up and hit his high-hat in a dramatically final manner, making a sudden lone sound, while the pianist looked round.

'Phillip—'

'*Yes?*'

The bespectacled face stared at the speaker, and even to Arietta the lack of expression on his face seemed to bode ill.

'Could we ask if we could have a little less of the Art Tatum and more Teddy Wilson, if you don't mind, Maestro?'

The pianist pushed his glasses up his nose and stared haughtily past the speaker. He said nothing for a minute, his expression grim.

*Ah, ah, trouble ahead, I think, time to move on.*

Arietta had hardly finished her thought and let herself into the house, when the door from the basement opened, and the drummer appeared at the top of the short flight of stairs, the expression on his face one of determined fury.

He stopped as he saw Arietta about to climb the first flight of stairs from the hall to her own flat.

'Who are you?' he demanded, as if he suspected her of being a burglar.

Arietta met his eye for a second before answering, 'Arietta Staunton. I am the new lodger on the first floor.'

'Well, you'll do.' He beckoned to her to follow him downstairs. 'Come on, you can be the judge.' He turned back. 'You're not tone deaf, are you?'

'I don't think so—'

'Good. Then you can come and adjudicate the row that is about to erupt below our feet.' He pulled at Arietta's arm, but she resisted his urging.

'Just a second, I have to go upstairs.'

'Oh, no, you don't.'

'Oh, yes, I do.'

'Not before you have settled the row.'

'I don't settle rows, and anyway, I have to brush my hair.'

Sam Finnegan stared at Arietta's hair.

'Your hair is perfectly all right,' he announced.

'I don't like it like this in the evening.'

The expression on her face must have been so stubborn that he seemed inclined to relent.

'Oh, very well,' he said reluctantly. 'Go and do your hair, or whatever you have to do, and then come straight down. I'm Sam Finnegan, by the way.'

'I know.'

Arietta nodded briefly at him, feeling a little ahead of the game as she did so, but this did not seem to make much impact on her new acquaintance, who didn't really seem surprised that she should know who he was.

'Don't be long,' he said, already moving towards the open basement door. 'Phillip is driving me nuts, and he just won't listen. You'll have to sit in on the next few sets and see if I'm not right. You like jazz, I take it?'

'I love jazz,' Arietta called back without turning, already mounting the stairs. 'But I have only two records. Louis Armstrong and Benny Goodman.'

'Benny Goodman is just the answer I wanted, Arietta Staunton. If you could get through to Phillip that it is more Teddy Wilson and less ruddy Art Tatum that is what is needed, I will fall in love with you for ever. But you know pianists, they *will* always conduct.'

But Arietta had closed her flat door by then and didn't hear his case against pianists. She was too busy tearing off her jacket and skirt, and unpinning her chignon, peeling off her dark stockings, and running towards the bathroom to have a quick dip.

When she reappeared in the basement, she looked quite different. No longer a replica of poor Mrs Ashcombe, instead she was wearing three-quarter-length matador pants with a bobble fringe, purchased during her lunch-time from a shop down the King's Road. These, together with a short-sleeved polo neck and hair dressed in a long flowing ponytail instead of a prim bun, gave her a hip bohemian look, more suited to the wrong end of the King's Road on a Friday night.

The three young musicians had stopped for drinks and cigarettes, the smoke from which was filling the basement with a pleasant fog. At first they were so busy arguing they did not turn as she reached the last step, so she was able to stand and take in their very different looks. Sam Finnegan was the tallest, dark-shirted with almost matching dark hair. The pianist, on the other hand, was practically a Benny Goodman look-alike, despite his obvious desire to play Art Tatum, his glasses on his nose giving him a lofty air. The bass player, of medium height and also dark-haired, but with intense dark eyes, was the first to spot Arietta, which meant that, having first taken care to wink at her, he turned and nudged Sam.

Sam turned towards him almost resentfully, until he saw that he was indicating the newly arrived and changed Arietta, at which point he stopped arguing with Phillip and stared.

'Good God, Miss Prism is fled, and we have a Vivien Leigh look-alike in her place!'

Arietta smiled at the compliment.

Sam stared at her briefly, and then he turned to Phillip and said, 'Listen, this cat here is hip, as you can see, so she's going to be sitting in on the next set, and she can be our judge.'

Phillip rolled his eyes behind his small wire glasses before leaning towards Arietta.

'He doesn't usually talk like this. He normally speaks English, really quite well.' He proffered a hand. 'Phillip Lane, bachelor of this parish.'

'Arietta Staunton, recently arrived spinster.'

They shook hands.

'Sit down, Miss Staunton, and give us the benefit of your crack,' the bass player said, stepping quite purposefully between them. 'I am Hart Dorling, also a bachelor of this parish, but that need not be a permanent state, really it need not.'

Sam rolled his eyes and, not just sensing competition but seeing it, he led Arietta away from Hart to a chair where he sat her down.

'Have nothing to do with the other two,' he commanded. 'They are not to be trusted. I, on the other hand, being the drummer, am a worthy sort that you can trust. The drummer, you see, is always late to the pub, because of packing up his kit, and as a consequence, however attractive, he never gets so much as a look in when the glamour's in town. So, always trust the drummer, Miss Staunton. Believe me, he will not two-time you.'

'Really? I've been told the drummer is always the one the girls flirt with from the floor when they're dancing with some-one else.'

'Don't you believe it. Since we never can get out from behind the kit,' Sam continued, once more seated behind his kit, 'we never have a hope.'

Phillip turned from the piano. 'One, two, one, two, three, four,' he commanded.

Sam rolled his eyes at Arietta, and she tried not to laugh as the set began.

Randy had given Arietta the first three hours of Saturday morning off, so it was he who rolled up the blind from the top half of the shop's front door, and it was he who took off the dustsheets, and he who wandered through to grapple with his ancient coffee pot, pouring in the hot water, and turning it upside down with lightning dexterity, before eventually pouring the coffee into a Parisian cup.

'Ah, the first cup of the morning, always the best,' said a voice behind him.

Randy turned. It was Gray Wyndham.

'Dear boy,' he said, his expression unchanging. 'And how are we this morning?'

'Strangely indifferent, I don't know why. Perhaps it is the hot weather, or perhaps it is the time of year, and the hot weather, neither August, nor May, neither autumn nor spring. Or perhaps it is the growing realisation that I am indifferent.'

'To everything, or someone?'

Gray shrugged. 'Perhaps to both.'

'Have we anything special that we want in the way of a book today?'

'No, no, you choose, you always choose things she likes.'

'Perhaps the new Angus Wilson collection? Very good. Most amusing, I thought.'

'If you thought them amusing, Randy, then that is enough for me.'

'You-know-who's husband home, is he?'

'Yes, and in crusty mood. Things are not well in the House of Zog.'

'Zog? Mmm? Can't quite see *that* gentleman being called Zog, but anything is possible.'

'I know what you mean. At any rate, whatever the reasons, I have been put in the out tray for the moment. At least I think it is only for the moment.'

'It happens from time to time.'

'Yes, it's happened before, and doubtless it will happen

again. As far as I can gather it's when things go wrong his end, he takes it out on her. So if you wouldn't mind affecting the usual sleight of hand because a coup de telephone is definitely going to be frowned on?'

'No, of course not, dear boy.' Randy took the single sheet of paper that Gray was offering him, and slipped it in between the back pages of the book. 'We will send this off for you, Mr Wyndham, sir,' he said lightly sarcastic. 'Just as soon as my assistant comes in, I will give it to her to take to the post office for you.'

'Angus Wilson, you *have* been a busy boy this week,' he murmured to the empty shop, once Gray had taken himself off. 'To my certain knowledge this is the fourth little *lettre d'amour* that your book has taken up this week. It has to be the fault of the weather. All this summer heat must be making everyone crotchety, particularly husbands kicking their heels in the country with no one but their wives to talk to, and all the mistresses away picking up tans in the South of France. And not just tans, methinks.'

The telephone rang. He picked it up.

'Yes?' A small pause, then he said after the voice the other end had said something, 'Well, speak of the devil, it is Mr Wilson himself, is it not? I was, but a minute or two ago, only busily recommending your delicious new short story collection to a gentleman customer to send round to a friend. That is number four this week, so we are in the way of being quite pleased, really . . . Yes, I know we're not Hatchards, Mr Wilson, but we do *try* – *au revoir.*'

Randy replaced the telephone, saying out loud to the empty shop, 'Nothing less than total ingratitude is all one can expect from writers,' just as Arietta, only half a mile away, was waking up with her first ever hangover.

There was a hand basin behind a curtain in the corner of her bedroom. She staggered to it blindly, throwing aside the curtain and running the tap. At first the water was brown and rusty coloured, and warm, but after a minute or so it ran clear and cold, at which point, head throbbing, mouth dry and eyes half closed, Arietta put a tooth mug underneath it.

The water tasted disgusting, not sweet and clean as it did in Rushington, but odd and dusty as if it had been in the taps or the tank, or wherever they kept water in London, for far too long.

There was a knock at the door, followed by a voice.

'Hallo, Miss Leigh, I mean, Miss Staunton?'

Arietta made a sound somewhere between 'uh-huh' and 'mmmm'.

'Can I come in?'

Arietta took the cold flannel off her head, and unlocked the door.

'No,' she said, opening it. 'There is a line,' she indicated the floor between them. 'Over that you may not pass.'

Sam stared at her solemnly, impassively, and for a second there was no emotion on his face or in his eyes, but he reached one hand forward and, taking one of hers, he tried to put something in it. Arietta immediately snatched her hand away from him.

'No, wait, please. I'm trying to give you some aspirin,' he said in a kind voice. 'I'm not trying to hold your hand, just to put something in it.'

Once again Arietta repeated the same sound as before.

'Well, I agree with that,' Sam said in a conciliatory tone. 'And funny you should mention it because I was thinking of ordering one myself.'

'What did I drink last night?'

Sam's face now registered emotion for the first time. He allowed it to exhibit undiluted guilt.

'I am afraid it was a wine that our accountant gets for us, from Morocco.'

'Morocco?' Arietta crossed the room and, taking the tooth mug up again, she drank down the two aspirin before sinking on to the studio couch, still clutching the flannel to her head. 'If this is what they give belly dancers no wonder they gyrate.'

Sam laughed, and sat down in a chair opposite her.

'If you can make jokes like that when all about you is spinning round then you are one hip cat, my friend.' He stared at the crumpled heap that was seated opposite him. 'I like your jams, they really are hip.'

'They're not jams, actually, they are my painting clothes,' Arietta stated from behind the flannel. 'I was in a bit of confusion when I went to bed last night.'

'You should think about marketing them – all those streaky bits down the side, they'd be good.' He paused, frowning. 'I didn't know you painted.'

'I don't paint. These are just my clothes for painting in, painting walls and so on. I packed them, in case.'

'I am a painter, you know.'

Arietta removed the flannel slightly.

'Really?' she asked, staring round the flannel, before replacing it.

'Yes, I paint. Quite well, really. I have sold some paintings recently – well, not paintings, portraits. Would you like me to paint you?'

'No.'

The riposte was so swift and forceful it gave rise to a small silence.

'Can't blame you, really. But, if you would like me to paint you, that is, I would very much like it, especially in those clothes, in your painting clothes, but without the flannel. Can I rinse it out for you?'

He walked across to the basin behind the curtain and, having rinsed out the flannel, he returned it to her.

'There we are, my dear, one cold flannel.'

It was because he said 'my dear' that Arietta came to suddenly.

'My dear! *Oh* dear, what is the time? Oh *dear*, get out of my way, get out of my way, I am going to be late for work!'

'It's half-past midday,' Sam stated, and seconds later found himself outside on the landing once more as Arietta shut her door and belted into her bedroom to dress.

Ten minutes later found Sam driving Arietta round to Beetle's Bookshop in his battered old Riley convertible. He turned to her at the traffic lights.

'I'm only doing this out of guilt. I don't want you to lose your job because I gave you bad wine.'

'I should think not. It doesn't seem possible that Morocco *has* wine, let alone that anyone drinks it,' Arietta finished crossly. 'You should be arrested, really you should.'

'How long have you worked at Beetle's Bookshop?' Sam asked hurriedly to take her mind off what he had given her to drink.

'All this week,' Arietta called to him as the car started off again. 'The lady I had worked for died after two days, but by that time I had met Mr Beauchamp, and the girl before me had gone, so he chose me.'

The car was still moving as she jumped out of it, leaving Sam to continue parking it, and flew into the shop.

'My, what *have* we come as?'

Randy stared at Arietta, who had, without thinking, and

probably because of her horrid headache, merely pulled on her clothes from the night before.

'Oh, I am so sorry, I didn't realise.'

There was a small silence as Randy stared at the matador pants, the tucked-in polo neck, the flat shoes and the ponytail.

'Turn round,' he commanded. 'Mmm.' Another silence, and then he said, 'I prefer it. You don't look so frumpish. Much better. Let's have lots more of *that* look, and less of the young-lady-dressed-as-mother look. There should be a move towards looking less old, really there should. I was thinking about that the other day. Since the war everyone seems determined to go round looking just like their mothers, or fathers. Clothing shortage is, of course, the problem, but it is also here.' He tapped his forehead. 'Everyone wants their children to be nine hundred and forty-two just because *they* are. It's such a pity, because it suffocates all originality. Before the war young girls were outrageous, cutting off their hair, and wearing shorts, and quite rightly they were *expected* to be so. I wouldn't have dreamed of taking out a young lady who didn't smoke, and have a deep mahogany tan.' He sighed in reminiscence, and then, turning back towards the stockroom, he said, 'Enough of that. Unpacking to do, my dear.'

At which point Sam came into the shop, and Randy smiled.

'Samuel Finnegan, of all the bars in all the world—'

'Uncle Randy, dost thou need help in the stockroom of this sunny Saturday?'

Randy stared at his nephew.

'Now here's a thing,' he announced to no one in particular, pronouncing his words slowly and clearly. 'To my certain knowledge, all the time Miss Grenville was working here, never, ever, was there any offer of help from this sometime jazz drummer-cum-Society portrait painter, *mais tout d'un coup,* there is a sudden and massive interest in helping out his poor old uncle. When the basement was flooded in the winter, where was Nephew Sam? In Morocco painting in kasbahs, smoking a hookah, and acquiring a taste for wearing a fez. When the lady upstairs came through the dry rot in the ceiling, where was Nephew Sam? In Cornwall painting fishermen, smoking Capstan, and acquiring a taste for wearing fisherman's jumpers. When the front door was bished in by two drunken yobs, where was Nephew Sam? Half a mile away painting Lady Finsborough in a scarlet cloak and acquiring an *expensive* habit of drinking champage at noon. Therefore what says Uncle Randy to himself? He says "Tiss, tiss, Mrs Tittlemouse, what's brought Nephew Sam therefore to my door with such humble mien and generous offers of help – not I think the welfare of his poor old Uncle Randy . . . ?" '

By now both Sam and Arietta were laughing, and Arietta was staring at him with new appreciation. Sam Finnegan had obviously led quite a life already, and he could only be a little older than herself.

'You can help front of shop, dear boy. It being Saturday it should be a lively affair. And Miss Staunton can go to the stockroom and start unpacking the new arrivals, and by that I do mean books . . .'

Randy's facial expression as he saw Nephew Sam's face fall remained admirably straight, but as Sam's expression turned to what threatened to be woebegone, he leaned forward and murmured to Sam, 'Don't worry, dear boy, once the closing-time whistle goes, I'll let you take her to the pub. But first she must wrap a couple of volumes for me, and take them to the post office. Miss Staunton!'

As Arietta turned at the stockroom door, he indicated the Angus Wilson for Gray Wyndham, and a leather-covered, obviously second-hand book, to be sent to the Duke of Somerton.

'Two labels to be written, one for this gentleman, address there, and one for this duke – his address there. See? Brown paper and string there, sealing wax and matches there. You may use my signet ring to stamp the wax. And please observe extreme caution when wrapping the books. We don't want any to-dos and dramas when the books reach their destinations.'

He slipped a letter into each of the volumes, and hurried off to help Sam, as not one but two customers had come into the shop, which was surely a minor miracle at this time of year?

Nothing had changed for Leandra. Dilke was still in a foul mood, not just at breakfast, which was standard for him, but at every meal, which meant, naturally, that nothing, but nothing, Leandra could do was right.

Normally, when one of Dilke's love affairs had finished, he came home, was a little morose for a few days, ate and slept too much, but then allowed himself to be cheered up. Such was not the case now. No matter what Leandra or Cook or anyone did to gentle him along, nothing seemed to be helping. Strangely, he had lost weight when normally in these circumstances he put on weight. Now he seemed to spend most of the time sleeping, and when at meals he pushed his food away, leaving Leandra solitary and alone to struggle through the pudding course – if only to keep on the right side of Cook – while Dilke made his way through the French windows into the garden where he was to be found wandering about smoking endless Du Maurier cigarettes.

'There seems very little point in planting all these sweet-smelling roses if we are to smoke them out, Dilke darling!'

Leandra joked, as she followed him out into the garden this particular night.

'Shut up, Leandra! Just, just – shut up, would you?'

Leandra stared at him, and then she too lit a cigarette from a small gold case that her escort before Gray had given her. Dilke might be offhand with other people, he might be charmless to a degree with Gray, but he was never, ever rude to her. Her manner did not allow it.

'What's the matter, Dilke?' she asked him finally after watching him pace up and down between the borders.

'I'm ruined, that's what the *matter* is!'

Leandra stared at him. Despite the bright light from the moon it was difficult to read his expression, but she did suddenly see how his face seemed to have fallen in, and as she did she wondered that she had not noticed it before. Dilke's skin, normally tanned in summer from holidaying abroad with his amours, now had a sallow tinge to it, and she saw that his eyes were staring at her as if it was all her fault, as if she had somehow brought about his ruin, if indeed ruined he was.

'Is it the supertax, Dilke darling?'

'Yes, it is the supertax, *Dilke darling*!' Dilke said, continuing to mimic her. 'Yes, it is. It is this bloody government, and the one before, and the one before that, and the war, and the way you spend money—'

'Which of course *you* don't!'

'The way you spend money one would think it was self-propagating; as if gold fell out of the sky every evening and you had only to come out here in the morning and pick it up, and start all over again.'

Leandra threw her cigarette to the ground and stamped on it. It could have been Dilke's face she was stamping on, but he didn't seem to notice.

Leandra decided to ignore Dilke's fantasy about gold.

'I knew everything was a bit wobbly, but I had no idea it was disastrous.'

'Wobbly? Wobbly? It is not wobbly, Leandra, it is crashed. I am ruined, finally, I am ruined. That accountant, God rot him, never let me know the final picture, never let me realise how deep we had sunk, or were sinking, too caught up with his divorce, and drink of course.' Dilke stared past her to the house, which he actually loved, perhaps even more than Leandra. 'This place will have to go, and that is just the start.'

'Oh, but it can't! Maydown is *us*.'

'Maydown *was* us.'

Another silence as Dilke lit another cigarette.

'Will we have to live abroad?'

'We certainly will, Leandra, probably in a backstreet in Marseilles, or Naples, or Basingstoke, somewhere where no one we know will find us.'

Leandra could not have said whether or not Dilke was being facetious, but she had known him long enough to know that he never made scenes, so he could not be stringing her along; their finances must truly have gone from being wobbly to being wiped out.

'Are we really ruined, Dilke darling?'

She put a gentle hand to his arm, and he turned, his eyes filled with tears.

'I am afraid so, Dippy.'

He hadn't called her Dippy since she didn't know when.

She frowned. 'Can't we do something about it? Is there nothing to be done, darling?'

'Not really,' Dilke sighed. 'It's simply a question of facing facts. This country does not like rich people, and there is no way round it. We are not like the Devonshires, we can't donate a great painting to the nation in lieu of tax. We cannot bargain; we are not in that position. In short, we are rich enough to be bled dry, but not wealthy enough to come to some arrangement. I bumped into Noël Coward at the Ritz the other evening, and he has just been told that he too may have to live abroad, that he might have to sell everything. Paintings, houses, everything may have to go. He is paying something like nineteen shillings in the pound. He can hardly afford a new pair of socks. Supertax has hijacked us all, Dippy. Supertax is the Robin Hood of our era, and while I am no Sheriff of Nottingham, and know that we must feed the poor, it seems we are now the poor because of this tax. No other country would stand for it. It is appalling. We create wealth, people like us, we employ, we keep up old houses, we endow the arts, we are not saints but we are necessary. If we all flee abroad the country will be poorer by everything, but that is what I think will have to happen. We will have to go into tax exile, or starve.'

As if suddenly reconciled, they sank down together on Leandra's favourite Lutyens-styled garden bench, with its curved back and swooping side arms, and Dilke dropped his head into his hands.

For a few seconds Leandra felt only sympathy for Dilke, of whom she had always been very fond, but once a half-minute had gone by, and she had speedily assessed the situation, she started to feel impatient, and then angry – first at him for not talking to her sooner, then at the accountant for getting divorced and taking to drink, and finally at the government.

'What a dreadful situation in which we find ourselves,' she said, at last, in a cool voice as the darkness around them seemed to mirror their despair. 'Quite dreadful.' She gave a small sigh, and the expression in her eyes hardened as she realised that Dilke might make her go and live abroad in tax exile, which meant that she and Gray could not possibly continue as they had. 'There is some small hope, however, Dilke darling.' She put a hand as cool as her voice on top of Dilke's hand, but he did not look round at her. 'I have been hatching a plan for some time, for Gray and myself and you, for all three of us.'

'Gray!' Dilke said, suddenly coming to and pronouncing his name in his customary manner. 'What possible good could Gray do us, outside of being charming at a Friday-to-Monday gathering? He is not rich enough to rescue us; he is not any-thing enough to do any good whatsoever.'

Leandra let that go. It wasn't worth defending Gray to Dilke. For some reason, despite Dilke's own infidelities, his endless extravagance as far as his love life was concerned, while she herself could not care who he was with, Dilke still managed to feel jealous of Gray. It was absurd.

'Dilke, we must be sensible. Gray is engaged to a nice young girl, of whom even his father approves. Once Gray is married, the family trust is such that he will be very, very wealthy indeed. His father, unlike yours, has been extremely clever. Their money is abroad in Switzerland; it is in gold, it is in paintings, it is anywhere except in an English bank paying English taxes. I know all this because Gray works for the trust, but should he not marry, it all goes to his cousin. Once he marries, he can buy Maydown from us, and we can continue in the old way. The girl knows this. She knows that Gray can never be a husband to her, that theirs will be an arranged marriage. It is often done, and is perfectly acceptable. She will be rich and happy, obviously, and we will be as we have been. Gray thinks it a splendid notion. The only pebble in the shoe is her father, who has insisted on a long engagement. But once that is over, it will all be as we wish. We just must not *panic*.'

Dilke straightened up. 'Do you really think all this could work?'

'I do. Always providing that you will stop pretending that you need me to be with you twenty-four hours a day.'

'Have I been a pest lately to my Dippy?'

'You have just a little, darling. But not meaning to, of course. And not you being a pest so much as Mr Whisky. Mr Whisky can make us behave in a way we wouldn't normally, don't you think?'

'I will be like Queen Victoria from now on, darling, I promise.'

Leandra stared ahead of her. Her plan must work. More now than ever she must get Gray married off, and all of them freed by the terms of his father's trust. But would it work? She cleared her throat. Of course it would work. It was her plan, she would not tolerate it *not* to work. Gray was the love of her life. Dilke was her husband, and although she had never loved him, on the whole he had behaved quite well throughout their marriage. The Little Puppy from Rushington needed a social and monetary leg-up. All in all, it was a good plan, a solid plan, and nothing must be allowed to interfere with it.

'I think I am feeling a little tired now, Dippy. I think it must be Mr Whisky; he is a bad friend to me.'

They stood up.

'You always make me feel better, do you know that, Dippy? Always, always make me feel better, and I dare say you always will.'

Leandra slipped her arm through his and they wandered back into the house. When they reached the landing, she leaned forward and kissed him as she always did when he was at home. It was a nice kind sort of kiss accompanied by a hug such as his nanny might have given him.

'Goodnight, darling.'

'Goodnight, Dippy.'

They smiled vaguely in each other's direction, and then wandered off to their separate rooms. Once in his room Dilke lay down on his bed and, reaching into his bedside cupboard, he pulled out a bottle of brandy and, without using a glass, started to drink from it. Leandra, on the other hand, once she was in her suite of rooms, reached for the neatly addressed brown-paper parcel that had arrived from Beetle's Bookshop.

She tore off the wrapping and stared at the book. How nice to be sent the new Angus Wilson. He was such an amusing author, and could always be counted on to be writing about his friends, about people she knew, who could be counted upon to read his books and writhe. She smiled at the choice, which she knew would have been Randy Beauchamp's choice for her, since Gray was not someone who would ever read fiction.

Inside the book was the expected letter from Gray. As always the sight of his writing gave her a *frisson*. Dilke had been impossible lately, drunk and abusive, demanding and rude. It had taken every bit of her strength to keep an eye on him, to stop him from upsetting the servants, to cope with his sudden jealous rages, but as always when he was going through one of his dark periods, one of the compensations had been that Gray and she had been forced to return to secret lovers' ways, and that was always exciting, adding a thrill to her life that she really enjoyed. She adored getting love notes from Gray in this way, hidden in a book. She opened the letter.

Darlingest – *Leandra loved that.*

I am writing this in some haste as you-know-who, the Little Puppy, may be coming to London. It seems she has stamped her tiny foot and does not wish to stay in her puppy kennel.

She is coming to London to work, and to be near me! This has put me in a muddled position, since I know from you that there is a 'complication', in other words I am sure that her real reason for coming to London is the 'complication' rather than yours truly. I think we should meet, but since I know that Dilke is doing his best to behave like a wounded bull in a very tiny china shop, it is probably quite difficult for you . . . nevertheless I think we must try.

Gray

Leandra put the letter down. The Little Puppy was not meant to go to London at this stage. She was meant to be a good puppy and stay at college, living in Rushington with her parents, being good and looking forward to making a marriage of convenience with an older man. She was not meant to be let off her lead.

Besides, there *was* no complication. Leandra herself had invented the complication because she felt jealous of Sunny, because she saw that Gray was speaking about her in a different way.

She picked up the telephone to ring Gray. Never mind the hour, she must tell him that, whatever happened, the Little Puppy must not come to London. He must insist that she stayed in her sweet little village, or wherever it was that she lived with her parents. She must be kept in her familial kennel and not allowed out until she was safely married, and Gray was wealthy beyond even her dreams.

She picked up the telephone. The line was dead. She rattled it desperately, trying to force it into life, but it was not having any. She replaced it. She must get in touch with Gray. They *must* stop the Little Puppy from going to London.

## Chapter Seven

John Chantry was feeling rather pleased with life. Some of the building restrictions were being lifted, and his partner had found a large supply of building materials which had been smuggled in from France. Not that its provenance was something that they could admit to officially knowing about – of course not – but nevertheless a supply of old building materials that could go to repair some of the war damage on the Fairview estate was making both himself and Lord Fairview very happy indeed. All in all John could not wait for Monday morning.

He hummed as he dead-headed the roses around the French windows, thinking as he did so that no one ever told the truth about dead-heading. When an actress in a West End play came through the French windows wearing a flowered hat, carrying an elegant basket on her arm, and remarking that she had just finished dead-heading her roses, she should, if she was half an actress, be covered with scratches and breathing heavily, not looking fresh from her makeup mirror without a hair out of place.

'John?'

John looked round at Mary. Despite the heat of the day, and

the fact that she was working all God's hours on a trousseau for Lady Finsborough's daughter, his wife of a quarter of a century was looking very fresh and pretty. He smiled at her.

'Yes, love?'

Mary too smiled, and then remembering why she had come out to the garden, she stopped smiling.

'We have a visitor.'

'Yes, love?'

'Yes, John. That Gray Wyndham man. He is outside the front door again, in his Bentley.'

John could not help approving of Mary leaving Gray Wyndham outside the front door. He also approved of her referring to him as 'that Gray Wyndham man'; that was just how someone *should* refer to a bounder like him.

'I suppose you will have to show him in,' he said in a purposefully bored voice.

'Either that or tell him to go back to London, or wherever he is staying at the moment.'

John thought for a minute.

'No, show him in, love.' He put down his secateurs, and removed his gardening gloves slowly and methodically, laying them down with care on the old oak garden table, as a boxer might lay his gloves.

'I will show him into the sitting room. That is what you want?'

'Yes, yes, love, by all means.'

'Do you want me to fetch ice and lemon for drinks?'

'Yes, yes, love, fetch ice and lemon.' John smiled, and Mary too smiled. 'And by the way, love. You look very, very sweet in that flower-printed frock. Have I seen it before?'

'Yes, dear. I wore it when we got engaged. Up on the Downs that day, remember?'

'Ah, yes, I thought I remembered it. Well, you look as young and pretty as you did then. Fallen in love with you all over again, really I have.'

'Thank you, John.'

Mary's smile broadened, and she hurried off, first to fetch the ice and lemon, and then to let in the Gray Wyndham man, whom she had deliberately left standing outside the front door, his wretched car parked too close for comfort to their beech hedge.

The ice and lemon having been laid out on the drinks tray, she walked slowly to the front door, and finally opened it.

She had to give the Gray Wyndham man his due, he was very good at pretending that she was behaving towards him in a normal fashion. His smile had never been more urbane, white teeth sparkling, tanned face, above the blue of his immaculate laundered shirt, handsome in every way.

'My husband will see you in the sitting room.'

Gray followed Mary into the increasingly familiar flowered chintz sitting room with its bowls of roses and *Alchemilla mollis*, its photograph of the Chantrys on their wedding day, and its charmingly quaint copper objects. Despite the fact that the sitting room was filled with warm, welcoming English style, Mrs Chantry's manner towards him made Gray feel just a little as if he was a patient following a nurse into a dentist's waiting room.

'There we are.' Mary stood back waiting for John, who was still loitering in the garden. 'My husband shouldn't be long.'

Gray thought, the dentist shouldn't be long.

'Would you like a gin and tonic?'

It was such a hot day, how could he refuse?

'I should love a gin and tonic, Mrs Chantry.'

Gray was still standing.

'Do sit down, please.'

He shook his head.

'No, thank you, I prefer to stand, if you don't mind. I have been sitting in the car for most of the day. I had to go to see my father on family business, but then I thought perhaps it would be a good idea to call on you.'

'You might have telephoned?'

'Yes, I might have, except my father will not allow guests to use his telephone.'

Mary looked at Gray. 'How strange,' she murmured, handing him a perfectly made gin and tonic.

'Yes, but then he is strange. Since my mother died he has become more than a little eccentric.'

'I believe people do. They lack the restraint of the other person. It can be tiresome.'

'Very tiresome.'

'Ah, here's my husband.'

*The dentist will see you now.*

Mary left the room, eager only to go back to her sewing, to the thing that she knew she did best, the thing that she enjoyed the most, the thing that proved to her that she was just a little more than 'Mrs Chantry, wife of John.'

'Good afternoon, Mr Wyndham.'

'Good afternoon, Mr Chantry.'

John strolled across to his drinks tray, and made himself a gin and tonic, very, very slowly, tortuously slowly, so slowly that Gray found himself reduced to sipping his own drink, despite the fact that he had a raging thirst and would normally have knocked it back in no time at all.

John strolled back to the other end of the sitting room, which was not a long walk, and joined Gray, who was now standing by the French windows staring out at the roses.

'The roses have been magnificent this year, have they not?'

John nodded slowly, smiling at his garden in a pleasant manner, as a vaguely proud mother might smile at the sight of her children playing.

'Yes, they have been quite magnificent,' he agreed, feeling almost bored at having to talk to this overelegant man who had come into their lives. He thought he must hurry things along, or he might have to offer him another drink, so he added quickly, 'How can I help you, Mr Wyndham? Or rather, should I say, *can* I help you?'

'As a matter of fact you can help me,' Gray agreed, and suddenly caring less than he should what the other man might think, he quickly finished the rest of his gin and put his glass down on the top of a nest of tables nearby.

'It's about Sunny, Mr Chantry, it's about your daughter.'

'Yes, I know Sunny is my daughter, Mr Gray.' John smiled. It was not a particularly pleasant smile, nor was it meant to be.

'She is affording me a great deal of worry.'

'Well, that is Sunny, Mr Wyndham. She is a worry. *We*, her father and mother, have always known that, whereas it would seem *you* are only now beginning to find this out for yourself. Sunny likes to cause worry, it is her forte. She is dedicated to causing concern in others. She does not mean it, really. It is just in her nature.'

Gray realised that Mr Chantry was telling him that Sunny was a troublemaker, although not in so many words. He did not like this. He did not like it for two reasons. The first was that he now thought of Sunny as being like her name, and the second was that it made Leandra's plan for them all just a little less certain. It made him doubt its efficacy.

'I have to tell you, Mr Chantry, that far from causing trouble, your daughter has won hearts wherever she goes. My father, who is a notorious recluse, almost, one could say, a thorough-going misogynist, was as putty in her hands. He did not want her to leave his house, whereas normally he wants everyone to leave after five minutes flat.'

Now it was John who was not enjoying what he was hearing, also for two reasons, although really rather different ones. First, he did not like to think that Gray Wyndham's father had seen a side to Sunny that he had not even glimpsed for some time, and secondly he did not like to think of Gray Wyndham being in charge of Sunny, when he, her father, had that duty.

'I am very glad to hear that Sunny has been behaving herself.'

Gray did not like that either. The idea of Sunny misbehaving herself was somehow belittling.

'I would not think that Sunny knew how to misbehave, Mr Chantry.'

'Then you obviously don't know her very well.'

'No, I do not know her very well, but as I just said, what I *have* seen of her is quite simply enchanting. What others have seen of her is quite the same. Sunny by name, Sunny by nature.'

John made a slight sound. It was neither approving nor disapproving, but nondescript in a way that made Gray turn to look at his host with greater scrutiny, trying to translate both the man and the noise.

'So what is it you want me to do?'

John drained his glass and put it down beside Gray's glass on the nest of tables. For a second their glasses looked almost friendly, as if the users had both been enjoying themselves, as if they had been having a good time, which was so far from the truth that had Gray been still at his father's house he would have rung the bell for Jones to come and take the wretched things away.

'I don't actually want you to do anything, Mr Chantry. I just wanted to warn you that I think that Sunny has it in her mind to go to London, and as her fiancé, this worries me, as I am sure that it worries you. I want to think of Sunny here with you, in Rushington, going to college, generally enjoying herself in her usual innocent way. I don't want to think of her in the great metropolis, being laid open to temptations of every kind. I am not a great lover of London, although I do live there, so I must admit that while my fears are probably quite groundless, I do know our great capital city like the back of my hand, and for a girl as pretty and personable as Sunny, there can only be temptations such as you and I, as her father and fiancé, would not wish for her.'

It was rather a pompous speech, and once he had finished it Gray realised it only too well. Perhaps he was so caught up in his own feelings, so embarrassed that he had begun to sound like some sort of modern version of Mr Barrett, the domineering father of Elizabeth Barrett who ran off with the poet Robert Browning, that he failed to notice that John Chantry's eyes had hardened in a most unattractive manner.

'You have overstepped the mark now, Mr Wyndham,' he said. His quiet tone was much more frightening than any heightened volume. 'You have overstepped the mark to such an extent that I really have no alternative but to call a halt to this whole charade of your engagement to my daughter. Because, let us face it, Mr Wyndham, it is a charade. I don't know what you are up to, and I don't know what your game is, but I do know that my instinct tells me you are up to no good at all.'

Gray looked at him amazed.

'But, but – but all I have just said was that I was worried

about Sunny going to London. That is all I have said. I would have thought that as her father you would have found that reasonable.'

'Well, you would have thought wrong, Mr Wyndham. The truth is that you have come here to be impertinent. You have come here prepared to criticise – and showing concern for Sunny in the way you have is quite definitely silent criticism, whatever you might think. And frankly, I have had enough of you. I didn't like you at first, and I don't like you now. Coming in here, with your swanky ways, parking your Bentley outside – making use of our *telephone* – and then having the gall to confide in me your fears for our daughter whom you have, God help her, persuaded to become engaged to you. Frankly, Mr Wyndham, whatever the outcome of your association – and I very much hope for your sake that it *is* only an association, that Sunny has nothing more to do with you, for her sake – if Sunny does fall into bad ways when she is in London, that is her business and not yours.'

Gray frowned. He did not like being told off, but he liked John Chantry's last words even less.

'You say "if Sunny does fall into bad ways".'

'That is exactly what I said,' John agreed, holding open the sitting-room door for Gray to walk through. 'Because Sunny left for London yesterday, Mr Wyndham.'

Gray stopped. 'She left yesterday?'

'Yes, Mr Wyndham, yesterday. She packed up her suitcase, and we gave her fifty pounds, which is a small inheritance left to her by a godmother. We wished her good luck and Godspeed, and now, we understand, she is in our great capital city, and having a rare old time of it, I am sure. I only hope that you never find her, and she never finds you.'

Gray walked out into the sunshine, feeling and looking

dazed. He had never dreamed that someone like John Chantry would or could be rude to him, but also he had never thought that Sunny would leave Rushington. He had always thought of Sunny as being the kind of small-town, or in her case, small-village, girl that stayed at home in the acknowledged manner, putting together a trousseau and embroidering her initials into hand towels until she married. But no, Sunny had gone. She had packed her bag, taken fifty pounds and gone, but – and this boded ill for Leandra's plan – she had not told either Leandra or Gray what she was going to do. She had, as it were, cut them out of her will.

Once outside he turned to say something to John Chantry, but he had closed the door. In the circumstances it was surprising that he had not slammed the front door behind Gray, but he hadn't; he had closed it, formally and obviously, as far as he was concerned, for ever.

Gray walked down the garden path feeling bewildered. Where was Sunny, and what was she doing? Why had the Little Puppy been let off her lead? The kennel door sprung behind his and Leandra's back? He had a feeling that Leandra would somehow blame him, that he would be considered to have put a foot wrong. He resolved not to say anything to Leandra until such time that he could find Sunny.

Inside the Chantrys' cottage Mary was kissing John.

'Well done, John, well done. You saw him off, all right.'

John sighed. 'Let's hope that he never finds poor Sunny until such time that she finds someone else.'

'Let's hope so,' Mary agreed.

It had been Mary's idea to let Sunny go to London after all. She had suddenly realised that if Sunny went to London, saw different people, had more excitement than she could possibly ever find in Rushington, she might forget the dreadful

Wyndham man, and John, bless his heart, had seen the light and gone along with it. Now they only had to cross their fingers and hope for the best.

## Chapter Eight

When Sunny stepped off the train at Victoria Station, she had been fully aware that the gentlemen commuters, who climbed out of their first-class carriage after her, were following her with slow tread and appreciative eyes towards the ticket barrier. In truth, since she had become nominally engaged to Gray and had grown so much in confidence, it seemed that she exuded something that she had not had before, and it was something she was really rather coming to take for granted. It was inevitable. She might have no engagement ring, she might have the profound disapproval of her parents, but she had still acquired the overt confidence of an engaged girl.

The truth was that she thought about Gray almost every hour of her day, trying to imagine what he might be doing, and not really succeeding, because when someone is so much older, and you are barely eighteen, the truth is you can't quite understand what their day might embrace, once the coffee and toast stage is over. Just a small part of her hoped that perhaps, as he went about his day, he might occasionally be thinking of her, but that is as far as it went. She knew that she had won his father's heart, and while she could not really understand why his father had told her to run from Gray, she could appreciate that her performance, which she recognised was what it had really been, had won Mr Wyndham Senior over to his son's cause, and that once married to her, they would be rich beyond anyone's dreams.

That too she couldn't imagine. Nevertheless she had been determined to arrive in London in style, hence the reason she had purchased a first-class ticket. The sum of fifty pounds, which her parents had passed on to her, seemed to provide wealth enough for anyone, and style.

Her parents' sudden acceptance of her leaving college had been surprising, but the haste with which they set about finding her a place in Arietta's lodgings, and the alacrity with which her mother packed her up, had been almost upsetting. On top of the speed of their dismissal of her, there had been the dinner they gave her at the George. Her parents never ate out, yet on Sunny's last evening in Rushington they had taken her to the George, and toasted her departure as if she was about to emigrate to America, which was perhaps how they thought of her leaving for London.

Certainly the whole dinner had had an air of finality about it. Her mother looking at her in a way that said 'Goodbye, darling' in every glance, and her father looking at her in a way that said 'Good luck, Sunny, and I hope you won't need it'.

There had been glasses raised in muted toasts – 'Here's to a happy outcome' – and murmured appreciation over the roast chicken, the strawberries and meringues – 'Do so love Eton mess; takes one back to before the war', and so on.

All very nice, yet all the time Sunny had had the feeling that her departure for London was freeing her parents in some way, that while not wanting to see the back of her, they were certainly not feeling upset. Indeed, the following morning they drove her to the station in the Vauxhall in such fine form, laughing and talking to each other in the front of the car, Sunny like a small reluctant child in the back, that they could have been at the start of a holiday, not seeing off their only child. Certainly they seemed more than happy to watch her buy a first-class ticket, and then disappear into the early light of a Sussex morning without so much as a backward glance.

'Much the best for you to go and take your chance in London,' her mother had murmured, as she sewed and ironed, washed and starched Sunny's clothes; and she had said it so many times that Sunny had found it difficult not to scream.

Now she stood in a queue waiting for a taxi, her suitcase by her side, her straw hat on the back of her head, short white gloves remaining miraculously unmarked after the train journey, hoping against hope that she would be able to find her way to the bookshop where Arietta worked. To someone who had hardly even been on a train, London seemed to be a maze, not a city, and she a figure lost within it, longing for a piece of string that she could follow and so find her way out of it.

'Beetle's Bookshop, off the King's Road.'

'Beetle's Bookshop? No idea. Any other address, miss?'

Sunny shook her head. 'No, all I know is that it's just off the King's Road.'

'There are quite a few places off of the King's Road, dear. Got to give me a bit more than that I am afraid, miss.'

Sunny felt in her handbag, and instead of the bookshop gave the address of the lodgings, which her mother had scribbled into the back of her diary.

'Oh, I know that street all right. Hop in.'

The taxi driver deposited her suitcase on the pavement

outside the tall, four-floored house, and drove off at what seemed to Sunny to be unseemly haste. She stared up at the house, and then down again at the address in her diary. It was the right place, but how to get in? The arrangement had been for Arietta to meet her at the bookshop, and take her round to the house. Arietta had the key to the front door. Sunny had no key. She walked towards the basement steps, hoping to be able to hide her suitcase behind the dustbins, but the gate to the area was firmly padlocked, and there was no sign of life behind the curtained window. She stared at her suitcase realising that with it in tow it was impossible to wander about trying to find the bookshop. Suddenly even the sight of her mother's writing in the back of her diary brought a feeling of homesickness that threatened to overwhelm her. She wanted to go home to Rushington, but knew that to do so meant that she would be seen to be cowardly; and worse than that, to her mother and father, her swift return would be about as welcome as a tax bill.

She sank slowly down on to her suitcase. The buckles were most uncomfortable, but had to be borne, because she knew there was only one thing she could do now, and that was to wait for someone or another to turn up and let her into the house.

In the ordinary way Arietta would have been looking forward to Sunny coming to London; would have resolved to put flowers in the room above her own, which was where Mr Beauchamp had agreed to let Sunny have a room, but she was now feeling really rather different. Her much altered feelings had everything to do with the parcel containing Angus Wilson's new short-story collection, which she had been given to despatch to a certain Mrs Dilke Fortescue, together with a letter written by a certain Mr Gray Wyndham, the whole having been sent on by Beetle's Bookshop.

Arietta knew, indeed she was certain, that she was not by nature a particularly curious person, but when Mr Beauchamp had handed her the single sheet of paper written by Mr Wyndham, within the back pages of the newly published book, she felt a curious sense of obligation to take it out and read it. Indeed, she felt it was almost a religious duty to do so. Sunny was, after all, meant to be engaged to Mr Wyndham, and as such Arietta felt she had a real duty to read what Mr Gray Wyndham had written to this Mrs Fortescue.

'*Darlingest*' the letter had begun. Arietta had been unable to believe her eyes. What a thing for an engaged man to put! Darlingest!

Naturally she had read on, feeling quite faint when she realised that it was Sunny of whom he was writing as 'the Little Puppy' and that Pear Tree Cottage was the 'puppy kennel'. It was hideous beyond anything to think of poor Sunny having made herself ill over this older man while all the time he was deceiving her with another woman, and a married woman at that.

Happily, once she had absorbed the letter and its contents and replaced it in the back pages of the novel, she was able to find a chair on which to sit to continue wrapping the wretched parcel. And she *had* sat down on it, after first clearing the over-crowded desk, and she had dutifully addressed the parcel, as also the one to the Duke of Somerton, although His Grace's missive to his mistress seemed quite mild in contrast to the throbbing intensity of Mr Gray Wyndham's to Mrs Fortescue.

My dear, I shall be at White's from Tuesday through to Thursday. Leave me one of your little missives there, and we can meet for a *cinq-à-sept* at Park Street. Your own Bear.

PS. I have a string of something very sweet which will suit a certain long white neck . . .

The parcels duly wrapped and sealed, Arietta had made her way to the post office, but although the sun was still shining, and the sky still blue, the King's Road looked suddenly shabby and second rate, rather, she imagined, like the people whose love letters she was now posting. She walked along, as a child might who has a stick that she is intent on running across the railings she passes, slowly and in a desultory fashion. The deception of the love letters, the furtive nature of the affairs had done more than shock her, it had disillusioned her. She had so hoped that once she came to London she would find that not everyone in the world would be like her mother, that they would be kind and straightforward, that they would care for each other, not want to deceive each other; but now she saw that wherever she went, the world would always be just as her mother had always said it was – full of people not caring how they hurt each other, wanting only to pleasure themselves, no matter at what cost to anyone else.

She had stood patiently in the queue of shabby people all with parcels they could probably hardly afford to post. While the queue moved up slowly the realisation had come to her, making her once again feel quite faint with the horror of it all. Sunny was coming to London any minute now. *What would she say to Sunny?* What?

That evening, after work, Sam and Arietta had retired to the pub. He had immediately noticed that she was not as she had been with him earlier in the day.

'Are you still holding it against me about the Moroccan wine?'

'Mmm?'

'I said, you seem to have grown so morose I thought you might well be holding it against me about the Moroccan wine, Miss Staunton.'

'You may call me Arietta, but you may not enquire further about why I am morose,' Arietta stated flatly and without humour, staring at the other customers without really seeing them.

'So what is it that eats at the heart of Miss Arietta Staunton?'

'Something pretty beastly, I can assure you.'

Sam pulled a face, and then started to tick off a list on his fingers.

'If it's not the Moroccan wine that's made you feel down in the mouth, let's see then . . .' He frowned. 'I know. You're feeling depressed because Uncle Randy made you go to the post office twice in one afternoon and the queues of people browned you off?'

'No, not that.' Arietta stopped, and pushed away her glass of tomato juice as if that too was getting on her nerves. 'Actually it *was* that, if you really want to know, but not exactly that.'

There was a small silence, but since he was a musician and quite used to waiting to blow, as the expression went, Sam let the silence rip. He actually didn't mind this because it gave him a small opportunity to stare at Arietta's lovely uneven face: her brown eyes with their slight astigmatism, her brown hair that had more than a shot of auburn in its lights, her beautiful complexion and elegant hands and figure. She might not be a beauty, but yet, he determined, she would be a brilliant subject for a painting.

He had to be honest with himself, he was attracted to her in every way, probably because she was *not* a beauty, but had an air of detachment, of not really wanting to be in the world, of hoping against hope that any minute now she would find herself elsewhere. It was this more than anything that interested him, that made him want not just to paint her, but to be with her a great deal, although not always in the bookshop.

'It was that, but it wasn't that? Is it possible to ask for a translation?'

'Yes.' Arietta frowned. 'If I tell you a secret you promise—'

'I promise, hand on heart, only to tell *one* other person.'

Sam's expression was serious; even so, Arietta sensed the opposite.

'How do you mean?'

'Do you not know the simple unavoidable fact, which is when someone is told a secret, they always tell at least *one* other person. Actually, it is not a fact, it is a rule.'

'Oh.' Arietta could not help looking impressed. 'That is honest. So who are you going to tell?'

Sam thought for a minute.

'I will tell Uncle Randy, because he probably knows already.'

'That *is* a good idea—' Arietta stopped. 'How do you know he knows already?'

'Because if it is something or other to do with the post office, he sent you there, after all. It does not take Sherlock Holmes or Dr Watson to work that one out, does it?'

'You're quite right. And it is to do with the post office, and also to do with the bookshop, and your uncle does know already, but – but he doesn't know *everything.*'

'Don't tell him that, for goodness' sake; he is quite sure he does.'

'Well, here's how it is.' Arietta took a deep breath and stared ahead of her. 'Back in Rushington where I come from, there is a girl called Sunny Chantry—'

'Dig the name, kid—'

'Well, I know, not quite fair if she'd turned out to be a lump of lard, but she's not. She's very, very pretty and very, very sweet – except when you wake her up in the morning, that is—'

'Shall we get on with the story?'

'Oh, yes, sorry. Anyway this man, much older than her – he must be about thirty – well, he broke down in his Bentley outside her parents' cottage and fell in love with her, well, that is, we *thought* he did. Anyway, there was the most awful shindig, because of his being older and her parents not approving and – and – so on. But at any rate, now they're engaged, although they have to wait a full year, except – except—'

Arietta stopped once more.

'Except?' Sam looked at her. 'Come on, stop looking tragic, spill the beans.'

'Well, this is where the post office comes in.'

'I thought it might.'

'One of those parcels, one of those books has a love letter from Sunny's fiancé to someone called *"Darlingest"*!' She stopped yet again. 'It's too awful, because he's a war hero, but he can't be a man.' Again another pause. 'But now I come to think of it, that can't be true, he *must* be able to be a man in some way or another if, well, if he's writing to this other person "darlingest" and so on. I mean, he must! Which means he must be deceiving Sunny for some dreadful reason, which we can only guess at, don't you think?'

Sam tried to keep a straight face, and failed.

'Arietta Staunton, you are a guinea a minute, do you know that?'

Arietta threw back her tomato juice and replaced the glass on the table.

'This is terrible. You mustn't laugh.' She stared ahead of her, then, seeing Sam's face, she too started to laugh. 'No, really, this is serious. I mean, Sunny really loves this chap. She thinks wherever he is the sun shines brightest. She is going to be heartbroken.'

They fell silent, both staring ahead.

'A fine mess someone's got someone in, then?'

'Well, if that's not stating the obvious – but what do we do now?'

Sam held up his hands. 'No "we" to it – you are in this thing alone, Arietta Staunton. I try to avoid post offices at all times, and as for reading other people's love letters, not my thing, kid, just not my thing.'

'No, I am not in this alone, I'm really not. You are in it too. After all, it's your uncle that owns the blooming bookshop that allows this sort of thing to happen.'

'Can't quite see that, but no doubt I will come round to it in a few centuries' time.'

Arietta shook her head, not really listening. 'And the worst of it is, she's coming up to London in a few days, so do I tell her then? What do I do?'

'No, no, you can't tell her! You can't possibly. It's not up to you. She has to find out for herself.'

'I *can* tell her, but *should* I? If I don't she might find out that I knew all along, and that will be that.' She stared not at Sam, but through him. 'Oh dear, this is a bit like something beastly in Shakespeare.'

'Never mind what it's like. You still can't tell her, you know you can't. You just can't. She probably wouldn't believe you anyway.'

'No, I can't tell her, I agree.'

'Something will happen,' Sam stated finally. 'It always does. Let's forget about it for a few hours. Do let's.' He paused for a second, changing tack. 'How about coming for a spaghetti bolognese instead of sitting agonising about this Sunny girl?'

At that Arietta stared at Sam, not through him. If you came from Rushington, spaghetti bolognese was exotic to a degree. You had heard about it, but you had never actually eaten it.

'Spaghetti bolognese? Are you sure?'

'I am sure I'm sure. Follow me. Giuseppe does the best, and he is only a few streets away. The secret is, well, there are two secrets to a spaghetti bolognese. One is the celery, and the other is chicken liver. But you must let him tell you . . .'

That was all a few days ago. Now Arietta was strolling home alone, staring up at the evening sky, and wondering why Sunny hadn't called round to the bookshop for her key, wondering if she had changed her mind about coming to London, wondering if she might have already found out about her beastly fiancé? It would be so good if she had. It would be better than good, it would be *frabjous*, as in 'frabjous day! Callooh! Callay!'

When she reached the house she rapped on the basement window, and called to where she could see Sam sitting reading some sheet music. He beckoned to her to come down and, going to the basement door, he let her in, at the same time placing his finger to his lips.

'I found your friend on the doorstep an hour or so ago. She'd been there for hours.'

'*What?*'

'You were wrong by the way.' Sam gave her a sly look. 'She's not pretty at all. She's beautiful.'

Arietta stared at him. It was probably true. Sunny probably was beautiful, but quite honestly, at that minute, she had other things on her mind.

'Where is she now?' she asked.

'She's asleep on the sofa in the other room.'

'Why is she asleep?'

Sam looked innocent and scratched his head in a comical fashion, which made Arietta feel suspicious.

'I don't know. I think it must be because she felt tired from sitting on her suitcase since heaven only knows when – since this morning. Since lunch-time I think she said, actually.'

'*You* can wake her up then, I'm not going to. Apparently she's lethal when she's woken up, always has been, can't help it.'

Sam nodded. 'Some people are. My father is the soul of sweetness, but my sister is beastly punchy when woken.'

Despite his cheerful tone, Sam was feeling rueful. He had hoped to make Arietta jealous by his observation about Sunny Chantry's being beautiful, which although true, had been a trifle unnecessary. He saw that he had failed to make Miss Staunton jealous. This impressed him. He was used to girls being jealous of each other, and the fact that she had not shown the slightest interest in his observation meant that she really was what Uncle Randy would call 'stalky'.

'Tell you what, we can both be stalky about this situation, really we can,' he went on as airily as he could. 'I'll leave my flatmate Hart a note to wake her when he gets in, and he can take the flak, savez?'

'But will he?'

'Hart? Hart will take anything from flak to your best evening jacket. He's the most stalky of us all, there is no biznai that he does not know about. Come on, off to the pub. I'm fed up with being cooped up inside this hellhole on a hot summer evening.'

'What about giving her the key?'

'I'll put it on the hall table with the note.'

Arietta nodded. She had hoped that Sam had been trying to make her jealous by extolling Sunny's beauty, and now she knew that she was right, or he would not be leaving Hart a note, and taking her to the pub.

She walked ahead of him up the area steps. The truth was

even if she didn't like being with Sam, which she did, she was actually feeling nervous and shy about seeing Sunny now that she knew that awful Wyndham man was deceiving her with 'darlingest' Mrs Fortescue. The morbid truth was that Sunny knew Arietta too well not to sense that something was wrong. Arietta had to prepare herself to be quite normal. She sighed, setting out towards the pub ahead of Sam. What a pickle it all was, and it was sure to end in everything being beastly rather than stalky.

Sam caught her up and took her arm as they walked along.

'Stop worrying,' he ordered, giving her arm a little shake. 'It's a fine evening, we're going to the pub. That's all that matters just now.'

He leaned over and kissed her on the cheek. Arietta pretended not to notice, just kept walking. Sam smiled. He knew that she had noticed, because she coloured a little, although she didn't bother to turn to look at him.

This he realised, as they walked along in companionable silence, was going to be the signature on their relationship, how it would always be. He would be the one to kiss, she would be the one to receive the kiss.

Arietta knew herself too well not to realise it also. She had been too hurt in her childhood ever to risk being hurt any more. Whoever liked her would have to come to her. She would go to no one.

'Come on!' Sam let go her arm and started to run. 'Race you to the pub!'

Although she was running well and fast, perhaps because she started later, Arietta found herself having to put on a great deal of speed in order to catch up with Sam.

Sam smiled as he heard her sprinting behind him, thinking that any girl who was that athletic had to make a great model.

By the time she was trying to overtake him he had already composed the painting. Perhaps because Arietta was at the centre of it, he finally let her win.

'Slow coach,' she said, turning to face him, her hand on the pub door, her face pink with the effort.

Sam smiled, and his green eyes glinted in the early evening London light. For a second Arietta caught the glint as she walked ahead of him into the pub. That smile reminded her of someone. Too late she realised who it might be. It was Beatrix Potter's foxy-whiskered gentleman. Was she then to play Jemima Puddle-Duck?

Leandra was furious, not just with Dilke for being so stupid, what with his disastrous affairs, both monetary and amatory, but she was also furious with Gray.

Gray had somehow let the Little Puppy slip through his fingers, and not just his fingers, he had let her slip through *their* fingers, and now the Little Puppy was doubtless gadding about London in a manner that, given her age and innocence, could surely only lead to trouble. There must have been some way that Gray could have stopped her from coming to London.

Gray was looking suitably miserable. Well, he looked as miserable as anyone with his looks *could* look, which was not really very miserable at all.

'How could I stop her from coming to London, darlingest, when it was her parents themselves who were actually sending her? They quite obviously do not want her at home any more; and really, considering their quite open dislike of me, you can't really blame the poor creatures, can you?'

Leandra felt quite able to blame them. In fact, she was sure that should they have been within a few feet of her, she might feel strongly tempted to bang their heads together, the idiotic couple!

'What could they be thinking, sending a young, stupid girl to London on her own that way?'

She started to walk up and down Gray's drawing room. She did not much like visiting Gray at home, for all sorts of reasons. The hall porter, she knew, must pass on information about visitors to all sorts of people in the know, gossip columnists, people in the security services, you name it, he would undoubtedly be in the market for receiving payments of any size for information, gossip – anything.

This was the drawback of being well known in polite circles, of always being mentioned and photographed in the press. A London hall porter would hardly need an Oxford degree to recognise her. Unfortunately, this particular day there had been no alternative to her visiting Gray rather than his being able to slip into her house by the servants' entrance, as was his habit. The reason for this was that the financial vultures were already visiting their latest victim – Dilke – pencils and pens poised over their notebooks as they added up the value of the Fortescues' many and beautiful *objets*.

Just before she left she had actually found Dilke trying to hide his jade collection. Despite his protestations, she had insisted that it be left out for assessment, and not just because she knew that his collection was both rare and valuable.

'Dilke was trying to hide his jade collection from the money men,' she murmured inconsequentially. 'I made him leave it out. They're welcome to it. I hate jade.'

Gray too disliked jade, almost as much as he knew Dilke disliked him, but for a second he felt sorry for the older man. The poor fellow's collection meant so much to him.

Gray frowned, lit a cigarette, and started to pace up and

down the drawing room, wondering why things were not going better.

His visit to Pear Tree Cottage in Rushington had been unfortunate, to say the least. In fact, driving back to London and Leandra with the news that the Little Puppy had fled her kennel had been really quite upsetting. He had found himself turning the events of the past days over and over in his mind, knowing that they were not going their way, and perhaps more importantly, they were not going *his* way.

It was not just the idea of Sunny Chantry alone in London that had been upsetting, it was the fact that despite the frigid atmosphere, the parental disapproval, Gray had actually spoken the truth to her father. He did not like to think of Sunny as being anywhere except at home with her parents, and now that it was obvious that her parents – who were looking extraordinarily chipper and spry – were more than happy for her to be let off her lead, it must mean that Sunny meant more to Gray than he could ever have imagined.

At first, in comparison to Leandra, Sunny had appealed only as a pretty little toy, but then seeing how adroit she had been at handling his father, she had started to appeal to him as being something rather more. A pretty little toy could not have won over his father, not to mention the whole household. A pretty little toy would have merely sat about making toylike noises, whereas Sunny Chantry, and in a very short space of time, had Jocelyn Wyndham eating out of her elegant little hand.

'Hope that poor sweet creature you've got in tow sees sense before it's too late,' was what Jocelyn had actually said to Gray before he took his leave of his father, a remark that suggested to Gray that Sunny was perhaps not as firmly nailed to the idea of marriage to him as Leandra and he had fondly imagined.

Remembering all this, the thought now came to Gray for the first time – was it possible that Sunny *had* seen sense? That she had gone to London not just at her parents' suggestion, but of her own volition? That she had, in other words, determined not just to escape from her parents, but to escape from Gray and Leandra too? Had his father warned her off Gray? He would be quite capable of so doing.

'Stupid, stupid girl,' Leandra was now murmuring to no one in particular as she too lit a cigarette and stared out into the Mayfair street.

Gray looked at Leandra. She suddenly seemed older, which was hardly surprising considering the strain she was under with Dilke's mismanagement of their finances, but it was not just that. Leandra seemed older, perhaps, because he had been thinking about Sunny. Her voice seemed older, and her eyes had an older look, and she smoked in a way that older women do, intensely, as if the nicotine was not getting to her fast enough. She lacked Sunny's freshness, she lacked her vivacity. Finally, he realised, she lacked Sunny's warmth and kindness.

'Sunny Chantry is not stupid, Leandra,' he announced, after a long pause. 'In fact, I would say that is the last thing that Sunny Chantry is. She may be innocent, but she is certainly not stupid.'

Leandra glanced up at him, for once not really paying much attention.

'She could be anywhere in this city, anywhere.' She stood up and, going to a heavy glass ashtray, she stubbed out her Turkish cigarette in its gleaming, immaculate centre, before starting to walk up and down the room, not looking at Gray or anything else in particular, as people don't when they are caught up in their own emotions. 'Do you realise that, thanks to the total irresponsibility of her parents, we have absolutely no idea of where to find this girl? Or even where to start looking for her?'

'Leandra,' Gray caught at her now cigarette-free hands, 'let's be frank. This was a crazy idea. I mean, you have had some great ideas in your time, some wonderful ideas, but this was mad, darling. How could we possibly expect this poor young girl to marry me and live a virgin's life while we carried on our affair? It is preposterous. Truly, it is.'

Leandra snatched her hands away from him.

'It is far from being preposterous,' she told him in a low voice. 'My plan is perfect. I told you at the start this sort of association is perfectly acceptable in Paris, in New York, and even in staid old London. But always to succeed one needs someone quite, quite innocent. The sophisticates that we know, know all about us, so they will never do. By chance, by good luck, we found just the one we needed. Nothing should have gone wrong. She is perfect for our plans. The only thing that has gone wrong with the plan is the parents of our innocent. It is they who have thrown a spanner in the works, and it is up to us to take the spanner out of the works, and throw it right back at them in Lustington—'

'Rushington actually.'

'In Rushington. Precisely. No, we have to keep our nerve. The debts are catching up on Dilke, and we are going to need to stick close together, you and I, darling.' She looked up at Gray with sudden passion. 'Not so difficult really, is it?'

Gray smiled, but it was an uneasy smile and he knew it. He just hoped that Leandra did not recognise it as such. To cover the moment he returned to the subject in hand.

'We cannot expect the Little Puppy's parents to be on our side. They have never pretended to be on our side. They have always said that they do not approve of me, that I am too old, that I am unsuitable – which, let's face it, I am.'

Even as he stated this Gray had to admit to himself that he felt that he was actually far from being too old for Sunny, and was certainly not unsuitable. He was, after all, quite a catch, now that his father had lost his heart to Sunny. But how could he find out whether she felt the same as he, if he couldn't find her, if he had indeed lost her?

It seemed that Leandra was determined to return to the subject that was most occupying her.

'The whole situation is now impossible, thanks to those *parents*!' Leandra paused. 'We can only hope that she will be in touch with you soon. That is our one hope. I know she was upset when you didn't telephone her, because she told me as much.' She paused again. 'But in the event of her not getting in touch with you, then we can only take it that she has changed her mind, or met someone else. Oh, but those parents, they have made such a mess of things, truly they have.'

Gray shook his head. 'Let us drop the subject of the Chantrys and concentrate on trying to find the Little Puppy ourselves,' he suggested. 'It is really not very attractive to go about blaming these poor folk who are, after all, only acting in what they believe to be their daughter's best interests. I cannot be a party to heaping blame on them, truly I can't.'

Leandra felt astonished, but was careful not to look it. She put her head on one side, and smiled.

'Mmm, indeed, darling, you're right,' she agreed after a little pause. 'That was very wrong of me.'

'Besides, you know and I know that there was someone else, was there not? The complication that you told me about? It is becoming more and more obvious that he is the reason she has come to London.'

'Oh, that was nothing,' Leandra said, a little too quickly even to her own ears as she remembered her lie. 'I found out about that. It was just a passing flirtation, nothing more. She told me about that. It was nothing. I shouldn't even have mentioned it, really I shouldn't.'

'No, perhaps you shouldn't. As a matter of fact, although we are meant to be keeping emotions out of it, it very nearly made me jealous. As I said, Sunny is still very innocent, you know. I'm quite sure she is incapable of having anything but the purest feelings for anyone. At the moment she is the proverbial rose at dawn.'

All of a sudden, Leandra caught on.

Gray was not just defending the parents of the Little Puppy, he was defending the Little Puppy herself, seeing her not as stupid, but innocent, which Leandra knew must be instantly appealing to an older man.

'Yes, you're right, darling. You're quite right. I'm being peevish and silly. Forgive me, won't you?' she asked with uncharacteristic humility.

She absented herself from the room for a short while, and when she returned, freshened and scented, Gray noticed that the cross look had gone from her beautiful violet-blue eyes and in its place was her usual sparkling amusement.

'I must tell you of a rumour I heard regarding the first family in the land,' she began, looking up at Gray in a way that she knew he loved.

Gray stared down at her. He loved the scent she wore. It was very, very special. It always excited him, made him feel marvellous, even when he was feeling much less than marvellous.

'Shall we forget about rumours for a while?' he asked her in a lowered tone.

'If you wish, sir?'

'I certainly do, madam.'

Gray took Leandra by her heavily ringed hand and they left the drawing room together, the Little Puppy at last forgotten.

Later, Leandra smiled to herself as she dressed. It was as well to be sophisticated. No matter how innocent the Little Puppy, she would never, ever be able to keep up with Gray. Whatever Gray said about her, Sunny Chantry was too young and stupid to understand how to please someone like Gray.

She kissed him goodbye. It was a kiss designed to remind him of the sensual hour that they had spent together, but without any sense of lingering passion. There was, after all, work to be done.

Gray watched Leandra crossing the street below him.

She was a beautiful woman who knew exactly how to please him, and, as always, please him she had, but what she could never do now was to take away a thirst that had been awakened in him for something else, something fresh and young. It was that which artlessly, and without perhaps meaning to, Sunny Chantry had awakened in him.

He sighed and, Leandra having rounded a corner and disappeared from sight, he went to the drinks tray and poured himself a Scotch.

One remark that Leandra had made during her tedious diatribe had hit home.

Supposing, Leandra had suggested, Sunny did *not* get in touch with Gray herself? Supposing she had left home because she had indeed found someone else? Her parents might even know this, and it might explain their proud intransigence.

He contemplated the idea for a few seconds and, finding it intolerable, he quickly finished his drink and went out to his club, just as Leandra found herself slipping unobtrusively back into her London house, only to discover that in the space of only a few hours, her situation was a great deal worse than she had thought.

She knew this the moment she saw Bennison, her London butler's, face. She knew it from the way his eyes could not look into hers, the way they strayed to the drawing-room door as a dog's eyes might stray reproachfully to an empty dinner bowl. She knew it from the sound of the low murmur of the voices, and how hurried the voices were at points, and excited, as voices always became when there was money at stake.

'They're all still here, are they, Bennison?' she asked, in a low voice.

Bennison nodded.

'I am afraid so, Mrs Fortescue,' he replied in an even lower tone. In fact he spoke so low that for a moment Leandra had the feeling that if he dropped his voice any more she would be reduced to lip reading.

'All of them?'

'All of them.'

Leandra nodded silently and then, quickly and quietly, she went to her bedroom suite and, without ringing for her maid, pulled down her suitcases and began to pack.

She would leave London for Maydown as soon as possible. Once at Maydown she would start to think of what to do. Rule would help her. They could hide a great many things against the creditors – the smaller paintings, the treasured *objets*. They could put the copy of the most valuable painting, *The Rape of the Sabines*, into the old frame, and roll up the original and put it somewhere safe, somewhere where no one else would think of finding it.

As she looked up train times and rang for a taxi – calling for the car would take far too long – Leandra found herself thinking of her grandmother, and she thanked her lucky stars that she had always told her granddaughter to have a contingency plan, that she had warned her, time and time again, that life could change suddenly and violently, and that being so, you always had to be ready to roll up paintings, hide precious objects such as jewellery and gold, and take to the hills, or in this particular case at this particular hour, the Sussex Downs.

## Chapter Nine

Hart was making coffee for Sunny, whom he had just woken up.

'I expect you're like me, you like it black?'

Back in Rushington Sunny normally took her coffee not only with milk, but with about four sugars. Now, however, she nodded in agreement because she did not want to appear unsophisticated.

'Oh, yes, coffee must always be black,' she agreed, watching Hart boiling a kettle and spooning a heaped spoon into an Alessi cafetiere.

'I get this blend from Soho. It is actually Jamaican, very, very tasty, very strong. I bribe the kitchen boy at the back door of Gianelli; where *he* gets it from we do not ask.' He smiled happily. 'This should wake you up for the rest of the evening all right. There, I hope it's strong enough?'

Sunny took a sip of the coffee and despite the assault on her senses, she managed to smile. Only minutes before she had opened her eyes to see a more than interested male face staring at her. For a few seconds she had smiled, probably because the face had been smiling at her, but then she had sat up, feeling odd, as if she had been caught trespassing.

'Just how I like my coffee.'

Now she was in London she must change, and change she would, in every way, no matter what. She would change her hair, her clothes, her tastes in food and drink – everything. She would become sophisticated, and therefore older, and more suitable for Gray. She would learn new manners and new words such as Arietta had used on the telephone to her, words like 'hip' and 'square'.

'Are you going to be a great jazz musician?' she asked Hart, after a minute or two during which the effects of the coffee took such strong hold she felt quite giddy.

Hart stared at her. He wanted her to hurry up with the coffee, because he was dying for a beer, but was too polite to say so.

'Good God, no! I'm never going to make it as a musician. Down here in the basement with the others, fine, anything more, no. We just like to have a bit of a blow. No, no, I could never make it. Just not good enough.'

'What are you going to be then?'

Hart looked at Sunny, his expression serious. 'You wouldn't want to know.'

'Oh, but I would, I would really. I am so interested in every-thing and everyone in this house, truly I am. What a bit of luck to have Arietta come here and then for her to find a room for me, and everything like that. Really, what a bit of luck, because I know no one in London, so I am interested, truly I am,' she assured him, the words tumbling over each other, again, because of the coffee.

'Very well, I will tell you if you promise not to tell anyone else, ever? I am working for an auction house.'

'Oh.'

'Yes, I know. Oh.'

'Living here, being here, I thought you would be doing something more exciting.'

'I know. Not exactly very bohemian, is it? Actually quite the opposite. I am not proud, though. I need to learn about Art, and this is the best opening I could find, slogging away in the basement with lots of other young men, all determined to uncover their very own masterpiece beneath centuries of old varnish.'

Sunny looked sober. 'It can't matter that much that you're doing something sensible, can it?'

'Down this end of the King's Road? You must be surely making *une* tiny little *blague*, or joke, as the French call it? The moment I get home I tear off the suit, the shirt, the whole caboodle, and plunge into the navy-blue polo neck and the jeans before anyone catches sight of me. Then, in the early morning, before anyone can see me, before anyone can note my square clothes, my hair slicked down, my demeanour of unholy capitalism, I creep out, under cover of early dawn, and slide off to the offices of Messrs Rookery and Co., and start wheeling fabulous works of art about the basement with a reverent gleam in my eye.'

'Auctions and auction houses are quite glam, aren't they?'

'Glam? My dear girl, whatever gave you that idea?' Hart's eyes widened and he laughed. 'The buying and selling of *objets* is what Sam calls "a terrible biznai". As a matter of fact, Sam is so embarrassed by my job he ignores the fact that I even leave the house to pursue my shameful calling. It is too sweet really. He is so protective of my hip status, if someone phones he always says, "He's just popped out," because he doesn't want them to know that I am gainfully employed. Finds it just so embarrassing. He is so idealistic, bless his nasty red socks. Just can't face the idea that I am working for someone who charges interest for handling someone else's possessions. Not that Sam's a socialist or anything, he's just so ultra *refined*. He makes it his special, special biznai to be so. It could almost be touching, except I can't help noticing that his sensitivities in monetary matters do not quite last out the month, and once he has run out of filthy lucre, he suddenly finds this fiendish capitalist friend Hart Dorling becomes just a little useful to him.'

'Oh, so it's one law for you, and a completely different one for him?'

'Naturally, but since, besides being my boyhood fishing friend, he's the best drummer around these parts, and Phillip is the best pianist, and I am by far the least talented, I have kept my observations to myself – until now, that is.' Hart gave Sunny a pretend soulful look.

Sunny laughed.

There was a pause as Sunny considered something very seriously. 'Can I say how much I like your boots? They are really chic.'

Hart looked down at his boots. 'I am so glad. I bought them in America. In New York, actually, on Second Avenue. They were pleasantly cheap.'

There was a longer silence this time, which Sunny finally thought should be filled because Hart was staring at her in a way that made her feel shy.

'Do you think that Sam and Arietta have gone to the pub?'

Hart, who had read Sam's note quite carefully, before having the pleasure of waking up surely the prettiest of sleeping beauties, nodded.

'I am quite sure they have gone to the pub.'

'Should we join them?'

'Well, we could, or I could show you to your room, and you could change, and then I could take you out to dinner.'

Sunny stood up, relieved to have broken the silence, and excited by the invitation to dinner. Suddenly London seemed really rather marvellous.

'What should I wear to dinner, do you think? I am a bit at sea in London,' she confessed as they walked up the long narrow flights of stairs to what would be her room for the next few months.

Hart put her key in the door of her flat, and then gave the door a little push.

'I would say a circular skirt with a petticoat that really rustles underneath, and a tight belt, and those flat ballerina-type shoes that make it easier to rock and roll, baby. Oh, and if possible, a Chinese-collared shirt. That would all suit where I am going to take you quite admirably.'

Sunny stared at him, amazed.

'How did you know that I have just that outfit in my suitcase?'

Hart smiled, and half closed his delightfully dark eyes. He knew that Sam would say that it was because Hart was stalky, and really, if he was honest, Hart might be forced to agree, but he was too modest to say so.

'I knew it because you have just the figure for a circular skirt,' he confessed, 'and because you are very, very pretty; and pretty girls always travel with petticoats that rustle, not to mention wide belts that can be pulled really tight.'

He started to walk back down the stairs, as Sunny closed her door, but she reopened it before he reached the turn.

'Before we go to dinner, I have to tell you – at least I think I *should* tell you – well, that I am meant to be engaged to a chap called, well, never mind what he's called. But I am meant to be engaged at least for the next year, so—' she stopped. 'Well, I just thought I ought to tell you, because it might mean that you wouldn't want to take me to dinner, once you knew.'

Hart stared at Sunny for a few seconds, astonished that her really rather bald announcement had had such an effect on him, and after such a short acquaintance.

Just for a few seconds he felt as if he had been kicked in the stomach, until he examined the statement a little closer, the way he was learning to examine paint, to stare at the varnish close up, to look at the tiniest detail, see where a painting had been repainted or revarnished too heavily, learning to recognise what had happened to a canvas over the years. On examining Sunny's statement in this increasingly professional manner he recognised that there was surely less need to panic than he might have thought, because what Sunny Chantry had actually said was, 'I am *meant* to be engaged . . .'

That did not smack of any kind of finality, or even formality. It did not sound ominous, it did not smack of notices posted in the *Daily Telegraph*, or rings about to be bought from Mappin and Webb. Indeed, it smacked of nothing more than a somewhat loose arrangement, a little like the way Miss Sunny Chantry wore her hair – loose and flowing. That was what her engagement sounded like – a loose and flowing arrangement, a little like the really rather dreamy look in her large eyes when he had finally woken her up, because he thought he should. And also because she was far too beautiful to leave lying around on a sofa by herself, let alone lying around on his sofa.

Last of all, he knew the moment he saw her that he would want to take her out to dinner, and that his life was about to change for ever. It had been that sort of moment.

'Never mind your engagement, I'll soon talk you out of it,' he told her after a brief pause, and gave a cheerful wave of his hand, before disappearing down the rest of the stairs, whistling a little too loudly.

Sunny closed her flat door behind her again. She had to confess to feeling excited. There was something about Hart that was electric. Something about him that made you sit up straight away, something elusive in his personality that really swung. It came to her what it was, what it must be, what it had to be. Hart was what Arietta would call 'hip'.

And now she was going out to dinner with him.

She gazed round her at the white painted walls of her little bed-sitter, at the cupboards, at the simple cotton curtains. Suddenly they seemed part of a tiny paradise, and she liked the room more than anywhere she had yet been.

Early morning at Beetle's Bookshop should have been a quiet time, but it actually wasn't. As Arietta soon discovered, early morning for the shop – that was from nine thirty onwards – was the time that old ladies, thieves and eccentrics made it their business to call. It was a time when, Randy Beauchamp had warned her, she must be at her most stalky. But of course she had yet to learn just *how* stalky.

'Oh, oh, here comes Silent Creeper.' Randy nodded at a tall, bespectacled, bearded figure who was hovering outside the window.

'Silent Creeper is so adept at sleight of hand, he should be on the Halls. You can stalk him this morning, while I shall take myself off to the back and make the coffee.'

Arietta nodded. Mr Beauchamp had taken up swapping jobs with her so often, and so relentlessly, she had soon come to realise that it was his subtly sporting way of teaching her the job, without actually teaching her.

'Silent Creeper is one of many who will spend hours reading

all the hardbacks, only to end up buying a Penguin for all of half a crown, but you will find with this one, after the first hour that he has been sunk in the new biography of the week, if you stand behind him and cough and, if at all possible, *sneeze*, he will run off because he is mortally afraid of germs.' As Arietta looked questioningly at Randy, he continued by way of explanation as the sound of the shop bell rang out in the silence, 'He has never been known to remove either of his two pairs of gloves, and wears a scarf over his face, whatever the weather. Good luck, Miss Staunton. You are now in charge.'

Arietta circled around the shop in what she now knew to be the acceptable manner used by Randy, who brought her through a cup of coffee, and then promptly disappeared back into the stockroom, leaving her to feel proudly in charge.

Next into the shop came a tall, slim, distinguished lady. Arietta knew at once that she was distinguished because she wore elegant clothes, a pearl necklace, and a hat at just the right angle. She also sported long white three-quarter-length gloves and a handbag with a gold cipher in the middle.

'*Do* you have, *might* you possibly have, a copy of Giovanni Bellini's *Arcadia di Amore* published by *Intime?*'

Arietta disappeared to look, frowning. Mr Beauchamp had already educated her enough to be prepared to be asked for some strange titles. It seemed that books were constantly being smuggled into the shop for loyal customers eager to read something that the censor had decided was unsuitable for genteel eyes.

'Mr British Censor is so sweet, always so anxious not to overexcite readers in Rye or Winchester with controversial books that would actually bore most people's great aunts so effectively they would be able to sleep serenely through an air raid. However, it seems it is his duty not to lead them into dark

paths by becoming interested in such matters as Irish martyrdom, or having a more imaginative love life such as the French
have always enjoyed. Not that Irish martyrdom and the secrets
of the bordello are necessarily one and the same thing, of
course.'

Arietta scaled the ladder to peruse the foreign section, and
then rushed down again, and hurried off into the back of the
shop to find Mr Beauchamp.

'There's a lady wanting to know if we have *Arcadia di Amore*
published by *Intime*? We don't seem to have it, so shall I tell her
that I will put it on order?'

She had hardly finished speaking when Randy shot past her,
Arietta following closely. They arrived at the front of the shop
just as the bell was sounding out a discreet farewell.

Randy pulled open the worn wooden drawer that housed
the cash.

'Oh, Dio mio,' he said, eyes closed, sighing heavily. 'She's
only done me over again, the female dog!'

Arietta stared at the empty drawer that had contained an
admittedly comfortingly small amount of cash.

'Miss Staunton,' Randy stood her in front of him,
straightening her shoulders as he did so, 'if you *ever*, ever see
that woman again, don't go looking for anything or anyone
except me. She is known as the Duchess of All Gone – and has
the lightest fingers of anyone you'll *ever* know. This must be
about the tenth time she has cleaned me out. Oh, the
annoyance of it all. Always beware the fact that she asks for
books published in Venice. Last time it was D. H. Lawrence's
*The Adventures of William*, would you believe? The poor
creature who was helping me at the time spent hours
looking for it, only to find that not only had Her Grace cleaned
out the cash drawer, dear, but she had also cleaned out the

poor girl's handbag. All her Christmas savings gone in a minute.'

'Oh dear, I am sorry.'

'And so you should be.' Randy smiled. 'Don't worry, you'll soon get used to these people.' He dropped his voice to a whisper. 'Now for your sins, you can take the white pepper pot we keep for the sandwiches, sniff hard, and then go and sneeze behind Silent Creeper.'

When she returned to the desk Randy was all smiles.

'What a good girl you are,' he said affectionately. 'Now see this?' He held up a copy of a book that Arietta did not recognise. 'You must take it to Lady Beatrice Bonnett, in Eccleston Street.' He took a wrapper off another book, and folded it carefully over. 'She will pay you for it as something quite other.' He sighed. 'This is what we are reduced to in this country, being treated like little smutty schoolchildren, not allowed to read the same things as people on the continent. What a silly business censorship is, but also how amusing it makes life. Smuggling is not a crime, it is a duty. Laces for my lady, brandy for the parson, a naughty book for teacher – dum, di, dum, di, dum, as the gentlemen ride by.'

Arietta grabbed her favourite straw hat with the black velvet trimming, and shot out into the street with the freshly wrapped brown parcel.

Randy watched her, smiling, holding his half-moon glasses at the ready, as he prepared to send out, for the fourth time, a bill to the millionaire Lord Cawston – who must imagine that everyone was as rich as he, or he would surely pay his account a little more readily. But before he folded the bill in two, and popped it in the envelope, Randy continued to smile at the disappearing sight of Arietta Staunton. She was what the Americans called 'a gas'. Certainly she was a breath of fresh air at Beetle's. All in all, not a bad place for a young country girl to grow up, really – always provided that he kept a firm avuncular eye on her.

The telephone rang. It was Arietta's mother. Randy pulled a face into the receiver. Mother wanted Arietta to go home to Rushington. Damn.

He turned as the shop bell finished ringing out its lazy welcome.

'Sam, Sam, pick up that tome for me, would you?'

Sam looked disappointed. 'How did you know it was me?' he asked, unwrapping himself from the false spectacles and woollen scarf in which he had hoped to disguise himself as his uncle's least popular customer.

'Silent Creeper does not wear Trumper's lime-based aftershave lotion, Sam. Nor does he smell strongly of garlic from a doubtless spanking spaghetti bolognese from the night before.'

'Damn.'

'Quite. Damn.'

'Oh, my—' Sam looked stricken. 'That means I must have breathed garlic all over Arietta.'

'And she has breathed garlic all over me this morning . . .'

Randy smiled.

'Happily I too partook of a *spag bol* last night, so we are duly all met. Ah. Now, time for you to vamoose to the stockroom. I have a bit of nifty negotiation to conduct, old boy. So off you go until this Americano gentleman goes.'

Sam watched from behind the stockroom door. He knew that Uncle Randy conducted some fairly fascinating deals on behalf of customers, but none was more fascinating than those he delicately negotiated on behalf of the adult books readers.

'I would like the sequel to this.'

'In the usual wrapper?'

'That will do nicely.'

Randy ran his index finger down a small black leather book. 'Let me see. *Flowers of Eastern China*, or *The Herbaceous Border in Summer?*' Randy looked over his spectacles at the American gentleman in his immaculate mackintosh. 'May I suggest the latter? I fear *Flowers of Eastern China* might encourage suspicion – too sensational perhaps?'

'Mr Beauchamp, if my wife sees me reading a book with either title it will encourage more than suspicion; it will encourage the outbreak of World War Three. Find me a title that will make her shy away from me as from a wasps' nest.'

Randy's finger continued to travel down a fresh page of the black leather book.

'How about *The European Monetary System 1650–1900?*'

'I think that would suit most perfectly, Mr Beauchamp, most perfectly.'

Randy effectively swapped both book wrappers and, having wrapped the sequel in brown paper, he watched his customer exit from the shop with a look of paternal pride.

'Bless him, he is *such* a DOM, and one of my best summer customers.' He turned and smiled at Sam. 'And what the silly old fool doesn't realise is that his wife comes here for just the same reasons as he.' He picked up his black leather book once more, and ran his finger down a list. 'She is currently reading that age-old classic *Old Men Forget* – and if you believe that, you are a better man than I, Gunga Din.'

Sam smiled. He had been coming to Beetle's since he was quite small, and for precisely the same purposes as the American gentleman. His mother having forbidden the reading of such gloriously entertaining books as *Five Go to Smuggler's Top* and *The Castle of Adventure*, Uncle Randy had taken it upon himself to keep his nephew supplied with Enid Blyton's popular classics.

Sam had regularly taken the number nine bus from Kensington, in company with his dog, and having been deposited in Knightsbridge, made the walk through the back streets to the shop.

'This is our secret,' Uncle Randy would murmur, handing him a mug of hot chocolate and the latest forbidden Blyton. 'Not a word to anyone.' Or a hurried phone call would reveal, 'Keep it under your hat – tell no one, dear boy – the latest Adventure is in.'

His secret forbidden life at Beetle's Bookshop, combined with the wonder of the children's adventures in the stories, became a magical part of Sam's London holidays, so much so that by contrast summers in Somerset spent riding and swimming, walking and rambling seemed positively ordinary by comparison.

Now he looked around the shop, searching for Arietta. Seeing this, Randy tapped him on the shoulder.

'I forgot to say, the poor child has been called home. I must tell her that her mother telephoned when she gets back from taking that book to Eccleston Street. It seems that her mother is far from better, and is calling for her only daughter.'

Sam frowned. Up until now it had not occurred to him that Arietta, she of the delightfully disdainful ways, had parents, particularly not a mother. For a second it seemed to make her ordinary, less in some way, until he realised that it was only practical, after all. Someone had to give birth to you. Even he had a mother, although not a father – the poor chap having copped it during the Normandy landings, which had probably been the reason his mother had been so strict. Purposefully intent on making up to him for no masculine presence in his life, she had assumed the role of a sergeant major, or in her particular case, now he came to think of it, a general.

Minutes later Sam left the shop and went round to his studio, which was situated among many studios in a cul-de-sac off the lower end of the King's Road. He climbed the dark stairs, thinking of Arietta, and having let himself into the re-assuring room that was both his bread and butter and his staff of life, his *raison d'être* and, until now, his greatest love, he started to prepare a canvas, or rather, he started to attack a large canvas. Before he had even started to draw he knew what he would call it – *Absence*.

Despite its being only a few weeks since she had left, Arietta found going back to Rushington an interesting experience, for not only, as is always the case, did it seem smaller, it seemed to her that she had never really lived there. She already felt as if she did not belong, or as if she was in some way a prodigal returning home, in want of forgiveness. Certainly her mother greeted her as such, opening the front door and, having seen who it was, walking off down the hallway to the kitchen, as if just the sight of her daughter was enough to make her flee.

'Hallo,' Arietta called to the retreating back.

There was no answer from the owner of the back.

Arietta followed Audrey into the kitchen where she had already placed a kettle on the stove.

'You said to come at once,' Arietta stated, gazing in some surprise at her perfectly healthy mother.

'I certainly did. Your Uncle Bob will be here before long. I had to call a family conference. We have a crisis on our hands.'

Arietta groaned inwardly. She knew exactly what the family conference would be about. It had always been the same. Ever since she'd been quite small her mother had taken it upon herself to call 'family conferences', and they had always been for one reason and one reason alone – what Uncle Bob always diplomatically referred to as 'Mummy's having difficulty managing'.

'Did you have to call Uncle Bob? Couldn't he have been told on the telephone?'

'Certainly not. What an appalling idea. I never discuss family matters on the telephone. You never know *who* may be listening.'

Arietta had long ago recognised this attitude to the telephone as being a direct offshoot of her mother's generation having, during the war, absorbed the government directive 'careless talk costs lives'; so, knowing of old that there was nothing she could do about it, she fell silent. There was a sound of a fly buzzing around the kitchen window, and somewhere outside someone in a nearby cottage was mowing their lawn. The kettle had boiled. Her mother now made them tea, which she knew Arietta disliked.

As they drank the tea, which in the silence sounded louder than it should, her mother's large eyes fell on Arietta's handbag.

'*What* an expensive item,' she murmured. '*I* can't afford such a handbag. As a matter of fact, I can hardly afford to pay the milkman.'

Arietta sighed inwardly. For some reason, ever since she was quite small, it had always been the milkman that Audrey had not been able to afford. If Uncle Bob or the Chantrys gave her a postal order for Christmas or her birthday, it was always palmed by her mother on the excuse that 'the milkman' needed paying.

Without saying a word Arietta took her wallet from her handbag, and carefully placed some notes on the kitchen table. Equally silently Audrey took the notes and put them in a jam jar. After which they continued to sip their tea.

'What time will Uncle Bob be here?' Arietta called, as she stood at the kitchen sink, washing up their tea things, and her mother went through to the hall to brush her hair and refresh her lipstick.

'Any minute. As a matter of fact, that will probably be him now.'

Arietta, wiping her hands on the roller towel, watched from the kitchen doorway as her mother hurried to open the front door. It was really too pathetic, but she found that she could not stop herself from hoping that her mother would greet Uncle Bob in precisely the same manner that she had greeted Arietta, but she was doomed to be disappointed. As soon as Uncle Bob's short, square, tweed-suited figure with its army haircut – one back hair of which always refused to sit down – was seen to be filling the cottage doorway with its comfortingly homely appearance, Audrey Staunton's expression changed to one of such warmth and charm that Arietta found herself turning away, not quite able to take the all-too-obvious contrast. Once again she wished passionately that she had been an orphan, brought up in some stark institution, owing nothing to anyone, able to make her own way in life without looking to the right or the left, seeing only ahead to some pin of light in the dark tunnel. The light being the future, the dark being the present.

For some reason they always went into the dining room for Audrey's 'family conferences'. Today was to be no exception.

'Well, there we have it, Bob. The bank manager is being really harsh. This poor little house, my only security, will have to be sold,' Audrey finished, laughing humourlessly.

They were seated around the small oak dining table whose

sides conveniently let down. Uncle Bob was looking grave but sympathetic. He always looked grave when it came to Audrey and her finances.

'That is most uncomfortable for you, Audrey,' he agreed. 'If the bank is being disagreeable that is most uncomfy for you.'

'Of course, now that Arietta is able to go out to work, it seems to me, after all I have done for her, that it is only right that she could contribute to the household, find a job locally, pay me weekly for her keep, help towards the expense of running the place. I heard only recently of a very good position with luncheon vouchers for a young woman with secretarial qualifications at the bacon factory near Steyning. They wanted someone presentable, with good speeds, which I must say Arietta has got, although of course she might have to be spruced up.'

She added the last observation with a disparaging glance at Arietta's Mrs Chantry-made suit.

Uncle Bob turned his grave owl-like gaze upon his only niece, and stared at her wordlessly for a few seconds, assessing her ability to earn money, before turning back to his sister-in-law.

'I would agree that, in theory, that would be a good idea, Audrey, of course it would.'

Arietta's heart sank. She dropped her eyes to the table. It was gate-legged and she had always hated it. Their cottage dining room was her least favourite room. She did not like the way it looked, or its stale unused smell; nor did she like the hatch through which she had, on occasion, had to push food for informal lunches or suppers, food that was served to visiting friends from the village. She could hear a fly buzzing some-where around the window. Judging from the sound it was making, it seemed like her, desperate to get out, to get away, to fly off. Money – it was always money with Audrey. Arietta could never understand why her mother could not manage better, why they always seemed to have lurched from one eternal financial crisis to another. Why did Audrey find it so difficult to do this thing called 'managing'? Everyone else's mother had managed, somehow, but Audrey never had. But where did the money go, for heaven's sake?

'How much are you earning in your little job?' Uncle Bob asked, taking out his pipe and lighting it.

Arietta thought with longing of Beetle's Bookshop, of making coffee for Mr Beauchamp, of the different customers that provided such colour to the day, of the bustle of the streets round about, the restaurants, and the shops. She hated the smell of pipe smoke. She hated her mother, and she even, fleetingly, hated poor old Uncle Bob.

She resolved to lie about how much she earned, it was the only way, but before she could lie or even try a little obfuscation, Uncle Bob had turned his gaze back to Audrey.

'I don't think we can call on Arietta for support in anything we might be planning, as yet, Audrey,' he went on gravely before Arietta could reply. 'Truly I don't. Arietta is but a fledgeling, only a fledgeling.'

'She can earn more. She must be able to earn more than she is doing at present, whatever it is that she is earning. She has to bring home more bacon,' Audrey insisted, her expression hardening, the idea of her daughter being a fledgeling leaving her palpably unmoved.

'I think what has to happen, Audrey, is that I will have to have a word with your bank manager,' Uncle Bob continued, as if Audrey had not spoken.

'And *I* think what will have to happen is that Arietta will have to come home and try and earn a decent wage,' Audrey said, staring at her daughter. 'That is what she will have to do.'

Uncle Bob removed his pipe from his mouth and set it in the ashtray in front of him.

'Is this a possibility, Arietta?'

'I don't know, Uncle Bob. I mean, I have only had two jobs so far, and they both paid the same. I don't know how much I *could* earn, but I do love my job, really I do. It is so interesting, and I meet such interesting people. I don't think I would like the bacon factory at Steyning much.'

It must have been the look in Arietta's eyes that could not have been very different from the look that she had used to give him when he took them both on holiday and a hungover Audrey had set about threatening Arietta with a myriad of undeserved punishments, because Uncle Bob promptly picked up his pipe again.

'Well, at any rate, Audrey, we must admit that this is at least good. The work Arietta is undertaking is obviously of great interest to her, and in my experience interesting work is always underpaid, for the very good reason that it puts the employer in the catbird seat, and he knows he can pay less. That being so, I suggest that *I* supplement Arietta's wage, and make it clear to the bank manager that *you*, Audrey, must not be bullied over your little account, which I will settle for you at once. What a horrid man. He must be treated like a flunkey, really he must, for that is all he is, his master being the board.'

He smiled, picked up his pipe and relit it, and as he did so Arietta realised that Uncle Bob really must like being called to Audrey's rescue, which meant that now he was really enjoying being called to Arietta's too. He liked being needed, he liked looking after what he would doubtless, when at his golf club, call his 'womenfolk'. He liked the dependency, which must mean that he did not really care too much to keep Audrey to any kind of financial plan, that he fully expected her to over-spend in order that he could be called in, and by doing so feel less lonely.

'Such a plain man, which is probably why he's never married,' Audrey said eventually, watching him driving off. 'I don't know what Bob would do without us. We are, after all, his only relatives, and really his only interest in life beside his golf club.' She stayed staring out of the window until the car disappeared from sight. 'There he goes off to his little house in Shere with only his antiques for company. Poor old Bob, he really needs us,' she added without either affection or satisfaction.

Arietta turned away, feeling miserable. She really did not want poor Uncle Bob to send her money, and she could not, as her mother obviously could, see his help as something that he enjoyed doing. She could only see it as miserably embarrassing. Once she returned to London she would write to him and tell him she had no need of anything, that at the moment she could rub along perfectly fine on her wage.

'Where are you going?'

'I must take the train back.'

'You're leaving now? Not spending the night?'

'I must get back to my job.'

'Job? I would hardly call being paid a pittance to sell books a job, Arietta, really I wouldn't.'

'I know, I know,' Arietta agreed, still making for the door. 'But, you see, I do. Goodbye.'

She closed the cottage door behind her, and started to run down the garden path, but as she did so she saw the Chantrys setting off from their cottage, and she waved to them. They waved back. They were a happy sight departing in their motor car, such a happy sight that it was only when the car had disappeared from vision that Arietta remembered Sunny's situation, and everything she knew, and her sudden exuberance evaporated. It was impossible to feel happy, even when shutting a door behind which she knew Audrey would be sitting fulminating, when she knew what she knew about poor Sunny: that she was being deceived by her older man who was busy writing letters beginning '*darlingest*'.

As she stood on the station platform waiting for the train, Arietta opened her strangely light handbag searching for a peppermint, and at once found that she had left her wallet with her return ticket tucked in it behind on the kitchen table. Inwardly groaning, she turned back from the platform and headed for her mother's cottage once more.

## Chapter Ten

Sunny had known right from the start that Hart was unusual. He was not handsome, as Gray was. People, most especially women, would not vie to sit next to him because of his looks, which were good rather than beautiful, but she instantly realised that he was possessed of a strangely electric personality; more than that, he seemed to *know* about everything. Although they had only known each other for half a day, an evening, and an early morning, he had already proved himself to be a mine of information about everything that Sunny – inevitably feeling at sea in London – needed to learn.

The morning following their dinner, Sunny found out many things. The first thing of which she could not help feeling intensely approving was that Hart had a way of dressing in front of a girl that was both elegant and discreet. He had asked her down to breakfast with him in the basement only after he had ascertained over dinner that she badly needed employment, that her mother was a dressmaker, and that she herself, while disclaiming any kind of talent in that direction, was nevertheless forced to admit that she was deft with a needle.

'With your figure you would make a great mannequin, but

until you are discovered by some genius photographer we must find you work. I have a godmother who is a hatter,' he announced as he poured coffee and pulled his tie through his shirt collar, more or less at the same time. 'Come with me this morning; I will introduce you. She always has need of people in her workroom. She uses a great many Italian and Spanish ladies, who are all too often great with child; so she is constantly having to replace them when they have to hurry off and give birth in their native Soho.'

Hart and Sunny's dinner together the night before had been delightful, not because of the food, although that had been delicious, but because they had talked non-stop. Sunny had hardly noticed this until she stood up to fetch her coat, and then she had paused by the table and, looking down at Hart she had said, in what she, rather too late, realised was a voice full of wonder, 'Do you realise we haven't *stopped* all evening.'

'Really? I thought dinner had all been quite awkward really,' Hart replied, straight-faced.

Sunny laughed, and wandered off to the cloakroom, leaving Hart to smile at everything and everyone, including the bill.

Of course they hadn't stopped, he said silently to himself, while writing the cheque for the dinner, of *course* they hadn't stopped. The moment he met Sunny he had known they would *never* stop. They were made for each other. *He* knew it. He just had to convince *her* that she knew it too. But perhaps even that would not now be necessary?

They had not kissed.

He would not kiss her on a first date, especially since she was meant to be engaged to someone else, but he would kiss her soon. He knew that. And he would kiss her well. Hart had always been a very good and dedicated kisser, so he knew that he could be sure of Sunny enjoying his kisses. He would make sure of it.

Now he made sure that she stepped into the Underground train carriage and found a seat, while he strap-hanged above her, smiling every now and then at her as she looked around her, fascinated. He knew from the way she was staring, first at him, and then at the other passengers, and without her having to confess to it, that it must be the first time she had been on an Underground train, the first time she had sat between regular commuters making their way to their all-too-regular jobs, the first time she had listened to the train stopping, hissing, swaying, stopping, hissing, swaying, making that latent clickety-clackety false-teeth sound that Underground trains make as they snake their way from stop to stop through frightening, blackened soot-laden tunnels only to re-emerge into what then seemed like blinding sunshine.

'Here we are.'

He guided her by the elbow out of the train carriage towards the escalator. Normally Sunny disliked anyone taking her by the elbow and guiding her anywhere, but for once she was grateful, for whether she liked to admit it or not, after Rushington the carriage had seemed dreadfully confined, the train overcrowded, and even the escalator all too eager to snag the heels of her new high-heeled shoes.

'Well, now, here we are.'

Hart stopped outside a darkly painted shop. It was a few steps down to the door, which led into a darkly painted interior. Nothing so indiscreet as a product name on the door, or anything more than a curtained window, proclaimed it to be what it was – a famous establishment frequented by beautiful women, tremulous debutantes and the mistresses of rich men.

'Titfers for the famous, the rich and the patrician classes

only, because, quite frankly, only they can afford them,' Hart murmured as he rang the top bell which said, in wobbly writing, 'Workroom'.

Sunny had no idea what 'titfers' meant.

Hart caught her puzzled look, and laughed. 'Titfer tat – hat?'

They both laughed as the door was opened by a tall woman wearing a bright red wig and glasses, both of which she promptly removed.

'But, Harty – *mon cher filleul,* you have come to see your poor old godmother.' She leaned forward. 'I put the wig on to confuse anyone I do not want, you understand?'

'Of course,' Hart agreed smoothly. 'I do quite the same at the gallery.'

'Come in. We must have a coffee. I still am hardly awake, *enfin.*' She stared at Sunny. 'But this beautiful girl, she is very awake, *hein?*'

'She needs a job, and since you are my magical godmother, who can turn pumpkins into hats, I know you will find her what she needs. She is very good at sewing.'

'But this is fantastique! Only this morning my beautiful Anna Maria gave birth to twins next door to the Windmill, so no more Anna Maria.' She shrugged.

'Did she die?' Hart asked in a vaguely disinterested voice.

'*Mon Dieu,* no. Of course not, no, but she die on *me.* She will not be allowed to come back here. Her husband insist on the lactation, no one can sew hats while lactating,' she added sadly.

Hart closed his eyes momentarily.

'I don't know why, but the idea of lactating at all near a hat seems vaguely offensive at this hour,' he murmured to Sunny, who promptly started to laugh helplessly, as did his godmother.

'Harty, you are a naughty boy, thank God,' she finally

managed. 'Your mother never lactated, *enfin*, that is why you are so different. You were lactated by the woman in the village near the castle.'

They were now standing in a large room off which, and more or less parallel, ran another room, glass panelled, and filled with activity. Here Sunny could see constant, if disciplined, movement. Small black-frocked ladies were surrounded by the gaiety of hats of every kind – flowers, veils, precious beads – as their small, neat brown-skinned hands flew in and out, sewing at a rate that Sunny appreciated was at least as fast as that of her mother – and that was fast.

'It is the end of the Season, the beginning of the next already, Harty. It play havoc with my nerves. So much tiny pieces of material arriving from the couturiers, all of which may be lost in a moment, and all of which must match my ladies' costumes. Ah, là là, I love it and I hate it too. So, Auguste will fetch us coffee, we will sit, and I will see your sewing, if you please, mademoiselle. For we have high standards here. *Voilà*, I will fetch you something, and you can show me your skill.'

Her mother might have made fun of Sunny's sewing because, it had to be faced, she had spent less time sewing than she had dreaming, and more time trying clothes on than putting stitches in them, but once presented with a fine needle, and a piece of thread, a button or a feather, Sunny found that her fingers were as quick and almost as neat as those of her mother.

Madame Charles, for that was the name of Hart's godmother, watched Sunny intently for little more than a minute.

'Ah, good, mademoiselle, *bon*. You may start at once, we are desperate for anyone.'

Sunny laughed, taking the remark as a lopsided

compliment, while Hart shook his head and murmured something in French to his godmother, which, in turn, made her laugh.

'Ah, but you know your godmother, Harty, she is no diplomat. Sometimes I think that is why my ladies come here. They know I will tell them the truth. If a hat is *affreuse*, if it is make them look ugly as a pill, I tell them, straight from the hatter's mouth, eh?'

As Sunny saw Hart off the premises, she leaned forward and kissed him quickly on the cheek.

'I can't thank you enough for the introduction, you know, really I can't.'

'Nor shall you try – at least not at this moment. You may save up the rest of your thanks for later – mademoiselle.'

Sunny turned and shot back up the stairs. Suddenly life had taken on a new and brighter turn. It was only as she settled down to the work that the thought came to her once more – she was *meant* to be engaged to Gray Wyndham. Oh *dear*.

Arietta was not looking herself that morning. Randy felt anxious. He liked his little assistant to look delightful, and the truth was she was looking rather less delightful than either of them would wish.

'Coffee?'

'No, no, I'll do it.'

'No, no, I'll do it. You've been travelling.'

Once the coffee was made to their mutual satisfaction, and because there were no customers in the shop, they retired together to the little room at the back to enjoy it.

There was a long pause. Randy sipped, Arietta sipped. Randy stared at Arietta's pale face, Arietta stared ahead of her at something she could see that he could not.

'How was Sussex?'

'Oh, you know Sussex . . .'

'As a matter of fact, hardly at all since the war.'

'It was there, you know.'

'Obviously or else you couldn't have come back.'

Silence was resumed, a long silence during which Randy waited for the words to come tumbling out, for the drama to unfold, for the hurt to surface, for surely only hurt, or a dread disease could change his bouncy little assistant into such a morose being overnight?

'You're in a scludge, my dear, and that will never do.'

'What is a scludge?'

'What you're in, and you mustn't be. It's not fair on either of us.'

Arietta coloured. 'I say, I am sorry, really I am.'

'Good, in that case we'll say no more about it, except to remind you, as we must *all* be reminded, that if we feel sorry for ourselves, as old Nanny Beauchamp used to say, then there's really nothing for anyone else to do.'

Arietta's colour remained heightened. She hated to think that her glum ambience had brought Mr Beauchamp down. She jumped up and hurried out of the shop, leaving Randy to stare after her, thinking, for a few minutes, that he might not see her again, but she was back again soon enough with a triumphant look, and a paper bag, which she thrust towards Randy.

'What are these?'

'So-sorry-for-being-glum buns . . .'

Randy stared at them. 'From now on that is what we will always call Chelsea buns – glum buns. Oh dear, here comes Nephew. Don't let him see, he'll scoff the lot.'

Arietta went to smile, and then stopped.

'Come to lunch at the studio?' Sam asked her.

Randy looked from one young face to the other. This was just what was needed, surely?

Arietta, still swathed in deepest remorse, shook her head. 'I don't think I'd better.'

'I'm shutting the shop for the afternoon, so if I was you, I *would* go to lunch with the dear boy. He's really quite a good cook. He might even give you his fish pie.'

Randy gave Sam his most innocent look. In return Sam looked daggers at his favourite uncle. It was a long-running joke between them that Sam could seduce most girls over his fish pie. It was that good.

'It's chicken pie today. Old English chicken pie, *not* fish pie.'

'Oh, well, *chicken* pie. In that case Arietta has to go.'

Sam had always told Randy that he would never make chicken pie for a girl unless he was serious about her.

'Are you sure it's all right?'

Randy looked down at the young anxious face looking up at him, and he sighed inwardly and hoped fervently for the best of all possible outcomes for her. There was nothing he, the older man, could possibly do to help her unhappiness, but perhaps a little loving from a younger man might do the trick?

'I will employ you until one of the clock and not a moment longer,' he said. 'As for you, Sam Finnegan, you can shoot off and start cooking.'

Sam did as he was told, and a few hours later Randy shut up the shop, and watched Arietta wandering off towards his nephew's studio. Dark stockings, a pinafore dress and white, wide-collared shirt, strappy shoes, and a black velvet ribbon in her hair, she looked every inch what she was – a nice girl about to be wooed by naughty Sam.

'You be good to her, Sam,' he murmured to himself. 'Or else

you will have to answer to your Uncle Randy – and what is more, there will be no more *Five Go to Smuggler's Top* or *The Castle of Adventure* stories coming your way.'

Sam had already explained to Arietta that his studio was actually only just off the King's Road, and that once you arrived outside number fifty-eight, all you had to do was cross under an archway, and then turn right to be faced with an old door which, after a few pushes gave into a dark hallway from where led a staircase. Arietta found herself on a dimly lit staircase walking up past two or three doors, all of which sported names that proclaimed them nothing to do with Sam Finnegan, until at last there was his door.

Of course! Despite the fact that his name was on the door – 'Samuel Finnegan, Portrait Painter, Artist' – she would always have known it was Sam's door, from the music she could hear he was playing rather too loudly.

'I love Duke Ellington,' she announced as he flung open the door wearing a Parisian-style apron, and brandishing a wooden spoon. 'He really swings like no other.'

'He certainly does.' Sam widened the gap in the door and bowed, indicating for Arietta to pass him.

As she did so he put his hand across her eyes.

'I want to play Little Blind Girl with you. Don't open your eyes until I tell you.'

He led Arietta into the room.

'One more step and then I will reveal my surprise, Miss Staunton.'

Arietta stared. On a large, old mahogany easel stood a canvas, and on the canvas, the beginnings of a drawing.

She turned and looked at Sam.

'Haven't you got better things to do with your time, Sam

Finnegan?' she asked, pulling a little face. But then he looked so cast down she immediately altered her tone. 'What a compliment, to have you draw me. But, but – why me?'

'Because I missed you,' Sam said simply, his eyes never leaving the canvas in front of them. 'I missed you so much, the only way I could cope was to draw you. Or begin to draw you, rather. I really needed you here, but it's not bad really, considering it is from memory.' He turned to look at her. 'Now you are going to make up for your absence – which, by the way, is the name I have given the painting – by sitting for me this afternoon.' He stared at her. 'Except I would far prefer to put you in something red.'

He went to an old wooden chest in the corner of the room and took out a red lace shawl heavily embroidered with imitation jewels of every colour and shape.

'Here.'

He swirled the shawl around him as a matador might. Arietta laughed, and he went to her and put the shawl around her shoulders, tying it at the back so that it covered her top half, after which he arranged her dark hair, removing the black velvet ribbon and tying it instead around her throat with the bow concealed under her long hair.

He stood back and stared.

'No lunch until I have worked.'

Arietta nodded, still feeling subdued and at the same time thrilled that Sam thought her worth painting. It was only when he had been at work for about an hour, and the smells from the little studio kitchen were wafting towards her and she realised how hungry she was, that she finally stood up and stretched.

'I'm sorry, Mr Modigliani, but your model is now so hungry that she is about to faint. And by hungry, I mean famished. I had no supper last night, and only a bun for breakfast. And what is worse is that the smells from your kitchen are making me feel positively ravenous.'

'Very well. If you must eat, you must. Do you want to see the—'

'No, I will only say the wrong thing, most particularly if I am hungry.'

Arietta helped Sam to serve chicken pie and new potatoes and peas, followed by small wild strawberries and Devon cream, and a delicious cheese with oat biscuits and unsalted butter.

'That was so good,' Arietta murmured, feeling more than a little woozy, both from the effects of the wine and the food. 'I think I have just been in heaven.'

Sam stared at her.

'No, you have not been in heaven – yet,' he told her gently, 'but very soon you might be.'


Earlier, Sunny's first morning in Madame Charles's workroom had made her all too aware that she was a foreigner in an alien country. Obviously the flow of Spanish and Italian that punctured the overlit, underventilated room contributed to this feeling, but it was also heightened by the fact that all the women seated at the tables were not only older, but married, the lights every now and then catching the thin gold bands that proclaimed their status, their figures advertising their post-maternal states, their hair already displaying thickened grey strands. For this reason Sunny knew she would have nothing in common with the ladies that surrounded her, so she resolved to keep her eyes down, and her mouth shut.

As she sewed she thought of what she would write to her

mother about her first days in London. She thought with sudden excitement that she could telephone her from the lodging house; she would actually love to telephone her, to hear her calm voice, until she remembered that a telephone call from her to Rushington would cause nothing but unease. However little the cost to Sunny, even if it was only sixpence, a London call from their daughter would seem shockingly prohibitive and extravagant to her parents, and that being so, the conversation would quickly become unbearably stilted. The fact was that her parents used their telephone as little as possible, regarding it as a sacred and costly instrument. When they did make use of it, it was strictly only to make business or social arrangements. It was never ever employed to hold a conversation.

As she bent to her work, which was effortlessly easy, it came to Sunny that she had actually never heard her father say either 'hallo' or 'goodbye'. Any kind of greeting or signing off would be considered by John to be both expensive and frivolous. Once the purpose of the call was at an end he would carefully and quietly replace the telephone on its cradle, and that would be very much that.

The idea of a telephone call to John and Mary therefore being quite out of the question, Sunny began an imaginary letter to her mother, writing it in her head as she stitched.

'Dear Ma, I have arrived in London, and am very well. The lodging house is great fun. There are about six flats in the building. Well, actually they are not flats so much as rooms with bathrooms, but you have your own latch key to your door, which makes it seem like your own flat. Arietta is working in the bookshop. She is very well, and I am too. I hope you are. Love Sunny.'

She stopped to rethread her needle. No point in stating the obvious. Obviously she was very well, otherwise she would not be writing to them. She would be coming home to be nursed by Mary, not writing to them. Or would she? She started to sew again. Suddenly home seemed strangely out of place in her new life. If she did go home now, she thought she would already feel out of place.

In the next minutes, as the noise and chatter swelled around her, and the sunlight filtered through the windows on to the variety of stuffs and feathers, sequins and buttons, tiny swathes of silk velvets, flowers and veiling, the realisation gradually came to her that she had been freed from her toys and her old school books, from the pink and white curtains of her room with the bobbled fringe that ran down the sides, from the steady, unvaried life of Rushington, from her parents' silently reproachful eyes, from the night-time sound of the hunting owl hooting on its way to the Downs; from the Vauxhall breaking down; from Clem Arkwright's Garage; from the butcher who liked to tease her as if she was still a schoolgirl. She had been freed from the whole tangle of her ordinary, happy childhood.

She knew that Arietta would call it a happy-sad moment, but to look back any more might mean turning to stone, so she wouldn't look back, she would jump into the future, flying from the hopscotch square marked 'past' to that marked 'today', landing safely on one foot, trying not to wobble as she looked ahead to the next square.

She quickly finished the piece she was sewing and, standing up preparatory to taking it over to Madame Charles, she realised that the time had whizzed by, and it was already one o'clock. Hart was taking her to lunch somewhere – anywhere, she didn't care. All that mattered was that she knew she was free, that in every essential except one, her life had really begun in earnest.

Hart was standing by the door through which Sunny bolted out into the suddenly sunny and demurely fashionable street outside. He took off his hat, and as Sunny raised her face to him, he leaned his dark, well-set, handsome head forward and kissed her.

'*Ah, mon Dieu,*' murmured Madame Charles, watching from above. '*L'amour, c'est bon, enfin!*' She smiled, remembering just such moments which now seemed long ago, before turning back to her workroom, and the increasingly wretched matter of the hideous flowers that the Duchess of G. was insisting upon having placed on her cartwheel hat. It would make Her Grace look like an ambulating garden trug, but would she listen to Madame Charles? *Non, enfin,* the silly woman!

Arietta had awoken to the late afternoon sun warming the pillow upon which her dark head of hair was resting. It had not taken more than a few seconds for her to realise that she was lying, clothed only in her petticoat, in Sam's sheets, in Sam's bed, and that being so, they must have made love.

She sat up feeling sensuous and miserable, both at the same time.

'Where are you?' she called out, eventually, because the studio seemed oddly silent.

Sam leaped up the stairs to the balconied area, which was his bedroom, high above the studio.

'I am here.'

He sat down on the bed and as he did so Arietta at once lay back against the pillows, closing her eyes. What had she done?

'What's the matter?'

Arietta kept her eyes closed. She could see colours and

sparks, dashes of light against the dark, she could see constellations, and she could also see her mother.

'Nothing's the matter,' she replied in a cold little voice, eyes still closed. 'What should the matter be?'

Sam leaned forward. 'I do love you, you know.'

'Yes, of course you do.'

Since her eyes were still closed, Arietta could not see Sam's look of hurt surprise at her lightly sarcastic tone.

'No, I mean I really do – love – you.'

'So you just said.'

Arietta stepped out of bed. Pulling fiercely on the top sheet, she extracted it from the bed before carefully and modestly wrapping it around herself, making of it a floor-length toga before walking it, and herself, across to the bathroom.

'I feel terribly sick. I think I must be pregnant,' she eventually called from the bathroom.

Sam waited for her to re-emerge, and then beckoned to her, still wrapped in the trailing sheet, to sit beside him on the bed, where he carefully, very carefully, refrained from touching her, while his eyes looked at her in such a tender manner that, had Arietta actually bothered to look at him, she might have felt better. But as it was she did not. She stared at the floor, tracing a constant pattern with one restless foot on the polished board.

'You cannot be pregnant, Arietta.'

'How do you know?'

Still the foot was tracing a design on the floor board.

'I know because nothing has happened that could make you pregnant.'

'How do you know?'

'Well, how can I best put it?' Sam hesitated. 'In order to make a girl pregnant certain things have to happen, and they didn't.'

'You can get pregnant from kissing, you know,' Arietta informed him angrily.

'Really? Well, in that case you are definitely pregnant.'

Arietta looked up for the first time. Sam was keeping an admirably straight face.

'Don't laugh. You're probably going to be a father ten times over by now.'

Sam nodded. Arietta's mouth set determinedly. She hated him. He saw that she did and waited, still straight-faced. Finally the sides of her mouth started to curl up, and she fell sideways on the bed still clutching the sheet, but laughing.

Sam joined her. They stared at each other. It was one of those long moments when each person realises, with some interest, just how long the other's eyelashes actually are; or that the small brown flecks that radiate from the middle of the eye are really rather like the minute markings on a feather; or that the other person's nose is really rather bigger than at first imagined; or smaller than first imagined; or the forehead broader, or the skin softer and pinker.

'What is the matter, Arietta of the ten babies? Tell your Uncle Sam. He might be able to help you,' Sam whispered.

A long silence, during which Arietta turned on her back and stared at the ceiling.

'Nothing,' she said eventually.

'If nothing why so sad?'

'You wouldn't understand.'

'I might.'

Arietta nodded up to the ceiling. Sam was right. She turned back to view him, sideways once more. She would try him, but without much confidence.

*

She had gone back for her purse, her wretched purse, and she had opened the front door with her key, very, very quietly, all the time hoping, it had to be said, that her mother had gone out, and she could grab her purse and flee.

It was as she tiptoed across the linoleum floor of the kitchen that she heard sounds from upstairs, and naturally froze. If she was in of an afternoon, rather than shopping, it was not like her mother to be anywhere except in the sitting room, listening to the wireless. Arietta had begun to creep across the parquet flooring in the hall when she heard the sounds drifting down from the bedroom, They were not sounds she had ever heard before, and yet she knew what they must be. She stood transfixed. She tried to move but her feet wouldn't do what she was asking of them. At last, at long, long last, they began to move towards the front door, which she closed behind her, so quietly, so slowly, that it was almost unbearable.

Once outside she started to run towards the station, towards the train, towards London, but not before she had recognised the car, which she now noticed parked opposite the house. It was the same one that had brought her mother home from the dinner party that early morning, what now seemed so long ago. God, oh God, the same car, belonging to some man, to some person, to that someone who was still upstairs with her mother.

'I see.'

Sam did not look shocked, he looked interested.

'So your mother has a lover.'

Arietta rolled on to her back once more.

'Yes.'

'And you don't think she should have a lover?'

'Well, no, of course not.'

'But, forgive me, she is a widow, is she not?'

'Well, yes.'

'In that case ask yourself why she should not have a lover. If she is anything like you she is a pretty woman, not yet old, probably attracted to men, and obviously attractive *to* them, so inevitably, one day, she and they will want to make love, wouldn't you say?'

'Well, yes.'

For a second Arietta wondered vaguely if she was becoming incapable of saying anything except 'well, yes'.

'So, what is upsetting you so much then? Why the Miss Glum face that you were wearing earlier?'

Arietta frowned. Well, quite. What *was* upsetting her so much? Given that Sam was right, that her mother was a very attractive woman and a widow, why shouldn't she have a lover? After all, Arietta now had a lover, why shouldn't Audrey have a lover?

'What is upsetting me so much is that . . .'

'Yes?'

Arietta bit her lip. The ceiling was very far above her. It was painted white. 'Is that I don't like the thought,' she finally admitted.

'Ah, yes. And perfectly understandable. My mother is amazingly beautiful, and I hate the thought of her having done anything more than hold hands with my father when he was alive. Uncle Randy has always said parents just don't do *it*. Not ever, not ever, ever, ever. They find us as babies behind cabbages, and we grow up to torment them, and that is that. Anything more is just not on, you understand. Just not on,' he repeated doing an excellent imitation of his Uncle Randy.

They both laughed, and Sam, thinking the matter at an end, kissed her.

'There, pregnant again, Miss Staunton!'

Arietta sighed. It was all very well for Sam the debonair painter to make light of everything, but it was not so simple for her.

'That's not exactly everything, and that is not what I meant, exactly. That is not exactly what is making me miserable – besides thinking I am pregnant, of course.'

'What then?'

'I can't say.'

'You must say.'

'I can't.'

'You must.'

'No, I can't.'

'Why?'

'Because it is probably blasphemous, or something.'

'Let's take the "or something" bit, and forget the blasphemy. I am in love with you, you must know that. You have to be able to tell me everything, as I have to be able to tell you everything, because one of these days you are going to realise that you are in love with me, so we might as well get on with it, don't you think?'

Arietta continued to stare up at the ceiling, thinking hard. Did she dare say what she knew had to be said? It would be so shocking to hear those words out loud, and yet if Sam was right, if they were to love each other, perhaps the words had to be said?

Finally she murmured the four shocking words.

Sam sat up and stared down at her. Happily he did not laugh, but nor did he look either shocked or serious. He looked vaguely disappointed.

'Is that all?'

'What do you mean – is that all?' Arietta too sat up.

'Just that – is that all? Everyone feels like that towards their mother. It's completely normal. We all feel like that, and most of the time. Uncle Randy says it's because they're the first people to punish us.'

'You don't feel like that.'

'How do you know?'

'Well, I don't,' she admitted. 'But I don't think you do.'

'I have felt like that more than you will ever know, I promise you. Ask Uncle Randy. He was my saviour, my hero, my best friend, without him I could never have survived my childhood, never have become a painter. He fought my mother for me tooth and nail because she was so possessive. It was Uncle Randy who gave me my freedom, my *joie de vivre*, my love of life.'

'Really?'

'Really. Now come on, get dressed. I want to get on with the canvas.'

Arietta dressed and went downstairs. Sam had made coffee. What a comfort that he had made coffee and not tea at tea-time. They sat opposite each other on large squishy chairs, saying nothing, sipping the strong coffee, until it was finished. Then Arietta washed up the cups and he tied the red shawl around her, and they went silently on with the day, he knowing that she must be about to love him as much as he knew he loved her, and she knowing that she was no longer alone.

And so began a swift succession of days and nights that Arietta spent between the studio, and Beetle's Bookshop, watched over with benign satisfaction by Mr Beauchamp. Days when Arietta learned to breakfast off crème caramel, to run to the new machine on the corner for snacks at midnight, to walk in the park before the sun got up, but most of all to take each hour as it came, to shy away from anxiety and the bolts of hideous thought, which normal people call conscience and which ruin so much that should be golden.

Meanwhile Sam began to paint what was to become his first famous painting. Inevitably, because Arietta was sitting for him, occupying his life and his thoughts all the time, he changed the title from *Absence* to *The Red Shawl.*

# Chapter Eleven

Leandra had slipped back into London. It was early morning and there was hardly anyone about, so there was a freshness in the summer air, and a sparkle to the swept streets as yet unadorned with either the rich or the fashionable, only the doormen standing outside the hotels and clubs, a lone gentleman walking his dog to the park, a briskly walking nanny pushing her charge to the gardens opposite her employer's apartment.

The taxi from the station having been paid off, Leandra walked quickly into the premises of Messrs Abel & Beddows, antique dealers to the upper classes.

'May I help you, madam?'

'Mr Abel, please. He is expecting me.'

Mr Abel was a tall man with matinée idol looks. He stood up behind his leather-topped partner's desk as Leandra was shown into his office and, walking from behind it, he extended one beautiful hand.

It was something that Leandra had always appreciated about him – not just that he was good-looking but he had extra-ordinarily beautiful hands. They were not the hands of a tradesman, and although he wore a wedding ring, in the continental manner, there was nothing about him that was not in the best possible taste. He was refined, in the best sense of the word, and if he had not been in trade, he might have married a daughter of the aristocracy, such were his manners, and his grace and charm.

'Mrs Fortescue. Good morning.'

He smiled, and indicated a graceful and perfectly upholstered chair.

Leandra sat down. She looked up at him, and she too smiled.

Mr Abel would know why she was there. She would not have to say anything. He was the soul of discretion. He knew, as they say, how to go on.

'I am in a bit of difficulty, Mr Abel.'

He returned to behind his desk and sat down, hands put together in a praying position.

'I am very sorry to hear that, Mrs Fortescue.'

Leandra knew this to be true. She knew that Mr Abel *would* be very sorry to hear of her difficulties. He had provided her, at every turn, with furniture both for Maydown, and her London address, always at hand, always seeming to understand just what she wanted, just what was needed. It had not been easy. Leandra knew that it had not been easy, because apart from anything else she had what he would call 'the eye', and nothing would go by her.

'Besides Lady Mountbatten, and Queen Mary, I know of no one who has such an eye as you, Mrs Fortescue.'

It was no empty compliment. Mr Abel was not one to flatter. He could spot a fake, whether it was a human being or a piece of furniture, from fifty yards. His predecessor had made a practice of passing off fakes to even the most discerning, but faking was not something of which Mr Abel was capable. He was not known as Able Abel for nothing.

Leandra knew all this, and she appreciated it, but she also appreciated that Mr Abel was a businessman. He could not buy back the furniture he had sold her for the same price that she had given for it. It would be impossible. Nevertheless, she could not help hoping.

'I wonder if it would be possible, without going to auction, for you to buy back some of the pieces that you found for me, which are presently at Maydown, Mr Abel?'

'I will certainly make sure that the company offer for them, Mrs Fortescue. Which particular pieces have you in mind?'

'There are the two matching gilt inlaid and marble-topped scagliola tables which you found for the end of the drawing room by the French windows, if you remember?'

Mr Abel reached into the drawer of his desk and pulled out the relevant folder. He had heard the rumours of the Fortescues' impending misfortune on the grapevine, and while, in common with the rest of the world, he could not stand Dilke Fortescue, he would do as much as possible to help his beautiful wife. Beautiful women should never be humiliated, and it was his rule to try to see that it never happened.

'I have in front of me now the sketches we prepared for your drawing room, Mrs Fortescue, and I see where we placed the Italian marble-topped tables. Very elegant too, if I may say so. Most appealing to be able to look down the room and see them, and that extraordinary mirror that we were able to find for you – that too is most attractive.'

'It is extraordinary, isn't it?'

Leandra stood up and went to his side of the desk to look at the specially prepared watercolours that had been done of the main rooms at Maydown. As she did so, her scent preceded her, and Mr Abel became aware, as every red-blooded man must, that her skirts were lined with silk, and her skin was a most beautiful hue. He quickly rang the bell under his desk.

'Ah, Miss Jenkins,' he said, careful to keep the relief out of his voice, 'can you have a table brought to Mrs Fortescue, so that she may study the sketches in this file more closely?'

He stood up, leaving Leandra to stay standing the other side of his desk. It was not unusual for patrician ladies in financial distress to proposition him; what was unusual was for him to feel even remotely tempted. Just at that moment he had actually felt that he might be tempted, which for a happily married man who always took care to go home at lunch-time was most distressing.

'There we are,' he said happily, as Miss Jenkins placed a slim table under the window for Leandra. 'I must say,' he went on, all of a sudden brought into a nostalgic mood as he gazed at the watercolours done by his men, 'ours was a most happy association at Maydown, was it not, Mrs Fortescue? The sun always seemed to be shining during that year, really it did seem so.'

Mr Abel instantly regretted what he had said, loose words that could after all be open to all sorts of interpretation, and indeed when he looked up and saw that Mrs Fortescue's beautiful blue eyes were brimming with tears, he could have taken his paper knife from the top of his desk and cut out his tongue.

'And shine again it shall, Mrs Fortescue,' he said, looking away. 'Shine again it shall.'

From the offices of Messrs Abel & Beddows, Leandra took a taxi to Madame Charles. If there was one thing upon which she and Dilke were determined, it was that they should, in the next few weeks, be seen to be carrying on as usual. It was essential, for many reasons. The London flat may already have been plundered, but Maydown, having been secured by Dilke in the past week and placed in Leandra's name, was, as yet, untouched by their disastrous downturn in fortune.

'We must go to the Melburys, as always. We must be seen at all our usual haunts, just as if nothing has happened. In this way people will begin to doubt the rumours. After all, at present, only tradespeople are in the know. None of our friends is aware of what has happened, Dilke darling.'

Leandra could hear her own voice lecturing poor Dilke, even as she stepped out of the taxi and down the steps to Madame Charles's establishment. She could only hope that Dilke would keep up the pretence, at any rate until such time that she had married Gray off to the Little Puppy, when they found her. She knew that when they did find her she would be hard put not to wring her neck, but that, in the event, it would not be practical. What she did have to do would be to bring such pressure to bear on her that she would marry Gray at once, by special licence in Scotland, or on a boat, anywhere, just as long as they tied the knot, and Gray finally came into his thankfully vast inheritance.

Once upstairs, with Madame Charles busily greeting her, and the familiar mirrored room ready and waiting, the heads of the old-fashioned felt models bearing all her new hats, Leandra was more than happy to forget about Gray and the tiresome Little Puppy.

'You have so much elegance, Madame Fortescue. Only you can carry off such a cartwheel worn on the side of the head. Truly, it needs your height and your beauty. So many of my customers, they are short and stumpy *comme des* dachshunds, and we place this *chapeau* on them and they disappear, only the legs showing!'

With her forefingers she imitated two legs moving over-swiftly across the room, at the same time making a vaguely musical running noise.

The *vendeuse*, Madame Charles, and of course Leandra, all laughed. Very few women could wear hats in such an elegant and perfect manner as Mrs Leandra Fortescue, the famous beauty now standing in the small room that acted as a salon.

Leandra stared at herself in the mirror, reassured. She was still beautiful, she was still the beautiful Leandra Fortescue; she had known misfortune before, she would carry the day, and the night, no matter what.

The hat for the York races having been duly admired, it was time to remove it, wrap it in tissue paper, place it in its perfectly sculpted, gold-embossed box, and turn to the next item on the list.

'With the John Cavanagh wedding for Wednesday of that following week, if you remember, madame, we chose this large wavy-line hat.'

Leandra stared at herself. Madame Charles had lined the inside of the hat with the identical yellow silk of the dress. All at once she knew she would look stunning. She would be photographed by everyone, as she so often had been. Nothing would change. No matter the temporarily annoying business of Dilke's misfortunes, life, her life, would go on as it had always done.

'And now we have the cartwheel, to be worn absolutely centre, which will carry you through from the luncheon to the cocktail party, and dinner. This is to be worn with the Dior. I love the Dior you have chosen, Madame Fortescue; I love the two tiers he has created for the dress. Such a beautiful idea, it seems to me, to put the camisole dress, and then to top it with the long tunic top, so flattering, and with this hat, I think you will be the toast of the day, as always, madame.'

Once again Leandra stared at herself. It was wonderful to look so beautiful. It made her once more believe in the fitness of things, forget the humiliation of the contents of the London flat disappearing, almost before her eyes, forget the looks in the creditors' eyes, the glee in that of their bank manager. How people like that loved to see people like them humiliated. Dilke had always said that bank people were chosen most especially for their chips. They loved to take possession of the houses of the rich, destroy their luxurious, easy way of life, which they saw as being an insult to themselves, not something to aim for nor indeed something beautiful which added to the value of civilised life, but something, once thankfully destroyed, which they could happily forget, reminding them, as it must, of their own failure, their own lack of taste.

'You have made me look more than I am, more than I could possibly hope for, as always.'

Leandra's glove passed lightly over Madame Charles's surprisingly careworn hand, for if her face portrayed her well-fed life, her enjoyment in her art, her love of and ease with the fashionable world, her hands betrayed a youth spent in long hours sewing.

'I am content that you are happy with what we have done, madame. We love all our customers, do we not?' she added, turning to her *vendeuse*. 'But most of all we love the so-beautiful Madame Fortescue.'

They walked together across the room, laughing and talking. Madame Charles stopped by the window, looking out, as she always did for her customers, to see what the weather might be like.

It was not an entirely altruistic habit, for the truth was, since her customers often insisted on wearing her hats as they left her premises, she could never bear to see the brand-new creations rained upon.

'*Tiens*, the sky is clouding over. We will call a taxi for you, madame.'

'No, really, I have an umbrella. I can find a cab outside.'

'You *can* find one, but you must not. *Enfin*, with so many boxes, no. I will not allow it. All might be ruined if you are caught in the rain.'

Leandra stood by the window, her expression tolerant, her mood mildly irritated. She loved Madame Charles, but really – the sun was still shining, hardly a cloud in the sky – what was she fussing about?

She stared out into the square, thinking of Gray and wondering if they could meet up for a perfectly delicious *cinq-à-sept* in his apartment. Or whether the fear of his father's arriving from the country might prevent such a meeting? The truth was that the further her fortunes had fallen, the more she longed for him.

She watched a couple crossing the square, arm in arm. He was tall and handsome, very correctly dressed, so he must be on his way back to his job. She, on the other hand, was more simply attired; plain dress, hair flowing, the sleeves of her cardigan rolled up. They stopped once they had crossed the road, and she stood looking up at him, both of them laughing and talking, until she reached up and kissed him chastely on the cheek. But it was a kiss that could fool no one. It was a kiss of a girl in love, and the girl was the Little Puppy.

'*Got you!*' The two vulgar words making up the whole cinematic vulgarism flashed into Leandra's sophisticated mind, astonishing her, repelling her, and at the same time determining her.

'Madame? Madame?'

Madame Charles looked round for Leandra, but she had gone, carrying the string of the hat boxes in pairs twisted over her suede-gloved fingers.

Once below, Leandra blocked the doorway just as Sunny stepped down into it.

'Sunny!'

Sunny paused. She paled, and then she recovered. The last person she had wanted to see just at that moment was Leandra Fortescue.

'My dear, I didn't know you were – in London?'

Sunny gave a lopsided smile. She knew it was lopsided because she saw that Leandra could not only sense her embarrassment at seeing her, but see it.

'Oh, am I?' she joked.

Leandra laughed, lightly and beautifully. She knew it was a light and beautiful laugh because she could hear it quite clearly. It was as if it did not come from her; not a top C of a laugh, a modulated laugh, perfectly pitched.

'How long have you been in London, Sunny?'

'Oh, just a little bit. I am working here in the sewing room. You know, earning enough to pay for my rent, and a meal or two. I can't imagine what my mother will think. She always said I would never make a seamstress, that I haven't the patience, but Madame Charles hasn't complained so far, so I can't be that bad.'

'I am sure you are quite brilliant,' Leandra replied smoothly. 'But my dear, Gray is looking for you. Don't you know that? He is desolated that you have disappeared from his life, albeit temporarily, of course.'

It was because she sounded so smooth, so affable, so completely at ease with the idea that Gray's fiancée was to be found in Madame Charles's sewing room that all at once Sunny knew, for certain, that somehow Leandra knew about herself and Hart. She didn't know how she knew, she just knew.

'Yes, of course, I was going to get in touch with him, once I had settled down here in London. I was going to surprise him, actually,' she lied.

'He is longing to see you, my dear,' Leandra told her, leaning forward and speaking in a lowered confidential manner. 'He is falling in love with you, you know. I am sure of it.'

Sunny was silenced. The truth was that having spent the last few days with Hart, doing nothing more sophisticated than travelling to work together, and meeting for lunch, and having supper with all the gang in the basement, she had quite forgotten Gray. Well, at least, she hadn't actually *forgotten* Gray, but she had forgotten that she was *meant* to be engaged to him, and that being so, it was now rather a shock to hear that he was falling in love with her, because that was not what she had understood would happen.

Seeing the confusion on Sunny's face, Leandra's suspicions were now confirmed. Sunny must have forgotten that she was meant to be engaged to Gray.

'I must have your address, my dear.'

Sunny went to tell her and then stopped.

'I don't have one at the moment, Mrs Fortescue. I just work here, and then I sleep – on people's floors.'

She had no idea why she had said something so ludicrous.

'In that case you must stop sleeping on people's floors,' Leandra replied smoothly. 'At least tell me which floor you will be sleeping on tonight?'

'I don't know yet, Mrs Fortescue.'

Leandra smiled, and touched her lightly on the cheek, at her most beguiling. 'You must know that Gray is waiting for you. Please get in touch with him, Sunny. You can imagine, for a man like him, it is not easy to be hurt.'

Sunny felt terrible, as she was meant to do.

'I really must go back to work,' she said, turning towards the door. 'Madame Charles has been so kind, I really must go back to work.'

'Of course, of course.'

Leandra leaned forward once again, but this time she kissed Sunny lightly on the cheek. 'I know you will not let poor Gray down.'

' "*And shall Trelawny die?*" '

'What did you say?'

'Oh, sorry, Mrs Fortescue.' Sunny paused. 'It's just something that my father always says, but I'm afraid I don't really know what it means, truly I don't. It is just something that he always says if he's – um, feeling—' she was just about to say 'cornered'. And then realising it would sound far too reflective of her own feelings, she stopped, and quickly changed. 'When he can't think of what to say next, he always says that, if there is a pause. "*And shall Trelawny die?*" '

Sunny thought of Rushington and her father, of Clem Arkwright, and the village green, of the flowers and the trees, the calmness of it all, while Leandra remembered John Chantry murmuring just that phrase when he had come to luncheon with her at Maydown.

Leandra smiled. 'My dear, I can't wait to tell Gray the good news that we have all found each other again. He will be overjoyed, truly he will.'

She waved a taxi down, and stepped into it, the driver putting the hat boxes in front of her.

Sunny turned towards Madame Charles's premises. She did not know why, but even as she waved goodbye to Leandra, she had a feeling of foreboding.

Up in the workroom she settled down to her sewing with some relief. The feathers that she was using were specially dyed for Madame Charles in Paris. They were so beautiful, and so special that they arrived wrapped in several layers, from velvet cloths to black tissue paper.

She fully expected the talk around her to be, as always, of who had given birth, who was about to give birth, and who was about to get married, and who would presumably, in nine months' time, be also giving birth, but for once fecundity seemed to have run into a blank wall, and the conversation turned to the winter Season, and who would be wearing what, and who was going to be seen in what, and the rival attractions of the new British designers as against the older more established French designers. It also, inevitably turned from there to the stars of the day, to women like Lady Docker and Mrs Leandra Fortescue, well known for either their extreme wealth or their fabulous looks, or both.

Sunny bent to her work, listening, always listening. For obvious reasons the talk had become a great deal more interesting to her, moving on from lactation to proper gossip, to innuendo and rumour.

'Madame Fortescue, she—'

No one in the room would know that Sunny knew Madame Fortescue, and of course she would be the last to tell them, for a great many reasons, most of all, because it might stop them from being indiscreet.

With increasing fury Leandra realised that the taxi driver was taking the longest route to her flat.

'Stop here, please!' she called to him, but not because of his silly cheating ways.

The taxi stopped, and the driver turned back to Leandra, his old walnut face attempting surprise. Rich ladies carrying shopping bags, hat boxes, bags from Aspreys in Bond Street did not usually mind him putting a few pennies on the clock, taking what was known in the trade as the 'scenic route'.

'Wait here, please!'

Somehow the 'please' at the end of her commands did nothing to ameliorate the imperious tone of his passenger, but the driver, mindful only of a large tip, did as she ordered, and stopped.

'I have your number so don't drive off with my hats, will you, please?'

It was Leandra's attempt at a joke, as she jumped out of the cab and headed towards the telephone box on the corner of the street.

Inside the box the smell of stale cigarettes was overpowering, and the myriad of messages and telephone numbers left written on every surface staggering in their design and complexity. For a second Leandra stared at the endless scribbles all written in different hands and different inks, and it came to her that put together they could make up a design that would be suitable for some mad wallpaper that would cause a sensation at any exhibition. Then, feeling vaguely dazed, because it was years since she had been in a telephone box, she took out the necessary money, and started to dial Gray's number.

*Oh, please, please, let him be in for once, and not at his club!*

At long, long last the telephone was picked up, and not by his butler, but, miraculously, by Gray himself.

As soon as she heard his mellifluous measured tones,

Leandra knew that it was vital that she did not sound hurried, that she must sound mischievously interesting, diplomatically calming, sweetly determined, anything rather than how she felt – desperate.

'Darlingest, I have some exciting news for us both!' she began, and then thinking it better not to wait for a response from Gray, she continued quickly. 'I have found our Little Puppy, and she is adorable, and waiting eagerly to see you.'

Gray sounded incredulous, and even more so when he heard where his Little Puppy, his sometime fiancée, was working, and what was worse, sleeping.

'I must say I do keep wondering what *can* her parents be thinking, allowing her to come to London, and then not even helping her to find proper lodgings. What *can* they be thinking?'

Leandra was anxious to deflect any blame from the Little Puppy, to make sure that Gray realised that it was her *parents'* fault that they had let loose an innocent creature upon the evil world.

'I must see her.'

'Of course you must see her, darlingest boy.'

Gray was far from being a boy, but like all men who had long ago left their boyhood behind he loved being so addressed.

'If you go to Madame Charles, in about an hour, she will just be finishing. She will be so thrilled to see you, I can't tell you.'

They finished the telephone call in the usual way, after which Leandra pushed her way out of the telephone box, finally leaning against the door for a few seconds, fighting both the panic the discovery of the Little Puppy had induced, and the almost overwhelming pain caused by her jealousy of Sunny.

She climbed back into the taxi, and ordered the driver to

take her home, sitting back in the seat with a dulled, flattened feeling. She had to face facts as they were. Dilke might well go bankrupt – at the moment the worst that had happened was that certain creditors had taken paintings, jewellery, and the blasted jade, thank God, in exchange for payment – but until she knew more she must only assume that this was merely the beginning, that pretty soon the remaining and quite substantial lease on their flat would have to be turned over to the bank for resale, and that would mean that she would finally be forced to put Maydown up for sale. This was obviously the number one fact. The second fact, and harder to face, was that Gray had quite obviously fallen in love with the Little Puppy. This should be a bonus, given her plan but, in fact, it could ruin everything. It all depended on the next few hours, when he and the Little Puppy would be reconciled, or would have re-met, she hoped, and he would charm her into realising that what he was offering would be a great deal more than any young man could ever offer her: a position in Society, wealth, clothes, motor cars, servants and a beautiful way of life.

Leandra thought for a brief second.

'Stop for a moment, please?' she called to the taxi driver. 'Stop here by this telephone box. I wish to make another urgent call.'

The taxi driver sighed inwardly. You would honestly have thought that a woman like her would be able to wait to make her telephone calls. Nevertheless he stopped.

Yet again Leandra found herself in an evil-smelling telephone box, and yet again reapplying herself to dropping yet more coins into yet another box – so humiliating, somehow – and dialling the number of Madame Charles's famous establishment. She knew she could trust Madame to fall in line with what Leandra wanted. After all, Leandra had not yet paid her.

*

Sunny looked up from her work.

'My dear, Miss Chantry? A gentleman has called for you. He is waiting outside in the square.'

Sunny smiled, unable to keep the delight from her face. Hart must have slipped away from work early. He had warned her that he might.

'If you don't mind, tell him I will be down in a minute, Madame Charles. I must just finish this.'

Madame Charles nodded. She had no idea why Mrs Fortescue had rung and asked her to let Sunny off work early, but she was not such a fool that she could not put two and two together. First the call, and then hardly any time later, round comes a soigné gentleman to call on the young Miss Chantry. Frankly she had no idea of what kind of private life Miss Chantry might like to enjoy, but she thought it impertinent, in view of the fact that Hart was her godson, and clearly what they nowadays called 'dotty' about Miss Chantry – not to mention the fact that he had taken the trouble to find work with his godmother for Miss Chantry – that both Mrs Fortescue and the young lady in question had thought it reasonable to have her meet another gentleman at her premises. But, if life in occupied France had taught her one thing, and one thing alone, it was to mind her own business and not ask questions, either of herself, or others. As far as she was concerned, Hart would have to take his chance. She only hoped that his heart would not be broken by this enchanting young seam-stress, but she feared that it might.

'Gray?'

Sunny looked more than surprised; she looked shocked.

Gray leaned forward and, taking her in his arms, he kissed her for the first time on the lips.

Sunny drew back, almost openly appalled, but he seemed oblivious.

'Darling little one, I thought I would never find you again.'

He flagged down a taxi and guided her into it, before she could say any more.

'This is wonderful – you here in London, finding you. I am the happiest man on earth.'

Sunny stared at Gray. It was too late to tell him that she had thought he was Hart. Too late to say anything, at any rate for the moment. After all she was *meant* to be engaged to him. She sat back in the taxi, staring ahead of her as he took her hand and kissed it, not letting it go.

Sunny left her hand in his while trying to think. She would have to tell Gray about Hart. She did not have to tell Hart about Gray. She had already done that, but she would have to tell Gray that she could no longer be engaged to him, that he must no longer consider her to be his fiancée.

They arrived at his flat without more than a desultory exchange of words, Sunny feeling increasingly confused, increasingly panicked.

'Mr Wyndham?' Gray's butler murmured, giving the young woman he had ushered into the elegant hall a surprised look. 'Mr Wyndham Senior is in the drawing room, already arrived, a little earlier than expected, as is his way.'

He gave Gray a familiarly old-fashioned look, the 'I am marking your card' look, and for once Gray could feel only grateful for it.

'My father, of course. How delighted he will be to see you with me, Sunny. I sometimes think if he was younger, he would marry you himself.'

Sunny's heart sank even further. Oh, for heaven's sake, whatever next? First Gray turning up unexpectedly, then his father.

She remembered Hart was meant to be coming to collect her, and hoped that Madame Charles would explain. She resolved to telephone him as soon as she could, once the embarrassment of drinks with both the Wyndhams had worn off, and she could find some excuse to leave – for leave she must, if only to find Hart and to escape the whole atmosphere of this very grown-up flat, with its heavy furniture and thick velvet curtains, which she was finding oppressive to a degree. She didn't know why, but she felt that at any minute the drawing-room ceiling would start to lower itself and finally suffocate her.

'Are you all right, my dear?'

'I wonder if I might have a glass of cold water?'

Sunny sat back in the chair, sipping the water, surrounded by anxious male faces.

'I am so sorry, so awfully sorry. I think I must have done too much close work today.'

'What does she mean by that? What has she been doing to feel unwell?' Father looked towards his son, accusingly, of course.

'She has been sewing.' Gray looked embarrassed. Sewing suddenly seemed the sort of thing no nice young girl should do.

'What has she been sewing?'

'Oh, it was just a little job she thought to take—'

'She must stop it at once. You can't have your future wife working! What can you be thinking?'

'It was just *un petit divertissement*, Father.'

'Very diverting I am sure – it has worn her to a thread paper.' Mr Wyndham leaned towards Sunny. 'No more work for you, young lady. This brute here is quite rich enough to keep half a dozen wives.' He looked up once more at Gray. 'Look at how pale she is. It must not go on, it really must not.'

Gray took one of Sunny's hands in his and patted it.

'No, of course it won't, Father. It was just a bit of fun, for the experience of it. You know young girls.'

'Sewing is never fun, Gray. Women only sew if they are unhappy, bored, poor, or in a nunnery, and that is a fact. Your mother always avoided sewing. It ruins the eyes and makes the sides of your fingers hard. So enough of this nonsense of sewing, please.'

Sunny closed her eyes. The two men hovering over her, the butler hovering behind her, Gray patting her hand all the time. It seemed that she would never make good her escape. Worst of all, she felt so unwell, her heart still racing, that the telephone call to Hart that she had to make was impossible. She opened her eyes and then quickly shut them again, realising that it was no good wishing the room, the men, the flat away somewhere over a rainbow, any rainbow, no good hoping that when she reopened them she would find herself in her new all-white room back at the lodging house, downstairs the sound of jazz being played, upstairs Arietta and she getting ready for the evening, nothing more interesting on the horizon than having to iron one of her new circular skirts.

Sam peered round the door at Hart.

'For why the absence from our nightly musical set-to in the sitting room?' he asked, puzzled. 'Has all desire to fracture the ears of the neighbours fled?'

Hart remained on his bed staring at the ceiling, silent, his eyes unmoving, while Sam noted that he had changed from 'civvies', as his work clothes – dark striped suit, white shirt, dark tie – were known to all his friends, into 'cool' – polo-necked jumper, American jeans, very, very hip boots, also from America.

'Has there been some biznai about which one needs to know, some unknown evil wrought in one's heavenly absence at the heavenly workplace known as the studio?' Sam persisted.

Silence remained the order of the day. It was such a silence that Sam, having plumped for facetiousness, now changed his manner to one of smooth concern, doing his best to imitate his Uncle Randy.

'I say, old boy, is something pushing you towards the window-ledge, something of which one should be cognisant?'

At last Hart turned his dark handsome head towards his old school friend, and Sam was embarrassed to see that he looked much as he had done after he had said goodbye to his dog at the start of term, eyes full of despair, mouth tightly buttoned, throat working a little overtime.

'She is seeing someone else, Sam.'

Sam frowned. He knew that the reference to 'she' must mean Sunny Chantry, and that being so, he must now tread with the feet of the sanctified, be as stalky as he had ever been.

He reached back in time to an Uncle Randy-ism. 'What evidence does one have for this, old boy?'

Hart cleared his throat. 'I went to meet her this afternoon. Went a bit early—'

'That can prove to be quite a bish with les girls, Harty, truly. I should have warned you. "Never surprise a lady" is what Uncle Randy wrote in my confirmation Bible. It didn't go down very well with Mr Vicar, I can tell you, but I have always adhered to the advice, as one should, coming as it did from a godfather and uncle.'

'We had lunch together, we walked in the park, I came back to collect her as arranged, and OK, it was a bit early – but, but did she need to do *that*.'

Sam was relieved to see that Hart was now sitting on the edge of the bed staring at his feet, and that the tone of his voice had gone from despair to anger.

'What did she do?'

'Kissed this chap in the middle of the street, before fleeing in a taxi with him.'

Sam sat down beside Hart on the bed, and the bed, being of a great age, promptly hit the floor, but neither of them moved. Women, as they both knew, could be fickle, but this was taking the biscuit, surely? To meet Hart and lunch and walk in the park with him (hand-holding *de rigueur*) to arrange to re-meet, and then to skip off with Another. It didn't seem possible that Sunny could have done such a thing. She had, after all, right from the first, appealed as the beautiful young girl of every-one's dreams.

'Is Miss Chantry La Belle Dame Sans Any Mercy, do you imagine, Harty?'

Hart stared ahead of him. 'I think she must be,' he offered finally.

'I think she must be too,' Sam agreed, his thoughts straying to Arietta. If Sunny Chantry was her best friend, was he going to discover that Arietta was cut from the same cloth? There was very little he could do to stop his heart from sink-ing, and his mouth going vaguely dry at just the thought. He was in love with Arietta, more than he had ever been in love with anyone, and the thought of turning up at Beetle's, albeit a trifle early, and discovering her kissing someone else made him feel – well, there was only one word to describe it – ill, very ill; if not totally nauseous.

Having personalised the issue that was tormenting his friend, Sam realised that all facetiousness must now be abandoned and he must get down to hard facts.

'What kind of man was she kissing?'

The expression on Hart's face was one of despair and he allowed it to be.

'A tall chap,' he said, after a small pause. 'Really quite tall, dark-haired, tanned, handsome, dressed to the tens, absolutely pukka, not a whisker out of place.'

'I never trust those kinds of men,' Sam announced with some feeling. 'I always think they're hiding something behind their immaculate exteriors – hearts of ice, minds like flints. You can be too well dressed, you know.'

'Not something you have ever suffered from,' Hart said, looking at Sam's paint-bespattered clothes with sudden humour.

Sam nodded, unsmiling. 'It's like exaggerated good manners, people who open doors too widely, and are always pulling out ladies' chairs halfway across the room, and whisking silk handkerchiefs out of their pockets at the slightest opportunity. I always think they're spies myself. Uncle Randy told me you could always tell a spy during the war because they talked English too beautifully.'

'Something else you have never suffered from . . .'

But Sam was warming to his theme, as well as feeling better about Hart, because Hart was now being a trifle rude, attempting the odd *bon mot*, which must mean he was feeling more cheerful.

'Very well, old boy,' Sam continued. 'I think I have now identified the spy in our midst, the rogue in the pack, the too-well-dressed chap that you spotted this afternoon. He is, he must be, none other than Miss Chantry's fiancé.'

If Sam imagined that he had produced the rabbit from the hat, the truth was that he was right. He had produced a dear little white bunny from the hat, the light catching its frightened eyes as the ghastly conjuror flourished the wretched creature.

'You must be right,' Hart agreed, after a moment. 'Of course. The tall Adonis in the perfect suiting must be the present incumbent in her love life.'

'She did warn you, old thing.'

'Yes,' Hart agreed, 'she did warn me, but I never thought, not for an instant, that she would go off with him again. I thought, I imagined, that what we were beginning to have together must obliterate everything else, that any minute now she must be going to give in to my far superior charms and put the fiancé back into the file marked "Past mistakes".'

Sam stood up, wiping his increasingly warm hands down his jeans.

'Look, old boy,' he said, starting to walk up and down. 'Look, I know it's a bit of a shock to you – more than a bit, obviously – but I think we must be cool about it. First of all, who is to say *she* was kissing *him?*'

Hart too stood up, lighting a cigarette and pulling on it too quickly.

'I saw him, Sam,' he said in a dead voice. 'I saw him.'

'Exactly.' Sam turned, pointing a finger at him. 'You saw him, Dr Watson. That is exactly what I mean, that is what Sherlock Holmes here is on about: you saw *him* kissing *her!*'

Hart paused in his perambulations, smoking too fast, walking up and down, giving every impression that he was an anxious father awaiting the arrival of his first baby.

'You mean to say, Holmes,' he said, warmth returning to his voice. 'You mean to say that *she* might not have wanted him to kiss *her?*'

'I mean exactly that. It happened to me once, at Cambridge. Came out of the door into the street, and this popsy straight off the morning train, the Popsy Express, ran up to me, flung her arms round me and gave me the old mouth-to-mouth, and for no better reason than she had taken a fancy to me the previous weekend at an informal party by the river where there had been a number of bottles sunk and a great deal of shoving and splashing in the river. I tell you, it played havoc with my sex life for the next week. The lady in my life walked out on me – well, she ran actually – and would not return until proof positive of my innocence had been established. Not that it made much difference in the long run,' he finished, looking nostalgic. 'The bitch ended up running off with my tutor, and they now live in married bliss on a Greek island, which is really, really too much to take, really it is, because I have always firmly held to the opinion that if someone is going to break your heart, they must end up *badly*. It is the rule, and rules must not be broken.'

Sam put a friendly arm across Hart's shoulders. Hart, who was busy stubbing out his cigarette in a large china ashtray with '*Goût de Gauloise*' round it, turned and as he did so Sam was relieved to see that the expression on his face was one of relief.

'Best to think that way, until you know better, Hart old boy, or one might head down the Othello route, don't you think?'

Hart nodded. He was still heart sore, but he could, none the less, see a glimmer of hope, just a glimmer. Perhaps Sunny hadn't *wanted* the fiancé to kiss her; perhaps Sam was right.

Hart gave a great deep sigh. The sort of sigh a horse can give when at long, long last he can feel a sensitive rider on his back, someone who has mounted him carefully, instead of plumping himself like a sack of potatoes in the saddle, someone who won't jab at his mouth, pull and kick as if demented, someone who will reward him either with a gentle pat, or a kind voice.

'Thank you, Sam—'

He turned to Sam but he had gone, haring up the stairs to find Arietta, to make sure she was still the same, that she had not suddenly changed overnight into something quite other, or someone quite other. She was not in her room, so he flung himself down the stairs and into the street just as Arietta was coming back down it, tired out from the shop, only too happy to be back at the lodging house.

'Oh, there you are.' Sam slid to a halt, at the same time trying to be nonchalant. 'I thought I might come to the shop to meet you, but you're here.'

Arietta looked at Sam. Something was the matter with Sam, but she was in too good a mood to anticipate what the particular matter might be.

'Why would you want to meet me at the shop? We said we would meet here, Sam,' she reminded him as he took hold of some of her shopping bags, and they walked along together.

'Did we? I wasn't too sure.'

'We said, at lunch-time if you remember, that we would meet here.'

Sam frowned, and looked and felt puzzled. 'Lunch-time seems a long time ago,' he offered, 'you know how it is, particularly if you've enjoyed it.'

It was Arietta's turn to frown and look puzzled.

'Sam,' she said, at last, giving in to the uneasiness of his mood, but only after they had walked along for a minute in silence, 'is something the matter?'

'Something the matter? No. Well, yes, actually.'

'Something I can do anything about, or rather, anything I can do something about?'

'As a matter of fact, yes. Some light shed on the matter, principally from the opposite sex, is needed in this case. Or to put it another way, since it involves him, we need to get to the Hart of the matter.'

Arietta groaned. 'Don't make bad jokes, and above all, please tell me Hart hasn't fallen in love with Sunny?'

'Yes, as a matter of fact he has.'

Arietta stopped, both to rest her arms from the shopping, and in order to stare gravely at Sam.

'But that's *fatal.* I mean, Hart must *know* that she's engaged to Gray Wyndham.'

They were now in the hall of the lodging house. Sam put his finger to his lips as Arietta went to speak.

'Ssh, *whisper.* Harty's downstairs trying to put a sticking plaster on his heart.'

'He's going to need more than sticking plaster, Sam. He's going to need a blooming great bandage. Gray Wyndham will *never* give up Sunny now.'

'But you know and I know that he's sending notes to this Fortescue woman in Beetle's books, and God knows what else is going on.'

'Yes, we do know that, but we can't say anything to her, or to him. We just have to keep our traps shut.'

They had crept upstairs and were now standing in Arietta's room.

'Why do we have to keep what you call our traps shut?'

'Because, Sam, your Uncle Randy says so. It is none of our biznai. None at all. Mr Beauchamp says it is a "where angels fear to tread department", and he should know. He's been running a bookshop long enough.'

Arietta sat down on her bed, counting off the emotional items on one finger after the other.

'First, we have Sunny who has got herself engaged to this chap Gray, who only wants to marry her so he can get his hands on his beastly family money, and then we have this woman '*darlingest*', as your Uncle Randy always refers to her now, who will be most disinclined to get her claws out of Gray Wyndham, and in the middle are the three of us, and poor Hart, who has fallen in love, albeit temporarily.'

'No, no, nothing temporary about Hart's feelings, Arietta. I know.'

'How do you know?'

'You can always tell.'

'How can you always tell?'

'Because his face has changed. He has become a man overnight.'

'What do you mean by that?'

'I mean since meeting Sunny Chantry my boyhood pal has stopped being a boy, and become a man. He's got it that bad.'

'Really?'

'Yes, really.'

Sam looked down at Arietta. 'And, Miss Staunton, as it happens, now the subject has come up, I looked in the mirror this morning after shaving, and realised – so has mine.'

Arietta stared up at Sam. She would have liked to have made a joke, turned away from the moment, but she couldn't, for the simple reason that she could see that it was true. Sam's face had changed. The expression in his eyes was different.

'So what shall we do next?' Arietta demanded after they had kissed for a little.

Sam thought for a moment. 'Why don't we go downstairs and find Hart and take him out to dinner at the bistro on the corner, and make him drink lots of red wine?'

Sam went ahead of Arietta, plunging down the stairs once more, all set to persuade Hart to come out for a jolly with them, leaving Arietta to brush her hair and change her clothes, before following him down, which, a little later she did, to find someone new in the hall.

'Sunny!'

Sunny was looking dishevelled and upset.

'Hallo, Arietta,' she said in a low voice.

'What are you doing here?'

'What should I be doing here? I am coming back to my lodgings, Ari, that's what.'

Arietta pulled her after her up the stairs, at the same time keeping one finger on her lips to indicate that she must not speak until they were back in her room. Once they were, she turned and faced her childhood friend.

'Look, Sunny, there has been the most awful to-do down-stairs with the boys.'

'Why?'

'*Why?*'

'Yes, why?'

'Because Hart saw you in the arms of your fiancé, being kissed, properly, in the street too, which actually is a bit cheap at the best of times, Miss Chantry.'

It was Sunny's turn to sink down on the bed, and stare up at Arietta.

'Oh, what a pill—'

'More than a pill, this is a whole bottle of the things. You truly seem to have broken Hart's heart – no, don't laugh. He thought you were gone on him, and now he's seen you in the arms of another, he has – to say the least – hit the deck. Despair is oozing from his every pore.'

Sunny stood up. 'I'd better go and explain, hadn't I?'

'Not for the minute, no. Better stay here and brush your hair, and calm down. You look a bit flustered. Why not go up to your room, and change and bath and all that, and by that time we can have thought out what to say.'

Sunny only nodded in reply because just for a moment she was finding talking difficult, and anyway, Arietta had turned away to brush her hair, which was just as well, because Sunny knew that if she so much as tried to utter, she would probably burst into tears of relief. It was so wonderful to be back at the lodging house, to be with Arietta, to be away from Gray and his father, and all the muddle she had made there. She had left them to come home and change into an evening dress because they were meant to be going to dinner at the Savoy.

God, how she dreaded going back again!

Minutes later, as she lay in the bath, she thought about what she should do, and what she must say, and how she must say it. She *must* first tell Gray that she could not marry him. Then she must tell Hart that Gray had kissed her against her will, and pushed her into the taxi, also against her will. She must tell everyone everything, but just at that moment all she actually felt like doing was sinking beneath the water, and staying there.

Arietta wandered down to the basement. Music was being played, which was good, since obviously this must mean that Hart had been persuaded to come out of the depths of his despair and blow a storm, which it seemed he was now doing. She went quietly into the room and sat down on the sofa, happy as always to sit in on a set and listen. After a while, when the three boys had paused to argue – which again was good because it meant that everything was as normal as blueberry pie – she picked up the evening newspaper. Inside there was a photograph of two buckled cars, and a caption above it.

### Socialite Killed in Car Crash

Dilke Fortescue, the well-known socialite, has been killed in a car crash on the Hog's Back in Surrey. On hearing the news, his wife, Mrs Leandra Fortescue, left London for Maydown, their magnificent country home. The driver of the other car is being treated in hospital. Mr Fortescue had a taste for fast cars, and was a well-known bon viveur. He leaves a widow but no children.

Arietta didn't know why, but her first reaction was panic. She quickly folded the newspaper and shoved it under the sofa. Darlingest's husband was obviously as dead as a nail. What would this mean to Sunny's fiancé, Gray? Now darlingest would be free to marry him, what would happen?

Happily the set had begun again, so Arietta was able to slip out of the room, and run up the stairs to find Sunny. She knocked on the door of her room, but there was no answer. She tried the handle, but the door was firmly locked. She turned away. It seemed that Sunny had gone, but where?

## Chapter Twelve

The silence in the room was such that had there been a wasp or a fly buzzing it would have sounded like a trumpet solo. Sunny heard the sound, but it did not register with her as a sound, nothing was registering with her outside of the fact that Gray was looking at her with longing, and hope, and it was breaking her heart, because, war hero that he was, she realised that he needed her, and perhaps always would. For this reason she must commit.

'Of course I will marry you, Gray. Not to marry you would be to go back on my word, and one must always, always stand by one's word, my father has always said that. Not to do so means you are quite beyond the pale, and the kind of person that no one wants to be.' Sunny's eyes were huge in her small heart-shaped face, her mouth dry, and her voice, although firm, sounded strained even to her own ears. 'I mean – I mean – I, er, I have made a commitment to you, Gray, and I will always stand by that. I will always love you in the way that you want, and I hate to think that I would ever hurt your feelings. Goodness knows, you have been far too hurt by the war, I know that. I could never ever live with the guilt of letting you down.

I want you to know that I will always stand by my promise to marry you, Gray.'

Gray stared into Sunny's eyes, and hearing the sincerity in her voice, he felt ashamed, and perhaps because of that he looked away, and took a different tack.

'Your father doesn't like me, Sunny. The last thing he takes me for is a man of honour.'

'In that case he is utterly mistaken in you. You are the personification of honour, and – and everything you stand for is what we should all stand for. What we should all be is what *you* are, Gray.'

'Sunny – I, er, have something to tell you, that might change your mind about me, I am afraid.'

But Gray could get no further because he was interrupted by the sound of the door opening. It was not his father returning for the evening paper or some such nonsense, but Fletcher, his butler.

'Sir, forgive me for interrupting?'

Gray said 'Yes?' in such a sharp voice that it implied, *this had better be important.*

'There is a lady on the telephone, and she wishes to speak to you, in private, sir.'

'Is it urgent?'

'I believe so, sir.'

'Very well, I will take it in my study.'

Gray turned back to Sunny. 'Please, don't move,' he begged her. 'It's probably my secretary about business. I will be back in a minute. Don't move.'

Sunny waited until Gray was out of the room, and then she snatched up her handbag, and started across to the drawing-room door.

She peered out into the hall, which thankfully was empty,

and then started to tiptoe across the hall as fast as she could.

'Where are you going, young lady?' a male voice demanded.

Sunny froze. 'I must just go to the aunt,' she said in an embarrassed voice.

'No need to tiptoe then, Miss Chantry. It is just through there.'

'Thank you.'

Sunny gave the butler a wan smile, and followed him obediently to the cloakroom. Once there she started to formulate a plan.

Gray picked up the telephone and was startled to hear Leandra. She began to talk, fast and low. He stared around his study. He could hardly believe what she was saying, but he had to because she was saying it over and over again.

'Dilke is dead, Gray, Dilke is dead. Poor Dilke is dead. He was killed in a car crash on the Hog's Back. Poor Dilke, I always did say that he drove too fast. It's terrible. Poor Dilke. But what it means is – is that we can marry. After all this time, we can now marry, Gray darling.'

Gray wanted to interrupt her to say, 'But I am not free to marry. I am engaged to Sunny Chantry,' but he couldn't, probably because Leandra was crying, and he didn't know whether she was crying from relief, or from grief.

Finally there was a pause as her voice steadied.

'We can do as we have always wanted,' she resumed, 'because you can now come into your inheritance, because you will be a married man. We are free at last to be respectable, and loved.'

Gray wanted to say, 'But I don't want to be respectable and loved by you, Leandra, I want to be loved by Sunny Chantry,' and then he remembered his lie, and he fell silent.

He and Leandra had constructed such a monumental lie that it was an Empire State Building of a lie, stretching right up to the sky; a lie as high as an elephant's eye, as the song had it. Christ! What was he to do? He was in love with a girl who was keeping to her promise to marry him because she imagined him unable to make love to her, in other words, she felt sorry for him. Yet he was really loved by Leandra, who knew only too well that he was very much a man, in every sense of the word.

All this flashed through his mind before he spoke, and then, perhaps understandably, he at once decided to back-pedal, to slow things down, while he tried to think of what to do.

'Leandra, do you mind if we meet rather than talk on the telephone?'

'No, of course, we *must* meet.' She lowered her voice. 'I long for you, but it can't be quite yet. So much to do, you know how it is, so much to do, so much to organise. Of course, Rule is going to take charge of the arrangements. He is, as you know, so good at it all. Everyone always says how busy one is at these times, and I am afraid it's true.'

They both replaced their receivers, as of old, with no effusive phrases or expressions of love, because old habits die hard, and they had always been careful in that way.

Leandra hurried off to repack for her return to the country. Having collected up her things once more she headed for the front door, but stopped as she remembered that she should be dressed in black. She paused, reluctant to delay her return to Maydown by even half an hour, but then turned back. Too awful to go back to Maydown dressed brightly. What would the servants think, particularly Rule, who knew all about Gray and as a consequence would hate her not to carry out her part, properly dressed as a grieving widow, heavy black veil and all?

Gray too hurried, back to the drawing room and, as he thought, Sunny, determined on telling her the truth, determined also that she should know how he now felt about her.

He pushed open the door and, thinking to call to the butler to fetch them some drinks, he did not at first register that the room was empty. He pushed the bell for his butler.

'Ah – could you tell me where our young guest, my fiancée, might now be, Fletcher? This is the second time she has left me in a matter of hours. Is she trying to tell me something, I wonder?' he ended, trying to joke. 'First she leaves me to go and change for dinner, and now, having brushed up, she leaves me once again.'

His butler stared at Gray.

'I showed her to the cloakroom a few minutes ago, sir,' he stated in a puzzled voice. 'I imagine she must have come back. I will check for you.'

On his return he looked embarrassed. 'I am afraid that the young lady must have left prematurely, sir.'

It was Gray's turn to look embarrassed. 'Is there no trace of her anywhere in the flat?'

'No, sir, but Mrs Fletcher thinks she saw her crossing the square in a bit of a hurry a few minutes back. Had we better check the silver, sir?'

'Good God, no, nothing like that. I will telephone her later, thank you.'

'Thank you, sir.'

Fletcher closed the drawing-room door. He'd had a funny feeling about that girl the moment Mr Wyndham had showed her into the flat. There was something about her, something that made him uneasy. She looked frightened, as if she didn't ought to be with Mr Wyndham, and after Mr Wyndham Senior left, she looked more frightened still. If Mrs Fletcher was right, and she had spotted her not just crossing the square outside, not as he had just said, 'in a bit of a hurry', but haring across it, then something was very wrong, although what it was neither he nor Mrs Fletcher could say.

'It's all just spectaculation at the moment, Ron,' his missus had warned him. 'And nothing more than that, but it's fishy, I have to say. That's what this is, fishy. First he brings this young girl back here, and then we see her leaving the place as soon as she can, shooting off heaven only knows where, and perhaps heaven is the only body who does know where, think of that.'

Certainly Gray had no idea where Sunny might have gone, and since it was Leandra who had found Sunny in the first place, he had no desire to tell her that he had lost the poor child, yet again.

For some reason he found himself sinking down into the chair his father had vacated. The cushion was flattened, as flattened as his feelings. He felt overwhelmed with despair, and with good reason. He was in love with Sunny, of that one thing he was quite certain, but now Dilke was dead there was no reason not to marry Leandra.

He remained seated in the chair, facing his inability to be anything except lightweight. It was no comfort, but it was probably the same with all the war generation, those of them that had managed, like him, somehow or other to survive. And then they had come home, realised they were alive, but not that something inside them was dead, and promptly confused the act of making love with real love. In his case he had happily given in to a situation that was both passionately pleasing and deliciously luxurious, that of being the lover of a rich and beautiful woman, without realising all along that he was merely hiding from the past, trying to put all the death and the killing, all the bloodshed behind him.

Too late he was realising what a sham it all was. You couldn't spend all your life crouching in an emotional bunker; you had to go over the top. He would have to go ahead and tell the truth, as he had begun to do earlier. He would tell Sunny the unlovely truth, and if she still wanted to marry him, well and good. But where was the elusive Sunny Chantry this time?

Sunny let herself quietly into the cottage. She could hear her mother's sewing machine going, and her father's wireless in the sitting room. She stood for a moment breathing in the familiar atmosphere once again. She was home, and what was more and what was better, she felt she was home.

'Sunny? Is that you?' her mother called.

'Yes, Ma.'

'Oh, good. Put the kettle on lovey, would you? I would love a cup of tea, and I am sure you would.'

Sunny went into the kitchen, and did as asked. She and her mother had often enjoyed a cup of tea after dinner. It was one of their little rituals, tea and biscuits at about nine o'clock at night. The train journey had been long and tiring, requiring a change, and a great many drunken soldiers in third class making insinuating remarks, but somehow she hadn't minded. She had felt in some odd way that she deserved it. She had made such a complete mess of things. Gray, Hart, everything so muddled, and no one knowing what she felt about them, least of all Sunny herself.

'I'm glad you could get home before the last train,' her mother said, smiling up at her as Sunny put down the tray with the cups of tea and the biscuits, as if nothing had happened, as if Sunny had not been away at all. 'I always think,' Mary continued, 'that the last train is the bottom, and one nearly always falls asleep and misses one's stop at that time of night.'

They neither of them attempted to kiss each other, because really, there was no need. They both knew that Sunny had run home, and that to become too emotional or too demanding at that point would be upsetting to both of them.

'How's the sewing?'

'Better than I thought, really. Better than I was at shorthand and typing, at any rate, which isn't saying much.'

'Well, that is good, then. I thought you might take to it one day, just didn't know which day.'

Mary took off her glasses and sat back, sipping her tea and nibbling elegantly at her biscuit, holding a small, flowered tea plate underneath it as she did.

'I heard from Arietta the other day. She's really enjoying helping in Beetle's Bookshop, isn't she?'

Sunny nodded.

Yes, Arietta was enjoying Beetle's Bookshop. She thought longingly of Ari and her seeming ability to handle everything – the bookshop, Sam, Mr Beauchamp. So unlike Sunny who, it seemed, could not handle *anything*.

'Why don't you hop up to bed, pet? You must be dog tired after your journey. I've put a hottie in between the sheets. And don't bother poking your nose round the sitting-room door. Pa is caught up in a concert on the wireless, and you know what he's like, goes into a trance, music on the knee, completely immersed, wouldn't register it was you if you dropped a bomb behind his chair.'

Sunny nodded, and putting down her teacup, she silently made her way up to bed as Mary, sighing inwardly, but only too relieved that she had come home safely, started to turn the handle of her sewing machine. She had no idea what the out-come of Sunny's dreadful muddle would be, but she had every idea that a good night's sleep would certainly not do it, or her, any harm.

Upstairs, Sunny stared around her room before slipping

between the covers, grateful, despite its being summer, for the comforting presence of Fido, her old dog hot-water bottle. She lay with her bedside light on for a few minutes, feeling herself to be a small girl again, staring at the moths busying themselves around her lamp, remembering how she had loved to hear her parents with their friends in the garden of a summer night, the low murmur of their voices, their laughter, drifting up to her as comforting as summer rain against the windowpanes, as she, in turn, drifted off to sleep.

She switched off her light, the moths fell silent, perhaps, like her, dazed by their recent experiences. Sunny pulled at the curtain, staring up at the moon. An owl hooted, a tree moved in the slight breeze, rustling its leaves as if to remind her that it was alive and awake, and that being so, she could go to sleep.

Randy Beauchamp was feeling in what he always, to himself at any rate, called his 'pasha mood'. In this mood he always felt that he would not be surprised to find, if he turned to see himself in a mirror, that he was wearing a fez and brandishing a rather elegant fly swat.

He had been following the little drama of 'darlingest' and Arietta's friend Sunny quite closely, and with some interest. For the most part – aside from letting the little lying deceivers put their love letters in Beetle's books – he never interfered with his customers' love lives, any more than he interfered with their ghastly taste in bad literature, but in this case, he had a feeling that now that it was clear that Dilke Fortescue had met a sticky end, he would have to do as instinct told him he must, and step in and inform his old friend Gray Wyndham that enough was enough.

As he had understood it from the happily indiscreet Sam, Miss Chantry, the beautiful friend of Arietta, had agreed to marry Gray on the understanding that he could not be a man. Could not be a man his foot – Gray, of all people! So that was a most unhappy start to a young life, because either the poor girl would marry him, thinking she could remain as chaste as a nun, and then get a dreadful fright, or she would marry him, and have to live out his lie, which was also not at all right.

Randy picked up the telephone.

'Gray?'

'Yes.'

'Your bookseller.'

'Randy. How are you?'

'Very perturbed, if you want to know. Would you care to come round and pay my bill?'

There was a small pause.

'But of course, Randy, whatever you say. Is it very outstanding?'

'As a matter of fact I find it to be extraordinarily so, Gray. Deplorably and inexcusably outstanding, if you really want to know.'

Gray and Randy had known each other, if not for ever, certainly from long ago. Randy had never yet asked him to pay his bill. It was a first, and that being so, Gray knew that Randy's demand to see him would have to be about something quite other than the bill.

Gray arrived at Beetle's Bookshop looking exactly as he always seemed to look since he got back from the war: polished, not a hair out of place, impeccably dressed, but today, for some reason, supremely uneasy.

'My dear friend, my dear bookseller in whom I trust utterly, what is it that I have done, or not done?' He paused as Randy surveyed him over the top of his glasses. 'I knew from your tone on the telephone – oh dear, that rhymes in such a hideous way – but at any rate I knew that you had something which you wished to discuss, which has absolutely nothing to do with the money I owe you – money I have to tell you that nevertheless I will pay over to you.'

He reached into the inner pocket of his overcoat and, Randy having presented him with a bill, he opened his immaculate leather wallet and paid out two beautifully new, clean five-pound notes.

'There we are, Randy, and if there is any change I beg you to put it towards your favourite charity.'

'My favourite charity is me, Gray.'

'Well then, if that is what you want, so be it . . .'

They hardly smiled because they both knew they were treading conversational water until such a moment arrived that Randy confessed why it was that he had wanted to see Gray so urgently.

'Why don't we go into the back room?'

'Oh, I don't think so, Randy. Ever since public school those sorts of invitations always fill me with dread. Whatever you have to say to me, over and above the hideous amounts of money I have owed you for far too long, should be said here.'

'Very well, dear boy. Why not therefore sit down?'

'Oh, no, Randy, thank you. And there is too much of the sadistic headmaster in that phrase too. No, let's battle it out here in full view and hearing of the gasping millions, don't you think?'

Since it was early in the shop's day, Randy agreed.

'You know that I know what it is that has been going on.'

Gray frowned. 'I dare say you do,' he agreed eventually.

'So why I sent for you was because I wanted you to understand that I am not for this situation continuing. I think I can say with some truth that I am tolerant and sophisticated, but I

always draw the line at the innocent being led to the slaughter
– or in this case, the altar rail, Gray.'

'Might we perhaps be treading where angels wouldn't dare,
Randy?' The look in Gray's eyes had changed from amusement
to warning.

'Oh, possibly,' Randy agreed cheerfully. 'Quite possibly. But
the truth is that I will none the less continue. I think you will
understand what I mean when I say that Miss Chantry is an
innocent little thing, and that no one, but no one, should
crush the innocent.'

'Nor shall anyone, Randy.'

'That's all that I wanted to know. You see, I saw that Leandra
Fortescue's poor husband had been killed – driving his motor
car too fast I'll be bound, I thought. And then next I thought,
this is going to make a difference to certain people's lives, and
I am quite sure it will.'

'Yes, Dilke has been killed. It is really quite sad.'

'Yes, it is, most particularly for Leandra, who I am sure was
really rather fond of him, in her way.'

'Yes, she was fond of him in many ways.'

'What is going to happen, Gray?' Randy insisted.

Gray looked at his old friend of many years, and noted that
the older man was looking, and doubtless feeling, at his most
pasha-like, and he was right.

Randy wanted Gray to know, and in no uncertain terms, that
he was going to be stern, that he was not on Gray's side,
that Miss Chantry was not to be used as a pawn in his doubtless
elaborate love life. Randy knew that Gray was playing both
ends against the middle, and that would never do.

'What is going to happen indeed?' Gray murmured after a
short pause, and the normally urbane expression on his face
changed. 'I imagine that there will be a funeral, and then

perhaps a wedding. That is what usually happens in these cases when someone dies and someone else is left.'

'It will be a white wedding, I hope, Gray?'

'Perhaps.'

'Or will it be a white *marriage*?'

'Who knows?'

'The innocent must not get caught in the crossfire. Over my beautifully opulent body does that happen,' Randy warned, his expression at its most stern.

'No, of course not. Nor must the guilty go unpunished.'

'Well, as long as you know it, Gray.'

Gray turned away. He knew it, all right, he just wondered whether Leandra also knew it. He turned back again.

'It may interest you to know that the innocent one has slipped through the net yet again. She must have been born under the sign of Pisces. There is no other explanation possible for her ability to disappear at a moment's notice, hiding beneath some water lily, no doubt.'

'Humph,' Randy muttered. 'Well, I am a Cancerian, and my pinch can make the bravest squeal.'

Gray left the shop, the bell tinkled behind him, and it began to rain. Randy stared out at the rain. Any minute now little Arietta would be back from her inevitable visit to the post office. He knew that she was as worried about her friend Sunny Chantry as he was. She had, apparently, left the house the previous evening, and had not been seen since.

'Phew!' Arietta shook herself, and folded the umbrella she had been carrying. 'Why is it that shops always seem further away when it's raining?'

'Why is it that it always rains when one has to go to a shop?' Randy smiled, and beckoned to Arietta. 'Come, let us take coffee together.'

Arietta followed him into the back room, and they began to make coffee and find biscuits in that comfortable way that people can who know exactly how to move about a small space without treading on each other's toes.

'You just missed seeing Miss Chantry's fiancé.'

Arietta put down her coffee cup. 'That stinker!'

'You know that, do you?'

She nodded, reddening. 'The letters in the Angus Wilson . . .'

'Of course . . . It seems you are not the only one to have lost your friend Miss Chantry. He too has lost her, he told me. Can't find her anywhere, which does not bode well for their engagement I should have thought, should you?'

'Really? Well, something good has happened, at any rate, because if he is not a stinker no one is.'

Randy laughed. 'You are very stern.'

'Well, you know. I mean to say. Sam thinks he's a stinker too,' she added, as if this justified her own hard-held opinion.

Randy laughed again, but then his expression changed to one of gravity.

'The gentleman in question knows that I will not stand for any nonsense. I have told him so, only minutes ago.'

Arietta turned and stared at Randy, realising that he meant what he said.

'Have you warned him off, Mr Beauchamp?'

'Yes, in essence. Yes, I have.'

'But supposing your warning doesn't do any good? Supposing this fiancé-person decides to push ahead with Sunny, what will happen then?'

'Nothing to be done. But I don't think she will.'

'Why?'

'Because if she was going to, she would have stayed put,

wouldn't you say? I mean, if your mind was made up, say, to marry my nephew, you wouldn't disappear, would you?'

Arietta's colour deepened. 'Well, no. No, of course not.'

'No,' Randy said, his voice nonchalant, his expression determinedly detached. 'You would stay put. You would make plans together, you would wonder when to tell the rest of the world, but what you wouldn't do is to run off into the metaphorical jungle and leave everyone to wonder where you were, would you?'

'No, no, absolutely not.'

'My case therefore rests. I do not think now, for one moment, your friend Miss Chantry will be in the mood to take Mr Wyndham up on his offer of marriage. As a matter of fact I think it is the last thing that she will do.' He fixed Arietta with a look. 'Now it is your turn to be quizzed, Miss Staunton. When are you going to say yes to marrying my nephew Sam?'

Arietta opened her mouth and closed it again.

'When he asks me – maybe?'

'That,' Randy said, after a joyous pause, and with much smiling satisfaction, 'is without doubt the most thoroughly feminine answer that I have yet come across.'

He sighed happily. He was more than fond of his nephew. He loved him. He wanted him to be happy. Sam was no plaster saint, but Randy knew now that he had found the girl whom the satin slipper fitted, the girl in a million whom every man in his right senses fell to dreaming of – a nice girl. And Arietta Staunton was just such.

As Leandra had comfortably predicted to Gray, Rule took the funeral arrangements for poor Dilke out of her hands and into his own, and left her alone to recover her senses.

Rule was pleased to do so. Not that he had ever wanted Mr

Fortescue to pass from this world prematurely, far from it, but now that he had been gathered, amid all the hurry and bustle that always accompanies such occasions, Rule and the rest of the staff could all feel a palpable feeling of relief. Certainly it was felt in the servants' quarters, because being servants, and therefore what Randy Beauchamp would call 'stalky', they had already sensed what they did not actually know, namely that all was not well at Maydown, that a monetary crisis had been brewing, but that now, for reasons they could not actually put their fingers on, the crisis was passing, and things would once more become settled.

Of course they knew nothing about insurances or wills, or trusts that were only entailed on those who achieved the marital status and so on, but what they did know for certain was that Mr and Mrs Dilke Fortescue's marriage had been unusual, to say the least, and that Mr Wyndham had not been asked down regularly for weekends with Mrs Fortescue just to play tiddlywinks.

However, there was one task that Rule could not perform for Leandra, and that was the delicate act of saying goodbye to the man who had picked her up when she was at her most low, when she had still been in mourning for her adored first husband, who had taken the lonely, grieving young girl and given her wealth beyond her dreams, and a position in Society, not to mention his name.

Leandra went to the church to kneel beside Dilke's coffin, and as she kneeled she realised that they had, in their way, loved each other. It had not been Dilke's fault that he was the way he was. That was probably no one's fault – although, of course, some people might say that it *had* been his fault that he had not told her until *after* they had married.

At first the young bride had been too naïve to know what a

'white marriage' might be, but after he had explained it to her, she had accepted it, as why should she not? Her great love, her poor young husband, Tom, was dead, as dead as Dilke was now, and she was being offered security, friendship, companionship in return for running his houses, and turning a blind eye to his amatory exploits. Of course she had accepted. She had been a poor girl, recently widowed, an only child herself born of a young widow, who had then died. Brought up in one foster home after another, always narrowly escaping the amatory attentions of the man of whatever house she had been in, she had learned to look after herself, and in that she had succeeded.

No one who had never been really poor knew what it was like, but once married to a man rich beyond anyone's dreams, Leandra had never forgotten. She had kept the one good white dress that she had owned when she first met her beloved Tom. It was still, to this day, hanging in her wardrobe at Maydown. A simple white dress, always there to remind her from where she had come, and to where she was resolved never, ever to return.

She walked slowly from the church and straight into Gray's arms.

'Gray!'

'Rule said you had come to church.'

'Yes, yes.' She looked away from him. 'Not where you might usually find me, but I came to say goodbye to Dilke.'

Gray looked down at Leandra, surprised. He had not expected to find her grieving, and yet unmistakably, the lines under her eyes were such, it was quite clear that she was grieving.

He hesitated to put his arm through hers. It didn't seem right. It didn't seem proper, not now that she was a widow. How ridiculous, though, because now it would be perfectly proper.

They walked along in sombre silence, Gray not wanting to break the silence, not thinking it fitting, and Leandra unable to do so. She had anticipated many things in her life, but not this, not that she would miss Dilke, and with all her heart.

She watched her feet sliding along in front of her. Of course they weren't sliding, they just seemed to be sliding because the path from the church was wet, and that being so, she was walking with care. She started to wonder if the pain would ever go. And having wondered that, silently, to herself, she started to wonder why seeing Gray had not been a pleasant surprise as it should have been – as it would have been only a few days before – but an intrusion.

'I didn't realise how much Dilke meant to me, Gray, not until now.'

Gray was silent. After all, what could he say to that?

'Actually, I didn't realise until now that I loved him at all. I always thought I coped with him, that I dealt with him, that I managed him, not that I loved him, but I must have done, or I wouldn't be feeling as I do now.'

'Which is?'

'Bereft.'

Gray tried not to look amazed, tried not to look astonished, tried not to look aggrieved, and ended up, he feared, looking all of those things.

'I suppose,' he murmured, finally, 'it is only to be expected. After all, you lived together for long enough, and although he was never a husband to you, he was always a friend.'

'Yes, yes, he was, the best friend I ever had.'

'And he certainly loved you. It used to amuse me to see how jealous he became when I was around. He had a way of saying my name which was so despising.'

343

'Oh I don't think so . . .'

'Well, maybe not that, but certainly if Dilke could love any woman, he loved you, Leandra. He loved you for your beauty, for your taste, for your ability, as Randy Beauchamp would say, to rise above it. That is a great quality in any human being. If you can rise above things, you will always be graceful and humane, you will never become a Nazi, or a lost cause, both of which have caused so much trouble in this world.'

They fell to silence once more, walking along, slowly, back up an all-too-familiar path through the woods, through the grounds back up to the house.

Gray glanced sideways at her once or twice, the only sound being their footfalls and the recent rain dripping from the trees. The sky was a light grey in contrast to Leandra's black dress, and Gray's black mood.

There were certain places that they were passing that he could not help remembering, as why should he not? Places where they had lain together on hot summer nights. He did not regret them, and yet, knowing himself a little better as he did now, he did deplore them.

What had he been doing wasting his time with poor Leandra when he could have been with someone young and innocent like Sunny? He could be married by now, with children, and a home, instead of which, for his sins – which he now realised must have been plentiful – he was walking through dripping woods with a grieving widow.

'I will leave you here, Leandra,' he said when they finally reached the house. 'I know you must wish to be alone.'

'Yes, I do wish to be alone. I am in pain. There is no other word for it. It's not that I want Dilke back again, Gray. It's not that I don't love you, it's just that I wish it had all been so different.'

'As do I.'

At that, Leandra looked up at him, astonished. 'Do you, Gray? Do you really?'

'Of course. Who wouldn't want everything to be different? No war, no older brother dying, no friends lost, no girlfriends killed in the bombing – who wouldn't want that to be different? Who wouldn't want Dilke to have loved you, as you deserved? Who would not want you to have been able to love Dilke as you wanted? Of course we all want it to be different, but all we have is the present, and at the moment –' he turned to leave her, and then turned back to her – 'just at the moment – well, just at the moment it has at least stopped raining.'

He walked off into the evening, and Leandra watched him for a few seconds, before ascending the steps into her house, because that was what it was now, *her* house. Beautiful, perfect Maydown, with its perfect choices of paintings and furniture, carefully supplied to her by dear Mr Abel, and yet now, its very perfection acted on her as a reproach, as if she had spent too much time worrying about all the things that did not matter, and too little thinking about the things that did matter.

'But what could I do? What could I do?' she muttered out loud to herself, as the old and lonely are always meant to do.

Rule heard her, and moved silently from his doorway to her side.

'You know, Mrs Fortescue, what Mr Fortescue always used to say when he felt a trifle down?' Mrs Fortescue's eyes were full of unshed tears, and Rule knew it and so did not wait for her to answer him. 'He used to say, "A little touch of champagne, I think, don't you, Rule?" And that is what we shall have, Mrs Fortescue. In the Yellow Drawing Room, a little touch of champagne, the way Mr Fortescue liked it, in the old glasses.'

He preceded her through the house, Leandra following.

Rule had had the maid light a fire in Mrs Fortescue's favourite room, the Yellow Drawing Room, and an array of her favourite flowers newly arranged on the Italian marble tables.

As Rule went to fetch the champagne, Leandra looked around her, and heard Gray's words echoing in her head as she did so. Who would not want it to be different? Who would not want that? Oh, for it to have been different!

And yet, as he had said, it had at least stopped raining.

## Chapter Thirteen

Audrey was in fine form. They were once more in the dining room, and Uncle Bob, his signature one hair standing up at the back of his head, was looking as always when a family conference had been called – owl-eyed and solemn.

'How can she possibly marry a painter, Bob? I mean, look at her!'

Uncle Bob was looking at Arietta anyway so there was really no need for this gun dog-type command. He removed his pipe and smiled at his niece.

'She looks very nice to me, Audrey.'

'She has no money, and he will have no money. No one can live off their earnings as a *painter*.'

Uncle Bob knocked the side of his pipe against the large glass ashtray always placed for his use in the middle of the oak table.

'I don't know that that is always the case, Audrey, I don't really,' he stated eventually, having made an elaborate ceremony out of cleaning out his pipe and restocking it, watched by the two women with varying interest. 'If we look at history, good painters have always made their way, via portraiture and so on.'

'Apparently he has painted Arietta.' Audrey made an unladylike snorting noise. 'He must be desperate if he's painted Arietta.'

Uncle Bob restocked his pipe with his favourite tobacco and, having pushed it down, relit it, pulling on it slowly and evenly until he had made the whole dining room smell of Fox's Best.

'What we have here, Audrey, is a love affair,' he told her, after several pulls, 'and that being so, what the painter sees is not what you see, Audrey, but what *he* sees. He sees the girl that he loves, so obviously your view and his view of Arietta is going to be quite different, and, frankly my view too. And my view is that Arietta is a very pretty girl, made even prettier now, by love.'

He turned and stared at Audrey, his expression almost grim. Audrey looked away. It was not like her brother-in-law to talk to her like that.

'Well,' she said, patting the back of her tightly permed hair and pulling it into place, 'what do you suggest that we do, Bob? What is your plan? If any?'

'I suggest that we let true love have its way, Audrey, as we all must.'

'How do we know that it is true love?'

'How do we ever know anything? Only when everything is over do we learn anything at all, and then it is always too late.'

Bob smiled at Audrey, but it was not a pleasant smile, as it was not meant to be. It was a putting-you-in-your-place sort of smile, but since Audrey never knew her place, and never would, the smile had very little effect. She therefore changed tack.

'I have no money for the wedding, you can be sure of that.'

'No, of course you have no money for the wedding, Audrey. You never have any money. I shall pay for Arietta's wedding. I set up a fund for just that eventuality years ago. It is quite a tidy sum now, I'm happy to tell you. Not just tidy, it has proved a most profitable investment fund, which will be quite enough for not just a wedding, but a honeymoon and a house too, perhaps.'

Audrey was furious. They could both see that. The last thing she wanted was for Uncle Bob to side with Arietta, and the fact that he had, secretly – for she would be sure to see the investment for Arietta as a dreadful deceit – saved up to help Arietta rather than Audrey, would be a source of fury to her. It would turn in on her in a bitter way, eating at her insides until she would want to scream.

'You never told me about this!'

The words shot out of Audrey, making a sound that reminded Arietta of a sheet being torn down the middle.

'No, I didn't tell you about this, Audrey,' Uncle Bob agreed calmly, 'for the simple reason it was between me and my bank manager, and no one else. But every sensible father, or in my case uncle, of a daughter or niece always makes provision for a daughter or niece. Always.' He put his pipe back in his mouth, and then, having had a fresh thought, in his usual unhurried manner, he took it out again, and said, 'So when is the happy day to be?'

Arietta shook her head. She had no idea. She just knew that Uncle Bob and herself were smiling at each other in a way that they had never smiled at each other before, and that her mother had left the room, the door slamming behind her.

Uncle Bob leaned forward. 'Ha, ha to her!'

They both started to laugh.


Hart had been to work, come back from work, been to work again, and come back again, and he was still so low that just the sight of him brought Sam down.

'Can't we cheer him up, Phillip?'

Phillip looked round from his piano. 'Oh, I don't think so, mate,' he said cheerfully. 'He's got it bad, and when someone's got it bad, nothing's to be done.'

Sam looked morose. He couldn't help feeling furious with Hart for being so depressed, most particularly because it affected *him*. How could *he* celebrate his engagement, talk about his future wedding, and generally go around feeling as if he was six feet above the ground, positively floating through the days and nights when, damn it, Hart was about as much fun as his mother's fish soufflé, and looked about as grey round the gills as that same soufflé.

It was boring, it was tedious, and he wanted it to stop.

'Surely we can ring Sunny up and ask her what the hell is happening?' he was now moaning to Arietta, but Arietta, taking her tone and her attitude from Mr Beauchamp, shook her head.

'We can do *nothing*, Sam. It is not our business to do anything about anything, and we can't make it our business, we just have to cross our fingers and hope that Sunny comes to her senses.'

'I can't believe she has gone back to Rushington! I can't tell Harty. If he knows that, I don't know what he would do.'

'It may not be to be near the fiancé.' Sam and Arietta always referred to Gray now as 'the fiancé' because it made him and the situation seem less real. 'I think she may have gone home not to be near the fiancé, but to tell him that she can't go through with the marriage.'

Sam looked hopeful. 'Do you really think so? Really, really?'

'I do think so. I think that she went home because she knew that he would be going to Maydown, the widow's house,

350

because she knew that the fiancé would be sure to go to see the widow to comfort her.'

'If only he would drop Sunny and marry the Fortescue lady, that *would* be a comfort.'

As it happened, Arietta could not have been more wrong. Sunny had gone home because she knew of nowhere else to go, and because she realised that she had made such a mess of things, there was nowhere else she *could* go, and because she wanted not to think, and when all was said and done, there was comfort in the familiar routines and small domestic disasters that she had once considered so dull and confining.

The Vauxhall still breaking down was comforting. Clem Arkwright calling to get her going was suddenly like Father Christmas being real and appearing down the fireplace.

Her mother's customers, Lady Finsborough in particular, coming for fittings, which required Sunny once again to model the gowns in question – that too was heart-warming in every way, as if nothing had really happened, as if time had not passed at all.

'You have filled out in a most elegant manner, Miss Chantry,' Lady Finsborough commented in admiring tones. 'You always were a beauty. Now turn, child, turn. Yes, yes, I see what your mother is trying to show me, the kick pleat is very much needed, whereas I would have found it a trifle too showy, but with the severity of the cut in the skirt, no, it is just what will be needed. Now, if you wouldn't mind modelling the coat and skirt for tomorrow's funeral, I have doubts about the belt at the back of the jacket.' She turned to Mary Chantry. 'What a shock for poor dear Leandra Fortescue that Dilke was killed like that.'

Sunny stared at the two women.

'Mrs Fortescue's husband has been killed?'

'Did you not know, my dear? Yes, he was killed driving that sports car of his too fast. It and he, I am afraid, were always an accident waiting to happen. But there we are. Nothing to be done now, and happily he has left her very well off, I believe.' Lady Finsborough nodded briskly. 'Now, as I said, if you wouldn't mind modelling the coat and skirt for me, my dear, I shall be most grateful.'

As Sunny went to change, Lady Finsborough smiled at Mary. 'What a good idea it was that I used my poor mother's illness as an excuse to get out of going to the Norells' ball that time. It will, I am sure, prove to have been dear Sunny's making, as things sometimes do.'

She smiled complacently at Mary, who, finding herself unable to tell the poor woman the truth, turned away, pretending to search for a pattern.

After Sunny had modelled the coat and skirt for Lady Finsborough and the lady had left, Sunny turned to her mother.

'Did you know that Mr Fortescue had been killed, Ma?'

'No, Sunny, I did not. I have far too much to do to keep looking through the arrivals and departures, matches and despatches in the *Daily Telegraph*, I am afraid. I only take it to do the crossword in bed at night, and you know your father, he only takes it to line his galoshes.'

Sunny stared out of the window, lost in thought.

'I will have to go and see Mrs Fortescue,' she said quietly and finally.

Once again Mary found herself turning away. She did not think it at all a good idea for Sunny to go to visit that awful Mrs Fortescue, although she had no idea *why* she didn't think it a good idea. It was just a feeling.

'Very well, Sunny, if you think it is a good idea . . .'

Mary allowed just a little, just a tincture of doubt to creep into her voice before turning back to the tiny alterations that the perfectionist Lady Finsborough wanted done to the pile of clothes she had brought in for Mary's attentions.

'It is not that it's a good idea, Ma. It probably isn't a good idea, but what it is, is something that has to be done.'

'In that case you had better keep on the black coat and skirt. I don't suppose Lady Finsborough will mind, and it is more in keeping than anything you have yourself.'

Sunny looked at herself in her mother's dressing mirror. It had all started like this, her modelling for Lady Finsborough, the yellow ball gown, Lady Finsborough not able to go, and now, in a way, it was all ending like it too, except she was now in black, not yellow.

Rule had answered the telephone, and he now walked quietly up to Leandra, who was staring into the fire, a position that it seemed to Rule that she had held for the past few days, with very few breaks.

'There's Miss Chantry on the telephone, Mrs Fortescue. She wonders if she might call on you this afternoon?'

'Miss Chantry? Oh, Miss *Chantry* – yes, yes, yes, of course she may call. Tell her to come here at four o'clock. We can take tea in the Small Dining Room, Rule.'

Rule bowed and, returning to the telephone, he relayed the message.

A few hours later he showed Sunny into the Small Dining Room with its Chinese wallpaper and elaborate Chinese vases, with its oriental lacquered chest, and its black lacquer chairs.

Leandra leaned forward to kiss Sunny on the cheek, but Sunny did not kiss her.

They sat down. The maid poured tea, and then left the two of them, black clothed, silent, both wondering who would begin.

'I am here because I have made the most awful mess of things, Mrs Fortescue.'

Sunny had decided to take the initiative. It was only fair since she was the one who had requested the interview, which was what, in truth, it was.

'I hardly think that, Sunny.'

Leandra felt her heartbeat quicken, and because of that was careful to keep her expression blank.

'Yes, I have, Mrs Fortescue. I have made the most awful mess of things. You see, I thought I loved Mr Wyndham – I mean, I thought I loved Gray – but I am awfully afraid that I don't love him as I should, but because of how he is – because of what you told me – I can't find it in me to tell him.'

Sunny's eyes were large, dark-lashed, and made to look even larger by the tension in her face.

'I should never have become engaged to him, I know that now, but all I can think is that at the time, I truly thought I was in love with him, but I'm not, I'm in love with someone else, someone I met at the lodging house, actually. He works in an auction house and plays jazz at night – well, you won't want to hear all about that – but you must see that I can't go through with going on being with Gray, as his fiancée, which is terrible, because this means that everything you told me – his trust and his father – well, it's all going to collapse, and he won't have what he should have, and all because of me.' Sunny sipped her tea, and then replaced the cup. 'I'm sure you will be going to be terribly angry with me, and I know that I should go to him myself, but I just can't face it.'

Leandra put her head on one side. 'It is going to be very

difficult to tell him, I do agree,' she agreed. 'But I also think that you may be right. It may be better if you let me do it, let me tell him, because I have known him so long, and because I put you two together in the first place. You seemed ideal, quite ideal, but now, as you say, you have found someone else.' She gave a little sad sigh. 'There is only one way to go, and that is to face the facts.' She put out a hand and patted Sunny's hand. 'Gray will be heartbroken,' she said sadly. 'But he will get over it, in time.'

'Will he, do you think? Will he be able to go back to his old life, having fun and being terribly popular, and all those things you said, in spite of everything? He is such an attractive man, so handsome—'

Leandra stopped her there. She had no need to be convinced of Gray's attractions.

'Of course, of course. We will all, all his friends, look after him, as we have always done. Now, my dear, you must go. I have so much to which to see.'

'Yes, yes, of course.'

As Sunny left Leandra watched her from the hall, walking back down the steps to the inevitable waiting taxi, with mixed feelings. On the one hand she had been relieved that the Little Puppy had been the one to call a halt to the now unnecessary engagement; on the other hand Leandra did not like the idea that it was she, Leandra, who would have to tell Gray. She did not want to see the look in his eyes.

She went back to the fire and sat staring into its comforting colours, watching the sparks occasionally fly up the chimney, wondering whether to wait until after the funeral, or to tell him before.

In the end, since it meant delaying for only a day or two, she waited until after the funeral when she and Gray had been left alone, when there were only the two of them in the twelve-bedroomed house, only the two of them with five servants, and four gardeners, only the two of them at last alone, how they had always thought they would want to be, alone at Maydown.

'She came to tell you that?'

To his amazement Gray heard that his voice was trembling slightly.

'Yes, Gray. She couldn't bear to tell you herself, she felt so bad. Because, well, she felt bad. She still believes she has let you down terribly, and that to tell you will wound your feelings beyond belief.'

Gray turned away. He had never felt worse. Like a man who has had an affair and wants only to confess to his wife and put it behind him, he found himself wishing that he had at least told Sunny that he had lied to her, but now, now there was no reason to tell her.

'So there was a complication after all?'

'Perhaps . . .'

'At any rate, if there wasn't, there is now.' Gray cleared his throat, and then taking out a gold cigarette case he lit a cigarette. 'I'm glad she's found someone her own age,' he said at last. 'I am glad, because she is such a sweet little thing, she deserves something better than us.'

Leandra went to him. 'Darling, I know it's all been rather a shock, but we can now be together, you realise that? We can now get married, and have all the security in the world. We can stay at Maydown, have all our comforts, Rule, the servants, the garden, everything that we love. We can have everything that we have ever wanted.'

Gray nodded, but he walked off down the length of the room towards the French windows, right away from her, still smoking.

How could he explain to Leandra what he was feeling? How could he tell her that in being with Sunny Chantry he had glimpsed a life that he knew now he could never have, a life of innocent love, of being and feeling young, of all the things that, as he had told her days before, the war had taken from his generation. How could he tell her that however beautifully she dressed, however magnificent her jewellery, she would never compare to the sight of a young girl in a simple dress trotting down the street with a straw hat on the back of her head?

Sunny was dawn breaking. Sunny was the first magnolia blossom. Sunny was summer sunshine, moonlight on snow, a trumpet solo. If he even tried to explain Leandra would never understand, not if she lived to be a thousand. She thought Sunny young and stupid. She called Sunny the Little Puppy, because she did not understand an inch of her.

Soon Leandra would be recovered from her mourning, and they would doubtless get married abroad, and travel for a while, after which they would return to Maydown, and everything would be the same, and more of the same would be just the same, and it would be fine, but there would be no tilt to the day, no feelings of intense excitement such as he had experienced, however briefly, for the first time, with Sunny. Comfort was not excitement, security was not joy, but that was what he had settled for, and perhaps after all he deserved it?

Sunny did not want to return to the lodging house immediately, and her mother seemed to understand this, but they both knew that she had to, that she was too old to live at home again. Besides, she had to earn her living, and while Mr Wyndham Senior had given it as his opinion that sewing was bad for ladies, Sunny could not put upon her parents to keep her, nor, she realised, should she interrupt their new-found freedom, and that being so, she returned to London.

This time she was not left sitting on her suitcase, waiting for someone to let her in; this time she returned home at precisely the same time as Hart was returning from his job.

'Ah, there you are,' he said coolly. 'I wondered where you had got to.'

Sunny nodded, not looking at him. She knew how he must have been hurt by her not punching Gray in the jaw when he kissed her, what now seemed like years ago. She knew from Arietta that he had been shocked, wounded, and probably, she half hoped, furious, but what she did not know was how he felt now.

He picked up her suitcase, which was she felt a good sign, and carried it up the steps into the hall of the house where he left it and prepared to proceed down to the basement, which was a bad sign.

'Any music tonight?' she asked, preparing to pick the case up herself.

'Sure.'

She picked up her suitcase for herself and started to struggle up the stairs with it. This was more than Hart could take, and he immediately leaped back up after her, and took it from her.

'Enough of the pathetic display,' he said, taking the suitcase and, proceeding in front of her, he climbed effortlessly to the top of the house, and placed it outside her door.

'There you are,' he said, and turned to go back down again.

'Would you like a cup of coffee?' Sunny asked, desperate to ask him anything rather than have him return downstairs.

'Well, as a matter of fact, I wouldn't mind, I wouldn't mind at all.'

Hart followed her into her room, and Sunny went straight to

put the kettle on, after which she stood looking at Hart as if she had never seen him before, because in a way, she hadn't, not like that, not looking half despairing and half adoring.

'I'd forgotten how beautiful you are, Sunny.'

'And I'd forgotten how handsome you are.'

'I'm not handsome—'

'And I'm not beautiful—'

'So, "Let's call the whole thing off."?'

Sunny shook her head. 'I don't think so, Hart. In fact, I think we should stay very cool, as you would say, and call the whole thing *on*.'

'There's no such thing as calling something *on*, Sunny.'

'Well, there should be,' she protested against the sound of the kettle whistling. 'And as far as I am concerned there is now,' she went on, going to make the coffee.

They sat down opposite each other, coffee cups in hand. Hart stared at her. Sunny stared at him.

'I have unmuddled my muddle, Hart,' she said, finally fracturing the silence, which was not a silence at all, but only a break in the music of their looks.

'Was it a very big muddle?' Hart asked.

'Rather. Huge, actually.'

Sunny looked past Hart to the view of the rooftops opposite. They were a very London set of rooftops, but comfortingly aged, as if the many faded colours had decided, over the centuries, to give in and become part of the gathering sky, and so their colours melted into it in a most gratifying manner, the whole making up a view that was neither city nor country, but vaguely both.

'The thing I never realised before was that you could stray into a situation that would then become something as big as anything you ever thought of, and that you could become so entangled that you might never, ever get out, that you would feel like a trapped animal who had walked into a net, or been caught in a snare, slowly suffocating, or bleeding to death, and no way out, no way out at all, and all you can think of is getting out, but you don't know how to get out, but then something happens that makes you realise how you were trapped, and you do get out, and you stop bleeding, and you go home, and everything is just as it always was, except probably better, and you know that you will never, ever let that happen to you again—'

'I love you terribly, Sunny.'

'And I love you terribly, Hart.'

'Let's hope we will improve with practice,' Hart joked as he took her in his arms.

'I thought I would never find you again,' Sunny confessed after they finished kissing and kissing.

'You thought you would never find me again. How did you think I felt seeing you—'

'No, no, we won't go into that. We can't go into that. It will be like unravelling a ball of wool; we'll never ever ravel it up the same again. It will always be too tight or too loose. Suffice it to say, we love each other. Shall we agree to let that suffice?'

'I think we should agree to let that suffice.'

They moved slowly towards the bed.

'Just a little bit more kissing.'

'Yes, just a little bit, only a very little, because—'

'Because I'm feeling quite hungry.'

Hart burst into laughter. 'Very well, just a little bit more kissing, and then—'

'And then?'

'And then we shall be married in your village church, and we will live in an old rectory that has benign spirits from the golden past, and they will smile down on us all our days, and we will have many joys, and only a few sorrows, and once we are gone everyone will say, "They were made for each other." '

That was such a delightful prediction that they found they went on kissing for rather longer than they perhaps should.

## *Epilogue*

As Gray had foreseen, a few months after Dilke Fortescue's funeral he and Leandra were married abroad, in Venice, by an aged priest who seemed only to speak Latin. After that they had lunch with their witnesses at the Gritti Palace, and everyone appreciated how beautiful the bride looked in her decorous hat, and perfectly matching coat and dress.

Life became very smooth for both of them, as they knew it had to, and since time is a great healer, Gray's heart mended, and he recovered from the pain that his passing engagement to Sunny Chantry had brought him. Only occasionally, over the years, if he saw a young girl walking down a side street, a straw hat on the back of her head, did the pain return, but it was only a fleeting pain that lasted a few seconds, after which, with a light sigh, he would turn away and make for his club, and the kind of congenial life to which he knew he was condemned.

Hart and Sunny, as Hart had hoped, were married in the little church at Rushington. The bride wore a magnificent tiara, belonging to Hart's great-aunt. It was very heavy, but she bore up wonderfully well, knowing that there would be very few other occasions when she would have the privilege of having so many diamonds on her head.

As dutifully reported in the local country newspaper and in the county magazine, the bride's dress was made of poult-de-soie, with a slight edging of pale pink organza sweeping through the waist, and it fell to the ground behind her in a large impressive sweep. Her veil was made of silk netting, and that too fell behind her in a large sweep. There were many pageboys – the Dorlings seeming to have a large number of male relatives from whom to select attendants – but only one bridesmaid, Arietta Staunton.

The reception was a joyful occasion, with many elegant speeches. After which, the happy couple left for their honeymoon in the old Vauxhall, Clem Arkwright having tuned her up so that she whizzed along to their honeymoon hotel in Brighton, only breaking down once they arrived.

Arietta and Sam did not marry until the following spring, Sam having determined that he would put together enough work to mount an exhibition, to impress Arietta's Uncle Bob. Arietta equally had determined not to leave Mr Beauchamp until he had found a proper replacement for her, which he now deemed impossible. The subject did not come up very often, but when it did Sam noticed that Uncle Randy looked more than forlorn at the idea of losing his little assistant; he looked bereft.

A solution had therefore to be found, and it was. Beetle's would move with them back to Rushington. This would mean that Uncle Randy would be able to ditch the dirty mac brigade and the serially unfaithful, and Arietta could go on helping him.

The wedding went off splendidly, particularly given that Audrey was the bride's mother. Uncle Bob gave Arietta away, managing to put out his pipe for the whole service, and giving a wonderfully warm and witty speech at the wedding breakfast.

The happy couple drove off in Sam's new purchase, an old racing-green Riley, which, much to Audrey's disappointment, gave them no trouble at all for the whole of their Cornish honeymoon.

On their return they helped Randy move into his new shop plumb in the middle of Rushington High Street. Business became so brisk that it was not long before his shop was joined by others of the same ilk, so that the people of Rushington were hard put to be able to find a grocery store that sold a bag of sugar among all the second-hand books and furniture shops.

Randy might have been able to ditch the dirty mac brigade, but not his habit of handing out advice to the lovelorn, and although he no longer allowed letters to be passed between hardcovers, he did allow for confessions, admissions, and out-pourings of emotion over cups of strong coffee, because that, as he often remarked, was what a bookseller was all about – getting to know his customers.

The cottage that Hart and Sunny eventually bought was within driving distance of Rushington, but not so near that they would feel tempted to visit friends and families too often. Hart commuted to London while Sunny painted the cottage white. White walls, white windows, white front door, white back door, nothing that she could paint that could be white was not white.

As she painted she sometimes thought of her few days spent sewing at Madame Charles's salon, wondering how many new babies would have come along, or new marriages made, remembering the singsong chatter in heavily foreign-accented English, the gossip meandering its way through the long hours, and how much she had learned by listening – not least about the private life of the famous Mrs Leandra Fortescue, and her long-time love, Mr Gray Wyndham.

In the light of her love for Hart it had not been difficult to forgive Gray and Leandra for deceiving her, and yet, understandably perhaps, she thought she must never forget the lesson that she had learned so early on in her young life, although what it was, she could never *quite* work out – Hart always seeming to come home earlier than expected, which naturally led to much happiness and lovemaking.